FEARSOME
FAIRIES

FEARSOME FAIRIES

Haunting Tales of the Fae

Edited by

ELIZABETH DEARNLEY

THE BRITISH LIBRARY

This collection first published in 2021 by
The British Library
96 Euston Road
London NW1 2DB

Selection, introduction and notes © 2021 Elizabeth Dearnley

Cataloguing in Publication Data
A catalogue record for this publication is available from the British Library

ISBN 978 0 7123 5430 1

Illustrations by Margery Lawrence from Fiona Macleod, *The Hills of Ruel* (1921); by Bernard
Sleigh from *The Faery Calendar* (1920), *A Faerie Pageant* (1924) and *The Dryad's Child*
(1936); by Jessie Willcox Smith from Frances Hodgson Burnett, *In the Closed Room* (1904);
by Claude A. Shepperson from "A Spell for a Fairy" in *Princess Mary's Gift Book* (1914).

Cover design by Mauricio Villamayor with illustration by Mag Ruhig
Text design and typesetting by Tetragon, London
Printed in the Czech Republic by Finidr

MIX
Paper | Supporting
responsible forestry
FSC
www.fsc.org
FSC® C014138

CONTENTS

INTRODUCTION   7

ACKNOWLEDGEMENTS   18

1   The Banshee's Warning (1867)
    Charlotte Riddell   19

2   Laura Silver Bell (1872)
    J. Sheridan Le Fanu   43

3   The White People (1904)
    Arthur Machen   59

4   In the Closed Room (1904)
    Frances Hodgson Burnett   103

5   Lock-out Time (1906)
    J.M. Barrie   135

6   By the Yellow Moonrock (1921)
    Fiona Macleod   147

7   After Dark in the Playing Fields (1924)
    M.R. James   163

8   The Case of the Leannabh Sidhe (1945)
    Margery Lawrence   169

9   The Trod (1946)
    Algernon Blackwood   253

10 The Erl-King (1979)
    Angela Carter   287

11 Concerning a Boy and a Girl Emerging from the Earth (1980)
    Randolph Stow   299

12 In Yon Green Hill to Dwell (2014)
    Jane Alexander   321

APPENDIX: The Cottingley Fairy Photographs   333

INTRODUCTION

In December 1920, Sir Arthur Conan Doyle published an article in *The Strand Magazine* recounting his discovery of photographs taken by two young girls from Yorkshire, who claimed they had taken pictures of fairies by Cottingley Beck during the summer of 1917. "Should the incidents here narrated ... hold their own against the criticism which they will excite," he wrote, "it is no exaggeration to say that they will mark an epoch in human thought." His story generated international attention, becoming a lightning rod for discussions about truth, photographic trickery, childhood, postwar grief, spiritualism, the supernatural, and belief versus scientific rationalism, hinging on a single question: do you believe in fairies?

The Spiritualist Conan Doyle came to believe wholeheartedly in the photographs, which he had acquired from leading Theosophist Edward L. Gardner. In September 1922 he published a book endorsing their authenticity, *The Coming of the Fairies*, followed three months later by *The Case for Spirit Photography*, an energetic defence of medium William Hope. His suggestion that any anomalies in the fairies' shadows could be explained by "ectoplasm [that] has a faint luminosity of its own" placed them on a continuum with other spirit entities, now seemingly capable of being captured on film. But fairies were not ghosts, he conjectured; they might, for instance, be part insect. Comparing the different species he observed in the photographs, Conan Doyle noted that "the elves are a compound of the human and the butterfly, while the gnome has more of the moth". But they ultimately remained a mystery: "I must confess", he concluded, "that after months of thought I am unable to get the true bearings of ... these little folk who appear to be our neighbours, with only some small difference of vibration to separate us."

A hundred years later, the Cottingley Fairies are usually remembered as one of the most famous hoaxes in photographic history, with the creator of Sherlock Holmes hoodwinked by a practical joke that got out of hand. But the story isn't quite so straightforward. The girls themselves, sixteen-year-old Elsie Wright and her nine-year-old cousin Frances Griffiths, stuck to their story until the 1980s, when as older women they admitted the fairies had been staged with paper cut-outs and hatpins. Yet until she died, Frances maintained that the fifth and final image they had taken was genuine. A paranormal researcher named Joe Cooper, who had followed the case for many years and had initially believed in the photographs himself, broke the news of the hoax in the December 1982 issue of *Unexplained* and published his own book about the case in 1990, but was devastated to learn that the pictures had been faked.[1] Conan Doyle's reputation certainly suffered as a result of his involvement; a mocking *Punch* cartoon from the time shows him with his head in the clouds while chained to a disapproving Sherlock Holmes. But the intensity of public debate following his publication of the photographs says a good deal about a collective desire to believe in the supernatural—particularly for a world reeling from the mass deaths of World War I—and also tapped into a much older uneasiness as to what fairies might be. Were they flimsy butterfly-winged creatures fluttering within the pages of children's books, or something altogether more ambiguous, hovering in the shadows?

Today, many popular images of fairies fall into the first category, from tinsel-skirted figures on Christmas trees to the Technicolor stardust of Disney magical helpers like Tinker Bell, the Blue Fairy, and *Sleeping Beauty's* Flora, Fauna and Merryweather. Like fairy tales themselves (the term coined by writer Marie-Catherine d'Aulnoy in 1697 for the title of her first collection *Les contes des fées*, literally "tales about fairies"), our perceptions of fairies have been shaped by developments in the children's book and entertainment industry over the last century, perhaps exemplified by J.M. Barrie's appeal to the audience to save Tinker Bell's life by believing in fairies in his 1904 play *Peter Pan*. But historically, fairies have always been much more unpredictable and formidable figures—and, as can be seen from the Barrie story in this book, even the most whimsical-seeming aspects of *Peter Pan* have a darker side.

Associations between fairies and the dead go back a long way. In many folklore traditions, fairies are described as coming from the otherworld, which is often also an underworld. The Irish term for fairies, *sídhe* (modern Irish *sí*), literally means "earthen mound", and there are many local legends of fairy realms reached through openings in rocks or hills. Other stories explicitly link fairies to the souls of the departed. They appear in several accounts of Scottish witch trials, where the borders between ghosts and fairies become blurred; Katherine Jonesdochter, an Orkney woman accused of witchcraft in the seventeenth century, was charged, among other things, with "haunting and seeing the trowis [fairies] rise out of the kirkyard".[2] A medieval retelling of Orpheus and Euridice, preserved in fourteenth-century Middle English poem *Sir Orfeo*, recasts their journey to Hades as fairy abduction: Orfeo's wife is stolen by the fairy king and taken through a rock three miles deep to a "castel [as] clere and schine as cristal", and only by playing the harp is he able to rescue her from this deceptively glittering underland.[3] Fairies appear to have acquired insect wings in the eighteenth century—appearing in Thomas Stothard's 1798 illustrations to Pope's *The Rape of the Lock*—giving them further associations with the souls of the dead, which are linked with butterflies or moths in numerous cultures.[4]

Another folk belief held that fairies were fallen angels. In the early 1690s, Scottish minister Robert Kirk's folklore treatise *The Secret Commonwealth of Elves, Fauns and Fairies* noted that "these sithes, or fairies … are said to be of a mid[d]le Nature betuixt Man and Angel, as were Dæmons thought to be of old", with "light changable Bodies … somewhat of the Nature of a condensed Cloud … seen in Twilight".[5] During the Romantic period, when scholars and writers across Europe made systematic attempts to collect folktales and weave them into their work, the novelist and fairy authority Sir Walter Scott described his banshee-undine hybrid White Lady of Avenel as

"Something betwixt heaven and hell … Neither substance quite, nor shadow, / Haunting lonely moor and meadow".[6] In all these accounts, fairies inhabit the in-between spaces—whether geographical, material or moral—flickering on the edges of the human world.

As folklore took shape as a discipline during the nineteenth century, Victorian Britain developed an enormous fascination with fairies, both building on these earlier explorations into supernatural heritage and using the otherness of fairies to deal with contemporary issues surrounding empire, race, gender, class and national identity.[7] Some theorists used the emerging social sciences of anthropology and archaeology to suggest pseudo-scientific explanations for belief in fairies. Darwin's *On the Origin of Species* was published in 1859, fuelling new theories of cultural evolution: could the original British fairies have been indigenous, pre-Celtic Britons, or beings which had taken a different evolutionary route to that of humans? Supported by the "discovery" of the Central African foragers who were called Pygmies by white explorers and colonizers in the 1870s, the so-called "pygmy theory" was popularized by folklorist David MacRitchie in *The Testimony of Tradition* (1890) and *Fians, Fairies and Picts* (1893). This argued that the Fians (i.e. pre-Scots) and Picts of Scotland and Ireland had been a short-statured race of people living in concealed underground houses until at least the eleventh century, leading to legends of fairies, brownies and dwarves. White anxieties about hierarchies of race fed in turn into racialised depictions of fairy creatures, particularly racist mythologies about threatening, "savage" dwarves and goblins inhabiting remote locations.[8]

Meanwhile, magical-seeming technologies like photography (1830s), the phonograph (1870s), moving pictures (1890s) and X-rays (1895) led to fresh questions about what might exist beyond human perception. Writing in 1910 that even if "nine out of every ten cases of experiences with fairies can be analysed and explained away—there remains the tenth", Manx folklorist Sophia Morrison suggested that "what used to be so called [supernatural] is simply something that we do not understand at present. Our forefathers would have thought the telephone, the X-rays, and wireless telegraphy things 'supernatural.'"[9] Numerous occultists, Spiritualists and Theosophists made similar arguments for belief in fairies on scientific grounds, often drawing on popularized ideas about evolution. The founder of Theosophy, Helena Blavatsky, suggested in her exploration of esoteric philosophy *Isis Unveiled* (1877) that elemental spirits "evolved in the four kingdoms of earth, air, fire and water … under the general designation of fairies, or fays", and "are the principal agents of disembodied but never visible spirits at seances".[10] In 1929, there was widespread media interest about fairy connections to the mysterious death of a young woman named Marie Emily ("Netta") Fornario on the Scottish island of Iona, who had travelled there after reading the work of fellow Hermetic Order of the Golden Dawn member William Sharp (as Fiona Macleod) and whose body was found naked near Sìthean Mòr wearing a blackened silver chain.[11] Seen within this wider context, it is easier to see how Conan Doyle's conviction that fairies might be invisibly all around us captured the public imagination.

It is out of this swirl of ideas about fairies, spirits, the occult, death, the otherworld and otherness that the stories in this collection were written. The earliest tale, Charlotte Riddell's "The Banshee's Warning", was first published in 1867, while the most recent—Jane Alexander's "In Yon Green Hill to Dwell"—is from 2014. Together, these stories chart a century and a half of unsettling encounters between the familiar human world and the unpredictable, potentially dangerous yet tempting fairy realm. Many draw directly on much older folktales—Alexander's story, for instance, revisits the Border ballad of Tam Lin to explore what happens next after the mortal Janet saves her lover Tam from the fairy queen—while also using these supernatural occurrences as a magic mirror in which to reflect on real-world fears, desires and anxieties.

Other than Frances Hodgson Burnett's "In the Closed Room", which takes place in a humid New York summer of elevated railroads and Central Park basements, all of the stories are set in the British Isles, frequently exploring resurfacings of fairy figures from British and Irish folklore in the modern world. Riddell's opening tale brings the death-heralding banshee, or *bean sí* ("fairy woman") of Ireland to the streets of Soho, while over a hundred years later, Randolph Stow's 1980 novel *The Girl Green as Elderflower*— an extract of which is reprinted here—weaves the strange medieval legend of the green children into his dreamlike story of 1960s Suffolk.

In nineteenth-century England, a nostalgia for the fairies of Shakespeare or Chaucer was coupled with a sense that there was no place for them in a rapidly industrializing society ("The age of piskays, like that of chivalry, is gone", lamented Cornish historian Samuel Drew in 1824, noting that "[t]here is, perhaps, at present hardly a house they are reputed to visit"[12])—and a hope, or fear, that they might still be there despite their displacement. The clash between urban modernity and remnants of older, darker forces buried in the landscape is a recurring folk horror theme, from the four-teenth-century poem *Sir Gawain and the Green Knight* to Ben Wheatley's 2021 psychedelic horror film *In the Earth*; ascribing such forces to fairies gives them a more tangible shape and name. M.R. James, whose ghost stories usually involve a sceptical academic being terrified into supernatural belief, is shown here making a rarer foray into the fairy world via Eton in his 1924 story "After Dark in the Playing Fields". Twenty years later, in Algernon Blackwood's "The Trod", a wealthy young Londoner is "whirled in one of the newest streamlined expresses towards the north", where his plans for a lux-urious weekend of grouse-hunting and moorland romance are thrown into disarray by his host's mysterious niece.

The Celtic Revival of the nineteenth and early twentieth centuries, meanwhile, revitalized interest in the fairy lore of Ireland and Scotland in particular, with writers from these countries reporting widely on—and sometimes openly endorsing—fairy beliefs. W.B. Yeats, who had a lifelong fascination with the occult, wrote in his 1902 edition of Irish fairy lore *The Celtic Twilight* that "the things a man has heard and seen are threads of life ... any who will can weave them into whatever garments of belief please them best".[13] Several of the tales in this collection are by Irish, Scottish and Welsh writers, including the Paisley-born writer and fellow Hermetic Order of the Golden Dawn member William Sharp, who wrote stories and poems inspired by Celtic folklore under the elaborately constructed female pseudonym Fiona Macleod. In 1897, Sharp travelled to Ireland where he recalled meeting "an old man [who] has often met 'the secret people,'" reflecting afterwards that "it is a haunted land."[14] Macleod's story included here, "By the Yellow Moonrock", takes the reader to the Scottish moorlands, where a young piper becomes captivated by a vampiric *"Bhean-Nimhir"* (serpent woman) he meets on St Bride's Night.

Macleod's *bhean-nimhir* is part of a lengthy tradition of seductively threatening female fairies; as with other alluringly sinister supernatural women found in myths and legends worldwide, such creatures invariably embody patriarchal fears about unruly female sexuality. However, seductive fairies are by no means always female. Sexually magnetic male fairies can be found in numerous guises, from the Scottish kelpies—shapeshifting water spirits who can transform themselves into handsome young men—to David Bowie's goblin king in the 1986 film *Labyrinth*. Examples in this collection can be found in Sheridan Le Fanu's chilly Northumbrian tale "Laura Silver Bell", where the orphan Laura becomes captivated by a mysterious lord with "clothes [that] were black and grand, and made o' velvet", and in Angela Carter's Erl-King, a mesmeric, green-eyed forest-dweller who, like Christina Rosetti's "whisk-tail'd merchant" in *Goblin Market*, promises "red berries, ripe and delicious" to anyone he entices into his lair. The young girl at the centre of Arthur Machen's "The White People", meanwhile, describes walking through a suggestively sensuous green valley, full of bubbling streams with ripples that kiss her like nymphs—in fairyland, even the landscape can seduce.

Further associations between fairies and non-heteronormative sexuality can be seen in the use of "fairy" to mean an effeminate or homosexual man in the late nineteenth and early twentieth centuries (the 1896 *American Journal of Psychology* reporting on a "secret organization" known as "'The Fairies' of New York"[15])—which came to be used as a pejorative term by the straight world, but was also one used during the period within the queer community itself.¹⁶ More recently, the term was reclaimed in the title of 2007 short story collection *So Fey: Queer Fairy Fiction*. The otherness of fairies has made them a stand-in for marginalized groups throughout history, but, as *So Fey*'s editor Steve Berman suggests, "Faeryland [also] promises freedom from the restraints of society and the dominant patriarchy and holds the illusive possibility of acceptance."¹⁷

Another fairy type found in this collection, often linked with children, is the changeling. A belief that fairies might steal a human child and leave a doppelgänger in its stead can be found in folk traditions from around the world, from the Nigerian *ogbanje* ("children who come and go") to Scandinavian legends of infants taken by trolls. Thought to have originated in part as a way of explaining congenital disabilities, neurodiversities such as autism, or any illness that might make someone appear "not themselves", these beliefs have sometimes had horrifying real-world consequences for those believed to be changelings. Perhaps the most notorious case was that of Bridget Cleary, a young Irish woman whose family burned her alive in 1895 after becoming convinced that a recent illness meant that she had been substituted for a fairy imposter.¹⁸ More recently, changeling stories have been revisited in twenty-first century reimaginings such as Victor LaValle's sinister New York fairy tale *The Changeling* (2017), Helen Oyeyemi's uncanny, double-pupiled Gretel in *Gingerbread* (2019) and the 2021 Icelandic Netflix drama *Katla*, where the eruption of a volcano leads to a strange series of long-missing people emerging from the ash.

Within this collection, four stories have connections with changelings. Margery Lawrence's 1945 "The Case of the Leannabh Sidhe", in which occult detective Dr Miles Pennoyer is called to investigate a young boy exhibiting disturbing behaviours, is the only one in which the term *leanbh sí* ("fairy child") is explicitly used. However, Frances Hodgson Burnett's haunting account of the delicate-featured, seven-year-old Judith, whose mother remarks that "Seems sometimes as if somehow she couldn't be mine", has several echoes of changeling tales, while Randolph Stow's "Concerning a boy and a girl emerging from the earth" recounts the consternation within the Suffolk village of Woolpit when two green-skinned children appear at the edge of the harvest field. Finally, J.M. Barrie's "Lock-out Time", originally written as part of his 1902 book *The Little White Bird*, introduces the character of Peter Pan that would become much better known in his 1904 play of the same name. Peter has left his mother of his own accord to live with the fairies, but his indecision about whether to return, and the eventual consequences of his leaving, gives it similar emotional resonances.

The story of Peter Pan, with its once-mortal child and "lost boys" frozen in time, remained popular throughout World War I (although the line "To die will be an awfully big adventure" was taken out in 1915), and chimes in many ways with the 1917 Cottingley photographs, another wartime bid to capture a fairy Neverland. A hundred years later, both stories continue to resonate—Peter was brought together with another human child visiting another world, Alice in Wonderland, in the 2020 fantasy film *Come Away*, and a live-action version of Peter Pan is currently in production with Disney. The Cottingley fairies, meanwhile, were the subject of the 1997 film *FairyTale* and a recent centenary exhibition at the University of Leeds' Brotherton Library, and the original cameras and photographs remain among the most popular artefacts in Bradford's National Science and Media Museum. The pictures have been reproduced in the appendix to this collection, including the final "fairy bower" image which Frances Griffiths always claimed was real—readers of this book can judge its veracity for themselves.

A century after Conan Doyle's *The Coming of the Fairies*, the tales in this collection invite you to explore the secretive, unsettling world of fairies in all their forms, from unearthly children to Fiona Macleod's bloodsucking *bhean-nimhir*. While they may start out in recognizable real-world locations—Guy's Hospital, the moors of Northumberland, the woods where teenage girls skive off school—the stories suggest that the hidden beings of the fairy world may never be far away.

NOTES

1 See e.g. a recent report in the local Bradford press, "Dark side of Cottingley hoax—by man who exposed it", *Telegraph & Argus*, 4 January 2017, available online <https://www. thetelegraphandargus.co.uk/news/15000794.dark-side-of-cottingley-fairy-hoax-by-family-of-the-man-who-exposed-it> [accessed 19 September 2021].

2 For further discussion see Diane Purkiss, "Birth and Death: Fairies in Scottish Witch Trials" in *Fairies and Fairy Stories: A History* (Stroud: Tempus, 2000, 2007), pp. 95–126, transcription on p. 114.

3 *Sir Orfeo*, in *The Middle English Breton Lays*, eds Anne Laskaya and Eve Salisbury (Kalamazoo, MI: Medieval Institute Publications, 1995), ll. 355, 358. Available online <https://d.lib. rochester.edu/teams/publication/laskaya-and-salisbury-middle-english-breton-lays> [accessed 12 September 2021].

4 This was the subject of Sam George's excellent keynote, "Fairy Lepidoptera: The Dark History of Butterfly-Winged Fae", presented at "'Ill met by moonlight': Gothic encounters with enchantment and the Faerie realm in literature and culture", 9 April 2021, to be published as an essay in *Gothic Encounters with Enchantment and the Faerie Realm in Literature and Culture*, eds Sam George and Bill Hughes (Manchester: Manchester University Press, forthcoming, 2022).

5 Robert Kirk, *The Secret Commonwealth of Elves, Fauns and Fairies: A Study in Folk-Lore and Psychical Research*, ed. Andrew Lang (London: David Nutt, 1893).

6 Sir Walter Scott, *The Monastery* (Edinburgh: Archibald Constable and John Ballantyne, 1820).

7 For an excellent study of fairies and their relationship with Victorian culture, see Carole G. Silver, *Strange and Secret Peoples: Fairies and Victorian Consciousness* (Oxford: Oxford University Press, 1999).

8 For a detailed discussion of this, see Carole G. Silver, "Little Goblin Men: On Dwarfs and Pygmies, Racial Myths and Mythic Races", in *Strange and Secret Peoples*, pp.117–47.

9 Sophia Morrison, writing in W.Y. Evans Wentz, *The Fairy Faith in Celtic Countries* (London: Oxford University Press, 1911).

10 Helena Blavatsky, *Isis Unveiled: A Master-Key to the Mysteries of Ancient and Modern Science and Theology*, Centenary Anniversary Edition (The Theosophy Company, 1931), p. 30, available online <https://www.theosophy-ult.org.uk/wp-content/uploads/2013/12/isis-unveiled-vol1. pdf> [accessed 18 September 2021].

11 For instance, *Reynold's Illustrated News* reported on 1 December 1929 that "Many weird stories are in circulation in the Western islands regarding Miss Farnario [sic] … Among the tales now circulated are mysterious remarks about blue lights and a cloaked man having been seen near the body."

12 Samuel Drew, *The History of Cornwall From the Earliest Records & Traditions, to the Present Time*, 2 vols (London: William Penaluna, 1824). It is worth noting that this argument has

always been made about fairies, including by Chaucer's Wife of Bath herself—at the beginning of her tale she remarks that "In th' olde dayes of the Kyng Arthour […] Al was this land fulfild of fayerye. […] I speke of manye hundred yeres ago / But now kan no man se none elves mo".

13 W.B. Yeats, *The Celtic Twilight* (London: A.H. Bullen, 1902).

14 Letter to his wife, quoted in *William Sharp (Fiona Macleod): A Memoir, compiled by his wife, Elizabeth A. Sharp* (New York: Duffield & Company, 1910), p. 289.

15 Cited in the Oxford English Dictionary, "fairy" (n.) 3.

16 For further discussion of the term "fairy" and its uses see George Chauncey, *Gay New York: Gender, Urban Culture, and the Making of the Gay Male World, 1890–1940* (New York: Basic Books, 1995), e.g. in his introduction.

17 Steve Berman (ed.), *So Fey: Queer Fairy Fiction* (Amhurst, MA: Lethe Press, 2007).

18 For a book-length analysis of the case, see Angela Bourke, *The Burning of Bridget Cleary: A True Story* (London: Pimlico, 1999, 2006).

FURTHER READING

Angela Bourke, *The Burning of Bridget Cleary: A True Story* (London: Pimlico, 1999, 2006)

Katharine Briggs, *The Fairies in Tradition and Literature* (London: Routledge, 1967)

Joe Cooper, *The Case of the Cottingley Fairies* (London: Simon & Schuster, 1990)

Arthur Conan Doyle, *The Coming of the Fairies* (New York: George H. Doran Company, 1922)

Diane Purkiss, *Fairies and Fairy Stories: A History* (Stroud: Tempus, 2000, 2007)

Carole G. Silver, *Strange and Secret Peoples: Fairies and Victorian Consciousness* (Oxford: Oxford University Press, 1999)

ELIZABETH DEARNLEY is a folklorist, artist and researcher based at the School of Advanced Study, University of London, and the University of Wolverhampton. Her work explores fairy tales, horror and collective story-telling, and she has curated several projects delving into these fields, including immersive 1940s Red Riding Hood retelling *Big Teeth*, and her uncanny restaging of E.T.A. Hoffmann's "The Sandman" for the Freud Museum London. Her previous anthology *Into the London Fog* was published in the British Library Tales of the Weird series.

ACKNOWLEDGEMENTS

Thank you to Jonny Davidson at the British Library for all his enthusiasm and support for this book, and for his numerous hunts for fairy material in the library collections as it took shape. Thanks are also due to Mauricio Villamayor and Mag Ruhig for their gorgeous cover design, and to the Tetragon typesetting team for pulling together all of the stories, folklore snippets and images to make such a beautiful-looking book.

This collection has developed alongside a wider ongoing project on the Cottingley Fairies, and I'm hugely fortunate to have such excellent and imaginative collaborators in Tamsin Dearnley and Amy Cutler. Many thanks are also due to Merrick Burrow, curator of the Brotherton Library's "The Cottingley Fairies: A Study in Deception" exhibition, for his inspiring key-note on the Cottingley Fairies at the 2021 Open Graves, Open Minds conference "'Ill met by moonlight': Gothic encounters with enchantment and the Faerie realm in literature and culture", as well as for his encouragement of my project. I'd also like to thank Sam George, co-convenor of the OGOM project, for her generosity in sharing her conference keynote with me, and for organizing such a fantastic conference.

Thanks are also due to Eilís Phillips for her invaluable reading sugges-tions on Victorian fairies and her generously shared PhD, "The Monstrous Economy: Guilt & Culpability in Representations of the British Working Classes, 1800–1901", to Kay McLeod for answering all my questions on Irish translation, and to Andy Johnson, Sasha Garwood Lloyd, Amy Cutler, Christopher Dearnley and Joan Dearnley for their careful reading of the introduction. Finally, I'd like to thank my great-grandparents Ellen and Stanley Dearnley, who lived in Fairy Dell, Cottingley, for my original family connection to the Cottingley fairies.

1867

THE BANSHEE'S WARNING

Charlotte Riddell

Charlotte Riddell (1832–1906) grew up in County Antrim, Northern Ireland, and moved to London in her early 20s after her father's death, determined to earn a living by writing. In 1856 her first book, *Zuriel's Grandchild*, was accepted by Thomas Cautley Newby, better known for being the first to publish Emily Brontë's *Wuthering Heights*. Riddell went on to publish over 50 novels, tale collections and short stories, and edited the literary periodical *St James's Magazine*, of which she was also co-proprietor.

Today, Riddell is remembered for her ghost stories and weird tales, modelled on those of Sheridan Le Fanu. Her supernatural plots often feature flawed yet sympathetic characters buffeted by modern urban life, with spirits from the past returning to redress long-buried wrongs. "The Banshee's Warning" was her first ghostly tale to be published, appearing in the Christmas 1867 edition of *London Society*, and brings the Irish banshee (*bean sí*, "fairy woman")—a female fairy who foretells death by wailing or shrieking—to Soho's Gerard Street. Cynical Irish surgeon Hertford O'Donnell is a rising star at Guy's Hospital, determined not to look back on his previous life, but as he discovers, the past has an eerie way of resurfacing.

As the Leanan-Sidhe was the acknowledged spirit of life, giving inspiration to the poet and the musician, so the Ban-Sidhe was the spirit of death, the most weird and awful of all the fairy powers.

[...]

Sometimes the Banshee assumes the form of some sweet singing virgin of the family who died young, and has been given the mission by the invisible powers to become the harbinger of coming doom to her mortal kindred. Or she may be seen as a shrouded woman, crouched beneath the trees, lamenting with veiled face; or flying past in the moonlight, crying bitterly: and the cry of this spirit is mournful beyond all other sounds on earth, and betokens mournful death to some member of the family whenever it is heard in the silence of the night.

Speranza (Lady Francesca Wilde), *Ancient Legends, Mystic Charms, and Superstitions of Ireland* (1887)

MANY a year, before chloroform was thought of, there lived in an old rambling house, in Gerrard Street, Soho, a clever Irishman called Hertford O'Donnell.

After Hertford O'Donnell he was entitled to write, M.R.C.S., for he had studied hard to gain this distinction, and the older surgeons at Guy's (his hospital) considered him one of the most rising operators of the day.

Having said chloroform was unknown at the time this story opens, it will strike my readers that, if Hertford O'Donnell were a rising and successful operator in those days, of necessity he combined within himself a larger number of striking qualities than are by any means necessary to form a successful operator in these.

There was more than mere hand skill, more than even thorough knowledge of his profession, then needful for the man, who, dealing with conscious subjects, essayed to rid them of some of the diseases to which flesh is heir. There was greater courage required in the manipulator of old than is altogether essential at present. Then, as now, a thorough mastery of his instruments, a steady hand, a keen eye, a quick dexterity were indispensable to a good operator; but, added to all these things, there formerly required a pulse which knew no quickening, a mental strength which never faltered, a ready power of adaptation in unexpected circumstances, fertility of resource in difficult cases, and a brave front under all emergencies.

If I refrain from adding that a hard as well as a courageous heart was an important item in the programme, it is only out of deference to general opinion, which, amongst other strange delusions, clings to the belief that courage and hardness are antagonistic qualities.

Hertford O'Donnell, however, was hard as steel. He understood his work, and he did it thoroughly; but he cared no more for quivering nerves and shrinking muscles, for screams of agony, for faces white with pain, and teeth clenched in the extremity of anguish, than he did for the stony countenances of the dead, which so often in the dissecting room appalled younger and less experienced men.

He had no sentiment, and he had no sympathy. The human body was to him, merely an ingenious piece of mechanism, which it was at once a pleasure and a profit to understand. Precisely as Brunei loved the Thames Tunnel, or any other singular engineering feat, so O'Donnell loved a patient on whom he had operated successfully, more especially if the ailment possessed by the patient were of a rare and difficult character.

And for this reason he was much liked by all who came under his hands, since patients are apt to mistake a surgeon's interest in their cases for interest in themselves; and it was gratifying to John Dicks, plasterer, and Timothy Regan, labourer, to be the happy possessors of remarkable diseases, which produced a cordial understanding between them and the handsome Irishman.

If he had been hard and cool at the moment of hacking them to pieces, that was all forgotten or remembered only as a virtue, when, after being discharged from hospital like soldiers who have served in a severe campaign, they met Mr. O'Donnell in the street, and were accosted by that rising individual just as though he considered himself nobody.

He had a royal memory, this stranger in a strange land, both for faces and cases; and like the rest of his countrymen, he never felt it beneath his dignity to talk cordially to corduroy and fustian.

In London, as at Calgillan, he never held back his tongue from speaking a cheery or a kindly word. His manners were pliable enough, if his heart were not; and the porters, and the patients, and the nurses, and the students at Guy's were all pleased to see Hertford O'Donnell.

Rain, hail, sunshine, it was all the same; there was a life and a brightness about the man which communicated itself to those with whom he came in contact. Let the mud in the Borough be a foot deep or the London fog as thick as pea-soup, Mr. O'Donnell never lost his temper, never muttered a surly reply to the gate-keeper's salutation, but spoke out blithely and cheerfully to his pupils and his patients, to the sick and to the well, to those below and to those above him.

And yet, spite of all these good qualities, spite of his handsome face, his fine figure, his easy address, and his unquestionable skill as an operator, the dons, who acknowledged his talent, shook their heads gravely when two or three of them in private and solemn conclave, talked confidentially of their younger brother.

If there were many things in his favour, there were more in his disfavour. He was Irish—not merely by the accident of birth, which might have been forgiven, since a man cannot be held accountable for such caprices of Nature, but by every other accident and design which is objectionable to the orthodox and respectable and representative English mind.

In speech, appearance, manner, taste, modes of expression, habits of life, Hertford O'Donnell was Irish. To the core of his heart he loved the island which he declared he never meant to re-visit; and amongst the English he moved to all intents and purposes a foreigner, who was resolved, so said the great prophets at Guy's, to rush to destruction as fast as he could, and let no man hinder him.

"He means to go the whole length of his tether," observed one of the ancient wiseacres to another; which speech implied a conviction that Hertford O'Donnell having sold himself to the Evil One, had determined to dive the full length of his rope into wickedness before being pulled to that shore where even wickedness is negative—where there are no mad carouses, no wild, sinful excitements, nothing but impotent wailing and gnashing of teeth.

A reckless, graceless, clever, wicked devil—going to his natural home as fast as in London any one can possibly speed thither; this was the opinion his superiors, held of the man who lived all alone with a housekeeper and her husband (who acted as butler) in his big house near Soho.

Gerrard Street—made famous by De Quincey, was not then an utterly shady and forgotten locality; carriage-patients found their way to the rising young surgeon—some great personages thought it not beneath them to fee an individual whose consulting rooms were situated on what was even then considered the wrong side of Regent Street. He was making money, and he was spending it; he was over head and ears in debt—useless, vulgar debt—senselessly contracted, never bravely faced. He had lived at an awful pace ever since he came to London, a pace which only a man who hopes and expects to die young can ever travel.

Life, what good was it? Death, was he a child, or a woman, or a coward, to be afraid of that hereafter? God knew all about the trifle which had upset his coach, better than the dons at Guy's.

Hertford O'Donnell understood the world pretty thoroughly, and the ways thereof were to him as roads often traversed; therefore, when he said that at the Day of Judgment he felt certain he should come off as well as many of those who censured him, it may be assumed, that, although his views of post-mortem punishment were vague, unsatisfactory and infidel, still his information as to the peccadilloes of his neighbours was such as consoled himself.

And yet, living all alone in the old house near Soho Square, grave thoughts would intrude into the surgeon's mind—thoughts which were, so to say, italicized by peremptory letters, and still more peremptory visits from people who wanted money.

Although he had many acquaintances he had no single friend, and accordingly these thoughts were received and brooded over in solitude—in those hours when, after returning from dinner, or supper, or congenial carouse, he sat in his dreary rooms, smoking his pipe and considering means and ways, chances and certainties.

In good truth he had started in London with some vague idea that as his life in it would not be of long continuance, the pace at which he elected to travel could be of little consequence; but the years since his first entry into the Metropolis were now piled one on the top of another, his youth was behind him, his chances of longevity, spite of the way he had striven to injure his constitution, quite as good as ever. He had come to that period in existence, to that narrow strip of tableland, whence the ascent of youth and the descent of age are equally discernible—when, simply because he has lived for so many years, it strikes a man as possible he may have to live for just as many more, with the ability for hard work gone, with the boon companions scattered, with the capacity for enjoying convivial meetings a mere memory, with small means perhaps, with no bright hopes, with the pomp and the circumstance and the fairy carriages, and the glamour which youth flings over earthly objects, faded away like the pageant of yesterday, while the dreary ceremony of living has to be gone through today and tomorrow and the morrow after, as though the gay cavalcade and the martial music, and the glittering helmets and the prancing steeds were still accompanying the wayfarer to his journey's end.

Ah! my friends, there comes a moment when we must all leave the coach, with its four bright bays, its pleasant outside freight, its cheery company, its guard who blows the horn so merrily through villages and along lonely country roads.

Long before we reach that final stage, where the black business claims us for its own especial property, we have to bid goodbye to all easy, thoughtless journeying, and betake ourselves, with what zest we may, to traversing the common of reality. There is no royal road across it that ever I heard of. From the King on his throne to the labourer who vaguely imagines what manner of being a king is, we have all to tramp across that desert at one period of our lives, at all events; and that period usually is when, as I have said, a man starts to find the hopes, and the strength, and the buoyancy of youth left behind, while years and years of life lie stretching out before him.

The coach he has travelled by drops him here. There is no appeal, there is no help; therefore, let him take off his hat and wish the new passengers good speed, without either envy or repining.

Behold, he has had his turn, and let whosoever will, mount on the box-seat of life again, and tip the coachman and handle the ribbons—he shall take that pleasant journey no more, no more for ever.

Even supposing a man's Spring-time to have been a cold and ungenial one, with bitter easterly winds and nipping frosts, biting the buds and retarding the blossoms, still it was Spring for all that—Spring with the young green leaves sprouting forth, with the flowers unfolding tenderly, with the songs of the birds and the rush of waters, with the Summer before and the Autumn afar off, and Winter remote as death and eternity, but when once the trees have donned their Summer foliage, when the pure white blossoms have disappeared, and the gorgeous red and orange and purple blaze of many-coloured flowers fills the gardens, then if there come a wet, dreary day, the idea of Autumn and Winter is not so difficult to realize. When once twelve o'clock is reached, the evening and night become facts, not possibilities; and it was of the afternoon, and the evening, and the night, Hertford O'Donnell sat thinking on the Christmas Eve, when I crave permission to introduce him to my readers.

A good-looking man ladies considered him. A tall, dark-complexioned, black-haired, straight-limbed, deeply divinely blue-eyed fellow, with a soft voice, with a pleasant brogue, who had ridden like a centaur over the loose stone walls in Connemara, who had danced all night at the Dublin balls, who had walked across the Bennebeola Mountains, gun in hand, day after day, without weariness, who had fished in every one of the hundred lakes you can behold from the top of that mountain near the Recess Hotel, who had led a mad, wild life in Trinity College, and a wilder, perhaps, while "studying for a doctor"—as the Irish phrase goes—in Edinburgh, and who, after the death of his eldest brother left him free to return to Calgillan, and pursue the usual utterly useless, utterly purposeless, utterly pleasant life of an Irish gentleman possessed of health, birth, and expectations, suddenly kicked over the paternal traces, bade adieu to Calgillan Castle and the blandishments of a certain beautiful Miss Clifden, beloved of his mother, and laid out to be his wife, walked down the avenue without even so much company as a Gossoon to carry his carpet-bag, shook the dust from his feet at the lodge gates, and took his seat on the coach, never once looking back at Calgillan, where his favourite mare was standing in the stable, his greyhounds chasing one another round the home paddock, his gun at half-cock in his dressing-room and his fishing-tackle all in order and ready for use.

He had not kissed his mother, or asked for his father's blessing; he left Miss Clifden, arrayed in her brand-new riding-habit, without a word of affection or regret; he had spoken no syllable of farewell to any servant about the place; only when the old woman at the lodge bade him good morning and God-blessed his handsome face, he recommended her bitterly to look at it well for she would never see it more.

Twelve years and a half had passed since then, without either Nancy Blake or any other one of the Calgillan people having set eyes on Master Hertford's handsome face.

He had kept his vow to himself; he had not written home; he had not been indebted to mother or father for even a tenpenny-piece during the whole of that time; he had lived without friends; and he had lived without God—so far as God ever lets a man live without him.

One thing only he felt to be needful—money; money to keep him when the evil days of sickness, or age, or loss of practice came upon him. Though a spendthrift, he was not a simpleton; around him he saw men, who, having started with fairer prospects than his own, were, nevertheless, reduced to indigence; and he knew that what had happened to others might happen to himself.

An unlucky cut, slipping on a piece of orange-peel in the street, the merest accident imaginable, is sufficient to change opulence to beggary in the life's programme of an individual, whose income depends on eye, on nerve, on hand; and, besides the consciousness of this fact, Hertford O'Donnell knew that beyond a certain point in his profession, progress was not easy.

It did not depend quite on the strength of his own bow and shield whether he counted his earnings by hundreds or thousands. Work may achieve competence; but mere work cannot, in a profession, at all events, compass fortune.

He looked around him, and he perceived that the majority of great men—great and wealthy—had been indebted for their elevation, more to the accident of birth, patronage, connection, or marriage, than to personal ability.

Personal ability, no doubt, they possessed; but then, little Jones, who lived in Frith Street, and who could barely keep himself and his wife and family, had ability, too, only he lacked the concomitants of success.

He wanted something or someone to puff him into notoriety—a brother at Court—a lord's leg to mend—a rich wife to give him prestige in Society; and in the absence of this something or someone, he had grown grey-haired and faint-hearted while labouring for a world which utterly despises its most obsequious servants.

"Clatter along the streets with a pair of fine horses, snub the middle classes, and drive over the commonalty—that is the way to compass wealth and popularity in England," said Hertford O'Donnell, bitterly; and as the man desired wealth and popularity, he sat before his fire, with a foot on each hob, and a short pipe in his mouth, considering how he might best obtain the means to clatter along the streets in his carriage, and splash plebeians with mud from his wheels like the best.

In Dublin he could, by means of his name and connection, have done well; but then he was not in Dublin, neither did he want to be. The bitterest memories of his life were inseparable from the very name of the Green Island, and he had no desire to return to it.

Besides, in Dublin, heiresses are not quite so plentiful as in London; and an heiress, Hertford O'Donnell had decided, would do more for him than years of steady work.

A rich wife could clear him of debt, introduce him to fashionable practice, afford him that measure of social respectability which a medical bachelor invariably lacks, deliver him from the loneliness of Gerrard Street, and the domination of Mr. and Mrs. Coles.

To most men, deliberately bartering away their independence for money seems so prosaic a business that they strive to gloss it over even to themselves, and to assign every reason for their choice, save that which is really the influencing one.

Not so, however, with Hertford O'Donnell. He sat beside the fire scoffing over his proposed bargain—thinking of the lady's age, her money bags, her desirable house in town, her seat in the country, her snobbishness, her folly.

"It would be a fitting ending," he sneered, "and why I did not settle the matter tonight passes my comprehension. I am not a fool, to be frightened with old women's tales; and yet I must have turned white. I felt I did, and she asked me whether I were ill. And then to think of my being such an idiot as to ask her if she had heard anything like a cry, as though she would be likely to hear *that*, she with her poor parvenu blood, which I often imagine must have been mixed with some of her father's strong pickling vinegar. What the deuce could I have been dreaming about? I wonder what it really was." And Hertford O'Donnell pushed his hair back off his forehead, and took another draught from the too familiar tumbler, which was placed conveniently on the chimney-piece.

"After expressly making up my mind to propose, too!" he mentally continued. "Could it have been conscience—that myth, which somebody, who knew nothing about the matter, said, 'Makes cowards of us all?' I don't believe in conscience; and even if there be such a thing capable of being developed by sentiment and cultivation, why should it trouble me? I have no intention of wronging Miss Janet Price Ingot, not the least. Honestly and fairly I shall marry her; honestly and fairly I shall act by her. An old wife is not exactly an ornamental article of furniture in a man's house; and I do not know that the fact of her being well gilded makes her look any handsomer. But she shall have no cause for complaint; and I will go and dine with her tomorrow, and settle the matter."

Having arrived at which resolution, Mr. O'Donnell arose, kicked down the fire—burning hollow—with the heel of his boot, knocked the ashes out of his pipe, emptied his tumbler, and bethought him it was time to go to bed. He was not in the habit of taking his rest so early as a quarter to twelve o'clock; but he felt unusually weary—tired mentally and bodily—and lonely beyond all power of expression.

"The fair Janet would be better than this," he said, half aloud; and then, with a start and a shiver, and a blanched face, he turned sharply round, whilst a low, sobbing, wailing cry echoed mournfully through the room. No form of words could give an idea of the sound. The plaintiveness of the Æolian harp—that plaintiveness which so soon affects and lowers the highest spirits—would have seemed wildly gay in comparison with the sadness of the cry which seemed floating in the air. As the Summer wind comes and goes amongst the trees, so that mournful wail came and went—came and went. It came in a rush of sound, like a gradual crescendo managed by a skilful musician, and died away in a lingering note, so gently that the listener could scarcely tell the exact moment when it faded into utter silence.

I say faded, for it disappeared as the coast line disappears in the twilight, and there was total stillness in the apartment.

Then, for the first time, Hertford O'Donnell looked at his dog, and beholding the creature crouched into a corner beside the fireplace, called upon him to come out.

His voice sounded strange even to himself, and apparently the dog thought so too, for he made no effort to obey the summons.

"Come here, sir," his master repeated, and then the animal came crawling reluctantly forward with his hair on end, his eyes almost starting from his head, trembling violently, as the surgeon, who caressed him, felt.

"So you heard it, Brian?" he said to the dog. "And so your ears are sharper than Miss Ingot's, old fellow. It's a mighty queer thing to think of, being favoured with a visit from a Banshee in Gerrard Street; and as the lady has travelled so far, I only wish I knew whether there is any sort of refreshment she would like to take after her long journey."

He spoke loudly, and with a certain mocking defiance, seeming to think the phantom he addressed would reply; but when he stopped at the end of his sentence, no sound came through the stillness. There was a dead silence in the room—a silence broken only by the falling of the cinders on the hearth and the breathing of his dog.

"If my visitor would tell me," he proceeded, "for whom this lamentation is being made, whether for myself, or for some member of my illustrious family, I should feel immensely obliged. It seems too much honour for a poor surgeon to have such attention paid him. Good Heavens! What is that?" he exclaimed, as a ring, loud and peremptory, woke all the echoes in the house, and brought his housekeeper, in a state of distressing dishabille, "out of her warm bed," as she subsequently stated, to the head of the staircase.

Across the hall Hertford O'Donnell strode, relieved at the prospect of speaking to any living being. He took no precaution of putting up the chain, but flung the door wide. A dozen burglars would have proved welcome in comparison with that ghostly intruder he had been interviewing; therefore, as has been said, he threw the door wide, admitting a rush of wet, cold air, which made poor Mrs. Coles' few remaining teeth chatter in her head.

"Who is there? What do you want?" asked the surgeon, seeing no person, and hearing no voice. "Who is there? Why the devil can't you speak?"

When even this polite exhortation failed to elicit an answer, he passed out into the night and looked up the street and down the street, to see nothing but the driving rain and the blinking lights.

"If this goes on much longer I shall soon think I must be either mad or drunk," he muttered, as he re-entered the house and locked and bolted the door once more.

"Lord's sake! What is the matter, sir?" asked Mrs. Coles, from the upper flight, careful only to reveal the borders of her night-cap to Mr. O'Donnell's admiring gaze. "Is anybody killed? Have you to go out, sir?"

"It was only a run-away ring," he answered, trying to reassure himself with an explanation he did not in his heart believe.

"Run-away—I'd run away them!" murmured Mrs. Coles, as she retired to the conjugal couch, where Coles was, to quote her own expression, "snoring like a pig through it all."

Almost immediately afterwards she heard her master ascend the stairs and close his bedroom door.

"Madam will surely be too much of a gentlewoman to intrude here," thought the surgeon, scoffing even at his own fears; but when he lay down he did not put out his light, and made Brian leap up and crouch on the coverlet beside him.

The man was fairly frightened, and would have thought it no discredit to his manhood to acknowledge as much. He was not afraid of death, he was not afraid of trouble, he was not afraid of danger; but he was afraid of the Banshee; and as he laid with his hand on the dog's head, he recalled the many stories he had been told concerning this family retainer in the days of his youth.

He had not thought about her for years and years. Never before had he heard her voice himself. When his brother died she had not thought it necessary to travel up to Dublin and give him notice of the impending catastrophe. "If she had, I would have gone down to Calgillan, and perhaps saved his life," considered the surgeon. "I wonder who this is for? If for me, that will settle my debts and my marriage. If I could be quite certain it was either of the old people, I would start tomorrow."

Then vaguely his mind wandered on to think of every Banshee story he had ever heard in his life. About the beautiful lady with the wreath of flowers, who sat on the rocks below Red Castle, in the County Antrim, crying till one of the sons died for love of her; about the Round Chamber at Dunluce, which was swept clean by the Banshee every night; about the bed in a certain great house in Ireland, which was slept in constantly, although no human being ever passed in or out after dark; about that

General Officer who, the night before Waterloo, said to a friend, "I have heard the Banshee, and shall not come off the field alive tomorrow; break the news gently to poor Carry;" and who, nevertheless, coming safe off the field, had subsequently news about poor Carry broken tenderly and pitifully to him; about the lad, who, aloft in the rigging, hearing through the night a sobbing and wailing coming over the waters, went down to the captain and told him he was afraid they were somehow out of their reckoning, just in time to save the ship, which, when morning broke, they found but for his warning would have been on the rocks. It was blowing great guns, and the sea was all in a fret and turmoil, and they could sometimes see in the trough of the waves, as down a valley, the cruel black reefs they had escaped.

On deck the captain stood speaking to the boy who had saved them, and asking how he knew of their danger; and when the lad told him, the captain laughed, and said her ladyship had been outwitted that time.

But the boy answered, with a grave shake of his head, that the warning was either for him or his, and that if he got safe to port there would be bad tidings waiting for him from home; whereupon the captain bade him go below, and get some brandy and lie down.

He got the brandy, and he lay down, but he never rose again; and when the storm abated—when a great calm succeeded to the previous tempest—there was a very solemn funeral at sea; and on their arrival at Liverpool the captain took a journey to Ireland to tell a widowed mother how her only son died, and to bear his few effects to the poor desolate soul.

And Hertford O'Donnell thought again about his own father riding full-chase across country, and hearing, as he galloped by a clump of plantation, something like a sobbing and wailing. The hounds were in full cry, but he still felt, as he afterwards expressed it, that there was something among those trees he could not pass; and so he jumped off his horse, and hung the reins over the branch of a Scotch fir, and beat the cover well, but not a thing could he find in it.

Then, for the first time in his life, Miles O'Donnell turned his horse's head *from* the hunt, and, within a mile of Calgillan, met a man running to tell him his brother's gun had burst, and injured him mortally.

And he remembered the story also, of how Mary O'Donnell, his great aunt, being married to a young Englishman, heard the Banshee as she sat one evening waiting for his return; and of how she, thinking the bridge by which he often came home unsafe for horse and man, went out in a great panic, to meet and entreat him to go round by the main road for her sake. Sir Everard was riding along in the moonlight, making straight for the bridge, when he beheld a figure dressed all in white crossing it. Then there was a crash, and the figure disappeared.

The lady was rescued and brought back to the hall; but next morning there were two dead bodies within its walls—those of Lady Eyreton and her still-born son.

Quicker than I write them, these memories chased one another through Hertford O'Donnell's brain; and there was one more terrible memory than any, which would recur to him, concerning an Irish nobleman who, seated alone in his great town-house in London, heard the Banshee, and rushed out to get rid of the phantom, which wailed in his ear, nevertheless, as he strode down Piccadilly. And then the surgeon remembered how that nobleman went with a friend to the Opera, feeling sure that there no Banshee, unless she had a box, could find admittance, until suddenly he heard her singing up amongst the highest part of the scenery, with a terrible mournfulness, and a pathos which made the prima donna's tenderest notes seem harsh by comparison.

As he came out, some quarrel arose between him and a famous fire-eater, against whom he stumbled; and the result was that the next afternoon there was a new Lord—vice Lord ——, killed in a duel with Captain Bravo.

Memories like these are not the most enlivening possible; they are apt to make a man fanciful, and nervous, and wakeful; but as time ran on, Hertford O'Donnell fell asleep, with his candle still burning, and Brian's cold nose pressed against his hand.

He dreamt of his mother's family—the Hertfords of Artingbury, Yorkshire, far-off relatives of Lord Hertford—so far off that even Mrs. O'Donnell held no clue to the genealogical maze.

He thought he was at Artingbury, fishing; that it was a misty Summer morning, and the fish rising beautifully. In his dreams he hooked one after another, and the boy who was with him threw them into the basket.

At last there was one more difficult to land than the others; and the boy, in his eagerness to watch the sport, drew nearer and nearer to the brink, while the fisher, intent on his prey, failed to notice his companion's danger.

Suddenly there was a cry, a splash, and the boy disappeared from sight.

Next instant he rose again, however, and then, for the first time, Hertford O'Donnell saw his face.

It was one he knew well.

In a moment he plunged into the water, and struck out for the lad. He had him by the hair, he was turning to bring him back to land, when the stream suddenly changed into a wide, wild, shoreless sea, where the billows were chasing one another with a mad demoniac mirth.

For a while O'Donnell kept the lad and himself afloat. They were swept under the waves, and came up again, only to see larger waves rushing towards them; but through all, the surgeon never loosened his hold, until a tremendous billow, engulphing them both, tore the boy from his grasp.

With the horror of his dream upon him he awoke, to hear a voice saying quite distinctly:

"Go to the hospital—go at once!"

The surgeon started up in bed, rubbed his eyes, and looked around. The candle was flickering faintly in its socket. Brian, with his ears pricked forward, had raised his head at his master's sudden movement.

Everything was quiet, but still those words were ringing in his ear:

"Go to the hospital—go at once!"

The tremendous peal of the bell over night, and this sentence, seemed to be simultaneous.

That he was wanted at Guy's—wanted imperatively—came to O'Donnell like an inspiration. Neither sense nor reason had anything to do with the conviction that roused him out of bed, and made him dress as speedily as possible, and grope his way down the staircase, Brian following.

He opened the front door, and passed out into the darkness. The rain was over, and the stars were shining as he pursued his way down Newport Market, and thence, winding in and out in a south-easterly direction, through Lincoln's Inn Fields and Old Square to Chancery Lane, whence he proceeded to St. Paul's.

Along the deserted streets he resolutely continued his walk. He did not know what he was going to Guy's for. Some instinct was urging him on, and he neither strove to combat nor control it. Only once did the thought of turning back cross his mind, and that was at the archway leading into Old Square. There he had paused for a moment, asking himself whether he were not gone stark, staring mad; but Guy's seemed preferable to the haunted house in Gerrard Street, and he walked resolutely on, determined to say, if any surprise were expressed at his appearance, that he had been sent for.

Sent for?—yea, truly; but by whom?

On through Cannon Street; on over London Bridge, where the lights flickered in the river, and the sullen plash of the water flowing beneath the arches, washing the stone piers, could be heard, now the human din was hushed and lulled to sleep. On, thinking of many things: of the days of his youth; of his dead brother; of his father's heavily-encumbered estate; of the fortune his mother had vowed she would leave to some charity rather than to him, if he refused to marry according to her choice; of his wild life in London; of the terrible cry he had heard overnight—that unearthly wail which he could not drive from his memory even when he entered Guy's, and confronted the porter, who said:

"You have been sent for, sir; did you meet the messenger?"

Like one in a dream, Hertford O'Donnell heard him; like one in a dream, also, he asked what was the matter.

"Bad accident, sir; fire; fell off a balcony—unsafe—old building. Mother and child—a son; child with compound fracture of thigh."

This, the joint information of porter and house-surgeon, mingled together, and made a boom in Mr. O'Donnell's ears like the sound of the sea breaking on a shingly shore.

Only one sentence he understood properly—"Immediate amputation necessary." At this point he grew cool; he was the careful, cautious, successful surgeon in a moment.

"The child you say?" he answered. "Let me see him."

The Guy's Hospital of today may be different to the Guy's Hertford O'Donnell knew so well. Railways have, I believe, swept away the old operating room; railways may have changed the position of the former accident ward, to reach which, in the days of which I am writing, the two surgeons had to pass a staircase leading to the upper stories.

On the lower step of this staircase, partially in shadow, Hertford O'Donnell beheld, as he came forward, an old woman seated.

An old woman with streaming grey hair, with attenuated arms, with head bowed forward, with scanty clothing, with bare feet; who never looked up at their approach, but sat unnoticing, shaking her head and wringing her hands in an extremity of despair.

"Who is that?" asked Mr. O'Donnell, almost involuntarily.

"Who is what?" demanded his companion.

"That—that woman," was the reply.

"What woman?"

"There—are you blind?—seated on the bottom step of the staircase. What is she doing?" persisted Mr. O'Donnell.

"There is no woman near us," his companion answered, looking at the rising surgeon very much as though he suspected him of seeing double.

"No woman!" scoffed Hertford. "Do you expect me to disbelieve the evidence of my own eyes?" and he walked up to the figure, meaning to touch it.

But as he essayed to do so, the woman seemed to rise in the air and float away, with her arms stretched high up over her head, uttering such a wail of pain, and agony, and distress, as caused the Irishman's blood to curdle.

"My God! Did you hear that?" he said to his companion.

"What?" was the reply.

Then, although he knew the sound had fallen on deaf ears, he answered: "The wail of the Banshee! Some of my people are doomed!"

"I trust not," answered the house-surgeon, who had an idea, nevertheless, that Hertford O'Donnell's Banshee lived in a whisky bottle, and would at some not remote day make an end of the rising and clever operator.

With nerves utterly shaken, Mr. O'Donnell walked forward to the accident ward. There with his face shaded from the light, lay his patient—a young boy, with a compound fracture of the thigh.

In that ward, in the face of actual danger or pain capable of relief the surgeon had never known faltering or fear; and now he carefully examined the injury, felt the pulse, inquired as to the treatment pursued, and ordered the sufferer to be carried to the operating room.

While he was looking out his instruments he heard the boy lying on the table murmur faintly:

"Tell her not to cry so—tell her not to cry."

"What is he talking about?" Hertford O'Donnell inquired.

"The nurse says he has been speaking about some woman crying ever since he came in—his mother, most likely," answered one of the attendants.

"He is delirious then?" observed the surgeon.

"No, sir," pleaded the boy, excitedly, "no; it is that woman—that woman with the grey hair. I saw her looking from the upper window before the balcony gave way. She has never left me since, and she won't be quiet, wringing her hands and crying."

"Can you see her now?" Hertford O'Donnell inquired, stepping to the side of the table. "Point out where she is."

Then the lad stretched forth a feeble finger in the direction of the door, where clearly, as he had seen her seated on the stairs, the surgeon saw a woman standing—a woman with grey hair and scanty clothing, and upstretched arms and bare feet.

"A word with you, sir," O'Donnell said to the house-surgeon, drawing him back from the table. "I cannot perform this operation: send for some other person. I am ill; I am incapable."

"But," pleaded the other, "there is no time to get anyone else. We sent for Mr. West, before we troubled you, but he was out of town, and all the rest of the surgeons live so far away. Mortification may set in at any moment, and—"

"Do you think you require to teach me my business?" was the reply. "I know the boy's life hangs on a thread, and that is the very reason I cannot operate. I am not fit for it. I tell you I have seen tonight that which unnerves me utterly. My hand is not steady. Send for someone else without delay. Say I am ill—dead!—what you please. Heavens! There she is again, right over the boy! Do you hear her?" and Hertford O'Donnell fell fainting on the floor.

How long he lay in that death-like swoon I cannot say; but when he returned to consciousness, the principal physician of Guy's was standing beside him in the cold grey light of the Christmas morning.

"The boy?" murmured O'Donnell, faintly.

"Now, my dear fellow, keep yourself quiet," was the reply.

"The boy?" he repeated, irritably. "Who operated?"

"No one," Dr. Lanson answered. "It would have been useless cruelty. Mortification had set in, and—"

Hertford O'Donnell turned his face to the wall, and his friend could not see it.

"Do not distress yourself," went on the physician, kindly. "Allington says he could not have survived the operation in any case. He was quite delirious from the first, raving about a woman with grey hair and—"

"I know," Hertford O'Donnell interrupted; "and the boy had a mother, they told me, or I dreamt it."

"Yes, she was bruised and shaken, but not seriously injured."

"Has she blue eyes and fair hair—fair hair all rippling and wavy? Is she white as a lily, with just a faint flush of colour in her cheek? Is she young and trusting and innocent? No; I am wandering. She must be nearly thirty now. Go, for God's sake, and tell me if you can find a woman you could imagine having once been as a girl such as I describe."

"Irish?" asked the doctor; and O'Donnell made a gesture of assent.

"It is she then," was the reply; "a woman with the face of an angel."

"A woman who should have been my wife," the surgeon answered; "whose child was my son."

"Lord help you!" ejaculated the doctor. Then Hertford O'Donnell raised himself from the sofa where they had laid him, and told his companion the story of his life—how there had been bitter feud between his people and her people—how they were divided by old animosities and by difference of religion—how they had met by stealth, and exchanged rings and vows, all for naught—how his family had insulted hers, so that her father, wishful for her to marry a kinsman of his own, bore her off to a far-away land, and made her write him a letter of eternal farewell—how his own parents had kept all knowledge of the quarrel from him till she was utterly beyond his reach—how they had vowed to discard him unless he agreed to marry according to their wishes—how he left his home, and came to London, and pushed his fortune. All this Hertford O'Donnell repeated; and when he had finished, the bells were ringing for morning service—ringing loudly, ringing joyfully, "Peace on earth, goodwill towards men."

But there was little peace that morning for Hertford O'Donnell. He had to look on the face of his dead son, wherein he beheld, as though reflected, the face of the boy in his dream.

Afterwards, stealthily he followed his friend, and beheld, with her eyes closed, her cheeks pale and pinched, her hair thinner but still falling like a veil over her, the love of his youth, the only woman he had ever loved devotedly and unselfishly.

There is little space left here to tell of how the two met at last—of how the stone of the years seemed suddenly rolled away from the tomb of their past, and their youth arose and returned to them, even amid their tears.

She had been true to him, through persecution, through contumely, through kindness, which was more trying; through shame, and grief, and poverty, she had been loyal to the lover of her youth; and before the New Year dawned there came a letter from Calgillan, saying that the Banshee's wail had been heard there, and praying Hertford, if he were still alive, to let bygones be bygones, in consideration of the long years of estrangement—the anguish and remorse of his afflicted parents.

More than that. Hertford O'Donnell, if a reckless man, was an honourable; and so, on the Christmas Day when he was to have proposed for Miss Ingot, he went to that lady, and told her how he had wooed and won, in the years of his youth, one who after many days was miraculously restored to him; and from the hour in which he took her into his confidence, he never thought her either vulgar or foolish, but rather he paid homage to the woman who, when she had heard the whole tale repeated, said, simply, "Ask her to come to me till you can claim her—and God bless you both!"

LAURA SILVER BELL

J. Sheridan Le Fanu

Dublin-born writer Joseph Thomas Sheridan Le Fanu (1814–73) published his first ghost story in the *Dublin University Magazine* at the age of 23, and is best known today for his 1872 collection *In a Glass Darkly*, which included the vampire novella *Carmilla* and his menacing story of a demonic monkey, "Green Tea". His macabre Gothic tales have influenced writers from Bram Stoker to Elizabeth Bowen, and E.F. Benson once wrote of him that "as a 'flesh-creeper' he is unrivalled. No one else has so sure a touch in mixing the mysterious atmosphere in which horror darkly breeds."

Le Fanu developed an interest in fairies during his teenage years spent in Abington, County Limerick, where his clergyman father had moved the family in 1826. The Le Fanu family were themselves involved in one fairy-related incident, when Le Fanu's brother William and his mother visited a local labourer who was concerned that his son had been switched for an imposter and had been instructed to hang him over a turf fire if he did not return to his body. The Le Fanus were on the verge of staging an "intervention" when the boy recovered.

Several of Le Fanu's stories are shot through with references to fairies and other Irish folklore, and in the final years of his life he published four fairy horror tales. "Laura Silver Bell", published in the *Belgravia Annual* the year before his death, is set in the moorlands of Northumbria, where unbaptized orphan Laura Lew encounters a mysterious young lord. But however fine his black velvet clothes, his intentions may be somewhat more sinister.

"Loke, dame, tomorwe thatow be
Right here under this ympe-tre,
And than thou schalt with ous go
And live with ous evermo.

And yif thou makest ous y-let,
Whar thou be, thou worst y-fet,
And totore thine limes al
That nothing help the no schal;
And thei thou best so totorn,
Yete thou worst with ous y-born."

["Make sure, lady, that tomorrow you are right here under this orchard tree, and then you'll go with us and live with us forever. And if you try to resist, wherever you are we'll find you, and tear you limb from limb so that nothing can help you; and however torn you are, we'll still take you with us."]

The fairy king of the Otherworld, *Sir Orfeo* (late thirteenth/ early fourteenth century), ll. 165–174. Translation by the editor.

I n the five Northumbrian counties you will scarcely find so bleak, ugly, and yet, in a savage way, so picturesque a moor as Dardale Moss. The moor itself spreads north, south, east, and west, a great undulating sea of black peat and heath.

What we may term its shores are wooded wildly with birch, hazel, and dwarf-oak. No towering mountains surround it, but here and there you have a rocky knoll rising among the trees, and many a wooded promontory of the same pretty, because utterly wild, forest, running out into its dark level.

Habitations are thinly scattered in this barren territory, and a full mile away from the meanest was the stone cottage of Mother Carke.

Let not my southern reader who associates ideas of comfort with the term "cottage" mistake. This thing is built of shingle, with low walls. Its thatch is hollow; the peat-smoke curls stingily from its stunted chimney. It is worthy of its savage surroundings.

The primitive neighbours remark that no rowan-tree grows near, nor holly, nor bracken, and no horseshoe is nailed on the door.

Not far from the birches and hazels that straggle about the rude wall of the little enclosure, on the contrary, they say, you may discover the broom and the rag-wort, in which witches mysteriously delight. But this is perhaps a scandal.

Mall Carke was for many a year the *sage femme* of this wild domain. She has renounced practice, however, for some years; and now, under the rose, she dabbles, it is thought, in the black art, in which she has always been secretly skilled, tells fortunes, practises charms, and in popular esteem is little better than a witch.

Mother Carke has been away to the town of Willarden, to sell knit stockings, and is returning to her rude dwelling by Dardale Moss. To her right, as far away as the eye can reach, the moor stretches. The narrow track she has followed here tops a gentle upland, and at her left a sort of jungle of dwarf-oak and brushwood approaches its edge. The sun is sinking blood-red in the west. His disk has touched the broad black level of the moor, and his parting beams glare athwart the gaunt figure of the old beldame, as she strides homeward stick in hand, and bring into relief the folds of her mantle, which gleam like the draperies of a bronze image in the light of a fire. For a few moments this light floods the air—tree, gorse, rock, and bracken glare; and then it is out, and grey twilight over everything.

All is still and sombre. At this hour the simple traffic of the thinly-peopled country is over, and nothing can be more solitary.

From this jungle, nevertheless, through which the mists of evening are already creeping, she sees a gigantic man approaching her.

In that poor and primitive country robbery is a crime unknown. She, therefore, has no fears for her pound of tea, and pint of gin, and sixteen shillings in silver which she is bringing home in her pocket. But there is something that would have frighted another woman about this man.

He is gaunt, sombre, bony, dirty, and dressed in a black suit which a beggar would hardly care to pick out of the dust.

This ill-looking man nodded to her as he stepped on the road.

"I don't know you," she said.

He nodded again.

"I never sid ye neyawheere," she exclaimed sternly.

"Fine evening, Mother Carke," he says, and holds his snuff-box toward her.

She widened the distance between them by a step or so, and said again sternly and pale,

"I hev nowt to say to thee, whoe'er thou beest."

"You know Laura Silver Bell?"

"That's a byneyam; the lass's neyam is Laura Lew," she answered, looking straight before her.

"One name's as good as another for one that was never christened, mother."

"How know ye that?" she asked grimly; for it is a received opinion in that part of the world that the fairies have power over those who have never been baptized.

The stranger turned on her a malignant smile.

"There is a young lord in love with her," the stranger says, "and I'm that lord. Have her at your house tomorrow night at eight o'clock, and you must stick cross pins through the candle, as you have done for many a one before, to bring her lover thither by ten, and her fortune's made. And take this for your trouble."

He extended his long finger and thumb toward her, with a guinea temptingly displayed.

"I have nowt to do wi' thee. I nivver sid thee afoore. Git thee awa'! I earned nea goold o' thee, and I'll tak' nane. Awa' wi' thee, or I'll find ane that will mak' thee!"

The old woman had stopped, and was quivering in every limb as she thus spoke.

He looked very angry. Sulkily he turned away at her words, and strode slowly toward the wood from which he had come; and as he approached it, he seemed to her to grow taller and taller, and stalked into it as high as a tree.

"I conceited there would come something o't", she said to herself. "Farmer Lew must git it done nesht Sunda'. The a'ad awpy!"

Old Farmer Lew was one of that sect who insist that baptism shall be but once administered, and not until the Christian candidate had attained to adult years. The girl had indeed for some time been of an age not only, according to this theory, to be baptized, but if need be to be married.

Her story was a sad little romance. A lady some seventeen years before had come down and paid Farmer Lew for two rooms in his house. She told him that her husband would follow her in a fortnight, and that he was in the mean time delayed by business in Liverpool.

In ten days after her arrival her baby was born, Mall Carke acting as *sage femme* on the occasion; and on the evening of that day the poor young mother died. No husband came; no wedding-ring, they said, was on her finger. About fifty pounds was found in her desk, which Farmer Lew, who was a kind old fellow and had lost his two children, put in bank for the little girl, and resolved to keep her until a rightful owner should step forward to claim her.

They found half-a-dozen love-letters signed "Francis," and calling the dead woman "Laura."

So Farmer Lew called the little girl Laura; and her *sobriquet* of "Silver Bell" was derived from a tiny silver bell, once gilt, which was found among her poor mother's little treasures after her death, and which the child wore on a ribbon round her neck.

Thus, being very pretty and merry, she grew up as a North-country farmer's daughter; and the old man, as she needed more looking after, grew older and less able to take care of her; so she was, in fact, very nearly her own mistress, and did pretty much in all things as she liked.

Old Mall Carke, by some caprice for which no one could account, cherished an affection for the girl, who saw her often, and paid her many a small fee in exchange for the secret indications of the future.

It was too late when Mother Carke reached her home to look for a visit from Laura Silver Bell that day.

About three o'clock next afternoon, Mother Carke was sitting knitting, with her glasses on, outside her door on the stone bench, when she saw the pretty girl mount lightly to the top of the stile at her left under the birch, against the silver stem of which she leaned her slender hand, and called,

"Mall, Mall! Mother Carke, are ye alane all by yersel'?"

"Ay, Laura lass, we can be clooas enoo, if ye want a word wi' me," says the old woman, rising, with a mysterious nod, and beckoning her stiffly with her long fingers.

The girl was, assuredly, pretty enough for a "lord" to fall in love with. Only look at her. A profusion of brown rippling hair, parted low in the middle of her forehead, almost touched her eyebrows, and made the pretty oval of her face, by the breadth of that rich line, more marked. What a pretty little nose! what scarlet lips, and large, dark, long-fringed eyes!

Her face is transparently tinged with those clear Murillo tints which appear in deeper dyes on her wrists and the backs of her hands. These are the beautiful gipsy-tints with which the sun dyes young skins so richly.

The old woman eyes all this, and her pretty figure, so round and slender, and her shapely little feet, cased in the thick shoes that can't hide their comely proportions, as she stands on the top of the stile. But it is with a dark and saturnine aspect.

"Come, lass, what stand ye for atoppa t' wall, whar folk may chance to see thee? I hev a thing to tell thee, lass."

She beckoned her again.

"An' I hev a thing to tell *thee*, Mall."

"Come hidder," said the old woman peremptorily.

"But ye munna gie me the creepin's" (make me tremble). "I winna look again into the glass o' water, mind ye."

The old woman smiled grimly, and changed her tone.

"Now, hunny, git tha down, and let ma see thy canny feyace," and she beckoned her again.

Laura Silver Bell did get down, and stepped lightly toward the door of the old woman's dwelling.

"Tak this," said the girl, unfolding a piece of bacon from her apron, "and I hev a silver sixpence to gie thee, when I'm gaen away heyam."

They entered the dark kitchen of the cottage, and the old woman stood by the door, lest their conference should be lighted on by surprise.

"Afoore ye begin," said Mother Carke (I soften her patois), "I mun tell ye there's ill folk watchin' ye. What's auld Farmer Lew about, he doesna get t' sir" (the clergyman) "to baptize thee? If he lets Sunda' next pass,

I'm afeared ye'll never be sprinkled nor signed wi' cross, while there's a sky aboon us."

"Agoy!" exclaims the girl, "who's lookin' after me?"

"A big black fella, as high as the kipples, came out o' the wood near Deadman's Grike, just after the sun gaed down yester e'en; I knew weel what he was, for his feet ne'er touched the road while he made as if he walked beside me. And he wanted to gie me snuff first, and I wouldna hev that; and then he offered me a gowden guinea, but I was no sic awpy, and to bring you here tonight, and cross the candle wi' pins, to call your lover in. And he said he's a great lord, and in luve wi' thee."

"And you refused him?"

"Well for thee I did, lass," says Mother Carke.

"Why, it's every word true!" cries the girl vehemently, starting to her feet, for she had seated herself on the great oak chest.

"True, lass? Come, say what ye mean," demanded Mall Carke, with a dark and searching gaze.

"Last night I was coming heyam from the wake, wi' auld farmer Dykes and his wife and his daughter Nell, and when we came to the stile, I bid them goodnight, and we parted."

"And ye came by the path alone in the night-time, did ye?" exclaimed old Mall Carke sternly.

"I wasna afeared, I don't know why; the path heyam leads down by the wa'as o' auld Hawarth Castle."

"I knaa it weel, and a dowly path it is; ye'll keep indoors o' nights for a while, or ye'll rue it. What saw ye?"

"No freetin, mother; nowt I was feared on."

"Ye heard a voice callin' yer neyame?"

"I heard nowt that was dow, but the hullyhoo in the auld castle wa's," answered the pretty girl. "I heard nor sid nowt that's dow, but mickle that's conny and gladsome. I heard singin' and laughin' a long way off, I consaited; and I stopped a bit to listen. Then I walked on a step or two, and there, sure enough in the Pie-Mag field, under the castle wa's, not twenty steps away, I sid a grand company; silks and satins, and men wi' velvet coats, wi' gowd-lace striped over them, and ladies wi' necklaces that would dazzle ye, and fans as big as griddles; and powdered footmen, like what the shirra hed behind his coach, only these was ten times as grand."

"It was full moon last night," said the old woman.

"Sa bright 'twould blind ye to look at it," said the girl.

"Never an ill sight but the deaul finds a light," quoth the old woman. "There's a rinnin brook thar—you were at this side, and they at that; did they try to mak ye cross over?"

"Agoy! didn't they? Nowt but civility and kindness, though. But ye mun let me tell it my own way. They was talkin' and laughin', and eatin', and drinkin' out o' long glasses and goud cups, seated on the grass, and music was playin'; and I keekin' behind a bush at all the grand doin's; and up they gits to dance; and says a tall fella I didna see afoore, 'Ye mun step across, and dance wi' a young lord that's faan in luv wi' thee, and that's mysel',' and sure enow I keeked at him under my lashes and a conny lad he is, to my teyaste, though he be dressed in black, wi' sword and sash, velvet twice as fine as they sells in the shop at Gouden Friars; and keekin' at me again fra the corners o' his een. And the same fella telt me he was mad in luv wi' me, and his fadder was there, and his sister, and they came all the way from Catstean Castle to see me that night; and that's t' other side o' Gouden Friars."

"Come, lass, yer no mafflin; tell me true. What was he like? Was his feyace grimed wi' sut? a tall fella wi' wide shouthers, and lukt like an ill-thing, wi' black clothes amaist in rags?"

"His feyace was long, but weel-faured, and darker nor a gipsy; and his clothes were black and grand, and made o' velvet, and he said he was the young lord himsel'; and he lukt like it."

"That will be the same fella I sid at Deadman's Grike," said Mall Carke, with an anxious frown.

"Hoot, mudder! how cud that be?" cried the lass, with a toss of her pretty head and a smile of scorn. But the fortune-teller made no answer, and the girl went on with her story.

"When they began to dance," continued Laura Silver Bell, "he urged me again, but I wudna step o'er; 'twas partly pride, coz I wasna dressed fine enough, and partly contrairiness, or something, but gaa I wudna, not a fut. No but I more nor half wished it a' the time."

"Weel for thee thou dudstna cross the brook."

"Hoity-toity, why not?"

"Keep at heyame after nightfall, and don't ye be walking by yersel' by daylight or any light lang lonesome ways, till after ye're baptized," said Mall Carke.

"I'm like to be married first."

"Tak care *that* marriage won't hang i' the bell-ropes," said Mother Carke.

"Leave me alane for that. The young lord said he was maist daft wi' luv o' me. He wanted to gie me a conny ring wi' a beautiful stone in it. But, drat it, I was sic an awpy I wudna tak it, and he a young lord!"

"Lord, indeed! are ye daft or dreamin'? Those fine folk, what were they? I'll tell ye. Dobies and fairies; and if ye don't du as yer bid, they'll tak ye, and ye'll never git out o' their hands again while grass grows," said the old woman grimly.

"Od wite it!" replies the girl impatiently, "who's daft or dreamin' noo? I'd a bin dead wi' fear, if 'twas any such thing. It cudna be; all was sa luvesome, and bonny, and shaply."

"Weel, and what do ye want o' me, lass?" asked the old woman sharply.

"I want to know—here's t' sixpence—what I sud du," said the young lass. "'Twud be a pity to lose such a marrow, hey?"

"Say yer prayers, lass; *I* can't help ye," says the old woman darkly. "If ye gaa wi' *the* people, ye'll never come back. Ye munna talk wi' them, nor eat wi' them, nor drink wi' them, nor tak a pin's-worth by way o' gift fra them— mark weel what I say—or ye're *lost!*"

The girl looked down, plainly much vexed.

The old woman stared at her with a mysterious frown steadily, for a few seconds.

"Tell me, lass, and tell me true, are ye in luve wi' that lad?"

"What for sud I?" said the girl with a careless toss of her head, and blushing up to her very temples.

"I see how it is," said the old woman, with a groan, and repeated the words, sadly thinking; and walked out of the door a step or two, and looked jealously round. "The lass is witched, the lass is witched!"

"Did ye see him since?" asked Mother Carke, returning.

The girl was still embarrassed; and now she spoke in a lower tone, and seemed subdued.

"I thought I sid him as I came here, walkin' beside me among the trees; but I consait it was only the trees themsels that lukt like rinnin' one behind another, as I walked on."

"I can tell thee nowt, lass, but what I telt ye afoore," answered the old woman peremptorily. "Get ye heyame, and don't delay on the way; and say yer prayers as ye gaa; and let none but good thoughts come nigh ye; and put nayer foot autside the door-steyan again till ye gaa to be christened; and get that done a Sunda' next."

And with this charge, given with grizzly earnestness, she saw her over the stile, and stood upon it watching her retreat, until the trees quite hid her and her path from view.

The sky grew cloudy and thunderous, and the air darkened rapidly, as the girl, a little frightened by Mall Carke's view of the case, walked homeward by the lonely path among the trees.

A black cat, which had walked close by her—for these creatures sometimes take a ramble in search of their prey among the woods and thickets—crept from under the hollow of an oak, and was again with her. It seemed to her to grow bigger and bigger as the darkness deepened, and its green eyes glared as large as halfpennies in her affrighted vision as the thunder came booming along the heights from the Willarden-road.

She tried to drive it away; but it growled and hissed awfully, and set up its back as if it would spring at her, and finally it skipped up into a tree, where they grew thickest at each side of her path, and accompanied her, high over head, hopping from bough to bough as if meditating a pounce upon her shoulders. Her fancy being full of strange thoughts, she was frightened, and she fancied that it was haunting her steps, and destined to undergo some hideous transformation, the moment she ceased to guard her path with prayers.

She was frightened for a while after she got home. The dark looks of Mother Carke were always before her eyes, and a secret dread prevented her passing the threshold of her home again that night.

Next day it was different. She had got rid of the awe with which Mother Carke had inspired her. She could not get the tall dark-featured lord, in the black velvet dress, out of her head. He had "taken her fancy"; she was growing to love him. She could think of nothing else.

Bessie Hennock, a neighbour's daughter, came to see her that day, and proposed a walk toward the ruins of Hawarth Castle, to gather "blaebirries." So off the two girls went together.

In the thicket, along the slopes near the ivied walls of Hawarth Castle, the companions began to fill their baskets. Hours passed. The sun was sinking near the west, and Laura Silver Bell had not come home.

Over the hatch of the farmhouse door the maids leant ever and anon with outstretched necks, watching for a sign of the girl's return, and wondering, as the shadows lengthened, what had become of her.

At last, just as the rosy sunset gilding began to overspread the landscape, Bessie Hennock, weeping into her apron, made her appearance without her companion.

Her account of their adventures was curious.

I will relate the substance of it more connectedly than her agitation would allow her to give it, and without the disguise of the rude Northumbrian dialect.

The girl said, that, as they got along together among the brambles that grow beside the brook that bounds the Pie-Mag field, she on a sudden saw a very tall big-boned man, with an ill-favoured smirched face, and dressed in worn and rusty black, standing at the other side of a little stream. She was frightened; and while looking at this dirty, wicked, starved figure, Laura Silver Bell touched her, gazing at the same tall scarecrow, but with a countenance full of confusion and even rapture. She was peeping through the bush behind which she stood, and with a sigh she said:

"Is na that a conny lad? Agoy! See his bonny velvet clothes, his sword and sash; that's a lord, I can tell ye; and weel I know who he follows, who he luves, and who he'll wed."

Bessie Hennock thought her companion daft.

"See how luvesome he luks!" whispered Laura.

Bessie looked again, and saw him gazing at her companion with a malignant smile, and at the same time he beckoned her to approach.

"Darrat ta! gaa not near him! he'll wring thy neck!" gasped Bessie in great fear, as she saw Laura step forward with a look of beautiful bashfulness and joy.

She took the hand he stretched across the stream, more for love of the hand than any need of help, and in a moment was across and by his side, and his long arm about her waist.

"Fares te weel, Bessie, I'm gain my ways," she called, leaning her head to his shoulder; "and tell gud Fadder Lew I'm gain my ways to be happy, and may be, at lang last, I'll see him again."

And with a farewell wave of her hand, she went away with her dismal partner; and Laura Silver Bell was never more seen at home, or among the "coppies" and "wickwoods," the bonny fields and bosky hollows, by Dardale Moss.

Bessie Hennock followed them for a time.

She crossed the brook, and though they seemed to move slowly enough, she was obliged to run to keep them in view; and she all the time cried to her continually, "Come back, come back, bonnie Laurie!" until, getting over a bank, she was met by a white-faced old man, and so frightened was she, that she thought she fainted outright. At all events, she did not come to herself until the birds were singing their vespers in the amber light of sunset, and the day was over.

No trace of the direction of the girl's flight was ever discovered. Weeks and months passed, and more than a year.

At the end of that time, one of Mall Carke's goats died, as she suspected, by the envious practices of a rival witch who lived at the far end of Dardale Moss.

All alone in her stone cabin the old woman had prepared her charm to ascertain the author of her misfortune.

The heart of the dead animal, stuck all over with pins, was burnt in the fire; the windows, doors, and every other aperture of the house being first carefully stopped. After the heart, thus prepared with suitable incantations, is consumed in the fire, the first person who comes to the door or passes by it is the offending magician.

Mother Carke completed these lonely rites at dead of night. It was a dark night, with the glimmer of the stars only, and a melancholy night-wind was soughing through the scattered woods that spread around.

After a long and dead silence, there came a heavy thump at the door, and a deep voice called her by name.

She was startled, for she expected no man's voice; and peeping from the window, she saw, in the dim light, a coach and four horses, with gold-laced footmen, and coachman in wig and cocked hat, turned out as if for a state occasion.

She unbarred the door; and a tall gentleman, dressed in black, waiting at the threshold, entreated her, as the only *sage femme* within reach, to come in the coach and attend Lady Lairdale, who was about to give birth to a baby, promising her handsome payment.

Lady Lairdale! She had never heard of her.

"How far away is it?"

"Twelve miles on the old road to Golden Friars."

Her avarice is roused, and she steps into the coach. The footman claps-to the door; the glass jingles with the sound of a laugh. The tall dark-faced gentleman in black is seated opposite; they are driving at a furious pace; they have turned out of the road into a narrower one, dark with thicker and loftier forest than she was accustomed to. She grows anxious; for she knows every road and by-path in the country round, and she has never seen this one.

He encourages her. The moon has risen above the edge of the horizon, and she sees a noble old castle. Its summit of tower, watchtower and battlement, glimmers faintly in the moonlight. This is their destination.

She feels on a sudden all but overpowered by sleep; but although she nods, she is quite conscious of the continued motion, which has become even rougher.

She makes an effort, and rouses herself. What has become of the coach, the castle, the servants? Nothing but the strange forest remains the same.

She is jolting along on a rude hurdle, seated on rushes, and a tall, big-boned man, in rags, sits in front, kicking with his heel the ill-favoured beast that pulls them along, every bone of which sticks out, and holding the halter which serves for reins. They stop at the door of a miserable building of loose stone, with a thatch so sunk and rotten, that the roof-tree and couples protrude in crooked corners, like the bones of the wretched horse, with enormous head and ears, that dragged them to the door.

The long gaunt man gets down, his sinister face grimed like his hands.

It was the same grimy giant who had accosted her on the lonely road near Deadman's Grike. But she feels that she "must go through with it" now, and she follows him into the house.

Two rushlights were burning in the large and miserable room, and on a coarse ragged bed lay a woman groaning piteously.

"That's Lady Lairdale," says the gaunt dark man, who then began to stride up and down the room rolling his head, stamping furiously, and thumping one hand on the palm of the other, and talking and laughing in the corners, where there was no one visible to hear or to answer.

Old Mall Carke recognized in the faded half-starved creature who lay on the bed, as dark now and grimy as the man, and looking as if she had never in her life washed hands or face, the once blithe and pretty Laura Lew.

The hideous being who was her mate continued in the same odd fluctuations of fury, grief, and merriment; and whenever she uttered a groan, he parodied it with another, as Mother Carke thought, in saturnine derision.

At length he strode into another room, and banged the door after him.

In due time the poor woman's pains were over, and a daughter was born.

Such an imp! with long pointed ears, flat nose, and enormous restless eyes and mouth. It instantly began to yell and talk in some unknown language, at the noise of which the father looked into the room, and told the *sage femme* that she should not go unrewarded.

The sick woman seized the moment of his absence to say in the ear of Mall Carke:

"If ye had not been at ill work tonight, he could not hev fetched ye. Tak no more now than your rightful fee, or he'll keep ye here."

At this moment he returned with a bag of gold and silver coins, which he emptied on the table, and told her to help herself.

She took four shillings, which was her primitive fee, neither more nor less; and all his urgency could not prevail with her to take a farthing more. He looked so terrible at her refusal, that she rushed out of the house.

He ran after her.

"You'll take your money with you," he roared, snatching up the bag, still half full, and flung it after her.

It lighted on her shoulder; and partly from the blow, partly from terror, she fell to the ground; and when she came to herself, it was morning, and she was lying across her own door-stone.

It is said that she never more told fortune or practised spell. And though all that happened sixty years ago and more, Laura Silver Bell, wise folk think, is still living, and will so continue till the day of doom among the fairies.

1904

THE WHITE PEOPLE

Arthur Machen

The weird fiction of Arthur Machen (1863–1947) has influenced generations of horror writers from H.P. Lovecraft to Stephen King, with other admirers including Rowan Williams, Aleister Crowley and The Fall's Mark E. Smith. Born in Caerleon in south-east Wales, Machen moved to London in his late teens, joining the 1880s precariat as a journalist, private tutor, publisher's clerk and cataloguer of occult books. His 1894 fantasy novella *The Great God Pan* scandalized the press with its Aubrey Beardsley cover and febrile visions of pagan sexuality, and has since been praised by King as "one of the best horror stories ever written".

Machen's fascination with "the eternal mysteries… hidden beneath the crust of common and commonplace things" is evident throughout his fairy fiction, from the seemingly innocuous, child-like arrangements of pebbles linked to the disappearance of a young girl in "The Shining Pyramid" (1895) to his late short story "N" (1936), in which a door to fairyland is discovered in north London's Stoke Newington.

First published in *Horlick's Magazine* in 1904, "The White People" is one of Machen's most eerie tales. Recent fans include film director Guillermo del Toro, whose 2006 *Pan's Labyrinth* bears certain similarities in its depiction of a girl drawn into a darkly magical otherworld. Presented as a diary of a teenage girl's experiences exploring a strange, sensuous landscape, where rocks have tongues and streams kiss like nymphs, Machen's stream-of-consciousness narrative teeters between dream and nightmare.

Believing herself to be possessed of occult powers, and wishing to get in touch with the unseen, Miss Emily Farnario (32), whose home was Kew, London, journeyed to the lonely isle of Iona, in the Hebrides—rich in mystic traditions—and was found dead there in amazing circumstances.

[...]

Her body was found at midnight by islanders, and although the cause of death has not yet been ascertained, it is believed that she died from exposure, after an attempt to exclude herself entirely from this world in order to get into closer touch with the unseen.

She lay unclothed on the bleak and lonely hillside. Round her neck was a silver chain and cross. Near at hand lay a large knife which had been used to cut in the turf a large cross on which the body was resting.

[...]

Miss Farnario thought she possessed the power of telepathy, and she went to the island to receive more power to cure by mental healing.

Two days before her body was found she wrote to the servant at her house at Kew Gardens, London, saying she would be away for a long time, as she had "a terrible healing case on."

Other letters of a similar mysterious kind have been received by friends.

Miss Farnario disappeared at 9 p.m. on Sunday, November 17.

Many weird stories are in circulation in the Western islands regarding Miss Farnario, who was regarded as a mysterious stranger, and much Highland superstition is being brought to light in connection with the mystery of her death.

Among the tales now circulated are mysterious remarks about blue lights and a cloaked man having been seen near the body.

Report on the mysterious death of Marie Emily ("Netta") Fornario, an Italian-British writer who had been drawn to Iona after reading Fiona Macleod's descriptions of a fairy portal on the island, from *Reynolds's Illustrated News*, 1 December 1929

"**S**ORCERY and sanctity," said Ambrose, "these are the only realities. Each is an ecstasy, a withdrawal from the common life."

Cotgrave listened, interested. He had been brought by a friend to this mouldering house in a northern suburb, through an old garden to the room where Ambrose the recluse dozed and dreamed over his books.

"Yes," he went on, "magic is justified of her children. There are many, I think, who eat dry crusts and drink water, with a joy infinitely sharper than anything within the experience of the 'practical' epicure."

"You are speaking of the saints?"

"Yes, and of the sinners, too. I think you are falling into the very general error of confining the spiritual world to the supremely good; but the supremely wicked, necessarily, have their portion in it. The merely carnal, sensual man can no more be a great sinner than he can be a great saint. Most of us are just indifferent, mixed-up creatures; we muddle through the world without realizing the meaning and the inner sense of things, and, consequently, our wickedness and our goodness are alike second-rate, unimportant."

"And you think the great sinner, then, will be an ascetic, as well as the great saint?"

"Great people of all kinds forsake the imperfect copies and go to the perfect originals. I have no doubt but that many of the very highest among the saints have never done a 'good action' (using the words in their ordinary sense). And, on the other hand, there have been those who have sounded the very depths of sin, who all their lives have never done an 'ill deed.'"

He went out of the room for a moment, and Cotgrave, in high delight, turned to his friend and thanked him for the introduction.

"He's grand," he said. "I never saw that kind of lunatic before."

Ambrose returned with more whisky and helped the two men in a liberal manner. He abused the teetotal sect with ferocity, as he handed the seltzer, and pouring out a glass of water for himself, was about to resume his monologue, when Cotgrave broke in—

"I can't stand it, you know," he said, "your paradoxes are too monstrous. A man may be a great sinner and yet never do anything sinful! Come!"

"You're quite wrong," said Ambrose. "I never make paradoxes; I wish I could. I merely said that a man may have an exquisite taste in Romanée Conti, and yet never have even smelt four ale. That's all, and it's more like a truism than a paradox, isn't it? Your surprise at my remark is due to the fact that you haven't realized what sin is. Oh, yes, there is a sort of connexion between Sin with the capital letter, and actions which are commonly called sinful: with murder, theft, adultery, and so forth. Much the same connexion that there is between the A, B, C and fine literature. But I believe that the misconception—it is all but universal—arises in great measure from our looking at the matter through social spectacles. We think that a man who does evil to *us* and to his neighbours must be very evil. So he is, from a social standpoint; but can't you realize that Evil in its essence is a lonely thing, a passion of the solitary, individual soul? Really, the average murderer, *quâ* murderer, is not by any means a sinner in the true sense of the word. He is simply a wild beast that we have to get rid of to save our own necks from his knife. I should class him rather with tigers than with sinners."

"It seems a little strange."

"I think not. The murderer murders not from positive qualities, but from negative ones; he lacks something which non-murderers possess. Evil, of course, is wholly positive—only it is on the wrong side. You may believe me that sin in its proper sense is very rare; it is probable that there have been far fewer sinners than saints. Yes, your standpoint is all very well for practical, social purposes; we are naturally inclined to think that a person who is very disagreeable to us must be a very great sinner! It is very disagreeable to have one's pocket picked, and we pronounce the thief to be a very great sinner. In truth, he is merely an undeveloped man. He cannot be a saint, of course; but he may be, and often is, an infinitely better creature than thousands who have never broken a single commandment. He is a great nuisance to *us*, I admit, and we very properly lock him up if we catch him; but between his troublesome and unsocial action and evil—Oh, the connexion is of the weakest."

It was getting very late. The man who had brought Cotgrave had probably heard all this before, since he assisted with a bland and judicious smile, but Cotgrave began to think that his "lunatic" was turning into a sage.

"Do you know," he said, "you interest me immensely? You think, then, that we do not understand the real nature of evil?"

"No, I don't think we do. We over-estimate it and we under-estimate it. We take the very numerous infractions of our social 'bye-laws'—the very necessary and very proper regulations which keep the human company together—and we get frightened at the prevalence of 'sin' and 'evil.' But this is really nonsense. Take theft, for example. Have you any *horror* at the thought of Robin Hood, of the Highland caterans of the seventeenth century, of the moss-troopers, of the company promoters of our day?

"Then, on the other hand, we underrate evil. We attach such an enormous importance to the 'sin' of meddling with our pockets (and our wives) that we have quite forgotten the awfulness of real sin."

"And what is sin?" said Cotgrave.

"I think I must reply to your question by another. What would your feelings be, seriously, if your cat or your dog began to talk to you, and to dispute with you in human accents? You would be overwhelmed with horror. I am sure of it. And if the roses in your garden sang a weird song, you would go mad. And suppose the stones in the road began to swell and grow before your eyes, and if the pebble that you noticed at night had shot out stony blossoms in the morning?

"Well, these examples may give you some notion of what sin really is."

"Look here," said the third man, hitherto placid, "you two seem pretty well wound up. But I'm going home. I've missed my tram, and I shall have to walk."

Ambrose and Cotgrave seemed to settle down more profoundly when the other had gone out into the early misty morning and the pale light of the lamps.

"You astonish me," said Cotgrave. "I had never thought of that. If that is really so, one must turn everything upside down. Then the essence of sin really is—"

"In the taking of heaven by storm, it seems to me," said Ambrose. "It appears to me that it is simply an attempt to penetrate into another and a higher sphere in a forbidden manner. You can understand why it is so rare. They are few, indeed, who wish to penetrate into other spheres, higher or lower, in ways allowed or forbidden. Men, in the mass, are amply content with life as they find it. Therefore there are few saints, and sinners (in the proper sense) are fewer still, and men of genius, who partake sometimes of each character, are rare also. Yes; on the whole, it is, perhaps, harder to be a great sinner than a great saint."

"There is something profoundly unnatural about sin? Is that what you mean?"

"Exactly. Holiness requires as great, or almost as great, an effort; but holiness works on lines that *were* natural once; it is an effort to recover the ecstasy that was before the Fall. But sin is an effort to gain the ecstasy and the knowledge that pertain alone to angels, and in making this effort man becomes a demon. I told you that the mere murderer is not *therefore* a sinner; that is true, but the sinner is sometimes a murderer. Gilles de Raiz is an instance. So you see that while the good and the evil are unnatural to man as he now is—to man the social, civilized being—evil is unnatural in a much deeper sense than good. The saint endeavours to recover a gift which he has lost; the sinner tries to obtain something which was never his. In brief, he repeats the Fall."

"But are you a Catholic?" said Cotgrave.

"Yes; I am a member of the persecuted Anglican Church."

"Then, how about those texts which seem to reckon as sin that which you would set down as a mere trivial dereliction?"

"Yes; but in one place the word 'sorcerers' comes in the same sentence, doesn't it? That seems to me to give the key-note. Consider: can you imagine for a moment that a false statement which saves an innocent man's life is a sin? No; very good, then, it is not the mere liar who is excluded by those words; it is, above all, the 'sorcerers' who use the material life, who use the failings incidental to material life as instruments to obtain their infinitely wicked ends. And let me tell you this: our higher senses are so blunted, we are so drenched with materialism, that we should probably fail to recognize real wickedness if we encountered it."

"But shouldn't we experience a certain horror—a terror such as you hinted we would experience if a rose tree sang—in the mere presence of an evil man?"

"We should if we were natural: children and women feel this horror you speak of, even animals experience it. But with most of us convention and civilization and education have blinded and deafened and obscured the natural reason. No, sometimes we may recognize evil by its hatred of the good—one doesn't need much penetration to guess at the influence which dictated, quite unconsciously, the 'Blackwood' review of Keats—but this is purely incidental; and, as a rule, I suspect that the Hierarchs of Tophet pass quite unnoticed, or, perhaps, in certain cases, as good but mistaken men."

"But you used the word 'unconscious' just now, of Keats' reviewers. Is wickedness ever unconscious?"

"Always. It must be so. It is like holiness and genius in this as in other points; it is a certain rapture or ecstasy of the soul; a transcendent effort to surpass the ordinary bounds. So, surpassing these, it surpasses also the understanding, the faculty that takes note of that which comes before it. No, a man may be infinitely and horribly wicked and never suspect it. But I tell you, evil in this, its certain and true sense, is rare, and I think it is growing rarer."

"I am trying to get hold of it all," said Cotgrave. "From what you say, I gather that the true evil differs generically from that which we call evil?"

"Quite so. There is, no doubt, an analogy between the two; a resemblance such as enables us to use, quite legitimately, such terms as the 'foot of the mountain' and the 'leg of the table.' And, sometimes, of course, the two speak, as it were, in the same language. The rough miner, or 'puddler,' the untrained, undeveloped 'tiger-man,' heated by a quart or two above his usual measure, comes home and kicks his irritating and injudicious wife to death. He is a murderer. And Gilles de Raiz was a murderer. But you see the gulf that separates the two? The 'word,' if I may so speak, is accidentally the same in each case, but the 'meaning' is utterly different. It is flagrant 'Hobson Jobson' to confuse the two, or rather, it is as if one supposed that Juggernaut and the Argonauts had something to do etymologically with one another. And no doubt the same weak likeness, or analogy, runs between all the 'social' sins and the real spiritual sins, and in some cases, perhaps, the lesser may be 'schoolmasters' to lead one on to the greater—from the shadow to the reality. If you are anything of a Theologian, you will see the importance of all this."

"I am sorry to say," remarked Cotgrave, "that I have devoted very little of my time to theology. Indeed, I have often wondered on what grounds theologians have claimed the title of Science of Sciences for their favourite study; since the 'theological' books I have looked into have always seemed to me to be concerned with feeble and obvious pieties, or with the kings of Israel and Judah. I do not care to hear about those kings."

Ambrose grinned.

"We must try to avoid theological discussion," he said.

"I perceive that you would be a bitter disputant. But perhaps the 'dates of the kings' have as much to do with theology as the hobnails of the murderous puddler with evil."

"Then, to return to our main subject, you think that sin is an esoteric, occult thing?"

"Yes. It is the infernal miracle as holiness is the supernal. Now and then it is raised to such a pitch that we entirely fail to suspect its existence; it is like the note of the great pedal pipes of the organ, which is so deep that we cannot hear it. In other cases it may lead to the lunatic asylum, or to still stranger issues. But you must never confuse it with mere social misdoing. Remember how the Apostle, speaking of the 'other side,' distinguishes between 'charitable' actions and charity. And as one may give all one's goods to the poor, and yet lack charity; so, remember, one may avoid every crime and yet be a sinner."

"Your psychology is very strange to me," said Cotgrave, "but I confess I like it, and I suppose that one might fairly deduce from your premises the conclusion that the real sinner might very possibly strike the observer as a harmless personage enough?"

"Certainly; because the true evil has nothing to do with social life or social laws, or if it has, only incidentally and accidentally. It is a lonely passion of the soul—or a passion of the lonely soul—whichever you like. If, by chance, we understand it, and grasp its full significance, then, indeed, it will fill us with horror and with awe. But this emotion is widely distinguished from the fear and the disgust with which we regard the ordinary criminal, since this latter is largely or entirely founded on the regard which we have for our own skins or purses. We hate a murderer, because we know that we should hate to be murdered, or to have any one that we like murdered. So, on the 'other side,' we venerate the saints, but we don't 'like' them as we like our friends. Can you persuade yourself that you would have 'enjoyed' St.

Paul's company? Do you think that you and I would have 'got on' with Sir Galahad?

"So with the sinners, as with the saints. If you met a very evil man, and recognized his evil; he would, no doubt, fill you with horror and awe; but there is no reason why you should 'dislike' him. On the contrary, it is quite possible that if you could succeed in putting the sin out of your mind you might find the sinner capital company, and in a little while you might have to reason yourself back into horror. Still, how awful it is. If the roses and the lilies suddenly sang on this coming morning; if the furniture began to move in procession, as in De Maupassant's tale!"

"I am glad you have come back to that comparison," said Cotgrave, "because I wanted to ask you what it is that corresponds in humanity to these imaginary feats of inanimate things. In a word—what is sin? You have given me, I know, an abstract definition, but I should like a concrete example."

"I told you it was very rare," said Ambrose, who appeared willing to avoid the giving of a direct answer. "The materialism of the age, which has done a good deal to suppress sanctity, has done perhaps more to suppress evil. We find the earth so very comfortable that we have no inclination either for ascents or descents. It would seem as if the scholar who decided to 'specialize' in Tophet, would be reduced to purely antiquarian researches. No palæontologist could show you a *live* pterodactyl."

"And yet you, I think, have 'specialized,' and I believe that your researches have descended to our modern times."

"You are really interested, I see. Well, I confess, that I have dabbled a little, and if you like I can show you something that bears on the very curious subject we have been discussing."

Ambrose took a candle and went away to a far, dim corner of the room. Cotgrave saw him open a venerable bureau that stood there, and from some secret recess he drew out a parcel, and came back to the window where they had been sitting.

Ambrose undid a wrapping of paper, and produced a green pocket-book. "You will take care of it?" he said. "Don't leave it lying about. It is one of the choicer pieces in my collection, and I should be very sorry if it were lost." He fondled the faded binding.

"I knew the girl who wrote this," he said. "When you read it, you will see how it illustrates the talk we have had tonight. There is a sequel, too, but I won't talk of that."

"There was an odd article in one of the reviews some months ago," he began again, with the air of a man who changes the subject. "It was written by a doctor—Dr. Coryn, I think, was the name. He says that a lady, watching her little girl playing at the drawing-room window, suddenly saw the heavy sash give way and fall on the child's fingers. The lady fainted, I think, but at any rate the doctor was summoned, and when he had dressed the child's wounded and maimed fingers he was summoned to the mother. She was groaning with pain, and it was found that three fingers of her hand, corresponding with those that had been injured on the child's hand, were swollen and inflamed, and later, in the doctor's language, purulent sloughing set in."

Ambrose still handled delicately the green volume.

"Well, here it is," he said at last, parting with difficulty, it seemed, from his treasure.

"You will bring it back as soon as you have read it," he said, as they went out into the hall, into the old garden, faint with the odour of white lilies.

There was a broad red band in the east as Cotgrave turned to go, and from the high ground where he stood he saw that awful spectacle of London in a dream.

THE GREEN BOOK

The morocco binding of the book was faded, and the colour had grown faint, but there were no stains nor bruises nor marks of usage. The book looked as if it had been bought "on a visit to London" some seventy or eighty years ago, and had somehow been forgotten and suffered to lie away out of sight. There was an old, delicate, lingering odour about it, such an odour as sometimes haunts an ancient piece of furniture for a century or more. The end-papers, inside the binding, were oddly decorated with coloured patterns and faded gold. It looked small, but the paper was fine, and there were many leaves, closely covered with minute, painfully formed characters.

I found this book (the manuscript began) in a drawer in the old bureau that stands on the landing. It was a very rainy day and I could not go out, so in the afternoon I got a candle and rummaged in the bureau. Nearly all the drawers were full of old dresses, but one of the small ones looked empty, and I found this book hidden right at the back. I wanted a book like this, so I took it to write in. It is full of secrets. I have a great many other books of secrets I have written, hidden in a safe place, and I am going to write here many of the old secrets and some new ones; but there are some I shall not put down at all. I must not write down the real names of the days and months which I found out a year ago, nor the way to make the Aklo letters, or the Chian language, or the great beautiful Circles, nor the Mao Games, nor the chief songs. I may write something about all these things but not the way to do them, for peculiar reasons. And I must not say who the Nymphs are, or the Dôls, or Jeelo, or what voolas mean. All these are most secret secrets, and I am glad when I remember what they are, and how many wonderful languages I know, but there are some things that I call the secrets of the secrets of the secrets that I dare not think of unless I am quite alone, and then I shut my eyes, and put my hands over them and whisper the word, and the Alala comes. I only do this at night in my room or in certain woods that I know, but I must not describe them, as they are secret woods. Then there are the Ceremonies, which are all of them important, but some are more delightful than others—there are the White Ceremonies, and the Green Ceremonies, and the Scarlet Ceremonies. The Scarlet Ceremonies are the best, but there is only one place where they can be performed properly, though there is a very nice imitation which I have done in other places. Besides these, I have the dances, and the Comedy, and I have done the Comedy sometimes when the others were looking, and they didn't understand anything about it. I was very little when I first knew about these things.

When I was very small, and mother was alive, I can remember remembering things before that, only it has all got confused. But I remember when I was five or six I heard them talking about me when they thought I was not noticing. They were saying how queer I was a year or two before, and how nurse had called my mother to come and listen to me talking all to myself, and I was saying words that nobody could understand. I was speaking the Xu language, but I only remember a very few of the words, as it was about the little white faces that used to look at me when I was lying in my cradle. They used to talk to me, and I learnt their language and talked to them in it about some great white place where they lived, where the trees and the grass were all white, and there were white hills as high up as the moon, and a cold wind. I have often dreamed of it afterwards, but the faces went away when I was very little. But a wonderful thing happened when I was about five. My nurse was carrying me on her shoulder; there was a field of yellow corn, and we went through it, it was very hot. Then we came to a path through a wood, and a tall man came after us, and went with us till we came to a place where there was a deep pool, and it was very dark and shady. Nurse put me down on the soft moss under a tree, and she said: "She can't get to the pond now." So they left me there, and I sat quite still and watched, and out of the water and out of the wood came two wonderful white people, and they began to play and dance and sing. They were a kind of creamy white like the old ivory figure in the drawing-room; one was a beautiful lady with kind dark eyes, and a grave face, and long black hair, and she smiled such a strange sad smile at the other, who laughed and came to her. They played together, and danced round and round the pool, and they sang a song till I fell asleep. Nurse woke me up when she came back, and she was looking something like the lady had looked, so I told her all about it, and asked her why she looked like that. At first she cried, and then she looked very frightened, and turned quite pale. She put me down on the grass and stared at me, and I could see she was shaking all over. Then she said I had been dreaming, but I knew I hadn't. Then she made me promise not to say a word about it to anybody, and if I did I should be thrown into the black pit. I was not frightened at all, though nurse was, and I never forgot about it, because when I shut my eyes and it was quite quiet, and I was all alone, I could see them again, very faint and far away, but very splendid; and little bits of the song they sang came into my head, but I couldn't sing it.

I was thirteen, nearly fourteen, when I had a very singular adventure, so strange that the day on which it happened is always called the White Day. My mother had been dead for more than a year, and in the morning I had lessons, but they let me go out for walks in the afternoon. And this afternoon I walked a new way, and a little brook led me into a new country, but I tore my frock getting through some of the difficult places, as the way was through many bushes, and beneath the low branches of trees, and up thorny thickets on the hills, and by dark woods full of creeping thorns. And it was a long, long way. It seemed as if I was going on for ever and ever, and I had to creep by a place like a tunnel where a brook must have been, but all the water had dried up, and the floor was rocky, and the bushes had grown overhead till they met, so that it was quite dark. And I went on and on through that dark place; it was a long, long way. And I came to a hill that I never saw before. I was in a dismal thicket full of black twisted boughs that tore me as I went through them, and I cried out because I was smarting all over, and then I found that I was climbing, and I went up and up a long way, till at last the thicket stopped and I came out crying just under the top of a big bare place, where there were ugly grey stones lying all about on the grass, and here and there a little twisted, stunted tree came out from under a stone, like a snake. And I went up, right to the top, a long way. I never saw such big ugly stones before; they came out of the earth some of them, and some looked as if they had been rolled to where they were, and they went on and on as far as I could see, a long, long way. I looked out from them and saw the country, but it was strange. It was winter time, and there were black terrible woods hanging from the hills all round; it was like seeing a large room hung with black curtains, and the shape of the trees seemed quite different from any I had ever seen before. I was afraid. Then beyond the woods there were other hills round in a great ring, but I had never seen any of them; it all looked black, and everything had a voor over it. It was all so still and silent, and the sky was heavy and grey and sad, like a wicked voorish dome in Deep Dendo. I went on into the dreadful rocks. There were hundreds and hundreds of them. Some were like horrid-grinning men; I could see their faces as if they would jump at me out of the stone, and catch hold of me, and drag me with them back into the rock, so that I should always be there. And there were other rocks that were like animals, creeping, horrible animals, putting out their tongues, and others were like words that I could not say, and others like dead people lying on the grass. I went on among them, though they frightened me, and my heart was full of wicked songs that they put into it; and I wanted to make faces and twist myself about in the way they did, and I went on and on a long way till at last I liked the rocks, and they didn't frighten me any more. I sang the songs I thought of; songs full of words that must not be spoken or written down. Then I made faces like the faces on the rocks, and I twisted myself about like the twisted ones, and I lay down flat on the ground like the dead ones, and I went up to one that was grinning, and put my arms round him and hugged him. And so I went on and on through the rocks till I came to a round mound in the middle of them. It was higher than a mound, it was nearly as high as our house, and it was like a great basin turned upside down, all smooth and round and green, with one stone, like a post, sticking up at the top. I climbed up the sides, but they were so steep I had to stop or I should have rolled all the way down again, and I should have knocked against the stones at the bottom, and perhaps been killed. But I wanted to get up to the very top of the big round mound, so I lay down flat on my face, and took hold of the grass with my hands and drew myself up, bit by bit, till I was at the top. Then I sat down on the stone in the middle, and looked all round about. I felt I had come such a long, long way, just as if I were a hundred miles from home, or in some other country, or in one of the strange places I had read about in the "Tales of the Genie" and the "Arabian Nights," or as if I had gone across the sea, far away, for years and I had found another world that nobody had ever seen or heard of before, or as if I had somehow flown through the sky and fallen on one of the stars I had read about where everything is dead and cold and grey, and there is no air, and the wind doesn't blow. I sat on the stone and looked all round and down and round about me. It was just as if I was sitting on a tower in the middle of a great empty town, because I could see nothing all around but the grey rocks on the ground. I couldn't make out their shapes any more, but I could see them on and on for a long way, and I looked at them, and they seemed as if they had been arranged into patterns, and shapes, and figures. I knew they couldn't be, because I had seen a lot of them coming right out of the earth, joined to the deep rocks below, so I looked again, but still I saw nothing but circles, and small circles inside big ones, and pyramids, and domes, and spires, and they seemed all to go round and round the place where I was sitting, and the more I looked, the more I saw great big rings of rocks, getting bigger and bigger, and I stared so long that it felt as if they were all moving and turning, like a great wheel, and I was turning, too, in the middle. I got quite dizzy and queer in the head, and everything began to be hazy and not clear, and I saw little sparks of blue light, and the stones looked as if they were springing and dancing and twisting as they went round and round and round. I was frightened again, and I cried out loud, and jumped up from the stone I was sitting on, and fell down. When I got up I was so glad they all looked still, and I sat down on the top and slid down the mound, and went on again. I danced as I went in the peculiar way the rocks had danced when I got giddy, and I was so glad I could do it quite well, and I danced and danced along, and sang extraordinary songs that came into my head. At last I came to the edge of that great flat hill, and there were no more rocks, and the way went again through a dark thicket in a hollow. It was just as bad as the other one I went through climbing up, but I didn't mind this one, because I was so glad I had seen those singular dances and could imitate them. I went down, creeping through the bushes, and a tall nettle stung me on my leg, and made me burn, but I didn't mind it, and I tingled with the boughs and the thorns, but I only laughed and sang. Then I got out of the thicket into a close valley, a little secret place like a dark passage that nobody ever knows of, because it was so narrow and deep and the woods were so thick round it. There is a steep bank with trees hanging over it, and there the ferns keep green all through the winter, when they are dead and brown upon the hill, and the ferns there have a sweet, rich smell like what oozes out of fir trees. There was a little stream of water running down this valley, so small that I could easily step across it. I drank the water with my hand, and it tasted like bright, yellow wine, and it sparkled and bubbled as it ran down over beautiful red and yellow and green stones, so that it seemed alive and all colours at once. I drank it, and I drank more with my hand, but I couldn't drink enough, so I lay down and bent my head and sucked the water up with my lips. It tasted much better, drinking it that way, and a ripple would come up to my mouth and give me a kiss, and I laughed, and drank again, and pretended there was a nymph, like the one in the old picture at home, who lived in the water and was kissing me. So I bent low down to the water, and put my lips softly to it, and whispered to the nymph that I would come again. I felt sure it could not be common water, I was so glad when I got up and went on; and I danced again and went up and up the valley, under hanging hills. And when I came to the top, the ground rose up in front of me, tall and steep as a wall, and there was nothing but the green wall and the sky. I thought of "for ever and for ever, world without end, Amen"; and I thought I must have really found the end of the world, because it was like the end of everything, as if there could be nothing at all beyond, except the kingdom of Voor, where the light goes when it is put out, and the water goes when the sun takes it away. I began to think of all the long, long way I had journeyed, how I had found a brook and followed it, and followed it on, and gone through bushes and thorny thickets, and dark woods full of creeping thorns. Then I had crept up a tunnel under trees, and climbed a thicket, and seen all the grey rocks, and sat in the middle of them when they turned round, and then I had gone on through the grey rocks and come down the hill through the stinging thicket and up the dark valley, all a long, long way. I wondered how I should get home again, if I could ever find the way, and if my home was there any more, or if it were turned and everybody in it into grey rocks, as in the "Arabian Nights." So I sat down on the grass and thought what I should do next. I was tired, and my feet were hot with walking, and as I looked about I saw there was a wonderful well just under the high, steep wall of grass. All the ground round it was covered with bright, green, dripping moss; there was every kind of moss there, moss like beautiful little ferns, and like palms and fir trees, and it was all green as jewellery, and drops of water hung on it like diamonds. And in the middle was the great well, deep and shining and beautiful, so clear that it looked as if I could touch the red sand at the bottom, but it was far below. I stood by it and looked in, as if I were looking in a glass. At the bottom of the well, in the middle of it, the red grains of sand were moving and stirring all the time, and I saw how the water bubbled up, but at the top it was quite smooth, and full and brimming. It was a great well, large like a bath, and with the shining, glittering green moss about it, it looked like a great white jewel, with green jewels all round. My feet were so hot and tired that I took off my boots and stockings, and let my feet down into the water, and the water was soft and cold, and when I got up I wasn't tired any more, and I felt I must go on, farther and farther, and see what was on the other side of the wall. I climbed up it very slowly, going sideways all the time, and when I got to the top and looked over, I was in the queerest country I had seen, stranger even than the hill of the grey rocks. It looked as if earth-children had been playing there with their spades, as it was all hills and hollows, and castles and walls made of earth and covered with grass. There were two mounds like big beehives, round and great and solemn, and then hollow basins, and then a steep mounting wall like the ones I saw once by the seaside where the big guns and the soldiers were. I nearly fell into one of the round hollows, it went away from under my feet so suddenly, and I ran fast down the side and stood at the bottom and looked up. It was strange and solemn to look up. There was nothing but the grey, heavy sky and the sides of the hollow; everything else had gone away, and the hollow was the whole world, and I thought that at night it must be full of ghosts and moving shadows and pale things when the moon shone down to the bottom at the dead of the night, and the wind wailed up above. It was so strange and solemn and lonely, like a hollow temple of dead heathen gods. It reminded me of a tale my nurse had told me when I was quite little; it was the same nurse that took me into the wood where I saw the beautiful white people. And I remembered how nurse had told me the story one winter night, when the wind was beating the trees against the wall, and crying and moaning in the nursery chimney. She said there was, somewhere or other, a hollow pit, just like the one I was standing in, everybody was afraid to go into it or near it, it was such a bad place. But once upon a time there was a poor girl who said she would go into the hollow pit, and everybody tried to stop her, but she would go. And she went down into the pit and came back laughing, and said there was nothing there at all, except green grass and red stones, and white stones and yellow flowers. And soon after people saw she had most beautiful emerald earrings, and they asked how she got them, as she and her mother were quite poor. But she laughed, and said her earrings were not made of emeralds at all, but only of green grass. Then, one day, she wore on her breast the reddest ruby that any one had ever seen, and it was as big as a hen's egg, and glowed and sparkled like a hot burning coal of fire. And they asked her how she got it, as she and her mother were quite poor. But she laughed, and said it was not a ruby at all, but only a red stone. Then one day she wore round her neck the loveliest necklace that any one had ever seen, much finer than the queen's finest, and it was made of great bright diamonds, hundreds of them, and they shone like all the stars on a night in June. So they asked her how she got it, as she and her mother were quite poor. But she laughed, and said they were not diamonds at all, but only white stones. And one day she went to the Court, and she wore on her head a crown of pure angel-gold, so nurse said, and it shone like the sun, and it was much more splendid than the crown the king was wearing himself, and in her ears she wore the emeralds, and the big ruby was the brooch on her breast, and the great diamond necklace was sparkling on her neck. And the king and queen thought she was some great princess from a long way off, and got down from their thrones and went to meet her, but somebody told the king and queen who she was, and that she was quite poor. So the king asked why she wore a gold crown, and how she got it, as she and her mother were so poor. And she laughed, and said it wasn't a gold crown at all, but only some yellow flowers she had put in her hair. And the king thought it was very strange, and said she should stay at the Court, and they would see what would happen next. And she was so lovely that everybody said that her eyes were greener than the emeralds, that her lips were redder than the ruby, that her skin was whiter than the diamonds, and that her hair was brighter than the golden crown. So the king's son said he would marry her, and the king said he might. And the bishop married them, and there was a great supper, and afterwards the king's son went to his wife's room. But just when he had his hand on the door, he saw a tall, black man, with a dreadful face, standing in front of the door, and a voice said—

Venture not upon your life,
This is mine own wedded wife.

Then the king's son fell down on the ground in a fit. And they came and tried to get into the room, but they couldn't, and they hacked at the door with hatchets, but the wood had turned hard as iron, and at last everybody ran away, they were so frightened at the screaming and laughing and shrieking and crying that came out of the room. But next day they went in, and found there was nothing in the room but thick black smoke, because the black man had come and taken her away. And on the bed there were two knots of faded grass and a red stone, and some white stones, and some faded yellow flowers. I remembered this tale of nurse's while I was standing at the bottom of the deep hollow; it was so strange and solitary there, and I felt afraid. I could not see any stones or flowers, but I was afraid of bringing them away without knowing, and I thought I would do a charm that came into my head to keep the black man away. So I stood right in the very middle of the hollow, and I made sure that I had none of those things on me, and then I walked round the place, and touched my eyes, and my lips, and my hair in a peculiar manner, and whispered some queer words that nurse taught me to keep bad things away. Then I felt safe and climbed up out of the hollow, and went on through all those mounds and hollows and walls, till I came to the end, which was high above all the rest, and I could see that all the different shapes of the earth were arranged in patterns, something like the grey rocks, only the pattern was different. It was getting late, and the air was indistinct, but it looked from where I was standing something like two great figures of people lying on the grass. And I went on, and at last I found a certain wood, which is too secret to be described, and nobody knows of the passage into it, which I found out in a very curious manner, by seeing some little animal run into the wood through it. So I went after the animal by a very narrow dark way, under thorns and bushes, and it was almost dark when I came to a kind of open place in the middle. And there I saw the most wonderful sight I have ever seen, but it was only for a minute, as I ran away directly, and crept out of the wood by the passage I had come by, and ran and ran as fast as ever I could, because I was afraid, what I had seen was so wonderful and so strange and beautiful. But I wanted to get home and think of it, and I did not know what might not happen if I stayed by the wood. I was hot all over and trembling, and my heart was beating, and strange cries that I could not help came from me as I ran from the wood. I was glad that a great white moon came up from over a round hill and showed me the way, so I went back through the mounds and hollows and down the close valley, and up through the thicket over the place of the grey rocks, and so at last I got home again. My father was busy in his study, and the servants had not told about my not coming home, though they were frightened, and wondered what they ought to do, so I told them I had lost my way, but I did not let them find out the real way I had been. I went to bed and lay awake all through the night, thinking of what I had seen. When I came out of the narrow way, and it looked all shining, though the air was dark, it seemed so certain, and all the way home I was quite sure that I had seen it, and I wanted to be alone in my room, and be glad over it all to myself, and shut my eyes and pretend it was there, and do all the things I would have done if I had not been so afraid. But when I shut my eyes the sight would not come, and I began to think about my adventures all over again, and I remembered how dusky and queer it was at the end, and I was afraid it must be all a mistake, because it seemed impossible it could happen. It seemed like one of nurse's tales, which I didn't really believe in, though I was frightened at the bottom of the hollow; and the stories she told me when I was little came back into my head, and I wondered whether it was really there what I thought I had seen, or whether any of her tales could have happened a long time ago. It was so queer; I lay awake there in my room at the back of the house, and the moon was shining on the other side towards the river, so the bright light did not fall upon the wall. And the house was quite still. I had heard my father come upstairs, and just after the clock struck twelve, and after the house was still and empty, as if there was nobody alive in it. And though it was all dark and indistinct in my room, a pale glimmering kind of light shone in through the white blind, and once I got up and looked out, and there was a great black shadow of the house covering the garden, looking like a prison where men are hanged; and then beyond it was all white; and the wood shone white with black gulfs between the trees. It was still and clear, and there were no clouds on the sky. I wanted to think of what I had seen but I couldn't, and I began to think of all the tales that nurse had told me so long ago that I thought I had forgotten, but they all came back, and mixed up with the thickets and the grey rocks and the hollows in the earth and the secret wood, till I hardly knew what was new and what was old, or whether it was not all dreaming. And then I remembered that hot summer afternoon, so long ago, when nurse left me by myself in the shade, and the white people came out of the water and out of the wood, and played, and danced, and sang, and I began to fancy that nurse told me about something like it before I saw them, only I couldn't recollect exactly what she told me. Then I wondered whether she had been the white lady, as I remembered she was just as white and beautiful, and had the same dark eyes and black hair; and sometimes she smiled and looked like the lady had looked, when she was telling me some of her stories, beginning with "Once on a time," or "In the time of the fairies." But I thought she couldn't be the lady, as she seemed to have gone a different way into the wood, and I didn't think the man who came after us could be the other, or I couldn't have seen that wonderful secret in the secret wood. I thought of the moon: but it was afterwards when I was in the middle of the wild land, where the earth was made into the shape of great figures, and it was all walls, and mysterious hollows, and smooth round mounds, that I saw the great white moon come up over a round hill. I was wondering about all these things, till at last I got quite frightened, because I was afraid something had happened to me, and I remembered nurse's tale of the poor girl who went into the hollow pit, and was carried away at last by the black man. I knew I had gone into a hollow pit too, and perhaps it was the same, and I had done something dreadful. So I did the charm over again, and touched my eyes and my lips and my hair in a peculiar manner, and said the old words from the fairy language, so that I might be sure I had not been carried away. I tried again to see the secret wood, and to creep up the passage and see what I had seen there, but somehow I couldn't, and I kept on thinking of nurse's stories. There was one I remembered about a young man who once upon a time went hunting, and all the day he and his hounds hunted every-where, and they crossed the rivers and went into all the woods, and went round the marshes, but they couldn't find anything at all, and they hunted all day till the sun sank down and began to set behind the mountain. And the young man was angry because he couldn't find anything, and he was going to turn back, when just as the sun touched the mountain, he saw come out of a brake in front of him a beautiful white stag. And he cheered to his hounds, but they whined and would not follow, and he cheered to his horse, but it shivered and stood stock still, and the young man jumped off the horse and left the hounds and began to follow the white stag all alone. And soon it was quite dark, and the sky was black, without a single star shining in it, and the stag went away into the darkness. And though the man had brought his gun with him he never shot at the stag, because he wanted to catch it, and he was afraid he would lose it in the night. But he never lost it once, though the sky was so black and the air was so dark, and the stag went on and on till the young man didn't know a bit where he was. And they went through enormous woods where the air was full of whispers and a pale, dead light came out from the rotten trunks that were lying on the ground, and just as the man thought he had lost the stag, he would see it all white and shining in front of him, and he would run fast to catch it, but the stag always ran faster, so he did not catch it. And they went through the enormous woods, and they swam across rivers, and they waded through black marshes where the ground bubbled, and the air was full of will-o'-the-wisps, and the stag fled away down into rocky narrow valleys, where the air was like the smell of a vault, and the man went after it. And they went over the great mountains and the man heard the wind come down from the sky, and the stag went on and the man went after. At last the sun rose and the young man found he was in a country that he had never seen before; it was a beautiful valley with a bright stream running through it, and a great, big round hill in the middle. And the stag went down the valley, towards the hill, and it seemed to be getting tired and went slower and slower, and though the man was tired, too, he began to run faster, and he was sure he would catch the stag at last. But just as they got to the bottom of the hill, and the man stretched out his hand to catch the stag, it vanished into the earth, and the man began to cry; he was so sorry that he had lost it after all his long hunting. But as he was crying he saw there was a door in the hill, just in front of him, and he went in, and it was quite dark, but he went on, as he thought he would find the white stag. And all of a sudden it got light, and there was the sky, and the sun shining, and birds singing in the trees, and there was a beautiful fountain. And by the fountain a lovely lady was sitting, who was the queen of the fairies, and she told the man that she had changed herself into a stag to bring him there because she loved him so much. Then she brought out a great gold cup, covered with jewels, from her fairy palace, and she offered him wine in the cup to drink. And he drank, and the more he drank the more he longed to drink, because the wine was enchanted. So he kissed the lovely lady, and she became his wife, and he stayed all that day and all that night in the hill where she lived, and when he woke he found he was lying on the ground, close to where he had seen the stag first, and his horse was there and his hounds were there waiting, and he looked up, and the sun sank behind the mountain. And he went home and lived a long time, but he would never kiss any other lady because he had kissed the queen of the fairies, and he would never drink common wine any more, because he had drunk enchanted wine. And sometimes nurse told me tales that she had heard from her great-grandmother, who was very old, and lived in a cottage on the mountain all alone, and most of these tales were about a hill where people used to meet at night long ago, and they used to play all sorts of strange games and do queer things that nurse told me of, but I couldn't understand, and now, she said, everybody but her great-grandmother had forgotten all about it, and nobody knew where the hill was, not even her great-grandmother. But she told me one very strange story about the hill, and I trembled when I remembered it. She said that people always went there in summer, when it was very hot, and they had to dance a good deal. It would be all dark at first, and there were trees there, which made it much darker, and people would come, one by one, from all directions, by a secret path which nobody else knew, and two persons would keep the gate, and every one as they came up had to give a very curious sign, which nurse showed me as well as she could, but she said she couldn't show me properly. And all kinds of people would come; there would be gentle folks and village folks, and some old people and boys and girls, and quite small children, who sat and watched. And it would all be dark as they came in, except in one corner where some one was burning something that smelt strong and sweet, and made them laugh, and there one would see a glaring of coals, and the smoke mounting up red. So they would all come in, and when the last had come there was no door any more, so that no one else could get in, even if they knew there was anything beyond. And once a gentleman who was a stranger and had ridden a long way, lost his path at night, and his horse took him into the very middle of the wild country, where everything was upside down, and there were dreadful marshes and great stones everywhere, and holes underfoot, and the trees looked like gibbet-posts, because they had great black arms that stretched out across the way. And this strange gentle-man was very frightened, and his horse began to shiver all over, and at last it stopped and wouldn't go any farther, and the gentleman got down and tried to lead the horse, but it wouldn't move, and it was all covered with a sweat, like death. So the gentleman went on all alone, going farther and farther into the wild country, till at last he came to a dark place, where he heard shouting and singing and crying, like nothing he had ever heard before. It all sounded quite close to him, but he couldn't get in, and so he began to call, and while he was calling, something came behind him, and in a minute his mouth and arms and legs were all bound up, and he fell into a swoon. And when he came to himself, he was lying by the roadside, just where he had first lost his way, under a blasted oak with a black trunk, and his horse was tied beside him. So he rode on to the town and told the people there what had hap-pened, and some of them were amazed; but others knew. So when once everybody had come, there was no door at all for anybody else to pass in by. And when they were all inside, round in a ring, touching each other, some one began to sing in the darkness, and some one else would make a noise like thunder with a thing they had on purpose, and on still nights people would hear the thundering noise far, far away beyond the wild land, and some of them, who thought they knew what it was, used to make a sign on their breasts when they woke up in their beds at dead of night and heard that terrible deep noise, like thunder on the mountains. And the noise and the singing would go on and on for a long time, and the people who were in a ring swayed a little to and fro; and the song was in an old, old language that nobody knows now, and the tune was queer. Nurse said her great-grandmother had known some one who remembered a little of it, when she was quite a little girl, and nurse tried to sing some of it to me, and it was so strange a tune that I turned all cold and my flesh crept as if I had put my hand on something dead. Sometimes it was a man that sang and sometimes it was a woman, and sometimes the one who sang it did it so well that two or three of the people who were there fell to the ground shrieking and tearing with their hands. The singing went on, and the people in the ring kept swaying to and fro for a long time, and at last the moon would rise over a place they called the Tole Deol, and came up and showed them swinging and swaying from side to side, with the sweet thick smoke curling up from the burning coals, and floating in circles all around them. Then they had their supper. A boy and a girl brought it to them; the boy carried a great cup of wine, and the girl carried a cake of bread, and they passed the bread and the wine round and round, but they tasted quite different from common bread and common wine, and changed everybody that tasted them. Then they all rose up and danced, and secret things were brought out of some hiding place, and they played extraordinary games, and danced round and round and round in the moonlight, and sometimes people would suddenly disappear and never be heard of afterwards, and nobody knew what had happened to them. And they drank more of that curious wine, and they made images and worshipped them, and nurse showed me how the images were made one day when we were out for a walk, and we passed by a place where there was a lot of wet clay. So nurse asked me if I would like to know what those things were like that they made on the hill, and I said yes. Then she asked me if I would promise never to tell a living soul a word about it, and if I did I was to be thrown into the black pit with the dead people, and I said I wouldn't tell anybody, and she said the same thing again and again, and I promised. So she took my wooden spade and dug a big lump of clay and put it in my tin bucket, and told me to say if any one met us that I was going to make pies when I went home. Then we went on a little way till we came to a little brake growing right down into the road, and nurse stopped, and looked up the road and down it, and then peeped through the hedge into the field on the other side, and then she said, "Quick!" and we ran into the brake, and crept in and out among the bushes till we had gone a good way from the road. Then we sat down under a bush, and I wanted so much to know what nurse was going to make with the clay, but before she would begin she made me promise again not to say a word about it, and she went again and peeped through the bushes on every side, though the lane was so small and deep that hardly anybody ever went there. So we sat down, and nurse took the clay out of the bucket, and began to knead it with her hands, and do queer things with it, and turn it about. And she hid it under a big dock-leaf for a minute or two and then she brought it out again, and then she stood up and sat down, and walked round the clay in a peculiar manner, and all the time she was softly singing a sort of rhyme, and her face got very red. Then she sat down again, and took the clay in her hands and began to shape it into a doll, but not like the dolls I have at home, and she made the queerest doll I had ever seen, all out of the wet clay, and hid it under a bush to get dry and hard, and all the time she was making it she was singing these rhymes to herself, and her face got redder and redder. So we left the doll there, hidden away in the bushes where nobody would ever find it. And a few days later we went the same walk, and when we came to that narrow, dark part of the lane where the brake runs down to the bank, nurse made me promise all over again, and she looked about, just as she had done before, and we crept into the bushes till we got to the green place where the little clay man was hidden. I remember it all so well, though I was only eight, and it is eight years ago now as I am writing it down, but the sky was a deep violet blue, and in the middle of the brake where we were sitting there was a great elder tree covered with blossoms, and on the other side there was a clump of meadowsweet, and when I think of that day the smell of the meadowsweet and elder blossom seems to fill the room, and if I shut my eyes I can see the glaring blue sky, with little clouds very white floating across it, and nurse who went away long ago sitting opposite me and looking like the beautiful white lady in the wood. So we sat down and nurse took out the clay doll from the secret place where she had hidden it, and she said we must "pay our respects," and she would show me what to do, and I must watch her all the time. So she did all sorts of queer things with the little clay man, and I noticed she was all streaming with perspiration, though we had walked so slowly, and then she told me to "pay my respects," and I did everything she did because I liked her, and it was such an odd game. And she said that if one loved very much, the clay man was very good, if one did certain things with it, and if one hated very much, it was just as good, only one had to do different things, and we played with it a long time, and pretended all sorts of things. Nurse said her great-grandmother had told her all about these images, but what we did was no harm at all, only a game. But she told me a story about these images that frightened me very much, and that was what I remembered that night when I was lying awake in my room in the pale, empty darkness, thinking of what I had seen and the secret wood. Nurse said there was once a young lady of the high gentry, who lived in a great castle. And she was so beautiful that all the gentlemen wanted to marry her, because she was the loveliest lady that anybody had ever seen, and she was kind to everybody, and everybody thought she was very good. But though she was polite to all the gentlemen who wished to marry her, she put them off, and said she couldn't make up her mind, and she wasn't sure she wanted to marry anybody at all. And her father, who was a very great lord, was angry, though he was so fond of her, and he asked her why she wouldn't choose a bachelor out of all the handsome young men who came to the castle. But she only said she didn't love any of them very much, and she must wait, and if they pestered her, she said she would go and be a nun in a nunnery. So all the gentlemen said they would go away and wait for a year and a day, and when a year and a day were gone, they would come back again and ask her to say which one she would marry. So the day was appointed and they all went away; and the lady had promised that in a year and a day it would be her wedding day with one of them. But the truth was, that she was the queen of the people who danced on the hill on summer nights, and on the proper nights she would lock the door of her room, and she and her maid would steal out of the castle by a secret passage that only they knew of, and go away up to the hill in the wild land. And she knew more of the secret things than any one else, and more than any one knew before or after, because she would not tell anybody the most secret secrets. She knew how to do all the awful things, how to destroy young men, and how to put a curse on people, and other things that I could not understand. And her real name was the Lady Avelin, but the dancing people called her Cassap, which meant somebody very wise, in the old language. And she was whiter than any of them and taller, and her eyes shone in the dark like burning rubies; and she could sing songs that none of the others could sing, and when she sang they all fell down on their faces and worshipped her. And she could do what they called shib-show, which was a very wonderful enchantment. She would tell the great lord, her father, that she wanted to go into the woods to gather flowers, so he let her go, and she and her maid went into the woods where nobody came, and the maid would keep watch. Then the lady would lie down under the trees and begin to sing a particular song, and she stretched out her arms, and from every part of the wood great serpents would come, hissing and gliding in and out among the trees, and shooting out their forked tongues as they crawled up to the lady. And they all came to her, and twisted round her, round her body, and her arms, and her neck, till she was covered with writhing serpents, and there was only her head to be seen. And she whispered to them, and she sang to them, and they writhed round and round, faster and faster, till she told them to go. And they all went away directly, back to their holes, and on the lady's breast there would be a most curious, beautiful stone, shaped something like an egg, and coloured dark blue and yellow, and red, and green, marked like a serpent's scales. It was called a glame stone, and with it one could do all sorts of wonderful things, and nurse said her great-grandmother had seen a glame stone with her own eyes, and it was for all the world shiny and scaly like a snake. And the lady could do a lot of other things as well, but she was quite fixed that she would not be married. And there were a great many gentlemen who wanted to marry her, but there were five of them who were chief, and their names were Sir Simon, Sir John, Sir Oliver, Sir Richard, and Sir Rowland. All the others believed she spoke the truth, and that she would choose one of them to be her man when a year and a day was done; it was only Sir Simon, who was very crafty, who thought she was deceiving them all, and he vowed he would watch and try if he could find out anything. And though he was very wise he was very young, and he had a smooth, soft face like a girl's, and he pretended, as the rest did, that he would not come to the castle for a year and a day, and he said he was going away beyond the sea to foreign parts. But he really only went a very little way, and came back dressed like a servant girl, and so he got a place in the castle to wash the dishes. And he waited and watched, and he listened and said nothing, and he hid in dark places, and woke up at night and looked out, and he heard things and he saw things that he thought were very strange. And he was so sly that he told the girl that waited on the lady that he was really a young man, and that he had dressed up as a girl because he loved her so very much and wanted to be in the same house with her, and the girl was so pleased that she told him many things, and he was more than ever certain that the Lady Avelin was deceiving him and the others. And he was so clever, and told the servant so many lies, that one night he managed to hide in the Lady Avelin's room behind the curtains. And he stayed quite still and never moved, and at last the lady came. And she bent down under the bed, and raised up a stone, and there was a hollow place underneath, and out of it she took a waxen image, just like the clay one that I and nurse had made in the brake. And all the time her eyes were burning like rubies. And she took the little wax doll up in her arms and held it to her breast, and she whispered and she murmured, and she took it up and she laid it down again, and she held it high, and she held it low, and she laid it down again. And she said, "Happy is he that begat the bishop, that ordered the clerk, that married the man, that had the wife, that fashioned the hive, that harboured the bee, that gathered the wax that my own true love was made of." And she brought out of an aumbry a great golden bowl, and she brought out of a closet a great jar of wine, and she poured some of the wine into the bowl, and she laid her mannikin very gently in the wine, and washed it in the wine all over. Then she went to a cupboard and took a small round cake and laid it on the image's mouth, and then she bore it softly and covered it up. And Sir Simon, who was watching all the time, though he was terribly frightened, saw the lady bend down and stretch out her arms and whisper and sing, and then Sir Simon saw beside her a handsome young man, who kissed her on the lips. And they drank wine out of the golden bowl together, and they ate the cake together. But when the sun rose there was only the little wax doll, and the lady hid it again under the bed in the hollow place. So Sir Simon knew quite well what the lady was, and he waited and he watched, till the time she had said was nearly over, and in a week the year and a day would be done. And one night, when he was watching behind the curtains in her room, he saw her making more wax dolls. And she made five, and hid them away. And the next night she took one out, and held it up, and filled the golden bowl with water, and took the doll by the neck and held it under the water. Then she said—

Sir Dickon, Sir Dickon, your day is done,
You shall be drowned in the water wan.

And the next day news came to the castle that Sir Richard had been drowned at the ford. And at night she took another doll and tied a violet cord round its neck and hung it up on a nail. Then she said—

> Sir Rowland, your life has ended its span,
> High on a tree I see you hang.

And the next day news came to the castle that Sir Rowland had been hanged by robbers in the wood. And at night she took another doll, and drove her bodkin right into its heart. Then she said—

> Sir Noll, Sir Noll, so cease your life,
> Your heart is piercèd with the knife.

And the next day news came to the castle that Sir Oliver had fought in a tavern, and a stranger had stabbed him to the heart. And at night she took another doll, and held it to a fire of charcoal till it was melted. Then she said—

> Sir John, return, and turn to clay,
> In fire of fever you waste away.

And the next day news came to the castle that Sir John had died in a burning fever. So then Sir Simon went out of the castle and mounted his horse and rode away to the bishop and told him everything. And the bishop sent his men, and they took the Lady Avelin, and everything she had done was found out. So on the day after the year and a day, when she was to have been married, they carried her through the town in her smock, and they tied her to a great stake in the market-place, and burned her alive before the bishop with her wax image hung round her neck. And people said the wax man screamed in the burning of the flames. And I thought of this story again and again as I was lying awake in my bed, and I seemed to see the Lady Avelin in the market-place, with the yellow flames eating up her beautiful white body. And I thought of it so much that I seemed to get into the story myself, and I fancied I was the lady, and that they were coming to take me to be burnt with fire, with all the people in the town looking at me. And I wondered whether she cared, after all the strange things she had done, and whether it hurt very much to be burned at the stake. I tried again and again to forget nurse's stories, and to remember the secret I had seen that afternoon, and what was in the secret wood, but I could only see the dark and a glimmering in the dark, and then it went away, and I only saw myself running, and then a great moon came up white over a dark round hill. Then all the old stories came back again, and the queer rhymes that nurse used to sing to me; and there was one beginning "Halsy cumsy Helen musty," that she used to sing very softly when she wanted me to go to sleep. And I began to sing it to myself inside of my head, and I went to sleep.

The next morning I was very tired and sleepy, and could hardly do my lessons, and I was very glad when they were over and I had had my dinner, as I wanted to go out and be alone. It was a warm day, and I went to a nice turfy hill by the river, and sat down on my mother's old shawl that I had brought with me on purpose. The sky was grey, like the day before, but there was a kind of white gleam behind it, and from where I was sitting I could look down on the town, and it was all still and quiet and white, like a picture. I remembered that it was on that hill that nurse taught me to play an old game called "Troy Town," in which one had to dance, and wind in and out on a pattern in the grass, and then when one had danced and turned long enough the other person asks you questions, and you can't help answering whether you want to or not, and whatever you are told to do you feel you have to do it. Nurse said there used to be a lot of games like that that some people knew of, and there was one by which people could be turned into anything you liked, and an old man her great-grandmother had seen had known a girl who had been turned into a large snake. And there was another very ancient game of dancing and winding and turning, by which you could take a person out of himself and hide him away as long as you liked, and his body went walking about quite empty, without any sense in it. But I came to that hill because I wanted to think of what had happened the day before, and of the secret of the wood. From the place where I was sitting I could see beyond the town, into the opening I had found, where a little brook had led me into an unknown country. And I pretended I was following the brook over again, and I went all the way in my mind, and at last I found the wood, and crept into it under the bushes, and then in the dusk I saw something that made me feel as if I were filled with fire, as if I wanted to dance and sing and fly up into the air, because I was changed and wonderful. But what I saw was not changed at all, and had not grown old, and I wondered again and again how such things could happen, and whether nurse's stories were really true, because in the daytime in the open air everything seemed quite different from what it was at night, when I was frightened, and thought I was to be burned alive. I once told my father one of her little tales, which was about a ghost, and asked him if it was true, and he told me it was not true at all, and that only common, ignorant people believed in such rubbish. He was very angry with nurse for telling me the story, and scolded her, and after that I promised her I would never whisper a word of what she told me, and if I did I should be bitten by the great black snake that lived in the pool in the wood. And all alone on the hill I wondered what was true. I had seen something very amazing and very lovely, and I knew a story, and if I had really seen it, and not made it up out of the dark, and the black bough, and the bright shining that was mounting up to the sky from over the great round hill, but had really seen it in truth, then there were all kinds of wonderful and lovely and terrible things to think of, so I longed and trembled, and I burned and got cold. And I looked down on the town, so quiet and still, like a little white picture, and I thought over and over if it could be true. I was a long time before I could make up my mind to anything; there was such a strange fluttering at my heart that seemed to whisper to me all the time that I had not made it up out of my head, and yet it seemed quite impossible, and I knew my father and everybody would say it was dreadful rubbish. I never dreamed of telling him or anybody else a word about it, because I knew it would be of no use, and I should only get laughed at or scolded, so for a long time I was very quiet, and went about thinking and wondering; and at night I used to dream of amazing things, and sometimes I woke up in the early morning and held out my arms with a cry. And I was frightened, too, because there were dangers, and some awful thing would happen to me, unless I took great care, if the story were true. These old tales were always in my head, night and morning, and I went over them and told them to myself over and over again, and went for walks in the places where nurse had told them to me; and when I sat in the nursery by the fire in the evenings I used to fancy nurse was sitting in the other chair, and telling me some wonderful story in a low voice, for fear anybody should be listening. But she used to like best to tell me about things when we were right out in the country, far from the house, because she said she was telling me such secrets, and walls have ears. And if it was something more than ever secret, we had to hide in brakes or woods; and I used to think it was such fun creeping along a hedge, and going very softly, and then we would get behind the bushes or run into the wood all of a sudden, when we were sure that none was watching us; so we knew that we had our secrets quite all to ourselves, and nobody else at all knew anything about them. Now and then, when we had hidden ourselves as I have described, she used to show me all sorts of odd things. One day, I remember, we were in a hazel brake, overlooking the brook, and we were so snug and warm, as though it was April; the sun was quite hot, and the leaves were just coming out. Nurse said she would show me something funny that would make me laugh, and then she showed me, as she said, how one could turn a whole house upside down, without anybody being able to find out, and the pots and pans would jump about, and the china would be broken, and the chairs would tumble over of themselves. I tried it one day in the kitchen, and I found I could do it quite well, and a whole row of plates on the dresser fell off it, and cook's little work-table tilted up and turned right over "before her eyes," as she said, but she was so frightened and turned so white that I didn't do it again, as I liked her. And afterwards, in the hazel copse, when she had shown me how to make things tumble about, she showed me how to make rapping noises, and I learnt how to do that, too. Then she taught me rhymes to say on certain occasions, and peculiar marks to make on other occasions, and other things that her great-grandmother had taught her when she was a little girl herself. And these were all the things I was thinking about in those days after the strange walk when I thought I had seen a great secret, and I wished nurse were there for me to ask her about it, but she had gone away more than two years before, and nobody seemed to know what had become of her, or where she had gone. But I shall always remember those days if I live to be quite old, because all the time I felt so strange, wondering and doubting, and feeling quite sure at one time, and making up my mind, and then I would feel quite sure that such things couldn't happen really, and it began all over again. But I took great care not to do certain things that might be very dangerous. So I waited and wondered for a long time, and though I was not sure at all, I never dared to try to find out. But one day I became sure that all that nurse said was quite true, and I was all alone when I found it out. I trembled all over with joy and terror, and as fast as I could I ran into one of the old brakes where we used to go—it was the one by the lane, where nurse made the little clay man—and I ran into it, and I crept into it; and when I came to the place where the elder was, I covered up my face with my hands and lay down flat on the grass, and I stayed there for two hours without moving, whispering to myself delicious, terrible things, and saying some words over and over again. It was all true and wonderful and splendid, and when I remembered the story I knew and thought of what I had really seen, I got hot and I got cold, and the air seemed full of scent, and flowers, and singing. And first I wanted to make a little clay man, like the one nurse had made so long ago, and I had to invent plans and stratagems, and to look about, and to think of things beforehand, because nobody must dream of anything that I was doing or going to do, and I was too old to carry clay about in a tin bucket. At last I thought of a plan, and I brought the wet clay to the brake, and did everything that nurse had done, only I made a much finer image than the one she had made; and when it was finished I did everything that I could imagine and much more than she did, because it was the likeness of something far better. And a few days later, when I had done my lessons early, I went for the second time by the way of the little brook that had led me into a strange country. And I followed the brook, and went through the bushes, and beneath the low branches of trees, and up thorny thickets on the hill, and by dark woods full of creeping thorns, a long, long way. Then I crept through the dark tunnel where the brook had been and the ground was stony, till at last I came to the thicket that climbed up the hill, and though the leaves were coming out upon the trees, everything looked almost as black as it was on the first day that I went there. And the thicket was just the same, and I went up slowly till I came out on the big bare hill, and began to walk among the wonderful rocks. I saw the terrible voor again on every-thing, for though the sky was brighter, the ring of wild hills all around was still dark, and the hanging woods looked dark and dreadful, and the strange rocks were as grey as ever; and when I looked down on them from the great mound, sitting on the stone, I saw all their amazing circles and rounds within rounds, and I had to sit quite still and watch them as they began to turn about me, and each stone danced in its place, and they seemed to go round and round in a great whirl, as if one were in the middle of all the stars and heard them rushing through the air. So I went down among the rocks to dance with them and to sing extraordinary songs; and I went down through the other thicket, and drank from the bright stream in the close and secret valley, putting my lips down to the bubbling water; and then I went on till I came to the deep, brimming well among the glittering moss, and I sat down. I looked before me into the secret darkness of the valley, and behind me was the great high wall of grass, and all around me there were the hanging woods that made the valley such a secret place. I knew there was nobody here at all besides myself, and that no one could see me. So I took off my boots and stockings, and let my feet down into the water, saying the words that I knew. And it was not cold at all, as I expected, but warm and very pleasant, and when my feet were in it I felt as if they were in silk, or as if the nymph were kissing them. So when I had done, I said the other words and made the signs, and then I dried my feet with a towel I had brought on purpose, and put on my stockings and boots. Then I climbed up the steep wall, and went into the place where there are the hollows, and the two beautiful mounds, and the round ridges of land, and all the strange shapes. I did not go down into the hollow this time, but I turned at the end, and made out the figures quite plainly, as it was lighter, and I had remembered the story I had quite forgotten before, and in the story the two figures are called Adam and Eve, and only those who know the story understand what they mean. So I went on and on till I came to the secret wood which must not be described, and I crept into it by the way I had found. And when I had gone about half-way I stopped, and turned round, and got ready, and I bound the handkerchief tightly round my eyes, and made quite sure that I could not see at all, not a twig, nor the end of a leaf, nor the light of the sky, as it was an old red silk handkerchief with large yellow spots, that went round twice and covered my eyes, so that I could see nothing. Then I began to go on, step by step, very slowly. My heart beat faster and faster, and something rose in my throat that choked me and made me want to cry out, but I shut my lips, and went on. Boughs caught in my hair as I went, and great thorns tore me; but I went on to the end of the path. Then I stopped, and held out my arms and bowed, and I went round the first time, feeling with my hands, and there was nothing. I went round the second time, feeling with my hands, and there was nothing. Then I went round the third time, feeling with my hands, and the story was all true, and I wished that the years were gone by, and that I had not so long a time to wait before I was happy for ever and ever.

Nurse must have been a prophet like those we read of in the Bible. Everything that she said began to come true, and since then other things that she told me of have happened. That was how I came to know that her stories were true and that I had not made up the secret myself out of my own head. But there was another thing that happened that day. I went a second time to the secret place. It was at the deep brimming well, and when I was standing on the moss I bent over and looked in, and then I knew who the white lady was that I had seen come out of the water in the wood long ago when I was quite little. And I trembled all over, because that told me other things. Then I remembered how sometime after I had seen the white people in the wood, nurse asked me more about them, and I told her all over again, and she listened, and said nothing for a long, long time, and at last she said, "You will see her again." So I understood what had happened and what was to happen. And I understood about the nymphs; how I might meet them in all kinds of places, and they would always help me, and I must always look for them, and find them in all sorts of strange shapes and appearances. And without the nymphs I could never have found the secret, and without them none of the other things could happen. Nurse had told me all about them long ago, but she called them by another name, and I did not know what she meant, or what her tales of them were about, only that they were very queer. And there were two kinds, the bright and the dark, and both were very lovely and very wonderful, and some people saw only one kind, and some only the other, but some saw them both. But usually the dark appeared first, and the bright ones came afterwards, and there were extraordinary tales about them. It was a day or two after I had come home from the secret place that I first really knew the nymphs. Nurse had shown me how to call them, and I had tried, but I did not know what she meant, and so I thought it was all nonsense. But I made up my mind I would try again, so I went to the wood where the pool was, where I saw the white people, and I tried again. The dark nymph, Alanna, came, and she turned the pool of water into a pool of fire…

EPILOGUE

"That's a very queer story," said Cotgrave, handing back the green book to the recluse, Ambrose. "I see the drift of a good deal, but there are many things that I do not grasp at all. On the last page, for example, what does she mean by 'nymphs'?"

"Well, I think there are references throughout the manuscript to certain 'processes' which have been handed down by tradition from age to age. Some of these processes are just beginning to come within the purview of science, which has arrived at them—or rather at the steps which lead to them—by quite different paths. I have interpreted the reference to 'nymphs' as a reference to one of these processes."

"And you believe that there are such things?"

"Oh, I think so. Yes, I believe I could give you convincing evidence on that point. I am afraid you have neglected the study of alchemy? It is a pity, for the symbolism, at all events, is very beautiful, and moreover if you were acquainted with certain books on the subject, I could recall to your mind phrases which might explain a good deal in the manuscript that you have been reading."

"Yes; but I want to know whether you seriously think that there is any foundation of fact beneath these fancies. Is it not all a department of poetry; a curious dream with which man has indulged himself?"

"I can only say that it is no doubt better for the great mass of people to dismiss it all as a dream. But if you ask my veritable belief—that goes quite the other way. No; I should not say belief, but rather knowledge. I may tell you that I have known cases in which men have stumbled quite by accident on certain of these 'processes,' and have been astonished by wholly unexpected results. In the cases I am thinking of there could have been no possibility of 'suggestion' or sub-conscious action of any kind. One might as well suppose a schoolboy 'suggesting' the existence of Æschylus to himself, while he plods mechanically through the declensions.

"But you have noticed the obscurity," Ambrose went on, "and in this particular case it must have been dictated by instinct, since the writer never thought that her manuscripts would fall into other hands. But the practice is universal, and for most excellent reasons. Powerful and sovereign medicines, which are, of necessity, virulent poisons also, are kept in a locked cabinet. The child may find the key by chance, and drink herself dead; but in most cases the search is educational, and the phials contain precious elixirs for him who has patiently fashioned the key for himself."

"You do not care to go into details?"

"No, frankly, I do not. No, you must remain unconvinced. But you saw how the manuscript illustrates the talk we had last week?"

"Is this girl still alive?"

"No. I was one of those who found her. I knew the father well; he was a lawyer, and had always left her very much to herself. He thought of nothing but deeds and leases, and the news came to him as an awful surprise. She was missing one morning; I suppose it was about a year after she had written what you have read. The servants were called, and they told things, and put the only natural interpretation on them—a perfectly erroneous one.

"They discovered that green book somewhere in her room, and I found her in the place that she described with so much dread, lying on the ground before the image."

"It was an image?"

"Yes, it was hidden by the thorns and the thick undergrowth that had surrounded it. It was a wild, lonely country; but you know what it was like by her description, though of course you will understand that the colours have been heightened. A child's imagination always makes the heights higher and the depths deeper than they really are; and she had, unfortunately for herself, something more than imagination. One might say, perhaps, that the picture in her mind which she succeeded in a measure in putting into words, was the scene as it would have appeared to an imaginative artist. But it is a strange, desolate land."

"And she was dead?"

"Yes. She had poisoned herself—in time. No; there was not a word to be said against her in the ordinary sense. You may recollect a story I told you the other night about a lady who saw her child's fingers crushed by a window?"

"And what was this statue?"

"Well, it was of Roman workmanship, of a stone that with the centuries had not blackened, but had become white and luminous. The thicket had grown up about it and concealed it, and in the Middle Ages the followers of a very old tradition had known how to use it for their own purposes. In fact it had been incorporated into the monstrous mythology of the Sabbath. You will have noted that those to whom a sight of that shining whiteness had been vouchsafed by chance, or rather, perhaps, by apparent chance, were required to blindfold themselves on their second approach. That is very significant."

"And is it there still?"

"I sent for tools, and we hammered it into dust and fragments."

"The persistence of tradition never surprises me," Ambrose went on after a pause. "I could name many an English parish where such traditions as that girl had listened to in her childhood are still existent in occult but unabated vigour. No, for me, it is the 'story' not the 'sequel,' which is strange and awful, for I have always believed that wonder is of the soul."

IN THE CLOSED ROOM

Frances Hodgson Burnett

Frances Hodgson Burnett (1849–1924) was born into a comfortable Manchester family whose circumstances abruptly changed following her father's sudden death, leaving her mother in charge of the family iron-mongery business. When the Lancashire cotton famine caused by the American Civil War reduced the Hodgsons' finances still further, her mother moved the family to join her brother in Knoxville, Tennessee. An invet-erate spinner of stories since early childhood, the young Frances turned to writing as a source of income in her late teens, becoming a regular contributor to periodicals like *Godey's Lady's Book*, *Peterson's Magazine* and *Harper's Bazaar*.

Best known today for her children's books featuring dramatic reversals of fortunes, such as *Little Lord Fauntleroy* (1885–6), *A Little Princess* (1905) and *The Secret Garden* (1911), Hodgson Burnett published a considerable number of other books, often exploring similar topics. *That Lass O' Lowrie's* (1877), set in a Lancashire mining village, addresses questions of social inequality through its "pit girl" heroine, while her delightful *The Making of a Marchioness* (1901) follows the fortunes of impoverished lady's companion Emily Fox-Seton. She also published a quartet of children's books about the adventures of the Queen of the Fairies, beginning with 1906's *Queen Silver-Bell*.

Hodgson Burnett turned to supernatural themes in her novella *The White People*, written during the First World War. Her tale of an isolated young girl living in a Scottish castle who sees ethereal "White People" invisible to those around her—"the ones whose fairness looks almost transparent"—brings together ghosts and fairies in a way that chimes with wider Spiritualist concerns of the period, which Hodgson Burnett herself had embraced following the death of her eldest son. Her earlier short story "In the Closed Room", first published in 1904, opens in modern-day New York rather than mist-covered Scottish moorlands, but its eerily dreamlike narrative takes the reader to some similar places.

I

N the fierce airless heat of the small square room the child Judith panted as she lay on her bed. Her father and mother slept near her, drowned in the heavy slumber of workers after their day's labour. Some people in the next flat were quarrelling, irritated probably by the appalling heat and their miserable helplessness against it. All the hot emanations of the sun-baked city streets seemed to combine with their clamour and unrest, and rise to the flat in which the child lay gazing at the darkness. It was situated but a few feet from the track of the Elevated Railroad and existence seemed to pulsate to the rush and roar of the demon which swept past the windows every few minutes. No one knew that Judith held the thing in horror, but it was a truth that she did. She was only seven years old, and at that age it is not easy to explain one's self so that older people can understand.

She could only have said, "I hate it. It comes so fast. It is always coming. It makes a sound as if thunder was quite close. I can never get away from it." The children in the other flats rather liked it. They hung out of the window perilously to watch it thunder past and to see the people who crowded it pressed close together in the seats, standing in the aisles, hanging on to the straps. Sometimes in the evening there were people in it who were going to the theatre, and the women and girls were dressed in light colours and wore hats covered with white feathers and flowers. At such times the children were delighted, and Judith used to hear the three in the next flat calling out to each other, "That's my lady! That's my lady! That one's mine!"

Judith was not like the children in the other flats. She was a frail, curious creature, with silent ways and a soft voice and eyes. She liked to play by herself in a corner of the room and to talk to herself as she played. No one knew what she talked about, and in fact no one inquired. Her mother was always too busy. When she was not making men's coats by the score at the whizzing sewing machine, she was hurriedly preparing a meal which was always in danger of being late. There was the breakfast, which might not be ready in time for her husband to reach his "shop" when the whistle blew; there was the supper, which might not be in time to be in waiting for him when he returned in the evening. The midday meal was a trifling matter, needing no special preparation. One ate anything one could find left from supper or breakfast.

Judith's relation to her father and mother was not a very intimate one. They were too hard worked to have time for domestic intimacies, and a feature of their acquaintance was that though neither of them was sufficiently articulate to have found expression for the fact—the young man and woman felt the child vaguely remote. Their affection for her was tinged with something indefinitely like reverence. She had been a lovely baby with a peculiar magnolia whiteness of skin and very large, sweetly smiling eyes of dark blue, fringed with quite black lashes. She had exquisite pointed fingers and slender feet, and though Mr. and Mrs. Foster were—perhaps fortunately—unaware of it, she had been not at all the baby one would have expected to come to life in a corner of the hive of a workman's flat a few feet from the Elevated Railroad.

"Seems sometimes as if somehow she couldn't be mine," Mrs. Foster said at times. "She ain't like me, an' she ain't like Jem Foster, Lord knows. She ain't like none of either of our families I've ever heard of—'ceptin' it might be her Aunt Hester—but she died long before I was born. I've only heard mother tell about her. She was a awful pretty girl. Mother said she had that kind of lily-white complexion and long slender fingers that was so supple she could curl 'em back like they was double-jointed. Her eyes was big and had eyelashes that stood out round 'em, but they was brown. Mother said she wasn't like any other kind of girl, and she thinks Judith may turn out like her. She wasn't but fifteen when she died. She never was ill in her life—but one morning she didn't come down to breakfast, and when they went up to call her, there she was sittin' at her window restin' her chin on her hand, with her face turned up smilin' as if she was talkin' to some one. The doctor said it had happened hours before, when she had come to the window to look at the stars. Easy way to go, wasn't it?"

Judith had heard of her Aunt Hester, but she only knew that she herself had hands like her and that her life had ended when she was quite young. Mrs. Foster was too much occupied by the strenuousness of life to dwell upon the passing of souls. To her the girl Hester seemed too remote to appear quite real. The legends of her beauty and unlikeness to other girls seemed rather like a sort of romance.

As she was not aware that Judith hated the Elevated Railroad, so she was not aware that she was fond of the far away Aunt Hester with the long-pointed fingers which could curl backwards. She did not know that when she was playing in her corner of the room, where it was her way to sit on her little chair with her face turned towards the wall, she often sat curving her small long fingers backward and talking to herself about Aunt Hester. But this—as well as many other things—was true. It was not secretiveness which caused the child to refrain from speaking of certain things. She herself could not have explained the reasons for her silence; also it had never occurred to her that explanation and reasons were necessary. Her mental attitude was that of a child who, knowing a certain language, does not speak it to those who have never heard and are wholly ignorant of it. She knew her Aunt Hester as her mother did not. She had seen her often in her dreams and had a secret fancy that she could dream of her when she wished to do so. She was very fond of dreaming of her. The places where she came upon Aunt Hester were strange and lovely places where the air one breathed smelled like flowers and everything was lovely in a new way, and when one moved one felt so light that movement was delightful, and when one wakened one had not quite got over the lightness and for a few moments felt as if one would float out of bed.

The healthy, vigorous young couple who were the child's parents were in a healthy, earthly way very fond of each other. They had made a genuine love match and had found it satisfactory. The young mechanic Jem Foster had met the young shop-girl Jane Hardy, at Coney Island one summer night and had become at once enamoured of her shop-girl good looks and high spirits. They had married as soon as Jem had had the "raise" he was anticipating and had from that time lived with much harmony in the flat building by which the Elevated train rushed and roared every few minutes through the day and a greater part of the night. They themselves did not object to the "Elevated"; Jem was habituated to uproar in the machine shop, in which he spent his days, and Jane was too much absorbed in the making of men's coats by the dozens to observe anything else. The pair had healthy appetites and slept well after their day's work, hearty supper, long cheerful talk, and loud laughter over simple common joking.

"She's a queer little fish, Judy," Jane said to her husband as they sat by the open window one night, Jem's arm curved comfortably around the young woman's waist as he smoked his pipe. "What do you think she says to me tonight after I put her to bed?"

"Search me!" said Jem oracularly.

Jane laughed.

"'Why,' she says, 'I wish the Elevated train would stop.'

"'Why?' says I.

"'I want to go to sleep,' says she. 'I'm going to dream of Aunt Hester.'"

"What does she know about her Aunt Hester," said Jem. "Who's been talkin' to her?"

"Not me," Jane said. "She don't know nothing but what she's picked up by chance. I don't believe in talkin' to young ones about dead folks. 'Tain't healthy."

"That's right," said Jem. "Children that's got to hustle about among live folks for a livin' best keep their minds out of cemeteries. But, Hully Gee, what a queer thing for a young one to say."

"And that ain't all," Jane went on, her giggle half amused, half nervous. "'But I don't fall asleep when I see Aunt Hester,' says she. 'I fall awake. It's more awake there than here.'

"'Where?' says I, laughing a bit, though it did make me feel queer.

"'I don't know,' she says in that soft little quiet way of hers. 'There.' And not another thing could I get out of her."

On the hot night through whose first hours Judith lay panting in her corner of the room, tormented and kept awake by the constant roar and rush and flash of lights, she was trying to go to sleep in the hope of leaving all the heat and noise and discomfort behind, and reaching Aunt Hester. If she could fall awake she would feel and hear none of it. It would all be unreal and she would know that only the lightness and the air like flowers and the lovely brightness were true. Once, as she tossed on her cot-bed, she broke into a low little laugh to think how untrue things really were and how strange it was that people did not understand—that even she felt as she lay in the darkness that she could not get away. And she could not get away unless the train would stop just long enough to let her fall asleep. If she could fall asleep between the trains, she would not awaken. But they came so quickly one after the other. Her hair was damp as she pushed it from her forehead, the bed felt hot against her skin, the people in the next flat quarrelled more angrily, Judith heard a loud slap, and then the woman began to cry. She was a young married woman, scarcely more than a girl. Her marriage had not been as successful as that of Judith's parents. Both husband and wife had irritable tempers. Through the thin wall Judith could hear the girl sobbing angrily as the man flung himself out of bed, put on his clothes and went out, banging the door after him.

"She doesn't know," the child whispered eerily, "that it isn't real at all."

There was in her strange little soul a secret no one knew the existence of. It was a vague belief that she herself was not quite real—or that she did not belong to the life she had been born into. Her mother and father loved her and she loved them, but sometimes she was on the brink of telling them that she could not stay long—that some mistake had been made. What mistake—or where was she to go to if she went, she did not know. She used to catch her breath and stop herself and feel frightened when she had been near speaking of this fantastic thing. But the building full of workmen's flats, the hot room, the Elevated Railroad, the quarrelling people, were all a mistake. Just once or twice in her life she had seen places and things which did not seem so foreign. Once, when she had been taken to the Park in the Spring, she had wandered away from her mother to a sequestered place among shrubs and trees, all waving tender, new pale green, with the leaves a few early hot days had caused to rush out and tremble unfurled. There had been a stillness there and scents and colours she knew. A bird had come and swung upon a twig quite near her and, looking at her with bright soft full eyes, had sung gently to her, as if he were speaking. A squirrel had crept up onto her lap and had not moved when she stroked it. Its eyes had been full and soft also, and she knew it understood that she could not hurt it. There was no mistake in her being among the new fair greenness, and the woodland things who spoke to her. They did not use words, but no words were needed. She knew what they were saying. When she had pushed her way through the greenness of the shrubbery to the driveway she had found herself quite near to an open carriage, which had stopped because the lady who sat in it was speaking to a friend on the path. She was a young woman, dressed in delicate spring colours, and the little girl at her side was dressed in white cloth, and it was at the little girl Judith found herself gazing. Under her large white hat and feathers her little face seemed like a white flower. She had a deep dimple near her mouth. Her hair was a rich coppery red and hung heavy and long about her cheeks and shoulders. She lifted her head a little when the child in the common hat and frock pressed through the greenness of the bushes and she looked at Judith just as the bird and the squirrel had looked at her. They gazed as if they had known each other for ages of years and were separated by nothing. Each of them was quite happy at being near the other, and there was not in the mind of either any question of their not being near each other again. The question did not rise in Judith's mind even when in a very few minutes the carriage moved away and was lost in the crowd of equipages rolling by.

At the hottest hours of the hot night Judith recalled to herself the cool of that day. She brought back the fresh pale greenness of the nook among the bushes into which she had forced her way, the scent of the leaves and grass which she had drawn in as she breathed, the nearness in the eyes of the bird, the squirrel, and the child. She smiled as she thought of these things, and as she continued to remember yet other things, bit by bit, she felt less hot—she gradually forgot to listen for the roar of the train—she smiled still more— she lay quite still—she was cool—a tiny fresh breeze fluttered through the window and played about her forehead. She was smiling in soft delight as her eyelids drooped and closed.

"I am falling awake," she was murmuring as her lashes touched her cheek.

Perhaps when her eyes closed the sultriness of the night had changed to the momentary freshness of the turning dawn, and the next hour or so was really cooler. She knew no more heat but slept softly, deeply, long—or it seemed to her afterwards that she had slept long—as if she had drifted far away in dreamless peace.

She remembered no dream, saw nothing, felt nothing until, as it seemed to her, in the early morning, she opened her eyes. All was quite still and clear—the air of the room was pure and sweet. There was no sound any-where and, curiously enough, she was not surprised by this, nor did she expect to hear anything disturbing.

She did not look round the room. Her eyes remained resting upon what she first saw—and she was not surprised by this either. A little girl about her own age was standing smiling at her. She had large eyes, a deep dimple near her mouth, and coppery red hair which fell about her cheeks and shoulders. Judith knew her and smiled back at her.

She lifted her hand—and it was a pure white little hand with long tapering fingers.

"Come and play with me," she said—though Judith heard no voice while she knew what she was saying. "Come and play with me."

Then she was gone, and in a few seconds Judith was awake, the air of the room had changed, the noise and clatter of the streets came in at the window, and the Elevated train went thundering by. Judith did not ask herself how the child had gone or how she had come. She lay still, feeling undisturbed by everything and smiling as she had smiled in her sleep.

While she sat at the breakfast table she saw her mother looking at her curiously.

"You look as if you'd slept cool instead of hot last night," she said. "You look better than you did yesterday. You're pretty well, ain't you, Judy?"

Judith's smile meant that she was quite well, but she said nothing about her sleeping.

The heat did not disturb her through the day, though the hours grew hotter and hotter as they passed. Jane Foster, sweltering at her machine, was obliged to stop every few minutes to wipe the beads from her face and neck. Sometimes she could not remain seated, but got up panting to drink water and fan herself with a newspaper.

"I can't stand much more of this," she kept saying. "If there don't come a thunderstorm to cool things off I don't know what I'll do. This room's about five hundred."

But the heat grew greater and the Elevated trains went thundering by.

When Jem came home from his work his supper was not ready. Jane was sitting helplessly by the window, almost livid in her pallor. The table was but half spread.

"Hullo," said Jem; "it's done you up, ain't it?"

"Well, I guess it has," good-naturedly, certain of his sympathy. "But I'll get over it presently, and then I can get you a cold bite. I can't stand over the stove and cook."

"Hully Gee, a cold bite's all a man wants on a night like this. Hot chops'd give him the jim-jams. But I've got good news for you—it's cheered me up myself."

Jane lifted her head from the chair back.

"What is it?"

"Well, it came through my boss. He's always been friendly to me. He asks a question or so every now and then and seems to take an interest. Today he was asking me if it wasn't pretty hot and noisy down here, and after I told him how we stood it, he said he believed he could get us a better place to stay in through the summer. Some one he knows has had illness and trouble in his family and he's obliged to close his house and take his wife away into the mountains. They've got a beautiful big house in one of them far up streets by the Park and he wants to get caretakers in that can come well recommended. The boss said he could recommend us fast enough. And there's a big light basement that'll be as cool as the woods. And we can move in tomorrow. And all we've got to do is to see that things are safe and live happy."

"Oh, Jem!" Jane ejaculated. "It sounds too good to be true! Up by the Park! A big cool place to live!"

"We've none of us ever been in a house the size of it. You know what they look like outside, and they say they're bigger than they look. It's your business to go over the rooms every day or so to see nothing's going wrong in them—moths or dirt, I suppose. It's all left open but just one room they've left locked and don't want interfered with. I told the boss I thought the basement would seem like the Waldorf-Astoria to us. I tell you I was so glad I scarcely knew what to say."

Jane drew a long breath.

"A big house up there," she said. "And only one closed room in it. It's too good to be true!"

"Well, whether it's true or not we'll move out there tomorrow," Jem answered cheerfully. "Tomorrow morning bright and early. The boss said the sooner the better."

A large house left deserted by those who have filled its rooms with emotions and life, expresses a silence, a quality all its own. A house unfurnished and empty seems less impressively silent. The fact of its devoidness of sound is upon the whole more natural. But carpets accustomed to the pressure of constantly passing feet, chairs and sofas which have held human warmth, draperies used to the touch of hands drawing them aside to let in daylight, pictures which have smiled back at thinking eyes, mirrors which have reflected faces passing hourly in changing moods, elate or dark or longing, walls which have echoed back voices—all these things when left alone seem to be held in strange arrest, as if by some spell intensifying the effect of the pause in their existence.

The child Judith felt this deeply throughout the entirety of her young being.

"How *still* it is," she said to her mother the first time they went over the place together.

"Well, it seems still up here—and kind of dead," Jane Foster replied with her habitual sociable half-laugh. "But seems to me it always feels that way in a house people's left. It's cheerful enough down in that big basement with all the windows open. We can sit in that room they've had fixed to play billiards in. We shan't hurt nothing. We can keep the table and things covered up. Tell you, Judy, this'll be different from last summer. The Park ain't but a few steps away an' we can go and sit there too when we feel like it. Talk about the country—I don't want no more country than this is. You'll be made over the months we stay here."

Judith felt as if this must veritably be a truth. The houses on either side of the street were closed for the summer. Their occupants had gone to the seaside or the mountains and the windows and doors were boarded up. The street was a quiet one at any time, and wore now the aspect of a street in a city of the dead. The green trees of the Park were to be seen either gently stirring or motionless in the sun at the side of the avenue crossing the end of it. The only token of the existence of the Elevated Railroad was a remote occasional hum suggestive of the flying past of a giant bee. The thing seemed no longer a roaring demon, and Judith scarcely recognized that it was still the centre of the city's rushing, heated life.

The owners of the house had evidently deserted it suddenly. The windows had not been boarded up and the rooms had been left in their ordinary condition. The furniture was not covered or the hangings swathed. Jem Foster had been told that his wife must put things in order.

The house was beautiful and spacious, its decorations and appointments were not mere testimonies to freedom of expenditure, but expressions of a dignified and cultivated thought. Judith followed her mother from room to room in one of her singular moods. The loftiness of the walls, the breadth and space about her made her, at intervals, draw in her breath with pleasure. The pictures, the colours, the rich and beautiful textures she saw brought to her the free—and at the same time soothed—feeling she remembered as the chief feature of the dreams in which she "fell awake." But beyond all other things she rejoiced in the height and space, the sweep of view through one large room into another. She continually paused and stood with her face lifted looking up at the pictured things floating on a ceiling above her. Once, when she had stood doing this long enough to forget herself, she was startled by her mother's laugh, which broke in upon the silence about them with a curiously earthly sound which was almost a shock.

"Wake up, Judy; have you gone off in a dream? You look all the time as if you was walking in your sleep."

"It's so high," said Judy. "Those clouds make it look like the sky."

"I've got to set these chairs straight," said Jane. "Looks like they'd been havin' a concert here. All these chairs together an' that part of the room clear."

She began to move the chairs and rearrange them, bustling about cheerfully and talking the while. Presently she stooped to pick something up.

"What's this," she said, and then uttered a startled exclamation. "Mercy! they felt so kind of clammy they made me jump. They *have* had a party. Here's some of the flowers left fallen on the carpet."

She held up a cluster of wax-white hyacinths and large heavy rosebuds, faded to discoloration.

"This has dropped out of some set piece. It felt like cold flesh when I first touched it. I don't like a lot of white things together. They look too kind of mournful. Just go and get the wastepaper basket in the library, Judy. We'll carry it around to drop things into. Take that with you."

Judith carried the flowers into the library and bent to pick up the basket as she dropped them into it.

As she raised her head she found her eyes looking directly into other eyes which gazed at her from the wall. They were smiling from the face of a child in a picture. As soon as she saw them Judith drew in her breath and stood still, smiling, too, in response. The picture was that of a little girl in a floating white frock. She had a deep dimple at one corner of her mouth, her hanging hair was like burnished copper, she held up a slender hand with pointed fingers and Judith knew her. Oh! she knew her quite well. She had never felt so near any one else throughout her life.

"Judy, Judy!" Jane Foster called out. "Come here with your basket; what you staying for?"

Judith returned to her.

"We've got to get a move on," said Jane, "or we shan't get nothin' done before supper time. What was you lookin' at?"

"There's a picture in there of a little girl I know," Judith said. "I don't know her name, but I saw her in the Park once and—and I dreamed about her."

"Dreamed about her? If that ain't queer. Well, we've got to hurry up. Here's some more of them dropped flowers. Give me the basket."

They went through the whole house together, from room to room, up the many stairs, from floor to floor, and everywhere Judith felt the curious stillness and silence. It can not be doubted that Jane Foster felt it also.

"It is the stillest house I was ever in," she said. "I'm glad I've got you with me, Judy. If I was sole alone I believe it 'ud give me the creeps. These big places ought to have big families in them."

It was on the fourth floor that they came upon the Closed Room. Jane had found some of the doors shut and some open, but a turn of the handle gave entrance through all the unopened ones until they reached this one at the back on the fourth floor.

"This one won't open," Jane said, when she tried the handle. Then she shook it once or twice. "No, it's locked," she decided after an effort or two. "There, I've just remembered. There's one kept locked. Folks always has things they want locked up. I'll make sure, though."

She shook it, turned the handle, shook again, pressed her knee against the panel. The lock resisted all effort.

"Yes, this is the closed one," she made up her mind. "It's locked hard and fast. It's the closed one."

It was logically proved to be the closed one by the fact that she found no other one locked as she finished her round of the chambers.

Judith was a little tired before they had done their work. But her wandering pilgrimage through the large, silent, deserted house had been a revelation of new emotions to her. She was always a silent child. Her mind was so full of strange thoughts that it seemed unnecessary to say many words. The things she thought as she followed her from room to room, from floor to floor, until they reached the locked door, would have amazed and puzzled Jane Foster if she had known of their existence. Most of all, perhaps, she would have been puzzled by the effect the closed door had upon the child. It puzzled and bewildered Judith herself and made her feel a little weary.

She wanted so much to go into the room. Without in the least understanding the feeling, she was quite shaken by it. It seemed as if the closing of all the other rooms would have been a small matter in comparison with the closing of this one. There was something inside which she wanted to see—there was something—somehow there was something which wanted to see her. What a pity that the door was locked! Why had it been done? She sighed unconsciously several times during the evening, and Jane Foster thought she was tired.

"But you'll sleep cool enough tonight, Judy," she said. "And get a good rest. Them little breezes that comes rustling through the trees in the Park comes right along the street to us."

She and Jem Foster slept well. They spent the evening in the highest spirits and—as it seemed to them—the most luxurious comfort. The space afforded them by the big basement, with its kitchen and laundry and pantry, and, above all, the specially large room which had been used for billiard playing, supplied actual vistas. For the sake of convenience and coolness they used the billiard room as a dormitory, sleeping on light cots, and they slept with all their windows open, the little breezes wandering from among the trees of the Park to fan them. How they laughed and enjoyed themselves over their supper, and how they stretched themselves out with sighs of joy in the darkness as they sank into the cool, untroubled waters of deep sleep.

"This is about the top notch," Jem murmured as he lost his hold on the world of waking life and work.

But though she was cool, though she was undisturbed, though her body rested in absolute repose, Judith did not sleep for a long time. She lay and listened to the quietness. There was mystery in it. The footstep of a belated passer-by in the street woke strange echoes; a voice heard in the distance in a riotous shout suggested weird things. And as she lay and listened, it was as if she were not only listening but waiting for something. She did not know at all what she was waiting for, but waiting she was.

She lay upon her cot with her arms flung out and her eyes wide open. What was it that she wanted—that which was in the closed room? Why had they locked the door? If they had locked the doors of the big parlours it would not have mattered. If they had locked the door of the library— Her mind paused—as if for a moment, something held it still. Then she remembered that to have locked the doors of the library would have been to lock in the picture of the child with the greeting look in her eyes and the fine little uplifted hand. She was glad the room had been left open. But the room upstairs—the one on the fourth floor—that was the one that mattered most of all. She knew that tomorrow she must go and stand at the door and press her cheek against the wood and wait—and listen. Thinking this and knowing that it must be so, she fell—at last—asleep.

II

Judith climbed the basement stairs rather slowly. Her mother was busy rearranging the disorder the hastily departing servants had left. Their departure had indeed been made in sufficient haste to have left behind the air of its having been flight. There was a great deal to be done, and Jane Foster, moving about with broom and pail and scrubbing brushes, did not dislike the excitement of the work before her. Judith's certainty that she would not be missed made all clear before her. If her absence was observed her mother would realize that the whole house lay open to her and that she was an undisturbing element wheresoever she was led either by her fancy or by circumstance. If she went into the parlours she would probably sit and talk to herself or play quietly with her shabby doll. In any case she would be finding pleasure of her own and would touch nothing which could be harmed.

When the child found herself in the entrance hall she stopped a few moments to look about her. The stillness seemed to hold her and she paused to hear and feel it. In leaving the basement behind, she had left the movement of living behind also. No one was alive upon this floor— nor upon the next—nor the next. It was as if one had entered a new world—a world in which something existed which did not express itself in sound or in things which one could see. Chairs held out their arms to emptiness—cushions were not pressed by living things—only the people in the pictures were looking at something, but one could not tell what they were looking at.

But on the fourth floor was the Closed Room, which she must go to—because she must go to it—that was all she knew.

She began to mount the stairs which led to the upper floors. Her shabby doll was held against her hip by one arm, her right hand touched the wall as she went, she felt the height of the wall as she looked upward. It was such a large house and so empty. Where had the people gone and why had they left it all at once as if they were afraid? Her father had only heard vaguely that they had gone because they had had trouble.

She passed the second floor, the third, and climbed towards the fourth. She could see the door of the Closed Room as she went up step by step, and she found herself moving more quickly. Yes, she must get to it—she must put her hand on it—her chest began to rise and fall with a quickening of her breath, and her breath quickened because her heart fluttered—as if with her haste. She began to be glad, and if any one could have seen her they would have been struck by a curious expectant smile in her eyes.

She reached the landing and crossed it, running the last few steps lightly. She did not wait or stand still a moment. With the strange expectant smile on her lips as well as in her eyes, she put her hand upon the door—not upon the handle, but upon the panel. Without any sound it swung quietly open. And without any sound she stepped quietly inside.

The room was rather large and the light in it was dim. There were no shutters, but the blinds were drawn down. Judith went to one of the windows and drew its blind up so that the look of the place might be clear to her. There were two windows and they opened upon the flat roof of an extension, which suggested somehow that it had been used as a place to walk about in. This, at least, was what Judith thought of at once—that some one who had used the room had been in the habit of going out upon the roof and staying there as if it had been a sort of garden. There were rows of flower pots with dead flowers in them—there were green tubs containing large shrubs, which were dead also—against the low parapet certain of them held climbing plants which had been trained upon it. Two had been climbing roses, two were clematis, but Judith did not know them by name. The ledge of the window was so low that a mere step took her outside. So taking it, she stood among the dried, withered things and looked in tender regret at them.

"I wish they were not dead," she said softly to the silence. "It would be like a garden if they were not dead."

The sun was hot, but a cool, little breeze seemed straying up from among the trees of the Park. It even made the dried leaves of the flowers tremble and rustle a little. Involuntarily she lifted her face to the blue sky and floating white clouds. They seemed so near that she felt almost as if she could touch them with her hand. The street seemed so far—so far below—the whole world seemed far below. If one stepped off the parapet it would surely take one a long time to reach the earth. She knew now why she had come up here. It was so that she might feel like this—as if she was upheld far away from things—as if she had left everything behind—almost as if she had fallen awake again. There was no perfume in the air, but all was still and sweet and clear.

Suddenly she turned and went into the room again, realizing that she had scarcely seen it at all and that she must see and know it. It was not like any other room she had seen. It looked more simple, though it was a pretty place. The walls were covered with roses, there were bright pictures, and shelves full of books. There was also a little writing desk and there were two or three low chairs, and a low table. A closet in a corner had its door ajar and Judith could see that inside toys were piled together. In another corner a large doll's house stood, looking as if some one had just stopped playing with it. Some toy furniture had been taken out and left near it upon the carpet.

"It was a little girl's room," Judith said. "Why did they close it?"

Her eye was caught by something lying on a sofa—something covered with a cloth. It looked almost like a child lying there asleep—so fast asleep that it did not stir at all. Judith moved across to the sofa and drew the cloth aside. With its head upon a cushion was lying there a very large doll, beautifully dressed in white lace, its eyes closed, and a little wreath of dead flowers in its hair.

"It looks almost as if it had died too," said Judith.

She did not ask herself why she said "as if it had died too"—perhaps it was because the place was so still—and everything so far away—that the flowers had died in the strange, little deserted garden on the roof.

She did not hear any footsteps—in fact, no ghost of a sound stirred the silence as she stood looking at the doll's sleep—but quite quickly she ceased to bend forward, and turned round to look at something which she knew was near her. There she was—and it was quite natural she should be there—the little girl with the face like a white flower, with the quantity of burnished coppery hair and the smile which deepened the already deep dimple near her mouth.

"You have come to play with me," she said.

"Yes," answered Judith. "I wanted to come all night. I could not stay downstairs."

"No," said the child; "you can't stay downstairs. Lift up the doll."

They began to play as if they had spent their lives together. Neither asked the other any questions. Judith had not played with other children, but with this one she played in absolute and lovely delight. The little girl knew where all the toys were, and there were a great many beautiful ones. She told Judith where to find them and how to arrange them for their games. She invented wonderful things to do—things which were so unlike anything Judith had ever seen or heard or thought of that it was not strange that she realized afterwards that all her past life and its belongings had been so forgotten as to be wholly blotted out while she was in the Closed Room. She did not know her playmate's name, she did not remember that there were such things as names. Every moment was happiness. Every moment the little girl seemed to grow more beautiful in the flower whiteness of her face and hands and the strange lightness and freedom of her movements. There was an ecstasy in looking at her—in feeling her near.

Not long before Judith went downstairs she found herself standing with her outside the window in among the withered flowers.

"It was my garden," the little girl said. "It has been so hot and no one has been near to water them, so they could not live."

She went lightly to one of the brown rose-bushes and put her pointed-fingered little hand quite near it. She did not touch it, but held her hand near—and the leaves began to stir and uncurl and become fresh and tender again, and roses were nodding, blooming on the stems. And she went in the same manner to each flower and plant in turn until all the before dreary little garden was bright and full of leaves and flowers.

"It's Life," she said to Judith. Judith nodded and smiled back at her, understanding quite well just as she had understood the eyes of the bird who had swung on the twig so near her cheek the day she had hidden among the bushes in the Park.

"Now, you must go," the little girl said at last. And Judith went out of the room at once—without waiting or looking back, though she knew the white figure did not stir till she was out of sight.

It was not until she had reached the second floor that the change came upon her. It was a great change and a curious one. The Closed Room became as far away as all other places and things had seemed when she had stood upon the roof feeling the nearness of the blueness and the white clouds—as when she had looked round and found herself face to face with the child in the Closed Room. She suddenly realized things she had not known before. She knew that she had heard no voice when the little girl spoke to her—she knew that it had happened, that it was she only who had lifted the doll—who had taken out the toys—who had arranged the low table for their feast, putting all the small service upon it—and though they had played with such rapturous enjoyment and had laughed and feasted—what had they feasted on? That she could not recall—and not once had she touched or been touched by the light hand or white dress—and though they seemed to express their thoughts and intentions freely she had heard no voice at all. She was suddenly bewildered and stood rubbing her hand over her forehead and her eyes—but she was happy—as happy as when she had fallen awake in her sleep—and was no more troubled or really curious than she would have been if she had had the same experience every day of her life.

"Well, you must have been having a good time playing upstairs," Jane Foster said when she entered the big kitchen. "This is going to do you good, Judy. Looks like she'd had a day in the country, don't she, Jem?"

Through the weeks that followed her habit of "playing upstairs" was accepted as a perfectly natural thing. No questions were asked and she knew it was not necessary to enter into any explanations.

Every day she went to the door of the Closed Room and, finding it closed, at a touch of her hand upon the panel it swung softly open. There she waited—sometimes for a longer sometimes for a shorter time—and the child with the coppery hair came to her. The world below was gone as soon as she entered the room, and through the hours they played together joyously as happy children play. But in their playing it was always Judith who touched the toys—who held the doll—who set the little table for their feast. Once as she went downstairs she remembered that when she had that day made a wreath of roses from the roof and had gone to put it on her play-mate's head, she had drawn back with deepened dimple and, holding up her hand, had said, laughing: "No. Do not touch me."

But there was no mystery in it after all. Judith knew she should presently understand.

She was so happy that her happiness lived in her face in a sort of delicate brilliance. Jane Foster observed the change in her with exceeding comfort, her view being that spacious quarters, fresh air, and sounder sleep had done great things for her.

"Them big eyes of hers ain't like no other child's eyes I've ever seen," she said to her husband with cheerful self-gratulation. "An' her skin's that fine an' thin an' fair you can jest see through it. She always looks to me as if she was made out of different stuff from me an' you, Jem. I've always said it."

"She's going to make a corking handsome girl," responded Jem with a chuckle.

They had been in the house two months, when one afternoon, as she was slicing potatoes for supper, Jane looked round to see the child standing at the kitchen doorway, looking with a puzzled expression at some wilted flowers she held in her hand. Jane's impression was that she had been coming into the room and had stopped suddenly to look at what she held.

"What've you got there, Judy?" she asked.

"They're flowers," said Judith, her eyes still more puzzled.

"Where'd you get 'em from? I didn't know you'd been out. I thought you was upstairs."

"I was," said Judith quite simply. "In the Closed Room."

Jane Foster's knife dropped into her pan with a splash.

"Well," she gasped.

Judith looked at her with quiet eyes.

"The Closed Room!" Jane cried out. "What are you saying? You couldn't get in?"

"Yes, I can."

Jane was conscious of experiencing a shock. She said afterwards that suddenly something gave her the creeps.

"You couldn't open the door," she persisted. "I tried it again yesterday as I passed by—turned the handle and gave it a regular shove and it wouldn't give an inch."

"Yes," the child answered; "I heard you. We were inside then."

A few days later, when Jane weepingly related the incident to awe-stricken and sympathizing friends, she described as graphically as her limited vocabulary would allow her to do so, the look in Judith's face as she came nearer to her.

"Don't tell me there was nothing happening then," she said. "She just came up to me with them dead flowers in her hand an' a kind of look in her eyes as if she was half sorry for me an' didn't know quite why.

"'The door opens for me,' she says. 'That's where I play every day. There's a little girl comes and plays with me. She comes in at the window, I think. She is like the picture in the room where the books are. Her hair hangs down and she has a dimple near her mouth.'

"I couldn't never tell any one what I felt like. It was as if I'd got a queer fright that I didn't understand.

"'She must have come over the roof from the next house,' I says. 'They've got an extension too—but I thought the people were gone away.'

"'There are flowers on our roof,' she said. 'I got these there.' And that puzzled look came into her eyes again. 'They were beautiful when I got them—but as I came downstairs they died.'

"'Well, of all the queer things,' I said. She put out her hand and touched my arm sort of lovin' an' timid.

"'I wanted to tell you today, mother,' she said. 'I had to tell you today. You don't mind if I go play with her, do you? You don't mind?'

"Perhaps it was because she touched me that queer little loving way—or was it the way she looked—it seemed like something came over me an' I just grabbed her an' hugged her up.

"'No,' I says. 'So as you come back. So as you come back.'

"And to think!" And Jane rocked herself sobbing.

A point she dwelt on with many tears was that the child seemed in a wistful mood and remained near her side—bringing her little chair and sitting by her as she worked, and rising to follow her from place to place as she moved from one room to the other.

"She wasn't never one as kissed you much or hung about like some children do—I always used to say she was the least bother of any child I ever knew. Seemed as if she had company of her own when she sat in her little chair in the corner whispering to herself or just setting quiet." This was a thing Jane always added during all the years in which she told the story. "That was what made me notice. She kept by me and she kept looking at me different from any way I'd seen her look before—not pitiful exactly—but something like it. And once she came up and kissed me and once or twice she just kind of touched my dress or my hand—as I stood by her. *She* knew. No one need tell me she didn't."

But this was an error. The child was conscious only of a tender, wistful feeling, which caused her to look at the affectionate healthy young woman who had always been good to her and whom she belonged to, though she remotely wondered why—the same tenderness impelled her to touch her arm, hand and simple dress, and folding her arms round her neck to kiss her softly. It was an expression of gratitude for all the rough casual affection of the past. All her life had been spent at her side—all her life on earth had sprung from her.

When she went upstairs to the Closed Room the next day she told her mother she was going before she left the kitchen.

"I'm going up to play with the little girl, mother," she said. "You don't mind, do you?"

Jane had had an evening of comfortable domestic gossip and joking with Jem, had slept, slept soundly and eaten a hearty breakfast. Life had reassumed its wholly normal aspect. The sun was shining hot and bright and she was preparing to scrub the kitchen floor. She believed that the child was mistaken as to the room she had been in.

"That's all right," she said, turning the hot water spigot over the sink so that the boiling water poured forth at full flow into her pail, with clouds of steam. "But when I've done my scrubbing I'm comin' up to see if it *is* the Closed Room you play in. If it is, I guess you'd better play somewhere else— and I want to find out how you get that door open. Run along if you like."

Judith came back to her from the door. "Yes," she said, "come and see. But if she is there," putting her hand on Jane's hip gently, "you mustn't touch her."

Jane turned off the hot water and stared.

"Her!"

"The little girl who plays. *I* never touch her. She says I must not."

Jane lifted her pail from the sink, laughing outright.

"Well, that sounds as if she was a pretty airy young one," she said. "I guess you're a queer little pair. Run on. I must get at this floor."

Judith ran up the three flights of stairs lightly. She was glad she had told her mother, though she wondered vaguely why it had never seemed right to tell her until last night, and last night it had seemed not so much necessary as imperative. Something had obliged her to tell her. The time had come when she must know. The Closed Room door had always shut itself gently after Judith had passed through it, and yesterday, when her mother passing by chance, had tried the handle so vigorously, the two children inside the room had stood still gazing at each other, but neither had spoken and Judith had not thought of speaking. She was out of the realm of speech, and without any sense of amazement was aware that she was out of it. People with voices and words were in that faraway world below.

The playing today was even a lovelier, happier thing than it had ever been before. It seemed to become each minute a thing farther and farther away from the world in the streets where the Elevated Railroad went humming past like a monster bee. And with the sense of greater distance came a sense of greater lightness and freedom. Judith found that she was moving about the room and the little roof garden almost exactly as she had moved in the waking dreams where she saw Aunt Hester—almost as if she was floating and every movement was ecstasy. Once as she thought this she looked at her playmate, and the child smiled and answered her as she always did before she spoke.

"Yes," she said; "I know her. She will come. She sent me."

She had this day a special plan with regard to the arranging of the Closed Room. She wanted all the things in it—the doll—the chairs—the toys—the little table and its service to be placed in certain positions. She told Judith what to do. Various toys were put here or there—the little table was set with certain dishes in a particular part of the room. A book was left lying upon the sofa cushion, the large doll was put into a chair near the sofa, with a smaller doll in its arms, on the small writing desk a letter, which Judith found in a drawer—a half-written letter—was laid, the pen was left in the ink. It was a strange game to play, but somehow Judith felt it was very pretty. When it was all done—and there were many curious things to do—the Closed Room looked quite different from the cold, dim, orderly place the door had first opened upon. Then it had looked as if everything had been swept up and set away and covered and done with forever—as if the life in it had ended and would never begin again. Now it looked as if some child who had lived in it and loved and played with each of its belongings, had just stepped out from her play—to some other room quite near—quite near. The big doll in its chair seemed waiting—even listening to her voice as it came from the room she had run into.

The child with the burnished hair stood and looked at it with her delicious smile.

"That is how it looked," she said. "They came and hid and covered everything—as if I had gone—as if I was Nowhere. I want her to know I come here. I couldn't do it myself. You could do it for me. Go and bring some roses."

The little garden was a wonder of strange beauty with its masses of flowers. Judith brought some roses from the bush her playmate pointed out. She put them into a light bowl which was like a bubble of thin, clear glass and stood on the desk near the letter.

"If they would look like that," the little girl said, "she would see. But no one sees them like that—when the Life goes away with me."

After that the game was finished and they went out on the roof garden and stood and looked up into the blue above their heads. How blue—how blue—how clear—how near and real! And how far and unreal the streets and sounds below. The two children stood and looked up and laughed at the sweetness of it.

Then Judith felt a little tired.

"I will go and lie down on the sofa," she said.

"Yes," the little girl answered. "It's time for you to go to sleep."

They went into the Closed Room and Judith lay down. As she did so, she saw that the door was standing open and remembered that her mother was coming up to see her and her playmate.

The little girl sat down by her. She put out her pretty fine hand and touched Judith for the first time. She laid her little pointed fingers on her forehead and Judith fell asleep.

It seemed only a few minutes before she wakened again. The little girl was standing by her.

"Come," she said.

They went out together onto the roof among the flowers, but a strange—a beautiful thing had happened. The garden did not end at the parapet and the streets and houses were not below. The little garden ended in a broad green pathway—green with thick, soft grass and moss covered with trembling white and blue bell-like flowers. Trees—fresh leaved as if spring had just awakened them—shaded it and made it look smiling fair. Great white blossoms tossed on their branches and Judith felt that the scent in the air came from them. She forgot the city was below, because it was millions and millions of miles away, and this was where it was right to be. There was no mistake. This was real. All the rest was unreal—and millions and millions of miles away.

They held each other's slim-pointed hands and stepped out upon the broad, fresh green pathway. There was no boundary or end to its beauty, and it was only another real thing that coming towards them from under the white, flowering trees was Aunt Hester.

In the basement Jane Foster was absorbed in her labours, which were things whose accustomedness provided her with pleasure. She was fond of her scrubbing, she enjoyed the washing of her dishes, she definitely entertained herself with the splash and soapy foam of her washtubs and the hearty smack and swing of her ironing. In the days when she had served at the ribbon counter in a department store, she had not found life as agreeable as she had found it since the hours which were not spent at her own private sewing machine were given to hearty domestic duties providing cleanliness, savoury meals, and comfort for Jem.

She was so busy this particular afternoon that it was inevitable that she should forget all else but the work which kept her on her knees scrubbing floors or on a chair polishing windows, and afterwards hanging before them bits of clean, spotted muslin.

She was doing this last when her attention being attracted by wheels in the street stopping before the door, she looked out to see a carriage door open and a young woman, dressed in exceptionally deep mourning garb, step onto the pavement, cross it, and ascend the front steps.

"Who's she?" Jane exclaimed disturbedly. "Does she think the house is to let because it's shut?" A ring at the front door bell called her down from her chair. Among the duties of a caretaker is naturally included that of answering the questions of visitors. She turned down her sleeves, put on a fresh apron, and ran upstairs to the entrance hall.

When she opened the door, the tall, young woman in black stepped inside as if there were no reason for her remaining even for a moment on the threshold.

"I am Mrs. Haldon," she said. "I suppose you are the caretaker?"

Haldon was the name of the people to whom the house belonged. Jem Foster had heard only the vaguest things of them, but Jane remembered that the name was Haldon, and remembering that they had gone away because they had had trouble, she recognized at a glance what sort of trouble it had been. Mrs. Haldon was tall and young, and to Jane Foster's mind, expressed from head to foot the perfection of all that spoke for wealth and fashion. Her garments were heavy and rich with crape, the long black veil, which she had thrown back, swept over her shoulder and hung behind her, serving to set forth, as it were, more pitifully the white wornness of her pretty face, and a sort of haunting eagerness in her haggard eyes. She had been a smart, lovely, laughing and lovable thing, full of pleasure in the world, and now she was so stricken and devastated that she seemed set apart in an awful lonely world of her own.

She had no sooner crossed the threshold than she looked about her with a quick, smitten glance and began to tremble. Jane saw her look shudder away from the open door of the front room, where the chairs had seemed left as if set for some gathering, and the wax-white flowers had been scattered on the floor.

She fell into one of the carved hall seats and dropped her face into her hands, her elbows resting on her knees.

"Oh! No! No!" she cried. "I can't believe it. I can't believe it!"

Jane Foster's eyes filled with good-natured ready tears of sympathy.

"Won't you come upstairs, ma'am?" she said. "Wouldn't you like to set in your own room perhaps?"

"No! No!" was the answer. "She was always there! She used to come into my bed in the morning. She used to watch me dress to go out. No! No!"

"I'll open the shutters in the library," said Jane.

"Oh! No! No! No! She would be sitting on the big sofa with her fairy story-book. She's everywhere—everywhere! How could I come! Why did I! But I couldn't keep away! I tried to stay in the mountains. But I couldn't. Something dragged me day and night. Nobody knows I am here!" She got up and looked about her again. "I have never been in here since I went out with *her*," she said. "They would not let me come back. They said it would kill me. And now I have come—and everything is here—all the things we lived with—and she is millions and millions—and millions of miles away!"

"Who—who—was it?" Jane asked timidly in a low voice.

"It was my little girl," the poor young beauty said. "It was my little Andrea. Her portrait is in the library."

Jane began to tremble somewhat herself. "That—?" she began—and ended: "She is *dead?*"

Mrs. Haldon had dragged herself almost as if unconsciously to the stairs. She leaned against the newel post and her face dropped upon her hand.

"Oh! I don't *know!*" she cried. "I cannot believe it. How *could* it be? She was playing in her nursery—laughing and playing—and she ran into the next room to show me a flower—and as she looked up at me—laughing, I tell you—laughing—she sank slowly down on her knees—and the flower fell out of her hand quietly—and everything went out of her face—everything was gone away from her, and there was never anything more—never!"

Jane Foster's hand had crept up to her throat. She did not know what made her cold.

"My little girl—" she began, "her name is Judith—"

"Where is she?" said Mrs. Haldon in a breathless way.

"She is upstairs," Jane answered slowly. "She goes—into that back room—on the fourth floor—"

Mrs. Haldon turned upon her with wide eyes.

"It is locked!" she said. "They put everything away. I have the key."

"The door opens for her," said Jane. "She goes to play with a little girl—who comes to her. I think she comes over the roof from the next house."

"There is no child there!" Mrs. Haldon shuddered. But it was not with horror. There was actually a wild dawning bliss in her face. "What is she like?"

"She is like the picture." Jane scarcely knew her own monotonous voice. The world of real things was being withdrawn from her and she was standing without its pale—alone with this woman and her wild eyes. She began to shiver because her warm blood was growing cold. "She is a child with red hair—and there is a deep dimple near her mouth. Judith told me. You must not touch her."

She heard a wild gasp—a flash of something at once anguish and rapture blazed across the haggard, young face—and with a swerving as if her slight body had been swept round by a sudden great wind, Mrs. Haldon turned and fled up the stairs.

Jane Foster followed. The great wind swept her upward too. She remembered no single intake or outlet of breath until she was upon the fourth floor.

The door of the Closed Room stood wide open and Mrs. Haldon was swept within.

Jane Foster saw her stand in the middle of the room a second, a tall, swaying figure. She whirled to look about her and flung up her arms with an unearthly rapturous, whispered cry:

"It is all as she left it when she ran to me and fell. She has been here—to show me it is not so far!"

She sank slowly upon her knees, wild happiness in her face—wild tears pouring down it.

"She has seen her!" And she stretched forth yearning arms towards the little figure of Judith, who lay quiet upon the sofa in the corner. "Your little girl has seen her—and I dare not waken her. She is asleep."

Jane stood by the sofa—looking down. When she bent and touched the child the stillness of the room seemed to have got into her blood.

"No," she said, quivering, but with a strange simplicity. "No! not asleep! It was this way with her Aunt Hester."

LOCK-OUT TIME

J.M. Barrie

Scottish novelist and playwright James Matthew Barrie (1860–1937) is
remembered above all for his creation of Peter Pan. His stories about "the
boy who wouldn't grow up" were initially inspired by his neighbours the
Llewelyn Davies boys, but also drew much of their emotional energy from
the tragic events of Barrie's own life.

When he was six years old, his elder brother David died in an ice-skating accident at the age of thirteen, an event which devastated his mother
and affected the rest of Barrie's life. In his 1896 biography of his mother,
Margaret Ogilvy, Barrie recounts how as a child he attempted to make up
for her loss by dressing in his brother's clothes and whistling in the same
manner, while his mother derived comfort from holding the family christen-
ing robe, "the one of her children that always remained a baby".

Starting his writing career as a staff journalist on the *Nottingham Journal*,
Barrie published his first novels in his late twenties and turned to theatre
soon afterwards. By this time he was living in London, where he met four-
year-old George Llewelyn Davies while walking his dog in Kensington
Gardens. Barrie soon became close friends with the whole family, entertain-
ing the older boys by inventing stories about their baby brother Peter.

The character of Peter Pan first appeared in Barrie's 1902 book *The Little
White Bird*, a strange, tonally complex adult novel narrated by a London
bachelor who develops a quasi-fatherly relationship with a boy called David.
A middle section introduces the fairy mythology of Kensington Gardens,
where David learns about the ageless boy Peter Pan: "though he was born
so long ago he has never had a birthday … The reason is that he escaped

from being a human when he was seven days' old; he escaped by the window and flew back to the Kensington Gardens." Following the runaway success of Barrie's 1904 play *Peter Pan; or, the Boy Who Wouldn't Grow Up*, these middle chapters were reworked as a standalone children's book, *Peter Pan in Kensington Gardens* (1906).

The "Lock-out Time" episode republished here is deceptively sweet, with its pastel depictions of diminutive fairies disguising themselves as flowers. But as the story continues, the costs of remaining with the fairy folk become increasingly clear.

I T is frightfully difficult to know much about the fairies, and almost the only thing known for certain is that there are fairies wherever there are children. Long ago children were forbidden the Gardens, and at that time there was not a fairy in the place; then the children were admitted, and the fairies came trooping in that very evening. They can't resist following the children, but you seldom see them, partly because they live in the daytime behind the railings, where you are not allowed to go, and also partly because they are so cunning. They are not a bit cunning after Lock-out, but until Lock-out, my word!

When you were a bird you knew the fairies pretty well, and you remember a good deal about them in your babyhood, which it is a great pity you can't write down, for gradually you forget, and I have heard of children who declared that they had never once seen a fairy. Very likely if they said this in the Kensington Gardens, they were standing looking at a fairy all the time. The reason they were cheated was that she pretended to be something else. This is one of their best tricks. They usually pretend to be flowers, because the court sits in the Fairies' Basin, and there are so many flowers there, and all along the Baby Walk, that a flower is the thing least likely to attract attention. They dress exactly like flowers, and change with the seasons, putting on white when lilies are in and blue for blue-bells, and so on. They like crocus and hyacinth time best of all, as they are partial to a bit of colour, but tulips (except white ones, which are the fairy-cradles) they consider garish, and they sometimes put off dressing like tulips for days, so that the beginning of the tulip weeks is almost the best time to catch them.

When they think you are not looking they skip along pretty lively, but if you look and they fear there is no time to hide, they stand quite still, pretending to be flowers. Then, after you have passed without knowing that they were fairies, they rush home and tell their mothers they have had such an adventure. The Fairy Basin, you remember, is all covered with ground-ivy (from which they make their castor-oil), with flowers growing in it here and there. Most of them really are flowers, but some of them are fairies. You never can be sure of them, but a good plan is to walk by looking the other way, and then turn round sharply. Another good plan, which David and I sometimes follow, is to stare them down. After a long time they can't help winking, and then you know for certain that they are fairies.

There are also numbers of them along the Baby Walk, which is a famous gentle place, as spots frequented by fairies are called. Once twenty-four of them had an extraordinary adventure. They were a girls' school out for a walk with the governess, and all wearing hyacinth gowns, when she suddenly put her finger to her mouth, and then they all stood still on an empty bed and pretended to be hyacinths. Unfortunately, what the governess had heard was two gardeners coming to plant new flowers in that very bed. They were wheeling a handcart with the flowers in it, and were quite surprised to find the bed occupied. "Pity to lift them hyacinths," said the one man. "Duke's orders," replied the other, and, having emptied the cart, they dug up the boarding-school and put the poor, terrified things in it in five rows. Of course, neither the governess nor the girls dare let on that they were fairies, so they were carted far away to a potting-shed, out of which they escaped in the night without their shoes, but there was a great row about it among the parents, and the school was ruined.

As for their houses, it is no use looking for them, because they are the exact opposite of our houses. You can see our houses by day but you can't see them by dark. Well, you can see their houses by dark, but you can't see them by day, for they are the colour of night, and I never heard of anyone yet who could see night in the daytime. This does not mean that they are black, for night has its colours just as day has, but ever so much brighter. Their blues and reds and greens are like ours with a light behind them. The palace is entirely built of many-coloured glasses, and is quite the loveliest of all royal residences, but the queen sometimes complains because the common people will peep in to see what she is doing. They are very inquisitive folk, and press quite hard against the glass, and that is why their noses are mostly snubby. The streets are miles long and very twisty, and have paths on each side made of bright worsted. The birds used to steal the worsted for their nests, but a policeman has been appointed to hold on at the other end.

One of the great differences between the fairies and us is that they never do anything useful. When the first baby laughed for the first time, his laugh broke into a million pieces, and they all went skipping about. That was the beginning of fairies. They look tremendously busy, you know, as if they had not a moment to spare, but if you were to ask them what they are doing, they could not tell you in the least. They are frightfully ignorant, and everything they do is make-believe. They have a postman, but he never calls except at Christmas with his little box, and though they have beautiful schools, nothing is taught in them; the youngest child being chief person is always elected mistress, and when she has called the roll, they all go out for a walk and never come back. It is a very noticeable thing that, in fairy families, the youngest is always chief person, and usually becomes a prince or princess; and children remember this, and think it must be so among humans also, and that is why they are often made uneasy when they come upon their mother furtively putting new frills on the basinette.

You have probably observed that your baby-sister wants to do all sorts of things that your mother and her nurse want her not to do: to stand up at sitting-down time, and to sit down at standing-up time, for instance, or to wake up when she should fall asleep, or to crawl on the floor when she is wearing her best frock, and so on, and perhaps you put this down to naughtiness. But it is not; it simply means that she is doing as she has seen the fairies do; she begins by following their ways, and it takes about two years to get her into the human ways. Her fits of passion, which are awful to behold, and are usually called teething, are no such thing; they are her natural exasperation, because we don't understand her, though she is talking an intelligible language. She is talking fairy. The reason mothers and nurses know what her remarks mean, before other people know, as that "Guch" means "Give it to me at once," while "Wa" is "Why do you wear such a funny hat?" is because, mixing so much with babies, they have picked up a little of the fairy language.

Of late David has been thinking back hard about the fairy tongue, with his hands clutching his temples, and he has remembered a number of their phrases which I shall tell you some day if I don't forget. He had heard them in the days when he was a thrush, and though I suggested to him that perhaps it is really bird language he is remembering, he says not, for these phrases are about fun and adventures, and the birds talked of nothing but nest-building. He distinctly remembers that the birds used to go from spot to spot like ladies at shop-windows, looking at the different nests and saying, "Not my colour, my dear," and "How would that do with a soft lining?" and "But will it wear?" and "What hideous trimming!" and so on.

The fairies are exquisite dancers, and that is why one of the first things the baby does is to sign to you to dance to him and then to cry when you do it. They hold their great balls in the open air, in what is called a fairy-ring. For weeks afterward you can see the ring on the grass. It is not there when they begin, but they make it by waltzing round and round. Sometimes you will find mushrooms inside the ring, and these are fairy chairs that the servants have forgotten to clear away. The chairs and the rings are the only telltale marks these little people leave behind them, and they would remove even these were they not so fond of dancing that they toe it till the very moment of the opening of the gates. David and I once found a fairy-ring quite warm.

But there is also a way of finding out about the ball before it takes place. You know the boards which tell at what time the Gardens are to close today. Well, these tricky fairies sometimes slyly change the board on a ball night, so that it says the Gardens are to close at six-thirty for instance, instead of at seven. This enables them to get begun half an hour earlier.

If on such a night we could remain behind in the Gardens, as the famous Maimie Mannering did, we might see delicious sights, hundreds of lovely fairies hastening to the ball, the married ones wearing their wedding-rings round their waists, the gentlemen, all in uniform, holding up the ladies' trains, and linkmen running in front carrying winter cherries, which are the fairy-lanterns, the cloakroom where they put on their silver slippers and get a ticket for their wraps, the flowers streaming up from the Baby Walk to look on, and always welcome because they can lend a pin, the supper-table, with Queen Mab at the head of it, and behind her chair the Lord Chamberlain, who carries a dandelion on which he blows when Her Majesty wants to know the time.

The table-cloth varies according to the seasons, and in May it is made of chestnut-blossom. The ways the fairy-servants do is this: The men, scores of them, climb up the trees and shake the branches, and the blossom falls like snow. Then the lady servants sweep it together by whisking their skirts until it is exactly like a table-cloth, and that is how they get their table-cloth.

They have real glasses and real wine of three kinds, namely, blackthorn wine, berberris wine, and cowslip wine, and the Queen pours out, but the bottles are so heavy that she just pretends to pour out. There is bread and butter to begin with, of the size of a threepenny bit; and cakes to end with, and they are so small that they have no crumbs. The fairies sit round on mushrooms, and at first they are very well-behaved and always cough off the table, and so on, but after a bit they are not so well-behaved and stick their fingers into the butter, which is got from the roots of old trees, and the really horrid ones crawl over the table-cloth chasing sugar or other delicacies with their tongues. When the Queen sees them doing this she signs to the servants to wash up and put away, and then everybody adjourns to the dance, the Queen walking in front while the Lord Chamberlain walks behind her, carrying two little pots, one of which contains the juice of wall-flower and the other the juice of Solomon's Seals. Wall-flower juice is good for reviving dancers who fall to the ground in a fit, and Solomon's Seals juice is for bruises. They bruise very easily and when Peter plays faster and faster they foot it till they fall down in fits. For, as you know without my telling you, Peter Pan is the fairies' orchestra. He sits in the middle of the ring, and they would never dream of having a smart dance nowadays without him. "P. P." is written on the corner of the invitation-cards sent out by all really good families. They are grateful little people, too, and at the princess's coming-of-age ball (they come of age on their second birthday and have a birthday every month) they gave him the wish of his heart.

The way it was done was this. The Queen ordered him to kneel, and then said that for playing so beautifully she would give him the wish of his heart. Then they all gathered round Peter to hear what was the wish of his heart, but for a long time he hesitated, not being certain what it was himself.

"If I chose to go back to mother," he asked at last, "could you give me that wish?"

Now this question vexed them, for were he to return to his mother they should lose his music, so the Queen tilted her nose contemptuously and said, "Pooh, ask for a much bigger wish than that."

"Is that quite a little wish?" he inquired.

"As little as this," the Queen answered, putting her hands near each other.

"What size is a big wish?" he asked.

She measured it off on her skirt and it was a very handsome length.

Then Peter reflected and said, "Well, then, I think I shall have two little wishes instead of one big one."

Of course, the fairies had to agree, though his cleverness rather shocked them, and he said that his first wish was to go to his mother, but with the right to return to the Gardens if he found her disappointing. His second wish he would hold in reserve.

They tried to dissuade him, and even put obstacles in the way.

"I can give you the power to fly to her house," the Queen said, "but I can't open the door for you."

"The window I flew out at will be open," Peter said confidently. "Mother always keeps it open in the hope that I may fly back."

"How do you know?" they asked, quite surprised, and, really, Peter could not explain how he knew.

"I just do know," he said.

So as he persisted in his wish, they had to grant it. The way they gave him power to fly was this: They all tickled him on the shoulder, and soon he felt a funny itching in that part and then up he rose higher and higher and flew away out of the Gardens and over the house-tops.

It was so delicious that instead of flying straight to his old home he skimmed away over St. Paul's to the Crystal Palace and back by the river and Regent's Park, and by the time he reached his mother's window he had quite made up his mind that his second wish should be to become a bird.

The window was wide open, just as he knew it would be, and in he fluttered, and there was his mother lying asleep. Peter alighted softly on the wooden rail at the foot of the bed and had a good look at her. She lay with her head on her hand, and the hollow in the pillow was like a nest lined with her brown wavy hair. He remembered, though he had long forgotten it, that she always gave her hair a holiday at night. How sweet the frills of her night-gown were. He was very glad she was such a pretty mother.

But she looked sad, and he knew why she looked sad. One of her arms moved as if it wanted to go round something, and he knew what it wanted to go round.

"Oh, mother," said Peter to himself, "if you just knew who is sitting on the rail at the foot of the bed."

Very gently he patted the little mound that her feet made, and he could see by her face that she liked it. He knew he had but to say "Mother" ever so softly, and she would wake up. They always wake up at once if it is you that says their name. Then she would give such a joyous cry and squeeze him tight. How nice that would be to him, but oh, how exquisitely delicious it would be to her. That I am afraid is how Peter regarded it. In returning to his mother he never doubted that he was giving her the greatest treat a woman can have. Nothing can be more splendid, he thought, than to have a little boy of your own. How proud of him they are; and very right and proper, too.

But why does Peter sit so long on the rail, why does he not tell his mother that he has come back?

I quite shrink from the truth, which is that he sat there in two minds. Sometimes he looked longingly at his mother, and sometimes he looked longingly at the window. Certainly it would be pleasant to be her boy again, but, on the other hand, what times those had been in the Gardens! Was he so sure that he would enjoy wearing clothes again? He popped off the bed and opened some drawers to have a look at his old garments. They were still there, but he could not remember how you put them on. The socks, for instance, were they worn on the hands or on the feet? He was about to try one of them on his hand, when he had a great adventure. Perhaps the drawer had creaked; at any rate, his mother woke up, for he heard her say "Peter," as if it was the most lovely word in the language. He remained sitting on the floor and held his breath, wondering how she knew that he had come back. If she said "Peter" again, he meant to cry "Mother" and run to her. But she spoke no more, she made little moans only, and when next he peeped at her she was once more asleep, with tears on her face.

It made Peter very miserable, and what do you think was the first thing he did? Sitting on the rail at the foot of the bed, he played a beautiful lullaby to his mother on his pipe. He had made it up himself out of the way she said "Peter," and he never stopped playing until she looked happy.

He thought this so clever of him that he could scarcely resist wakening her to hear her say, "Oh, Peter, how exquisitely you play." However, as she now seemed comfortable, he again cast looks at the window. You must not think that he meditated flying away and never coming back. He had quite decided to be his mother's boy, but hesitated about beginning tonight. It was the second wish which troubled him. He no longer meant to make it a wish to be a bird, but not to ask for a second wish seemed wasteful, and, of course, he could not ask for it without returning to the fairies. Also, if he put off asking for his wish too long it might go bad. He asked himself if he had not been hardhearted to fly away without saying goodbye to Solomon. "I should like awfully to sail in my boat just once more," he said wistfully to his sleeping mother. He quite argued with her as if she could hear him. "It would be so splendid to tell the birds of this adventure," he said coaxingly. "I promise to come back," he said solemnly and meant it, too.

And in the end, you know, he flew away. Twice he came back from the window, wanting to kiss his mother, but he feared the delight of it might waken her, so at last he played her a lovely kiss on his pipe, and then he flew back to the Gardens.

Many nights and even months passed before he asked the fairies for his second wish; and I am not sure that I quite know why he delayed so long. One reason was that he had so many goodbyes to say, not only to his particular friends, but to a hundred favourite spots. Then he had his last sail, and his very last sail, and his last sail of all, and so on. Again, a number of farewell feasts were given in his honour; and another comfortable reason was that, after all, there was no hurry, for his mother would never weary of waiting for him. This last reason displeased old Solomon, for it was an encouragement to the birds to procrastinate. Solomon had several excellent mottoes for keeping them at their work, such as "Never put off laying today, because you can lay tomorrow," and "In this world there are no second chances," and yet here was Peter gaily putting off and none the worse for it. The birds pointed this out to each other, and fell into lazy habits.

But, mind you, though Peter was so slow in going back to his mother, he was quite decided to go back. The best proof of this was his caution with the fairies. They were most anxious that he should remain in the Gardens to play to them, and to bring this to pass they tried to trick him into making such a remark as "I wish the grass was not so wet," and some of them danced out of time in the hope that he might cry, "I do wish you would keep time!" Then they would have said that this was his second wish. But he smoked their design, and though on occasions he began, "I wish—" he always stopped in time. So when at last he said to them bravely, "I wish now to go back to mother for ever and always," they had to tickle his shoulders and let him go.

He went in a hurry in the end because he had dreamt that his mother was crying, and he knew what was the great thing she cried for, and that a hug from her splendid Peter would quickly make her to smile. Oh, he felt sure of it, and so eager was he to be nestling in her arms that this time he flew straight to the window, which was always to be open for him.

But the window was closed, and there were iron bars on it, and peering inside he saw his mother sleeping peacefully with her arm round another little boy.

Peter called, "Mother! mother!" but she heard him not; in vain he beat his little limbs against the iron bars. He had to fly back, sobbing, to the Gardens, and he never saw his dear again. What a glorious boy he had meant to be to her. Ah, Peter, we who have made the great mistake, how differently we should all act at the second chance. But Solomon was right; there is no second chance, not for most of us. When we reach the window it is Lock-out Time. The iron bars are up for life.

BY THE YELLOW MOONROCK

Fiona Macleod

Fiona Macleod was an elaborately constructed literary *alter ego* created by Scottish writer William Sharp (1855–1905), a novelist, art critic, Hermetic Order of the Golden Dawn member and associate of Dante Gabriel Rossetti and W.B. Yeats. Arguing in *The Pagan Review* of 1892 for gender equality and a world in which "women no longer have to look upon men as usurpers, men no longer to regard women as spiritual foreigners", the following year he began to develop a female persona named Fiona Macleod, who came to occupy much of his imaginative life.

Sharp preserved the fiction that Macleod was a real person for over a decade, even going so far as to compose letters for his sister to copy in her handwriting and post from Edinburgh to Macleod's increasingly large circle of correspondents. Macleod presented herself as a well-educated young woman steeped in Celtic folklore, married to a wealthy Scotsman. The deception's success was due to Sharp's ability to project a fully rounded, wholly believable personality into his Macleod writings; the University of London's Fiona Macleod Archive sees her as "William Sharp's most impressive literary achievement."

Fiona Macleod's literary output encompassed novels, poetry and short stories influenced by Scottish and Celtic lore, and became a significant part of the Celtic Revival of the late nineteenth and early twentieth centuries. A number of her works explore the more fearsome aspects of fairies, and "By the Yellow Moonrock" contains a particularly terrifying example. Macleod's *bhean-nimhir*, or "serpent woman", is a bloodsucking lamia similar to the *bao-bhan sìth*, a female vampire-fairy from the Scottish Highlands.

A particularly fierce female demon called *baobhan sith* might appear as a hoodie crow or raven, or as a beautiful girl of human stature clad in a long, trailing, green dress which concealed the deer hoofs she had instead of feet. Like a vampire, she drank the blood of her human victims.

There are many stories regarding this class of demon. The Rev. C.M. Robertson ... tells of four men who had been hunting and sought shelter for the night in a lonely shieling. One supplied vocal music (*puirt-a-beul*) and one of the others, who danced, expressed the wish that they had partners. Four women entered the shieling and three of them danced with the men, while the fourth sat beside the music maker. One of the men saw blood drops falling from a companion and fled from the shieling, taking refuge in a horse-fold. His demon partner pursued him, but "once he got in alongside of the horses she was powerless to harm him". When daylight came he and others went to the shieling and found the lifeless remains of the other hunters. "The creatures with whom they had associated had sucked the blood from their bodies."

Donald Mackenzie, *Scottish Folk-Lore and Folk Life* (1935)

R ory MacAlpine the piper had come down the Strath on St. Bride's
Eve, for the great wedding at the farm of his kinsman Donald
Macalister. Every man and woman, every boy and girl, who could
by hook or by crook get to the big dance at the barns was to be seen there:
but no one that danced till he or she could dance no more had a wearier joy
than Rory with the pipes. Reels and strathspeys that everyone knew gave
way at last to wilder strathspeys that no one had ever heard before… and
why should they, since it was the hill-wind and the mountain-torrent and
the roar of pines that had got loose in Rory's mind, and he not knowing it
any more than a leaf that sails on the yellow wind.

He played with magic and pleasure, and had never looked handsomer, in
his new grandeur of clothes, and with his ruddy hair aflame in the torchlight,
and his big blue eyes shining as with a lifting, shifting fire. But those who
knew him best saw that he was strangely subdued for Rory MacAlpine, or
at least, that he laughed and shouted (in the rare intervals when he was not
playing, and there were two other pipers present to help the Master) more
by custom than from the heart.

"What is't, Rory?" said Dalibrog to him, after a heavy reel wherein he
had nearly killed a man by swinging upon and nigh flattening him against
the wall.

"Nothing, foster-brother dear; it's just nothing at all. Fling away,
Dalibrog; you're doing fine."

Later old Dionaid took him aside to bid him refresh himself from a
brew of rum and lemons she had made, with spice and a flavour of old

brandy—"Barra Punch" she called it—and then asked him if he had any sorrow at the back of his heart.

"Just this," he said in a whisper, "that Rory MacAlpine's fëy."

"Fëy, my lad, an' for why that? For sure, I'm thinking it's fëy with the good drink you have had all day, an' now here am I spoiling ye with more."

"Hush, woman; I'm not speaking of what comes wi' a drop to the bad. But I had a dream, I had; a powerful strange dream, for sure. I had it a month ago; I had it the night before I left Strathanndra; and I had it this very day of the days, as I lay sleepin' off the kindness I had since I came into Strathraonull."

"An' what will that dream be, now?"

"Sure, it's a strange dream, Dionaid Macalister. You know the great yellow stone that rises out of the heather on the big moor of Dalmonadh, a mile or more beyond Tom-na-shee?"

"Ay, the Moonrock they call it; it that fell out o' the skies, they say."

"The Yellow Moonrock. Ay, the Yellow Moonrock; that's its name, for sure. Well, the first time I dreamed of it I saw it standing fair yellow in the moonshine. There was a moorfowl sitting on it, and it flew away. When it flew away I saw it was a ptarmigan, but she was as clean brown as though it were summer and not midwinter, and I thought that strange."

"How did you know it was a ptarmigan? It might have been a moorhen or a—"

"Hoots, woman, how do I know when it's wet or fine, when it's day or night? Well, as I was saying, I thought it strange; but I hadn't turned over that thought on its back before it was gone like the shadow o' a peewit, and I saw standing before me the beautifullest woman I ever saw in all my life. I've had sweethearts here and sweethearts there, Dionaid-nic-Tormod, and long ago I loved a lass who died, Sine MacNeil; but not one o' these, not sweet Sine herself, was like the woman I saw in my dream, who had more beauty upon her than them altogether, or than all the women in Strathraonull and Strathanndra."

"Have some more Barra punch, Rory," said Miss Macalister drily.

"Whist, ye old fule, begging your pardon for that same. She was as white as new milk, an' her eyes were as dark as the two black pools below Annora Linn, an' her hair was as long an' wavy as the shadows o' a willow in the wind; an' she sat an' she sang, an' if I could be remembering that song now it's my fortune I'd be making, an' that quick too."

"And where was she?"

"Why, on the Moonrock, for sure. An' if I hadn't been a good Christian I'd have bowed down before her, because o'—because—well, because o' that big stare out of her eyes she had, an' the beauty of her, an' all. An' what's more, by the Black Stone of Iona, if I hadn't been a God-fearin' man I'd have run to her, an' put my arms round her, an' kissed the honey lips of her till she cried out, 'For the Lord's sake, Rory MacAlpine, leave off!'"

"It's well seen you were only in a dream, Rory MacAlpine."

At another time Rory would have smiled at that, but now he just stared.

"She said no word," he added, "but lifted a bit of hollow wood or thick reed. An' then all at once she whispered, 'I'm bonnie St. Bride of the Mantle,' an' wi' that she began to play, an' it was the finest, sweet, gentle, little music in the world. But a big fear was on me, an' I just turned an' ran."

"No man'll ever call ye a fool again to my face, Rory MacAlpine. I never had the thought you had so much sense."

"She didna let me run so easy, for a grey bitch went yapping and yowling at my heels; an' just as I tripped an' felt the bad hot breath of the beast at my throat, I woke, an' was wet wi' sweat."

"An' you've had that dream three times?"

"I've had it three times, and this very day, to the Stones be it said. Now, you're a wise woman, Dionaid Macalister, but can you tell me what that dream means?"

"If you're really fëy, I'm thinking I can, Rory MacAlpine."

"It's a true thing: Himself knows it."

"And what are you fëy of?"

"I'm fëy with the beauty o' that woman."

"There's good women wi' the fair looks on them in plenty, Rory; an' if you prefer them bad, you needna wear out new shoon before you'll find them."

"I'm fëy wi' the beauty o' that woman. I'm fëy wi' the beauty o' that woman that had the name o' Bride to her."

Dionaid Macalister looked at him with troubled eyes.

"When she took up the reed, did you see anything that frighted you?"

"Ay. I had a bit fright when I saw a big black adder slip about the Moonrock as the ptarmigan flew off; an' I had the other half o' that fright when I thought the woman lifted the adder, but it was only wood or a reed, for amn't I for telling you about the gentle, sweet music I heard?"

Old Dionaid hesitated; then, looking about her to see that no one was listening, she spoke in a whisper:

"An' you've been fëy since that hour because o' the beauty o' that woman?"

"Because o' the sore beauty o' that woman."

"An' it's not the drink?"

"No, no, Dionaid Macalister. You women are always for hurting the feelin's o' the drink. It is not the innycent drink I am telling you; for sure, no; no, no, it is not the drink."

"Then I'll tell you what it means, Rory MacAlpine. It wasn't Holy St. Bride—"

"I know that, ye old—, I mean, Miss Macalister."

"It was the face of the *Bhean-Nimhir* you saw, the face of *Nighean-Imhir*, an' this is St. Bride's Night, an' it is on this night of the nights she can be seen, an' beware o' that seeing, Rory MacAlpine."

"*The Bhean-Nimhir*, the *Nighean-Imhir*... the Serpent Woman, the Daughter of Ivor—" muttered Rory; "where now have I heard tell o' the Daughter of Ivor?" Then he remembered an old tale of the isles, and his heart sank, because the tale was of a woman of the underworld who could suck the soul out of a man through his lips, and send it to slavery among the people of ill-will, whom there is no call to speak of by name; and if she had any spite, or any hidden wish that is not for our knowing, she could put the littleness of a fly's bite on the hollow of his throat, and take his life out of his body, and nip it and sting it till it was no longer a life, and till that went away on the wind that she chased with screams and laughter.

"Some say she's the wife of the Amadan-Dhu, the Dark Fool," murmured Dionaid, crossing herself furtively, for even at Dalibrog it was all Protestantry now.

But Rory was not listening. He sat intent, for he heard music—a strange music.

Dionaid shook him by the shoulder.

"Wake up, Rory, man; you'll be having sleep on you in another minute."

Just then a loud calling for the piper was heard, and Rory went back to the dancers. Soon his pipes were heard, and the reels swung to that good glad music, and his face lighted up as he strode to and fro, or stopped and tap-tapped away with his right foot, while drone and chanter all but burst with the throng of sound in them.

But suddenly he began to play a reel that nigh maddened him, and his own face was wrought so that Dalibrog came up and signed to stop, and then asked him what in the name o' Black Donald he was playing.

Rory laughed foolishly.

"Oh, for sure, it's just a new reel o' my own. I call it 'The Reel of Ivor's Daughter.' An' a good reel it is too, although it's Rory MacAlpine says it."

"Who is she, an' what Ivor will you be speaking of?"

"Oh, ask the Amadan-Dhu; it's he will be knowing that. No, no, now, I will not be naming it that name; sure, I will call it instead the Serpent-Reel."

"Come, now, Rory, you've played enough, an' if your wrist's not tired wi' the chanter, sure, it must be wi' lifting the drink to your lips. An' it's time, too, these lads an' lasses were off."

"No, no, they're waiting to bring in the greying of the day—St. Bride's Day. They'll be singing the hymn for that greying, 'Bride bhoidheach muime Chriosda.'"

"Not they, if Dalibrog has a say in it! Come, now, have a drink with me, your own foster-brother, an' then lie down an' sleep it off, an' God's good blessing be on you."

Whether it was Dalibrog's urgency, or the thought of the good drink he would have, and he with a terrible thirst on him after that lung-bursting reel of his, Rory went quietly away with the host, and was on a mattress on the floor of a big, empty room, and snoring hard, long before the other pipers had ceased piping, or the last dancers flung their panting breaths against the frosty night.

An hour after midnight Rory woke with a start. He had "a spate of a head-ache on," he muttered, as he half rose and struck a match against the floor. When he saw that he was still in his brave gear, and had lain down "just as he was," and also remembered all that had happened and the place he was in, he wondered what had waked him.

Now that he thought of it, he had heard music: yes, for sure, music—for all that it was so late, and after every one had gone home. What was it? It was not any song of his own, nor any air he had. He must have dreamed that it came across great lonely moors, and had a laugh and a moan and a sudden cry in it.

He was cold. The window was open. That was a stupid, careless thing of Donald Macalister to do, and he sober, as he always was, though he could drink deep; on a night of frost like this Death could slip in on the back of a shadow and get his whisper in your ear before you could rise for the stranger.

He stumbled to his feet and closed the window. Then he lay down again, and was nearly asleep, and was confused between an old prayer that rose in his mind like a sunken spar above a wave; and whether to take Widow Sheen a packet of great thick Sabbath peppermints, or a good heavy twist of tobacco; and a strange delightsome memory of Dionaid Macalister's brew of rum and lemons with a touch of old brandy in it;

when again he heard that little, wailing, fantastic air, and sat up with the sweat on his brow.

The sweat was not there only because of the little thin music he heard, and it the same, too, as he had heard before; but because the window was wide open again, though the room was so heavy with silence that the pulse of his heart made a noise like a jumping rat.

Rory sat, as still as though he were dead, staring at the window. He could not make out whether the music was faint because it was so far away, or because it was played feebly, like a child's playing, just under the sill.

He was a big, strong man, but he leaned and wavered like the flame of a guttering candle in that slow journey of his from the mattress to the window. He could hear the playing now quite well. It was like the beautiful, sweet song of "Bride bhoidheach muime Chriosda," but with the holy peace out of it, and with a little, evil, hidden laugh flapping like a wing against the blessed name of Christ's foster-mother. But when it sounded under the window, it suddenly was far; and when it was far, the last circling peewit-lilt would be at his ear like a skiffing bat.

When he looked out, and felt the cold night lie on his skin, he could not see because he saw too well. He saw the shores of the sky filled with dancing lights, and the great lighthouse of the moon sending a foam-white stream across the delicate hazes of frost which were too thin to be seen, and only took the sharp edges off the stars, or sometimes splintered them into sudden dazzle. He was like a man in a sailless, rudderless boat, looking at the skies because he lay face upward and dared not stoop and look into the dark, slipping water alongside.

He saw, too, the hornlike curve of Tom-na-shee black against the blueness, and the inky line of Dalmonadh Moor beyond the plumy mass of Dalibrog woods, and the near meadows where a leveret jumped squealing, and then the bare garden with ragged gooseberry-bushes like scraggy, hunched sheep, and at last the white gravel-walk bordered with the withered roots of pinks and southernwood.

Then he looked from all these great things and these little things to the ground beneath the window. There was nothing there. There was no sound. Not even far away could he hear any faint, devilish music. At least—

Rory shut the window, and went back to his mattress and lay down.

"By the sun an' wind," he exclaimed, "a man gets fear on him nowadays, like a cold in the head when a thaw comes."

Then he lay and whistled a blithe catch. For sure, he thought, he would rise at dawn and drown that thirst of his in whatever came first to hand.

Suddenly he stopped whistling, and on the uplift of a lilting turn. In a moment the room was full of old silence again.

Rory turned his head slowly. The window was wide open.

A sob died in his throat. He put his hands to his dry mouth; the back of it was wet with the sweat on his face.

White and shaking, he rose and walked steadily to the window. He looked out and down: there was no one, nothing.

He pulled the ragged cane chair to the sill, and sat there, silent and hopeless.

Soon big tears fell one by one, slowly, down his face. He understood now. His heart filled with sad, bitter grief, and brimmed over, and that was why the tears fell.

It was his hour that had come and opened the window.

He was cold, and as faint with hunger and heavy with thirst as though he had not put a glass to his lips or a bit to his mouth for days instead of for hours; but for all that, he did not feel ill, and he wondered and wondered why he was to die so soon, and he so wellmade and handsome, and unmarried too, and now with girls as eager to have him as trouts for a May fly.

And after a time Rory began to dream of that great beauty that had troubled his dreams; and while he thought of it, and the beautiful, sweet wonder of the woman who had it, she whom he had seen sitting in the moonshine on the yellow rock, he heard again the laughing, crying, fall and lilt of that near and far song. But now it troubled him no more.

He stooped, and swung himself out of the window, and at the noise of his feet on the gravel a dog barked. He saw a white hound running swiftly across the pasture beyond him. It was gone in a moment, so swiftly did it run. He heard a second bark, and knew that it came from the old deerhound in the kennel. He wondered where that white hound he had seen came from, and where it was going, and it silent and white and swift as a moonbeam, with head low and in full sleuth.

He put his hand on the sill, and climbed into the room again; lifted the pipes which he or Donald Macalister had thrown down beside the mattress; and again, but stealthily, slipped out of the window.

Rory walked to the deerhound and spoke to it. The dog whimpered, but barked no more. When the piper walked on, and had gone about a score yards, the old hound threw back his head and gave howl upon howl, long and mournful. The cry went from stead to stead; miles and miles away the farm-dogs answered.

Perhaps it was to drown their noise that Rory began to finger his pipes, and at last let a long drone go out like a great humming cockchafer on the blue frosty stillness of the night. The crofters at Moor Edge heard his pibroch as he walked swiftly along the road that leads to Dalmonadh Moor. Some thought it was uncanny; some that one of the pipers had lost his way, or made an early start; one or two wondered if Rory MacAlpine were already on the move, like a hare that could not be long in one form.

The last house was the gamekeeper's, at Dalmonadh Toll, as it was still called. Duncan Grant related next day that he was wakened by the skreigh of the pipes, and knew them for Rory MacAlpine's by the noble, masterly fashion in which drone and chanter gave out their music, and also because that music was the strong, wild, fearsome reel that Rory had played last in the byres, that which he had called "The Reel of the Daughter of Ivor."

"At that," he added, each time he told the tale, "I rose and opened the window, and called to MacAlpine. 'Rory,' I cried, 'is that you?'

"'Ay,' he said, stopping short an' giving the pipes a lilt. 'Ay, it's me an' no other, Duncan Grant.'

"'I thought ye would be sleeping sound at Dalibrog?'

"But Rory made no answer to that, and walked on. I called to him in the English: 'Dinna go out on the moor, Rory! Come in, man, an' have a sup o' hot porridge an' a mouthful with them.' But he never turned his head; an' as it was cold an' dark, I said to myself that doited fools must gang their ain gait, an' so turned an' went to my bed again, though I hadn't a wink so long as I could hear Rory playing."

But Duncan Grant was not the last man who heard "The Reel of the Daughter of Ivor."

A mile or more across Dalmonadh Moor the heather-set road forks. One way is the cartway to Balnaree; the other is the drover's way to Tom-na-shee and the hill countries beyond. It is up this, a mile from the fork, that the Yellow Moonrock rises like a great fang out of purple lips. Some say it is of granite, and some marble, and that it is an old cromlech of the forgotten days; others that it is an unknown substance, a meteoric stone believed to have fallen from the moon.

Not near the Moonrock itself, but five score yards or more away, and per-haps more ancient still, there is a group of three lesser fang-shaped boulders of trap, one with illegible runic writing or signs. These are familiar to some as the Stannin' Stanes; to others, who have the Gaelic, as the Stone Men, or simply as the Stones, or the Stones of Dalmonadh. None knows anything certain of this ancient cromlech, though it is held by scholars to be of Pictish times.

Here a man known as Peter Lamont, though commonly as Peter the Tinker, an idle, homeless vagrant, had taken shelter from the hill-wind which had blown earlier in the night, and had heaped a bed of dry bracken. He was asleep when he heard the wail and hum of the pipes.

He sat up in the shadow of one of the Stones. By the stars he saw that it was still the black of the night, and that dawn would not be astir for three hours or more. Who could be playing the pipes in that lonely place at that hour?

The man was superstitious, and his fears were heightened by his igno-rance of what the unseen piper played (and Peter the Tinker prided himself on his knowledge of pipe music) and by the strangeness of it. He remem-bered, too, where he was. There was not one in a hundred who would lie by night among the Stannin' Stanes, and he had himself been driven to it only by heavy weariness and fear of death from the unsheltered cold. But not even that would have made him lie near the Moonrock. He shivered as memories of wild stories rose ghastly one after the other.

The music came nearer. The tinker crawled forward, and hid behind the Stone next the path, and cautiously, under a tuft of bracken, stared in the direction whence the sound came.

He saw a tall man striding along in full Highland gear, with his face death-white in the moonshine, and his eyes glazed like those of a leistered salmon. It was not till the piper was close that Lamont recognized him as Rory MacAlpine.

He would have spoken—and gladly, in that lonely place, to say nothing of the curiosity that was on him—had it not been for those glazed eyes and that set, death-white face. The man was fëy. He could see that. It was all he could do not to leap away like a rabbit.

Rory MacAlpine passed him, and played till he was close on the Moonrock. Then he stopped, and listened, leaning forward as though strain-ing his eyes to see into the shadow.

He heard nothing, saw nothing, apparently. Slowly he waved a hand across the heather.

Then suddenly the piper began a rapid talking. Peter the Tinker could not hear what he said, perhaps because his own teeth chattered with the fear that was on him. Once or twice Rory stretched his arms, as though he were asking something, as though he were pleading.

Suddenly he took a step or two forward, and in a loud, shrill voice cried:

"By Holy St. Bride, let there be peace between us, white woman!

"I do not fear you, white woman, because I too am of the race of Ivor:

"My father's father was the son of Ivor mhic Alpein, the son of Ivor the Dark, the son of Ivor Honeymouth, the son of Ruaridh, the son of Ruaridh the Red, of the straight, unbroken line of Ivor the King:

"I will do you no harm, and you will do me no harm, white woman:

"This is the Day of Bride, the day for the daughter of Ivor. It is Rory MacAlpine who is here, of the race of Ivor. I will do you no harm, and you will do me no harm:

"Sure, now, it was you who sang. It was you who sang. It was you who played. It was you who opened my window:

"It was you who came to me in a dream, daughter of Ivor. It was you who put your beauty upon me. Sure, it is that beauty that is my death, and I am hungering and thirsting for it."

Having cried thus, Rory stood, listening, like a crow on a furrow when it sees the wind coming.

The tinker, trembling, crept a little nearer. There was nothing, no one.

Suddenly Rory began singing in a loud, chanting, monotonous voice:

> "An diugh La' Bride
> Thig nighean Imhir as a chnoc,
> Cha bhean mise do nighean Imhir,
> 'S cha bhean Imhir dhomh."

> (To-day the day of Bride,
> The daughter of Ivor shall come from the knoll;
> I will not touch the daughter of Ivor,
> Nor shall the daughter of Ivor touch me.)

Then, bowing low, with fantastic gestures, and with the sweep of his plaid making a shadow like a flying cloud, he sang again:

"La' Bride nam brig ban
Thig an rigen ran a tom
Cha bhoin mise ris an rigen ran,
'S cha bhoin an rigen ran ruim."

> (On the day of Bride of the fair locks,
> The noble queen will come from the hill;
> I will not molest the noble queen,
> Nor will the noble queen molest me.)

"An' I, too, Nighean Imhir," he cried in a voice more loud, more shrill, more plaintive yet, "will be doing now what our own great forbear did, when he made *tabhartas agus tuis* to you, so that neither he nor his seed for ever should die of you; an' I, too, Ruaridh MacDhonuill mhic Alpein, will make offering and incense." And with that Rory stepped back, and lifted the pipes, and flung them at the base of the Yellow Moonrock, where they caught on a jagged spar and burst with a great wailing screech that made the hair rise on the head of Peter the Tinker, where he crouched sick with the white fear.

"That for my *tabhartas*," Rory cried again, as though he were calling to a multitude; "an' as I've no *tuis*, an' the only incense I have is the smoke out of my pipe, take the pipe an' the tobacco too, an' it's all the smoke I have or am ever like to have now, an' as good incense too as any other, daughter of Ivor."

Suddenly Peter Lamont heard a thin, strange, curling, twisting bit of music, so sweet for all its wildness that cold and hunger went below his heart. It grew louder, and he shook with fear. But when he looked at Rory MacAlpine, and saw him springing to and fro in a dreadful reel, and snapping his fingers and flinging his arms up and down like flails, he could stand no more, but with a screech rose and turned across the heather, and fluttered and fell and fell and fluttered like a wounded snipe.

He lay still once, after a bad fall, for his breath was like a thistledown blown this way and that above his head. It was on a heathery knoll, and he could see the Moonrock yellow-white in the moonshine. The savage lilt of that jigging wild air still rang in his ears, with never a sweetness in it now, though when he listened it grew fair and lightsome, and put a spell of joy and longing in him. But he could see nothing of Rory.

He stumbled to his knees and stared. There was something on the road.

He heard a noise as of men struggling. But all he saw was Rory MacAlpine swaying and swinging, now up and now down; and then at last the piper was on his back in the road and tossing like a man in a fit, and screeching with a dreadful voice, "Let me go! let me go! Take your lips off my mouth! take your lips off my mouth!"

Then, abruptly, there was no sound, but only a dreadful silence; till he heard a rush of feet, and heard the heather-sprigs break and crack, and something went past him like a flash of light.

With a scream he flung himself down the heather knoll, and ran like a driven hare till he came to the white road beyond the moor; and just as dawn was breaking, he fell in a heap at the byre-edge at Dalmonadh Toll, and there Duncan Grant found him an hour later, white and senseless still.

Neither Duncan Grant nor any one else believed Peter Lamont's tale, but at noon the tinker led a reluctant few to the Yellow Moonrock.

The broken pipes still hung on the jagged spar at the base. Half on the path and half on the heather was the body of Rory MacAlpine. He was all but naked to the waist, and his plaid and jacket were as torn and ragged as Lamont's own, and the bits were scattered far and wide. His lips were blue and swelled. In the hollow of his hairy, twisted throat was a single drop of black blood.

"It's an adder's bite," said Duncan Grant.

None spoke.

AFTER DARK IN THE PLAYING FIELDS

M. R. James

Montague Rhodes James (1862–1936), provost of King's College Cambridge and Eton, director of the Fitzwilliam Museum, and cataloguer of Cambridge medieval manuscripts, has become one of the names most closely associated with the English ghost story. Composing his first chilling tales as Christmas entertainments for his friends (and possibly the King's choristers), he began to publish them in magazines during the 1890s, and in 1904 he brought out his first collection, *Ghost Stories of an Antiquary*. Its huge success led to several more volumes, and an enduring reputation for James as the master of eerie tales featuring quiet country towns, sceptical scholars and ominous supernatural forces.

Though best known today for his horror tales, James also experimented with children's literature, writing fantasy novella *The Five Jars* (1922) for a friend's daughter. Featuring talking streams, magical ointments, helpful fairy folk known as the "Right People" and the occasional terrifying swarm of bats, it met with limited success upon publication, falling into the uneasy space of being deemed too frightening for children and not frightening enough for adults.

Explaining at the end of *The Five Jars* that he came to write the story after having "heard something from the owls", he returns to this idea in his 1924 tale "After Dark in the Playing Fields". This short piece, originally published in Eton's *College Days*, has a lighter tone than James' better-known tales, but there is still an underlying darkness to this midsummer night's encounter.

THE hour was late and the night was fair. I had halted not far from
Sheeps' Bridge and was thinking about the stillness, only broken
by the sound of the weir, when a loud tremulous hoot just above
me made me jump. It is always annoying to be startled, but I have a kindness
for owls. This one was evidently very near: I looked about for it. There it was,
sitting plumply on a branch about twelve feet up. I pointed my stick at it and
said, "Was that you?" "Drop it," said the owl. "I know it ain't only a stick,
but I don't like it. Yes, of course it was me: who do you suppose it would be
if it warn't?" We will take as read the sentences about my surprise. I lowered
the stick. "Well," said the owl, "what about it? If you will come out here of
a Midsummer evening like what this is, what do you expect?" "I beg your
pardon," I said, "I should have remembered. May I say that I think myself very
lucky to have met you tonight? I hope you have time for a little talk?" "Well,"
said the owl ungraciously, "I don't know as it matters so particular tonight.
I've had me supper as it happens, and if you ain't too long over it—ah-h-h!"
Suddenly it broke into a loud scream, flapped its wings furiously, bent forward
and clutched its perch tightly, continuing to scream. Plainly something was
pulling hard at it from behind. The strain relaxed abruptly, the owl nearly
fell over, and then whipped round, ruffling up all over, and made a vicious
dab at something unseen by me. "Oh, I *am* sorry," said a small clear voice in a
solicitous tone. "I made sure it was loose. I do hope I didn't hurt you." "Didn't
'urt me?" said the owl bitterly. "Of course you 'urt me, and well you know it,
you young infidel. That feather was no more loose than—oh, if I could git at
you! Now I shouldn't wonder but what you've throwed me all out of balance.
Why can't you let a person set quiet for two minutes at a time without you
must come creepin' up and—well, you've done it this time, anyway. I shall

go straight to 'eadquarters and"—(finding it was now addressing the empty air)—"why, where have you got to now? Oh, it is too bad, that it is!"

"Dear me!" I said, "I'm afraid this isn't the first time you've been annoyed in this way. May I ask exactly what happened?"

"Yes, you may ask," said the owl, still looking narrowly about as it spoke, "but it 'ud take me till the latter end of next week to tell you. Fancy coming and pulling out anyone's tail feather! 'Urt me something crool, it did. And what for, I should like to know? Answer me that! Where's the *reason* of it?"

All that occurred to me was to murmur, "The clamorous owl that nightly hoots and wonders at our quaint spirits." I hardly thought the point would be taken, but the owl said sharply: "What's that? Yes, you needn't to repeat it. I 'eard. And I'll tell you what's at the bottom of it, and you mark my words." It bent towards me and whispered, with many nods of its round head: "Pride! stand-offishness! that's what it is! *Come not near our fairy queen*" (this in a tone of bitter contempt). "Oh, dear no! we ain't good enough for the likes of them. Us that's been noted time out of mind for the best singers in the Fields: now, ain't that so?"

"Well," I said, doubtfully enough, "*I* like to hear you very much: but, you know, some people think a lot of the thrushes and nightingales and so on; you must have heard of that, haven't you? And then, perhaps—of course I don't know—perhaps your style of singing isn't exactly what they think suitable to accompany their dancing, eh?"

"I should kindly 'ope not," said the owl, drawing itself up. "Our family's never give in to dancing, nor never won't neither. Why, what ever are you thinkin' of!" it went on with rising temper. "A pretty thing it would be for me to set there hiccuppin' at them"—it stopped and looked cautiously all round it and up and down and then continued in a louder voice—"them little ladies and gentlemen. If it ain't sootable for them, I'm very sure it ain't sootable for me. And" (temper rising again) "if they expect me never to say a word just because they're dancin' and carryin' on with their foolishness, they're very much mistook, and so I tell 'em."

From what had passed before I was afraid this was an imprudent line to take, and I was right. Hardly had the owl given its last emphatic nod when four small slim forms dropped from a bough above, and in a twinkling some sort of grass rope was thrown round the body of the unhappy bird, and it was borne off through the air, loudly protesting, in the direction of Fellows' Pond. Splashes and gurgles and shrieks of unfeeling laughter were heard as I hurried up. Something darted away over my head, and as I stood peering over the bank of the pond, which was all in commotion, a very angry and dishevelled owl scrambled heavily up the bank, and stopping near my feet shook itself and flapped and hissed for several minutes without saying anything I should care to repeat.

Glaring at me, it eventually said—and the grim suppressed rage in its voice was such that I hastily drew back a step or two—"'Ear that? Said they was very sorry, but they'd mistook me for a duck. Oh, if it ain't enough to make anyone go reg'lar distracted in their mind and tear everythink to flinders for miles round." So carried away was it by passion, that it began the process at once by rooting up a large beakful of grass, which alas! got into its throat; and the choking that resulted made me really afraid that it would break a vessel. But the paroxysm was mastered, and the owl sat up, winking and breathless but intact.

Some expression of sympathy seemed to be required; yet I was chary of offering it, for in its present state of mind I felt that the bird might interpret the best-meant phrase as a fresh insult. So we stood looking at each other without speech for a very awkward minute, and then came a diversion. First the thin voice of the pavilion clock, then the deeper sound from the Castle quadrangle, then Lupton's Tower, drowning the Curfew Tower by its nearness.

"What's that?" said the owl, suddenly and hoarsely. "Midnight, I should think," said I, and had recourse to my watch. "Midnight?" cried the owl, evidently much startled, "and me too wet to fly a yard! Here, you pick me up and put me in the tree; don't, I'll climb up your leg, and you won't ask me to do that twice. Quick now!" I obeyed. "Which tree do you want?" "Why, my tree, to be sure! Over there!" It nodded towards the Wall. "All right. Bad-calx tree do you mean?" I said, beginning to run in that direction. "'Ow should I know what silly names you call it? The one what 'as like a door in it. Go faster! They'll be coming in another minute." "Who? What's the matter?" I asked as I ran, clutching the wet creature, and much afraid of stumbling and coming over with it in the long grass. "*You'll* see fast enough," said this selfish bird. "You just let me git on the tree, *I* shall be all right."

And I suppose it was, for it scrabbled very quickly up the trunk with its wings spread and disappeared in a hollow without a word of thanks. I looked round, not very comfortably. The Curfew Tower was still playing St. David's tune and the little chime that follows, for the third and last time, but the other bells had finished what they had to say, and now there was silence, and again the "restless changing weir" was the only thing that broke—no, that emphasized it.

Why had the owl been so anxious to get into hiding? That of course was what now exercised me. Whatever and whoever was coming, I was sure that this was no time for me to cross the open field: I should do best to dissemble my presence by staying on the darker side of the tree. And that is what I did.

All this took place some years ago, before summertime came in. I do sometimes go into the Playing Fields at night still, but I come in before true midnight. And I find I do not like a crowd after dark—for example at the Fourth of June fireworks. You see—no, you do not, but I see—such curious faces: and the people to whom they belong flit about so oddly, often at your elbow when you least expect it, and looking close into your face, as if they were searching for someone—who may be thankful, I think, if they do not find him. "Where do they come from?" Why, some, I think, out of the water, and some out of the ground. They look like that. But I am sure it is best to take no notice of them, and not to touch them.

Yes, I certainly prefer the daylight population of the Playing Fields to that which comes there after dark.

THE CASE OF THE
LEANNABH SIDHE

Margery Lawrence

Wolverhampton-born writer and illustrator Margery Lawrence (1889–1969) published widely in the romance, horror, fantasy and detective genres, but is best known for her creation of occult detective Dr Miles Pennoyer, whose case histories are recorded by his assistant Jerome Latimer.

During the early 1940s, Lawrence wrote several articles on Spiritualism for *Psychic News*, and in 1944 published Spiritualist primer *Ferry Over Jordan*. Here she explained that she had been "deeply interested in what … I have called the 'Other Side'" since receiving a message from a recently deceased relative some years previously: "*Somewhere* that man was obviously still alive … and I was determined to find out *where*". Her Spiritualist beliefs infuse her novels and short stories, which frequently involve mediums, spirits, and communications between the living and the dead.

Lawrence's work also explored folklore themes, including illustration projects such as drawings for Fiona Macleod's *The Hills of Ruel, and Other Stories*, and writings like 1926's tale of threatening wood spirit "Robin's Rath" and her 1967 *Rosemary's Baby*-esque novel of modern-day witchcraft, *Bride of Darkness*. "The Case of the Leannabh Sidhe", from her 1945 Pennoyer collection *Number Seven, Queer Street*, turns to Irish folklore, with Latimer recounting a case involving a changeling or *leanbh sí* ("fairy child"). When widow Mrs. Flaherty's eleven-year-old son starts behaving strangely, she turns to Pennoyer for advice.

The Sidhe often strive to carry off the handsome children, who are then reared in the beautiful fairy palaces under the earth, and wedded to fairy mates when they grow up.

The people dread the idea of a fairy changeling being left in the cradle in place of their own lovely child; and if a wizened little thing is found there, it is sometimes taken out at night and laid in an open grave till morning, when they hope to find their own child restored, although more often nothing is found save the cold corpse of the poor outcast.

Sometimes it is said the fairies carry off the mortal child for a sacrifice, as they have to offer one every seven years to the devil in return for the power he gives them. And beautiful young girls are carried off, also, either for sacrifice or to be wedded to the fairy king.

Speranza (Lady Francesca Wilde), *Ancient Legends, Mystic Charms, and Superstitions of Ireland* (1887)

T HIS case that I am going to tell you about (said my friend Pennoyer) happened in the earlier years of this queer career of mine. I remember I had returned from a difficult but interesting case of exorcism (I believe I told you about it, the case of the Dumb Child), and it had taken a good deal out of me, and I'd promised myself a week-end in the country to rest and replenish my "psychic batteries." But I found there was a letter amongst those awaiting me that rather interested me. It was from a woman—a woman of what the French call "a certain age", I decided, from the slender slanting writing that belonged to the age of our aunts rather than that of our sisters: it was headed "Brown's Hotel, Albemarle Street", and was brief—but very much to the point.

"Dear Dr. Pennoyer,
   "I understand that you make a speciality of dealing with cases that baffle the ordinary medical practitioner. My sister, Mrs. Flaherty, with whom I live, has a young son who is giving us both a considerable amount of anxiety, and we should welcome a talk to you about him, if you could spare the time to call upon us here—or if you prefer, we will call upon you. If you will telephone us we will make our time yours.
                                        "Yours sincerely,
                                        "Catherine Cargill."

I needed a few days' rest rather badly—and though I liked the agreeably direct flavour of the note, I think I might have refused the case on the plea of too much work; but it concerned a child, and while the psychic maladies, ills or evils that attack mankind at any age are serious, they are most serious when they attack children, whose minds and souls are so pliant, so terribly vulnerable to the Outer Forces. So I threw up my week-end, telephoned saying I would call, and next day made my way about tea-time to Brown's Hotel. I was shown up to a pleasant suite of rooms on the first floor, and found two ladies, the elder about fifty, the younger, I should say, about forty-two or three, awaiting me in the sitting-room. They greeted me both kindly and warmly and ordered tea at once—it was plain they were people with plenty of money, for the room was full of flowers, a handsome mink coat lay across the back of one of the chairs, and the large diamond brooch that pinned the collar of the younger lady's, Mrs. Flaherty's, gown was definitely not purchased at Ciro's!

The sisters were very different in type. Mrs. Flaherty had obviously been pretty in a pink-and-white, rather Christmas-card fashion in her youth, but had run to fat in her thirties, and now looked rather like a wax doll that had been left too long before the fire. But she seemed a pleasant, kindly little woman enough, though shy and rather scared and clinging close to her sister, Miss Cargill, who was as tall and lean as she was plump and small; grey-haired and rather grim-looking, but with a surprisingly charming smile to set off her horn-rimmed glasses and somewhat governessy grey tailored gown.

The waiter brought tea, and as he handed round the cakes and scones we talked trivialities—indeed, it seemed that Mrs. Flaherty would have gone on talking trivialities even after he had left the room, as she was evidently dreading the opening of the subject about which I had called. But as I began upon my second muffin, Miss Cargill, despite an imploring glance from her sister, spoke bluntly.

"Dr. Pennoyer, we want your help, please. It's as I wrote you—about my nephew. My sister's boy."

"So I gathered," I said. "And if I can give you any help I shall be only too delighted. So please be frank and tell me what the trouble is."

The sisters glanced at each other.

"That is the difficulty," said Miss Cargill slowly. "We don't know!"

I raised my brows as Mrs. Flaherty laughed uncertainly and looked at her sister.

"You must think us too stupid," she murmured. "And after all, perhaps…"

"Nonsense, Aggie!" said Miss Cargill firmly. "Don't try and back out now. You know as well as I do it's neither stupid *nor* nonsense! There is something definitely wrong with Patrick…"

"If you could give me some idea—some of the symptoms, however trivial?" I suggested.

Miss Cargill frowned and hesitated a moment.

"There's nothing *physically* wrong with him in the least," she said at last. "He's perfectly *healthy*! He can spend hours—days—in the open in all weathers and seasons without a coat and never catches even a cold. It's difficult to describe, but the whole thing is that he's never been quite like other boys and that recently he's getting worse. And… we are getting seriously worried." Her level grey eyes met mine. "Again, I don't mean to suggest that he's in the least mental—on the contrary. But there's *something*… something definitely not right, and it's come to such a pitch that we are appealing to you to come and try and find out what it is, and if possible put it right."

"How old is he?" I asked.

"Eleven," said Mrs. Flaherty in a small voice. "And well-grown for his age. But old…" She checked herself as though about to say something better left unsaid and glanced at her sister as I went on.

"Has he been educated at school—or at home?"

It appeared that he had been to school—to several schools indeed, both as a day-boy and as a boarder; but somehow he had never stayed long at any school. He was clever enough, his reports were first-class… indeed he was described as "mentally in many ways far in advance of the average boy of his years"… but somehow he did not seem to get on with either boys or masters. I asked for details, but none were forthcoming. There were "stories", apparently—possibly mere boys' chatter, or perhaps jealousy or antagonism of some sort, but there it was; somehow he never stayed long. The last two schools he had been to the Headmasters had written and asked that he might be taken away—oh, no positive accusation was ever made, that was what made it so maddening! Simply that he "had an influence they didn't like" or some lame excuse like that. Now it had become quite difficult to get him accepted at any school… it was unfair, of course, and likely to do the boy harm…

Mrs. Flaherty's voice died away and Miss Cargill took up the tale in her refreshingly-direct manner. Tutors also he had had—but there again, none of them stayed very long. None of them had anything definite to say against the lad; but there seemed to be a feeling… almost a sort of fear mingled with dislike… Only one had had the courage to put what he felt into words. The last, who had only recently left…

"Oh, Cathie!" pleaded Mrs. Flaherty.

But Miss Cargill went on firmly.

"Nonsense, Aggie! If Mr. Pennoyer takes up the case he *must* hear all we can tell him, whether it sounds nonsense or not!"

"That's what I want," I said at once. "Go on, Miss Cargill. What did this tutor say?"

"He was a Scot," said Miss Cargill slowly, "and he said something to me just as he was standing at the door ready with his bag in his hand to go. He said that he'd tutor any honest-to-God boy… but that yon wasn't a boy at all, and he wasn't staying to handle anything uncanny! And that he pitied us and wondered how on earth such a being could be born of such a nice normal mother."

Mrs. Flaherty emitted a small sob. She was twisting her plump little hands together over a lace-edged handkerchief.

"My only boy!" she murmured. "And I'm sure he's really all right, if we could only…"

"The thing is this," said Miss Cargill, silencing her more emotional sister with a warning glance, "that if you consent to take the case, Mr. Pennoyer, it won't be any use bringing you into contact with him as a—as a sort of doctor? He's too sharp—uncannily so! He would be against you at once and you could do no good. I… we wondered… whether perhaps you could, if you would, play the part of a resident tutor for a while? We have come up to London ostensibly to engage a new tutor, and in that capacity you would be able to study him at your leisure and draw your own conclusions? But of course it would mean leaving your other work and concentrating entirely on him. And I don't know…"

She glanced at her sister and went on after a faint pause, almost hesitatingly, "Of course we realize that this would be asking a great deal of you. But it is urgent, and my sister's only son, and we would pay anything…"

"I've not taken up this career for the money I might make out of it, though I appreciate what you say, Miss Cargill," I said. "And if I can get through my immediate work within, say, a week, I feel that I should like to see what I can do—that is, providing I *can* do anything, which of course I can't say until I have studied the child."

I considered a moment. Yes, there was only the Scott haunting case that was all but cleared up, and the obsession case merely needed a hypnotic treatment or two to complete the cure. I would refuse to take on anything fresh till this was dealt with… I nodded.

"I will take the case," I said. "And I think you're very wise to suggest I come as a new tutor. I took my degree in my time, and I've no doubt I can play the part well enough while I watch the boy's reactions."

Both ladies burst out into profuse thanks, which I silenced at once with the repeated warning that I could promise nothing. But I would come and try my best.

Well, within the week I was on my way. My destination was Church Detton—a remote country town in the Cotswolds, where I arrived about six o'clock at night at a pretty little station where rambler roses clustered about the stationmaster's cottage, and the name of the place was blazoned in blue lobelia and yellow calceolaria along the bank opposite. An elderly porter awoke from a profound sleep to transport my baggage outside the station, where, in the dusty road, a handsome brown Daimler, driven by a smart chauffeur in brown dustcoat and cap to match, awaited me. The luggage-carrier on the back of the car took my suitcases easily enough. I tipped the porter and climbed in, and for over an hour we travelled through charming old-world English lanes high-hedged with flowering bushes, dog-roses, honeysuckle, hawthorn and the like, to turn at last between two stone gate-posts into a gravel drive that ended before a dignified brick manor-house set in a large and rambling garden.

A pretty little maid opened the door, and I walked into a low, wide hall with walls panelled in oak, a polished oak floor and two or three handsome pieces of old Jacobean furniture set about with bowls of flowers to lighten and scent what was otherwise a rather gloomy, if handsome interior. It was roughly square in shape, and several doors opened off it, both right and left, while a flight of oaken stairs with lovely corkscrew balusters and low, comfortable treads wound upwards into the upper portion of the house… Even as I entered, one of the doors opened and Mrs. Flaherty and her sister emerged.

Both ladies greeted me with such relief and gratitude that I felt quite touched, and followed Miss Cargill up the stairs to find my room, whither the chauffeur and maid had already transported my modest baggage, with a feeling that I was definitely and pleasantly welcome.

I noticed as the elder lady climbed the stairs that she had a slight but unmistakable limp, and wondered why, deciding to ask for myself when I had grown to know her a little better. She left me in a charming low-ceiled room boasting a carved oak fourposter bed, hung with ancient red and white printed linen, that made my mouth water, and Hammond the chauffeur, who had slipped off his brown dustcoat, revealing a neat dark suit, proceeded to unpack my things with neatness and despatch.

I chatted to him as he worked, and found that he played rôles other than that of chauffeur at the Manor House! There was actually little driving to be done, and he performed various house duties such as valeting occasional visitors, waiting at table, even occasional gardening if the gardener needed help. He was a nice, open-faced fellow of about forty-five or six and talked to me cheerfully as he arranged my clothes. He had been a long time with Mrs. Flaherty—who (he declared) was "one of the nicest ladies God ever put breath into". He had known her husband too, before he was killed in a motor-car in Ireland. Miss Cargill, too—that was a nice lady, for all she looked so severe, and it had been a godsend for poor Madam when she came to live with her after the Master's death in Ireland…

"It sounds a nice family you're working for," I said. "Is young Master Patrick as nice as his mother and aunt?"

I had put the question deliberately, watching his face. As I had half expected, he paused suddenly in his work of laying my shirts and collars, handkerchiefs and underwear into their respective drawers, and his answer, when it came, was obviously guarded.

"I don't see much of Master Patrick, sir. He's generally out rabbiting or wandering about, like… unless he's at his lessons."

"But if you've been with the Flahertys so long, you must have seen a good deal of him, surely?" I persisted.

Hammond hesitated, laid the last of my shirts neatly on the top of the others, and, shutting the drawer, replied without looking at me.

"I used to, sir, when he was a little 'un. But he's changed a good bit since then, and since we came to live in England—here, I mean—he's mostly out and about on his own concerns and don't stay around the house very much. And if that's all I can do for you, sir, I'll go and help Molly lay the dinner."

He was obviously anxious to get away, so I said no more, but dressed leisurely and found my way down to the drawing-room, where I found both sisters awaiting me before a wood-fire—welcome, despite the fact that the month was June, since the evening was distinctly chilly—beside which was a small table set with glasses and a lovely Waterford decanter of brown sherry.

I refused the drink and asked for fruit-juice instead, and sat talking to the sisters, feeling that as far as creature comforts went my lines had certainly fallen into pleasant places.

The drawing-room was a fine large room with white woodwork, and walls painted a delicate sparrow-egg blue. It had long windows opening upon a wooden verandah with posts set at intervals along the edge that supported a wide green-and-white striped linen awning that jutted out from the house-front above the window-frame, which verandah was furnished with a green-painted table and various wicker chairs that proved that it was in constant use in warm weather as an annexe to the drawing-room. Three shallow steps ran down from the verandah to a long, sloping lawn with a handsome herbaceous border on each side, and at the bottom of the lawn was a sort of small planta-tion of flowering shrubs, almond, cherry, prunus, forsythia and so on. Beyond that was a fence that marked the end of the garden proper, and on the other side of the fence was a belt or patch of woodland in which, I subsequently found, a miniature lake lay hidden that fed the stream that, marked by a row of pollard willows, meandered away through the distant green fields towards where a line of telegraph-poles along the skyline showed the road down which I had just driven. There was a grand piano in one corner of the drawing-room, its top heaped with music; deep-blue curtains picked up the colour of the blue delphiniums that patterned the cretonne sofa-and chair-covers; the furniture was an attractive mixture of old and new; there was a long range of well-filled bookshelves, on the walls were one or two good pictures, and a lovely Venetian mirror gleamed over the high white Adams mantelpiece.

I looked about for my pupil, but finding no sign of him, put the obvious question. There was a quick interchange of glances between the sisters, and Miss Cargill answered with, I thought, a hint of rather overdone casualness, that she was "afraid Patrick was running rather wild these days. We never wait dinner for him—he comes in to meals more or less as he likes. He is probably fishing with one of the local farmers' boys, or collecting birds' eggs, or something of that sort."

As she spoke, Hammond came into the room, and I saw a queer look flash across his face as he caught her sentence—a look almost sardonic. But it was gone even as I noted it. He announced dinner, and I followed the ladies into an attractive little dining-room, where a handsome oval walnut table was laid for four, with lace mats and red candles in silver candlesticks, and Molly, the pretty maid, stood beside the sideboard to assist Hammond in serving the dinner.

The dinner was as good as the surroundings, and the conversation pleasant, though I confess to devoting most of my attention to Miss Cargill, who was vastly more interesting as a companion than her sister. Her reading was wide, she had travelled considerably and learnt much in her travels—had also had a certain amount of experience in psychic work and study, so much that she was not prepared to pooh-pooh any belief, no matter how apparently fantastic—for which I was grateful. I felt that I might need her help in dealing with my "pupil", and the fact that as regards these matters she was not encased in the armour of mingled fear and distaste that bound her less intelligent sister, was a source of considerable satisfaction to me.

We had returned to the drawing-room and were sitting over our coffee talking easily and pleasantly when I brought up the subject of Patrick again. By this time I was getting definitely curious to see the boy…

"It's getting late, and I haven't made the acquaintance of my pupil yet, Mrs. Flaherty," I said. "What time does he generally come in at night?"

"I'm afraid," said Mrs. Flaherty uncomfortably, "I—he's not very regular in his habits. I don't…" She glanced uneasily at her sister and that lady spoke easily, airily.

"Oh, he'll be about somewhere! He comes and goes as he likes. You see, my sister doesn't believe in too much 'cabining and confining' for a growing boy…"

As she spoke I heard Hammond, who had come in to remove the coffee-tray, draw in his breath quickly. He was standing close to me and I don't think the ladies heard it, but I glanced up sharply and saw that he was staring at the French windows, closed now but still uncurtained to the night, and following his glance I saw that against the glass of the window a face was pressed. A child's face crowned with a tossing mane of light hair, with wide eyes fixed intently upon us as we sat cosily around the fire, talking and laughing, already on a footing of old and trusted friends... I got the swift impression of an outcast looking in—and it was not for a long time that I realized how right, in a sense, I was!

He stood wedged up against the thick-growing ivy at one side of the window, so that his body was concealed and only that face, white, intent, unblinking, hung close against the window-pane, backed by the dark of the night, like a mask suspended in air, staring.

And there was something about that grim, unwinking stare that made me draw in my breath as Hammond had done... I opened my mouth to speak, but Miss Cargill anticipated me. She had followed my glance to the window...

"Patrick!" she said, and her voice was loud and firm. "Patrick, come in and shake hands with Mr. Pennoyer!"

As Hammond, putting down the coffee-tray, went down the room to open the window to the peering creature outside, I sensed not only in Mrs. Flaherty, but in Miss Cargill also, a strange sense of sudden tension; it was as though they braced themselves to meet something...

Yet when a sturdy young figure in flannel shorts and shirt slipped into the room I felt a momentary rush of relief and could have kicked myself for imagining things. For here, surely, stood the most normal and ordinary eleven-year-old, snub-nosed, light-haired, blue-eyed, with grass-stains on shirt and shorts and scratches on his sunburnt knees, and the toes of his brown shoes scuffed and dirty with scrambling... He nodded at me rather casually and held out a grubby paw.

"You're my new tutor, aren't you?" he said and, glancing up at Mrs. Flaherty, smiled brilliantly.

I saw her look at him with an expression of pitiful, adoring love that was shot through at the same time with a most strange hint of fear—but she slipped her arm around him and he leant affectionately back against her as he continued his inquisition.

"You're Mr. Pennoyer, I know. They call me Patrick Flaherty." (The odd phrasing of this sentence, "they call me", stuck curiously in my mind, to be explained later.) "I hope you don't expect me to know too much. Or do you?"

"That depends," I said cautiously, "on what sort of response you've made to the efforts of my predecessors!"

He laughed suddenly and glanced at Miss Cargill, who sat quite still and upright on the further side of the fire, watching him.

"That's easy," he said. "I haven't made any response—or at least not much. I'm what they call a problem child—aren't I, mother?" He twisted his head round to smile afresh at Mrs. Flaherty, and I saw her eyes fill as she held him close to her side. "*Don't* they, mother?" he insisted, watching her with intent bright eyes, and she muttered something and turned her head away. He turned to me again with the same glittering smile.

"You see, I never stay at schools—and I don't keep tutors very long. They don't like me—or there's something *about* me they don't like..." The glittering smile positively blazed... "and they don't stay. I wonder if you will?"

"I—I'm sure I hope so," I said rather feebly.

But to tell the truth, for the moment I was completely disconcerted. I had been prepared for wariness, sulks, shyness, open dislike or distrust, for a dozen things—but not for this *dégagé* mockery, this unchildlike *blague*. I remembered Mrs. Flaherty's murmur when I asked her son's age. "Eleven... but old..." I realized its truth. Old? There *was* something incredibly old— and uncanny—behind that wide and gleaming smile.

The boy's eyes never moved from my face as he went on smoothly, evenly, leaning back against his mother. I saw her arm tremble, but she kept it valiantly round him as he went on.

"I don't think you will! The betting's all against it in the servants' hall." Those blue, unblinking eyes were fixed on Hammond now. "In fact,

Hammond's got his next week's wages on your leaving before the month's out. Aren't I right, Hammond?"

Hammond's brown face flushed darkly, but before he could speak Miss Cargill broke in.

"You are talking rather too much for a small boy, aren't you, Pat?" she said firmly. "And what Hammond or any of the staff like to do or say is no concern of yours! Take the coffee away, Hammond."

I saw two pairs of eyes meet, the lady's steady, dominant, the child's... well, it's difficult to say quite what I read into those blue, childish eyes raised to Miss Cargill's. I would have said defiance—but when I say that I don't mean the ordinary wilful defiance of a naughty child. I mean the surly, furtive defiance of something quite unchildlike, and with that defiance a look of venomous dislike—nay, a look of hate so profound and bitter that it gave me a feeling as though someone had laid a chilly hand down the centre of my spine. It was as though someone had slipped the boyish mask aside and shown me something on the further side that was not only unboyish, but not quite human...

However, the child made no reply beyond that one glance, but turned away and, apparently losing interest in me, squatted down upon a velvet *pouffe* on the further side of the fire, and taking a flat drawing-book from under his arm, proceeded to devote himself to sketching or scribbling while I resumed my talk with the ladies. But I was anxious to try to establish some sort of contact with the boy for whose sake I had set aside all my other work, and after a while I spoke to him across the firelight.

"I see you're interested in drawing, Patrick—may I see some of your things?"

He raised his head and looked at me across the rosy gleam of the fire. There was a little pause before he answered.

"I only scribble," he said evasively. "Nothing worth while. It wouldn't interest you."

He shut the book, slipped an elastic band round it and sat with his arms folded over it almost as though to protect it.

"Patrick can draw and paint and carve all sorts of pretty things out of wood, and whistle so that any bird will come to him," said Mrs. Flaherty with a rather pathetic sort of pride. "He's very artistic…"

The child laughed abruptly as he rose and, tucking the book under his arm, strolled over to the piano.

"I may not have been as great a success in school as some boys," he said, "but I can do lots of things that other boys can't. Can't I, mother? Eh?"

There was an odd hint of challenge in his voice, and Mrs. Flaherty's voice was faint as she replied, after a pause.

"Yes. Yes! Oh my God, yes…"

The last words were a mere whisper, and I knew not intended for me to catch. But my hearing is peculiarly sharp and I glanced quickly at the woman… and then back to the piano, where the boy was just opening the great instrument. I was surprised and distinctly impressed.

"It appears my pupil is gifted," I laughed to Miss Cargill. "Does Patrick really play as well as draw? And are his drawings really mere scribble?"

Miss Cargill nodded slowly.

"He plays—well," she said briefly. "As regards his drawings—you would have to judge for yourself—*if* he shows them to you. He doesn't—often."

The answer was cryptic—but the first half of it was certainly true. The boy's small hands took control of the instrument with the sureness of a master, and astonished and impressed. I settled myself down for a treat, as from Liszt to Beethoven, from Chopin to Mozart he wandered, and the two women sat listening, their shadowed eyes on the fire, their hands idle on their laps… at least the hands of Miss Cargill were idle. But I saw that Mrs. Flaherty's hands were restless. They twitched and trembled, clasped together, twisted over each other, played with and plucked at the stuff of her dress… a terribly nervy woman, poor soul, I decided, and wondered how much of her nervousness was justified by facts, or whether, like many women, she had allowed herself to exaggerate a situation that was capable of a normal explanation into a semi-hysterical obsession? Was there real and serious reason for her to worry over Patrick?

Of course I had barely made his acquaintance yet, but though he seemed precocious, certainly, and inclined to pertness and over-assurance, I had as yet seen no signs of anything more positively disquieting—barring my own inner instincts, which had certainly sent out the signal "danger". I had not liked that steely, unmirthful smile, nor the look in his eyes when he had "measured" Miss Cargill, as she snubbed him about Hammond—but after all, that might be childish rebellion or dislike, and up to date I had seen nothing really tangible to justify the suggestion of "queerness". Yet even as the thought passed through my mind, as though in answer to it, I became aware that the boy was playing something new—and playing it with a subtle difference. He was playing that supremely eerie masterpiece—Sibelius' "Valse Triste".

I had heard it before, but never in my life had I heard it played with such uncanny and unpleasant power! The room was shadowed, lighted only by the gleam of the fire, a handsome Sèvres reading-lamp and candles, which Mrs. Flaherty considered far more beautiful than modern electric lighting, and I heartily agreed with her. And somehow that child was filling that shadowed room with *other* shadows—shadows that seemed to glide and swirl about us, closer and closer, dimming the lights and bringing with them the very essence of the haunted music.

One could see the dying woman cowering, too terrified to shriek, while one by one the grim ghosts stole in at her bedroom door and danced their silent saraband about her bed. One could positively hear the grisly rustle of their garments, the murmur of their gloating laughter as they circled about their cringing victim, whose eyes, bulging with mortal terror, showed the light of reason departing as she awaited the entrance of Death, the last and most terrific figure of the horrible troupe…

I found myself shivering unaccountably, and a nasty damp sweat gathered in the palms of my hands and beaded my forehead, and I tried to move and found I could not. Alarmed, I forced myself to turn my head and look at the child as he played—and I saw that over the corner of the great instrument he was watching us, and smiling as he watched! Smiling that queer inhuman smile. A cold shiver ran down my back for the second time that evening, and yet his eyes were not upon me, but upon his mother—and I saw she was looking back at him, with the gaze horrified, fascinated, of a rabbit before a snake. Her pleasant round face had gone quite white, and her twisting hands were still as her eyes, fixed, terrified…

Miss Cargill rose sharply to her feet, and walking over to the piano, swept the boy's hands from the keys and shut down the piano-lid with a crash. I heard her voice, firm, dominant, rising over the blur of notes that still re-echoed within the piano.

"You've played quite enough for tonight, Pat," she said evenly. "And it's time for you to go to bed. Run along."

For a moment the boy crouched there on the stool, staring up at the tall woman who stood over him, and I could sense as sharply as though I heard the actual clashing of steel in mortal combat, the clash and challenge of their two wills as they met and held—but the woman's was the stronger. His face was dark with fury, but without a word he slipped off the piano-stool and, tucking his sketch-book under his arm, departed without a word to any of us—and I admit that as the door closed behind him I heaved a sigh of relief!

The two ladies were obviously shaken, so I hastily suggested the wireless, and under the cheerful normal clamour of dance-music from London the tensity of the atmosphere slowly cleared; and when at last I rose to make my good-night bow, Miss Cargill, rather to my surprise, volunteered to show me to my room. I guessed that this was merely an excuse to speak to me alone, and I was right, for directly we left the drawing-room and the door was safely closed behind us, she looked at me and spoke at once.

"My sister—as perhaps you can see—is in such a state of nerves about Patrick that she isn't quite balanced. He can reduce her to absolute jitters if he likes—and he *does* like, as you can see. She's like a rabbit before a snake…"

"How does he do it?" I said, "and does he do it often?"

"He can do it not only by playing the piano, but in a dozen different ways," said Miss Cargill grimly, "and with dozens of different people, barring myself and Hammond the chauffeur! He can't affect either of us in the least—though he's tried. The villagers are mortally scared of him, and nobody will speak to him if they can avoid it... that's why Hammond looked so odd when I said he was out fishing with the farmers' boys! I said that, of course, because of my sister... I try to keep up some sort of fiction about his being quite a normal boy before her, it seems to help her to bear it."

"Why does he try to influence people?" I asked. "To satisfy a sense of power?"

"Partly that, perhaps," said the lady, "but really he seems to have some queer sort of spite against humanity. And though in an odd way he's fond of his mother, I'm sure in certain moods he is more cruel to her than to anybody, as though he were revenging himself on her for that very fondness."

"I'll admit," I said, "that at first, to be honest, I wondered whether you ladies weren't perhaps, in your love and anxiety over the boy, making a mountain out of a really quite ordinary molehill. But you are right. There *is* something queer about that boy, and I'll do my best to find out what it is and where it springs from—without that we cannot hope to find a cure."

"You've given me a little hope already," said the lady gratefully, "by not laughing the whole thing off at once! You don't know how many doctors, child-experts, psychiatrists, psychoanalysts and all sorts of healers of various sorts and kinds we've had down here on one pretext or another. Now please let me help in every way I can. Is there anything I or my sister can tell you, about Patrick's early life, about his surroundings and upbringing or anything else, that may be useful?"

I hesitated.

"Not for the moment, I think, frankly," I said at last. "It's better not to know *too* much at the start. I want to get my impressions completely fresh—uncoloured by anything I'm told by *anybody*. Later on, when I've made some progress and want to collate and sum up those impressions, I shall ask you or your sister—both of you probably—to give me as many details of the boy's early life and history as you can. But at the moment I want to keep the slate absolutely untouched and let what comes write itself as it likes."

"I think you're very wise—and we shall be guided entirely by you," said Miss Cargill, "so now I'll wish you a really good night!"

I *did* sleep well—but only, I am convinced, because I did what I always do when I am conscious of being near some creature or influence that I do not understand and have reason to distrust. I built round myself before I slept a "ring" or fence of psychic power that would act as a guard against any inimical force that tried to come near me—and it was needed! On waking I remembered dimly that all through the early part of the night I had been aware of something prowling, circling, and poking, trying to come near me… for what reason I had no idea. Possibly mere curiosity, possibly something quite different… but it could not pierce the barrier of power behind which I lay, so I awoke refreshed to a lovely day. Had a pleasant breakfast with the two sisters and Patrick—looking, in clean shirt and shorts and well-brushed hair, the very pattern of exemplary small boys—and afterwards adjourned to the schoolroom upstairs to put my pupil through his paces.

In the sunny morning light, as he sat facing me while I questioned him, he seemed so very ordinary a boy that I wondered afresh whether I was not perhaps being influenced by two rather nervy, over-anxious women into reading more into the situation than was actually there. After all, what precisely *had* happened last night? A clever child had played a sinister piece of music remarkably well, and various hints, none very coherent, had been dropped by two women who were obviously so tensely concentrated upon him that their outlook might well be a little out of balance—nothing more substantial!

I resolved to maintain my own judgement as unbiassed as possible. I started the morning's lessons—and soon found myself agreeably surprised by the quick and mobile quality of my pupil's mind.

His education up to date seemed to have been oddly patchy. For instance, he had little knowledge of arithmetic, and less of grammar and general literature, and his knowledge of history and geography was extraordinarily uneven. He knew, for instance, accurately and in detail, the lives of Nero, of Julian the Apostate, of the Borgias, Cagliostro and Nostradamus and Catherine de Medici—in these and other of the less pleasant characters in history he took an almost morbid interest. But as regards the lives of William the Conqueror, of Richard Cœur de Lion, Elizabeth or Edward the Confessor, his knowledge was nil, and when questioned he merely looked blank, and said they "bored him, so he couldn't remember anything about them." Therefore, on certain periods of history he was a positive authority, whereas others simply didn't seem to "register"—and it was just the same with geography. (It was not till considerably later that I began to understand the underlying reason for all this, and to piece it together with other matters to make a coherent pattern.)

Certain countries held his attention, while other countries interested him not at all. For instance, he was passionately interested in Haiti, and knew a startling amount about the history of the Voodoo and Obeah-worship said still to prevail there; and he knew every detail—far more than I knew myself— about the grim and bloodstained figure of the "Black Emperor" of Haiti. The Spain of Inquisition days also interested him, and he would pore for hours over books that dealt with the old slave-days in America, in Africa, Jamaica and Brazil, when torture, superstition and kindred horrors were rife. The period of European and English history that deals with witches and witch-finding in the Middle Ages fascinated him, and he possessed an uncanny knowledge of folk-lore, legends, beliefs of all sorts, belonging to almost every country. But the one country—and that surprised me, knowing its wealth of folk-lore and fairy legend, quite apart from his own Irish blood—that he resolutely refused to discuss or learn anything about, was Ireland.

He was a born actor and mimic, and could, as his mother had said, imitate the call or cry of any bird or animal with uncanny accuracy. He adored music and poetry and would recite by the hour, in a queer chanting sort of rhythm, the pieces he loved—mostly blank verse, to which his odd method of reciting gave a curious, almost hypnotic effect. I already knew he could draw, though in what sort of a fashion I had no idea, as he still refused to show me his sketch-book—a refusal I put down to a child's, innate shyness, and refrained from pressing the point. His knowledge of flowers and plants, animal life, birds and fishes was profound in so young a boy—and I was told that he possessed an amazing power over animals of every kind, except dogs, who refused to go near him. This explained the absence of any dog at the Manor House—which had rather surprised me at first, as I should have imagined so typical a country house and such typical country women as Mrs. Flaherty and her sister possessing at least two or three dogs. It also emphasized my inner feeling that despite any arguments, *something* was wrong with Patrick—and that something definitely "bad". Dogs, those animals nearest of all to the human in development, are remarkably sure barometers of evil…

Altogether I found my pupil a curious and interesting problem, and was so busy studying him and trying to plan his lessons so as to fill in the gaps in his education, that the best part of a week passed by quite uneventfully— nothing at all on the lines of my first rather eerie evening occurred, to my knowledge at least. Perhaps nothing actually *did* occur, and he was "lying low"—it is quite possible, as he might well have been equally busy studying me and trying to make me out, as I was with him. Anyway the next few days passed peacefully enough, and but for one or two nights, when I was again conscious of that prowling entity trying to get past my protective circle, there was nothing of interest to report.

But one morning about a week later something rather startling happened. I had been out for a walk the previous afternoon and run across Molly, the pretty little housemaid who shared the waiting at table with Hammond. She was standing talking agitatedly with a good-looking gipsyish fellow in green corduroys with silver buttons on his coat—I put him down as somebody's gamekeeper—and avoided my glance as I passed, so I pretended not to notice her and walked on. But the meeting had a startling sequel on the following morning when, on descending the stairs to breakfast in the dining-room, I found Hammond stationed at the sideboard, not Molly, as was usual.

The two ladies had just entered the room before me, and an agitated conversation was in progress between them and Hammond, during which I gathered that "George" ("George" being Rider the gardener, to whom apparently Molly had been engaged) had had a fight over the girl with "Gipsy Bert"—whom I had no difficulty in identifying as Molly's escort of the previous afternoon. "George" had got the worst of it and was lying half-dead in his cottage, and "Bert" had fled. It appeared that the news had been telephoned to the Manor House from Rider's cottage by George's mother, who had found him lying bleeding from a serious knife-wound on the threshold of his cottage, and Molly, who had answered the telephone, had gone into hysterics and was now lying in a state of collapse in the kitchen…

With exclamations of distress Mrs. Flaherty and her sister hurried out of the room in the direction of the servants' quarters, and Hammond turned to me.

"You waiting breakfast for Master Patrick, sir?" he said—and it struck me that there was something faintly pointed in the way he spoke.

"Why of course, he isn't down yet," I said, and felt surprised, as it was the only meal at which Patrick made, as a rule, a fairly regular appearance.

I glanced round the room and out upon the terrace, but there was no sign of him and I went on apparently casually—though actually I was on the alert. Up to date, I suppose, out of loyalty, as he thought it, towards his employer, Hammond had carefully stone-walled any attempts on my part to pump him—but he was evidently at breaking-point now.

"I suppose he's overslept and you ought to go up and shake him," I said. Hammond snorted.

"Overslept? No fear! He's up and about—he's been up these two hours like he always is! Don't seem to need sleep like regular boys… but *I* know where he is. George's mother just told me on the 'phone. He's down there… by the cottage. Hiding in the thicket near by, and gloating…"

A thrill of horror ran through me. The picture was truly hateful, sketched in those few crude words. Gloating upon the broken figure asprawl across that neatly white-stoned doorstep, with the ugly stain of blood spoiling its purity…

"What do you mean?" I asked quietly. "Go on, Hammond—you've said too much now not to say more. You must know that, surely."

"Well… I guess you had to know, sir." He looked at me deprecatingly.

"It may help you," I said, "to know that the ladies have already confided in me their trouble about Master Patrick, and I am trying to find some way of helping them. I'm not merely here to give him lessons! So if you're worrying about telling their secrets, your mind may be relieved, my good fellow. Anything you can tell me may be more useful than you can guess."

The look of surprise and relief that spread over his honest, rugged face was good to see. He opened his mouth to speak, but at the same moment shut it and stood listening. A faint whistle came across the lawn from the belt of trees at the far end, beyond which lay the tragic cottage, and thrusting a dish of hot porridge he had but a moment before taken from the electric heater that stood upon the sideboard, back into its place, Hammond turned towards the door.

"Come up, sir—come to my room, if you don't mind, and watch him come up the lawn… now, quick. Come on!"

We ran out of the room, down a passage, and up a narrow flight of stairs like lamplighters, and into a neat little bedroom over the kitchen—one of a group of similar rooms occupied by the staff of the Manor House. Hammond closed the door behind us and led me to the window, which was neatly curtained in white muslin and overlooked the lawn.

Hammond peered through the curtains and nodded, his lips compressed into a bitter line. From the kitchen below the sound of weeping came, and the murmur of voices as the women tried to comfort the weeper…

"There he comes—now, see, watch him! Often and often I've watched him come up the lawn to the house with that look on his face—and always I've known there was some devilry doing when he looked like that!"

The boy was strolling leisurely up the lawn, hands in pocket, whistling idly, a shrill lilting little tune, a nasty little tune that sent a pringling sensation along one's nerves. He paused now and then to sniff at a flower or kick a tuft of grass, and to all appearances he was nothing but an ordinary youngster idling his way along, in no particular hurry, and with nothing particularly remarkable about him. But as he came nearer, and the sound of Molly's weeping stole out upon the air and met his ear, he paused and stood still a minute, looking up at the house and smiling... and a cold shiver went down my spine! For the look on that listening, smiling face, for all its round and sunburnt youth, was the look of a cool devil hearing, and relishing as he heard them, the cries of one of his helpless victims as he tortured them...

I shrank away from the window with a sudden exclamation of horror, and Hammond, looking at me, nodded with satisfaction.

"You see?" he said. "Gloating—just gloating! He's done it again... just as he's done it God knows how many times before, that I know of and the village knows of. And as many times again that we can guess but can't prove..."

"How do you mean 'he's done it'?" I asked. "A mere child surely couldn't have had a hand in anything so tragic as this?"

"*Couldn't* he?" said Hammond grimly. "I tell you, there hasn't been a wicked thing happen in the village since he come to live here that he hasn't had a hand in—though I know it can't always be proved, worse luck! He pulled the strings to make Bert and Molly meet—just because she was tokened to George, and they was as happy as the day was long, and he couldn't bear it! Had to do something to spoil it—that's his way. I guessed from the way he grinned when he heard she and George was fixing the wedding-day that he'd be up to something, and I told him if he didn't keep his meddling, wicked little fingers out of this I'd break his neck. But it didn't do no good." His honest face was troubled. "He was too sharp! First thing

I knew he was teasing Molly about throwing herself away on a lout like George when she ought to have had some fun first, and talking about gipsies and what gay, romantic chaps they were, and how Bert was handsome wasn't he, and how he thought her the prettiest girl in the village... I told him off good and sharp, and Molly too, for listening, but it wasn't no kind of use. He just grinned at me, and Molly tossed her head. And later on I found that whenever she was out for her half-day, Bert 'ud be dangling outside in the lane—though God knows how that young devil got word to him she'd be there—and Bert never was a slow worker as far as women were concerned!" He drew a long breath. "Well, there you are. The girl's in the family way, and Bert can't marry her even if he wanted, which I doubt... he's got a hedgerow sort of a wife of his own somewhere and a row of kids..."

"It's a tragic story," I said hesitatingly, "but not necessarily due to the string-pulling of a boy, Hammond. These things happen."

"Then why do they happen so often when he's somewhere in the background?" said Hammond. "I'm not asking you to believe me, 'cause of this one isolated case, sir—this is only one of dozens where he's had a finger in the pie, somehow, somewhere, though you can't always pin down exactly where."

"How did this tragedy finally blaze up—do you know?" I asked.

Hammond nodded.

"Molly came crying and howling into the kitchen last night—that must 'a' been after you'd seen her talking to Bert in the lane, sir. She told him she was in for a baby—and *he* told her there was nothing doing in the way o' marriage and went off whistling, and she came back here and collapsed before the whole lot of us—we were too sorry for the girl to say 'I told you so', though we *had* and all, a dozen times over. And later she wrote out a letter to George telling him what had happened and sent it down by the gardener's boy to leave at George's cottage, and of course George lays for Bert early this morning and gets the worst of it—as anybody might have told him, dealing with that slippery devil with his knife."

"They're positive it was Bert who did it then?" I said.

"George had one of his silver buttons with a bit of green stuff still stuck to it clutched in one hand," Hammond said. "And there's nobody else wears that sort of rig in the village—nor uses a knife. So there we are! George either dead or dying, Bert on the run from the police, and Molly carrying a bastard, poor girl—and my lord comes up the garden grinning like a Cheshire cat! D'you wonder I get the creeps when he comes near me? If it wasn't for being sorry for Madam and her sister I wouldn't stay. But I can't leave 'em to *that*—alone…"

"I don't blame you for feeling that way," I said sincerely.

"And I'm not the only one," continued Hammond. "There's nobody calls on the ladies now, though there was plenty in the beginning—but they all dropped off, scared of him or something about him, and now everybody fights shy of the Manor House. It don't seem reasonable to think that the whole village has got the wrong idea, now do it, sir?"

"What idea exactly *have* they got?" I said downrightly.

Hammond hesitated.

"I can't rightly put it into words," he said. "But Master Patrick's got *something* about him that's not like ordinary boys. Even as a very little chap, when he came here first, he was queer and horrid—cruel, sort of, and yet not the ordinary sort of little-boy cruel that sticks caterpillars into spiders' webs or pulls the wings off flies. He don't hurt animals—it's humans he seems to have a down on."

I remembered Miss Cargill's words, "seems to have a spite against humanity"—but Hammond was going on.

"He's always had it in for his auntie, now—and it's my belief he's responsible for her being lame like what she is!"

I uttered an incredulous exclamation and Hammond nodded firmly.

"Well, you listen to me a minute, sir! It happened when Miss Aggie had to go over to Ireland and see about some business connected with the estate; about four years ago it was. Miss Aggie didn't want to go without her sister, but that meant taking Master Patrick, and the hubbub that child raised at the thought of going back to Ireland, the place where he was born... well, it u'd have to ha' been seen to be believed! Miss Cargill was all for over-riding his whims, as she called it, and the three of them going, lock, stock and barrel, whatever he said. But Master Pat had worked himself into such a state that he frightened his mother, and she said she wouldn't force him, and then they tried to arrange things so that Miss Cargill—she was always the one with the business head—could go to Ireland and see to the business there, instead of Miss Aggie. But it couldn't be done, because Miss Aggie being the owner of Killeen, it was only her could sign and decide things. So over she had to go, and Miss Cargill had to stay behind to look after Master Patrick."

"Couldn't they have left him in charge of a well-trained nurse?" I asked. "Or a nursery governess?"

Hammond glanced at me half-scornfully.

"*Nurse?*" he said. "He used to scare his nurses so they wouldn't stay more than a few months, and it was the same with governesses. He had a string of 'em going and coming till he grew old enough to go to school... don't ask me what he done to them, because I don't know. And maybe at that it isn't just anything actual he *done* so much as the sort of thing he *is*... whatever it may be."

I glanced appreciatively at the speaker. It is often given to the simple and unlettered to put the whole gravamen of a matter into a single graphic phrase. "The sort of thing he is"... how completely that described Patrick! He was a "thing" rather than a human child...

"Well," said Hammond, "Master Patrick was simply livid when he found he was going to be left with his auntie! As far as he's got any sort of affection for anybody he seems to have it for his mother, poor lady—or maybe it's just because he can do what he likes with her, and with Miss Cargill he has to toe the line, for all his cunning. But for all his scenes and pleadings, Miss Aggie went off to Ireland with her maid and I stayed here with Miss Cargill and him.

"Well now, Master Patrick had a pet cat in those days—a nasty slinking little ginger beast we all hated, and the villagers specially. They used to hint it was a what-d'you-call-it… you know, sir, the sort of creature them old witches was supposed to have with 'em."

"Familiars!" I nodded. "Sort of special little animal given them by the Devil to help them in their work for him. Yes, go on…"

"Well, however that may be, it was a sly, vicious beast, but Master Patrick he always had it with him, walking by him or on his shoulder or cuddling up to him like. He used to stroke it and whisper to it and laugh with it… odd it was to watch! And I remember as well as if it was yesterday that one night about a week after Miss Aggie went away to Ireland Miss Cargill was going out to dinner. Quite a party it was to be—*then*, the ladies was still asked out now and again, though their list of invitations was beginning to thin out—so she was all dressed up in her best, and I'd brought the car round and was standing by it, waiting for her outside the front door. The door was open, because it was very hot weather, and I could see right into the hall, and I saw Master Patrick crouched in a corner of the hall, just below the stairs. He had this cat in his arms, and he was whispering to it and stroking it—and there was a sort of gleam in his eyes I'd learned not to like! I was in two minds to step in and tell him to run along out and play, and I wish I'd done it now… but I was too late. Just as I moved forward, he let the cat go and she ran upstairs and jumped on the square newel-post at the top of the stairs just as Miss Cargill came rustling along the landing from her room.

"She was a handsome lady in those days, and she looked fine in her evening dress—black velvet it was, with a trailing skirt and long gloves and a cloak trimmed with white fur and lots of diamonds—and as she came to the top of the stairs she saw the cat sitting on the post and said, 'Hullo, pussy' or something of the sort and put out her hand to stroke it. She didn't like the beast any more than the rest of us, but she was always one to be kind to animals, was Miss Cathie. And you can bet my blood fairly ran cold when that damned cat reared up like a demon and flew straight at her face!

"By the Lord's mercy its claws missed her eyes… I've always had it in mind that that young limb of Satan meant to 'a' got her blinded… but though it wasn't as bad as that, it was quite bad enough. The brute's claws tore one eyebrow open and she staggered back, half blinded with her own blood, flinging out her arms to fight the creature off—but she caught her foot in her long skirt, and in doing it she somehow got turned sideways, lost her balance and came hurtling down the stairs! She landed on her head in the hall and lay like a stone—and if you'd seen the look on Master Patrick's face as he looked down at her as she lay at his feet, you'd know I was telling you the plain truth. Gloating, sir… fair gloating! Of course there was a frightful how-d'ye-do, and the cat was drowned, and Miss Cathie had the best doctors that could be got, but it was all no use. She got over it… but she'd broken her hip-bone, and she'll walk lame, as you see, all the rest of her life."

"Of course," I said cautiously, "there's no proof that that was due to him? Cats have been known to go temporarily mad in hot weather."

"I know," said Hammond. "But if you'd lived with him, sir—and *watched* him, same as I have, you wouldn't have no doubts. And that's not the only story I could tell you. I remember soon after he first came, when he wasn't no more'n about four, he was caught putting nettles into the Weddell baby's crib, and Big Ned, Farmer Edge's son, picked him up and spanked him till he squawked. And that night a chunk of tiling from the porch over the farmhouse door crashed down on Ned and knocked him flat, and he's never been right in his head since. And you can call that coincidence *if* you like—and so did we, *then*! But it's happened too often to be coincidence *all* the time! Sure as a gun, if Master Patrick's crossed, and especially if he's struck, *something* nasty'll happen to whoever touches him—so the whole village leaves him alone. The Vicar hung on longest, and talked of the power of the Church and all, and the ladies used to go regularly to St. Aidan's down in the village— especially Madam, it seemed to comfort her. But it's three years since they went, and the Vicar never sets foot in the Manor House now."

"Why not?" I asked.

"Well, it was after another school—there's been lots of 'em!—had sent Master Patrick back saying they didn't want him," said Hammond. "And the Reverend offered to take him with his own boy and three or four others in special classes—he's a great scholar, is Mr. Percival, and makes quite a bit of money doing what they call private coaching. But he hadn't had my lord more than two or three months when he brought him back late one night with one hand on his shoulder and his mouth set grim—and for once Master Patrick looked a bit scared too, and was I glad!"

"What was it all about?" I asked curiously.

Hammond had the grace to blush.

"I suppose I shouldn't 'a' listened," he said. "But they were in the drawing-room—the ladies were waiting for Master Patrick to come in, and Madam was a bit fussed because it was after eleven, and he's not often out so late. And I didn't like to lock up till he *was* in, and when I let the Vicar in with him, marchin' him in like a prisoner, well... I waited about to show his Reverence off, and I couldn't help but hear. Seems one night Mrs. Wakely— that's the Vicar's wife—took it into her head to have a look at Master Eddy, him having a cold or some such, on her way up to bed. Him being the one-and-only, naturally she fretted a bit about him... and he wasn't there! So she came rushing downstairs in a regular fantigue to get hold of the Vicar. Now, Vicar was taking his final stroll in the garden before turning in, and for once he took it into his head to go right down to the bottom of the garden, by the orchard, instead of just strolling round the lawn—and he heard voices and saw some funny-looking lights in the meadow beyond the orchard.

"He thought it might be gipsies, so he went quietlike and looked over the hedge, and there he saw his own Master Eddy sitting in the middle of one of them Rings the locals call Fairy Dancing Floors! He was staring in front of him like a dummy, all white and fixed, and that Master Patrick and *some others*—though the Vicar couldn't rightly see just what they were, he knew they weren't right things, they was dark and lean and had funny lights on their heads—and they were all dancing widder-shins, if you know what that means, sir?"

"I do!" I said grimly. "But go on…"

"Well, the Vicar saw red and either jumped over the hedge or crashed through it—he's a big strong gentleman for all he's over fifty—and seized hold of Master Patrick, and there was a sort of whistle in the air and them *others* was gone in a flash, and just then Mrs. Wakely came screaming down the garden and Master Patrick said something quick-like and Master Eddy woke up—though he'd been sitting still as a stone staring in front of him, in spite of his father bouncing over the hedge! So it's plain there was some funny business going on if he couldn't wake till Master Patrick told him."

"Funny business is the word all right," I said. "And then?"

"Well," said Hammond. "After that, Vicar brought his lord-ship back here and told his mother and aunt the whole thing, with *him* sitting and glowering on a stool between 'em—Madam crying like a pump, poor lady, and Miss Cathie sitting looking frozen, and Vicar talking about dabbling with the powers of evil and quoting yards of Latin what I couldn't make head nor tail of… And when the Vicar stumped off at last it was plain it was all over with any goings and comings between the Vicarage and here. And maybe you'll say that it's just another coincidence that less than a month later there was a fire in the Vicar's study—*only* in his study!—that burnt up a whole lot of valuable books and curios he'd got there, and worst of all, the manuscript of a big book he'd been working on for years, together with the notes and stuff so he couldn't ever rewrite it!" He drew a long breath. "Lord, sir, I could tell you scores of other tales, if I'd the time, about him and his nasty slimy ways. But I hope I said enough anyway to put you on your guard, sir, to prove that I'm not just pitching a tale when I say there's something queer—*very* queer—about Master Patrick. You start from where I left off, sir, and go on. You'll find plenty!"

Hammond was right—I *did* find plenty. A good deal of it was impossible to check and corroborate, of course, and there was much that I had to dismiss as either sheer invention or gross exaggeration—but out of the rest there emerged enough to prove that the boy Patrick was undoubtedly the core, the central focus around which revolved a whole list of ugly tales, adventures, episodes, incidents and whatnot. Some merely childishly unpleasant, showing a twisted sort of prankishness, but there was a sinister percentage that seemed to show a mind or force definitely evil, inimical towards humanity, deliberately using its powers, whatever they were, for its own macabre ends, and rejoicing in its power and the helplessness of those who feared it. It was quite plain that Master Patrick had got the entire village, besides his mother and the staff of the Manor House, entirely under his thumb. They dreaded and feared him without in the least knowing what they feared, and he walked amongst them alone, accompanied only by the shadow of their fear and hate, and he seemed to rejoice in that loneliness, to bask and smile in the sense of power that it gave him…

Only three people stood out against him. Myself, Hammond, and his aunt Miss Cargill. And while he watched me as yet guardedly, not sure of his ground or of me, and Hammond he affected to deride, he hated his aunt with a hatred very definite and most unchildlike—and this hate was presently to show itself in a manner both startling and unpleasant.

After the tragic episode of Molly and Bert Master Patrick was remarkably quiet and obedient for some days—the tiger temporarily sated, I wondered? and kicked myself for being melodramatic! He came regularly in to meals, did his lessons, and behaved towards his mother, his aunt and myself with impeccable politeness. He even, on hearing the news that George—who, thanks to an assiduous doctor and a strong constitution, did *not* die—insisted upon marrying Molly and shouldering the responsibility of Bert's child, suggested giving the girl a pound out of his pocket-money as a wedding-present. He was loudly applauded by his mother for his generosity—but as he went out of the room to carry out his suggestion, Hammond went softly after him, and I was just near enough to hear the dialogue between them.

"If you've got the bleeding cheek to go near that girl, let alone offer her that damn money after what you have done to her," said Hammond fiercely, "I'll wait till I get a chance and pretty well break your ruddy neck. D'ye hear?"

The boy looked up into the angry face of the man, scowled and hesitated. Whatever dwelt behind that round ingenuous face—and I knew now it was a soul evil, old as the hills and quite without the ordinary human sensitiveness to love, kindness, affection—was longing to deride him, to challenge and defy! But the body that housed it was still that of a small boy, and could suffer pain and indignity just as the bodies of ordinary boys may suffer, and Hammond was a sturdy fellow, standing well on to six feet high. So at last Patrick shrugged his shoulders, gave a malicious little grin, thrust the note back into his pocket and turned away.

"What are you making such a fuss about, Hammond?" he said airily. "If you like to prevent Molly having a quid to spend, *I* don't care—it's her loss. But why are you doing the gallant-protector act? I suppose we aren't all on the wrong track and it's your baby after all?"

And while Hammond was fuming at the insult, he strolled whistling back to the drawing-room.

Shortly after this I made an interesting discovery. Evidently tired of trying to pierce the protective "ring" that I built about myself every night, the young man let me alone after a while—and I was able to set a watch on him for a change!

I discovered that he frequently left his bedroom at night—without his mother's knowledge, of course; he had perfected a method of climbing out of his window over the balcony rail and sliding down a penthouse roof that stretched below it, by means of a knotted rope that he kept hidden somewhere in his room, and departing into the night, returning sometimes hours later with leaves and twigs in his curly hair and his pyjamas damp with dew and green with moss. He would climb up, helped by his rope, and regain his room—but sometimes he would linger on the balcony outside, staring out over the garden with eyes alight with that uncanny brightness, singing to himself under his breath and laughing now and then, quiet, unpleasant laughter. Several nights I watched him go and come... my room was on a level with his, though it had no balcony... and once or twice I was by no means sure that he returned alone. At any rate, two or three times as he came up from the belt of trees that stretched across the fields just below where the garden ended, a small dark figure walking slowly through the silver dawn mist, I got the impression that beside him came... others. Flickering, intangible shadows that faded and vanished into the mist as he approached the house...

I made use of one of these nightly absences to have a look round his room while he was away. He always locked it carefully behind him, but that was no hindrance to me—as you know, there is nothing in the trick of making a skeleton key once you have been taught!—and I found several things that interested me greatly during my search. First, I found his sketch-book... and its contents startled me! I had expected, from the pains he had taken to keep it out of my way, that he probably shared the usual young boy's liking for making drawings of a more or less "smutty" type—but I got a considerable surprise. The pages were covered with scribbled sketches—mostly ordinary things enough, scenes, geometric designs, one or two portrait heads, including one of Molly and another of Bert, the gipsy, a group of flowers, a fanciful pair of figures... but somehow, though it is quite impossible to explain quite *how*, they were—evil! Uncanny and horrible, as though the ordinary pleasant shapes and forms of life were seen through a twisted vision...

I don't mean to say they were foul and obscene, though there was a hint of this aspect, too, about them. But it was not a *sexual* sort of obscenity—more a mental, though this is difficult to describe in words. I mean that they were drawings done by a mind entirely removed from the human. A mind that held within its eerie byways strange twists and turns down which the normal, ordinary mind would never, could never dream of wandering...

I flicked hastily over the pages—and just before the end came upon three drawings more carefully executed than any of the others. One was a rough sketch of a landscape, a wild, untamed mountain-side with a stream in the foreground, and on the further side of the stream a mass of tangled bushes, and behind them a high-curving bank, like a curling wave, crowned with two great trees. Beneath this was written the mysterious words *"Dail-sheomra ruit Sidhe".** The second was a flight of arrowy figures, lean, graceful, eerie, merely indicated and yet profoundly and disturbingly vivid—and the third was a sketch of a head. But what a head! Though it was a mere tangled mass of lines that formed hair, and a vague shadowy face that was narrow and foxy, its eyes, even as mere pencilled scribbles, made something in one curl and shrink! Under these last two drawings, as under the first, were two or three lines of strange characters—I studied them for a moment and recognized them as Gaelic. *"An Ciar"†* was written beneath the head, and beneath the drawing of the flying figures *"Nai aluinn an sluagh Sidhe ar mhuin na gaoithe".‡*

I spelt them out slowly—I knew a little Gaelic, through my Scottish grandmother—and stared, astonished. This from the lad who seemed to dislike the very name of Ireland? I felt I was hot on the track of something, and putting the sketch-book carefully back where I had found it, rummaged further. My discoveries were interesting. I found a dictionary of Celtic words and phrases, a scribbled book in which he had obviously laboriously tried to set himself exercises in the ancient Irish tongue, two or three books on Irish folk-lore and history, pictures and photographs of Irish beauty spots… and all this from a boy who declared that he hated Ireland!

This puzzled me so much that next day I went straight to Miss Cargill and tackled her.

"Look here, Miss Cargill," I said, "if you remember, I didn't want you to tell me too much at the outset; but I've been here several weeks now and

---

* "The Council Room of the Shee."
† "The Dark One."
‡ "How beautiful are the Shee, as they ride the winds."

gathered quite a lot—and now I want you to tell me, please, all you can about Patrick—and Ireland."

She looked puzzled.

"I shouldn't have thought he had much connection with Ireland," she began. "He was only five when he left the country, and he remembers so little about the place that he never even speaks about it. He used to have a violent antipathy to any idea of returning there, certainly, that used to puzzle me and my sister a good deal—why a mere child should take a dislike to a country he left at five years old seems absurd, but so it was. But now I think the antipathy has given place to plain boredom. He simply doesn't take any interest in Ireland any more."

"That is pure camouflage—for some reason," I told her, and went on to recount my discoveries in his room.

She was startled and interested.

"Then you think…"

"I don't think anything positive as yet," I said, "but the care with which he hides his secret passionate interest in Ireland means *something*—and I want to get at what it means. Hate of a thing is often only an inverted form of love, you know. It may easily mean that Ireland means a great deal to him—so much that he daren't admit it even to himself. Go on, please. I want to go back to the root of things—before Patrick was born."

We had an interesting and informative talk. Miss Cargill told me the story of her sister's marriage—a marriage that had taken place sorely against their parents' will, as Dick Flaherty, though a good-hearted fellow enough and handsome in a flashy, dashing style, was only a bookmaker, and not a very successful bookmaker at that, and the match was considered a terrible *mésalliance* for pretty Agnes Cargill, younger daughter of a wealthy north-country business man.

Mr. and Mrs. Cargill resisted the idea for as long as they could, and for some time successfully, as Dick Flaherty had nothing to offer beyond a family name that he boasted ranked amongst the best in Ireland—and in point of fact Dick Flaherty, despite his flamboyant vulgarity and race-course standards of life and living, was actually an offshoot of a good old Irish family, though so minor an offshoot, and so far away from the regular line of succession to the family estate, that any idea of inheriting it had never entered his head. And yet, after the fashion of such things, that is actually what happened! The Cargill parents were still trying to persuade their daughter to break off her engagement when three unexpected deaths left the way free for Dick Flaherty to inherit the family estate, Killeen, a handsome property in County Kerry. The Cargills, dismayed, found their strongest arguments against the marriage silenced, and Agnes was led triumphantly to the altar by her swaggering Irish groom.

Apparently little Mrs. Flaherty had not been too anxious to go to live in Ireland, and her parents urged her husband to sell or let the place and get a nice farm somewhere on the outskirts of Oxford so that they could keep in touch with their daughter… but that did not suit Flaherty at all. He was all agog to take his place amongst the nobs, he said—where he'd always belonged by rights, as he'd told them, and bejabers he was right, for all they'd thought him a liar! Was it now that he'd the chance to hold up his head to his own place, run his own horses and drink his own whisky, that he'd stand back? Not he! So off to Killeen they went, and shortly afterwards old Mr. and Mrs. Cargill died, within a short time of each other—their deaths hastened by worry about their daughter, so rumour said—and there was left only Catherine to go to her sister's help when the advent of the baby was announced…

"What sort of a success was Flaherty in Ireland?" I asked.

Miss Cargill pursed her lips and shook her head.

"Directly I got there," she said, "I knew the whole thing was a miserable flop. The 'gentry' wouldn't have Dick Flaherty at any price, and Dick was only staying on out of a mixture of defiance and refusal to admit failure. He was drinking heavily too, and poor Aggie was dreadfully unhappy…"

"Did he ill-treat her?" I asked.

"Oh *no!*" Miss Cargill assured me at once. "On the contrary, he adored her, and one of his special hates against the neighbours was that they 'treated his wife like dirt when she was worth a million of them'. But poor, stupid, well-meaning Dick would never, and *did* never, see that the whole thing was his own fault."

"Had people cold-shouldered him from the very beginning?" I asked.

"Not entirely," said Miss Cargill. "Irish society is pretty hard up, and Aggie had plenty of money, and Killeen was a charming place, and they held open house—heaps of drinks, parties, cards, gambling, and so on—so at first plenty of people rallied round them. And of course everybody was glad the place was to be carried on by a Flaherty, even if he were rather an odd specimen! But Dick was one of those maddening people who *must* boast and swank and try to throw their weight about—you know the type—and he couldn't keep his temper when he got drunk, either, which he did very easily. He was the sort of man who always went about with a chip on his shoulder—I think that having been a bookmaker, he got an inferiority-complex when he found himself amongst a lot of 'landed gentry' and exaggerated this aggressive manner just to hide it." She sighed. "So after a while 'society' decided he was totally impossible and left him severely alone, and then, of course, in a fury he flew off at a tangent, back to his old crowd, the gambling and racing, horsy set, and Killeen was filled with a mob of race-course toughs and their women, and poor Aggie simply hated them all! She used to take refuge with the peasants and cottagers on the estate—they liked her, but they had no time for Dick. The lower classes are quicker than anybody to spot a fake... and for all his boasted Flaherty blood, poor Dick was only a 'fake' gentleman, and the peasantry simply ignored him. Dick spent a long and very expensive year trying to 'get back' on local society for snubbing him, and when he was refused membership of the local golf club, that was the last straw—Aggie told me he stamped up and down the room, hysterical with rage, and swore that he'd be even with 'em! If his countrymen wouldn't have him, he'd bring his own friends over from England, by God, and be independent of 'em! He'd turn the house into an English Club! There was shooting and fishing in plenty on his property. And more than that, if he couldn't play golf on their damn links, he'd lay out a nine-hole course on his own land that should be the envy of those bloody Irish, and *that* would show 'em!

"When I arrived," she went on, "they were more or less isolated. People were coolly polite to them when they had to meet, but nobody would speak to them if they could avoid it—poor Aggie was looking dreadfully white and depressed, and nearly cried with joy at seeing me. Dick's racing friends had grown tired of Killeen after a while and departed, and Aggie had been alone with Dick, surly and morose and drinking harder than he should, for weeks and weeks, with nobody but the servants and the cottagers to speak to. And the baby was due in a few weeks' time…" She heaved a sigh. "Poor Aggie, I felt so sorry for her! But after I'd been there a day or so and we were deep in plans for the coming baby, she cheered up a lot and we frankly didn't bother about Dick, who was engrossed in his plans for the new golf-course. I'd got Hammond and my own car with me, so we were independent…"

"Tell me a little about Hammond?" I said.

"Oh, he was first of all bootboy in our house, before Agnes was married," Miss Cargill said, "and later on he learnt house work and valeted my father, and when my father and mother died I had him taught to drive a car and made him my chauffeur. He's the most faithful fellow—would do anything for either of us. But of course his real devotion is to Agnes… always has been."

I nodded. I remembered the gleam in the good fellow's eyes as he said "the nicest lady God ever put breath into!"

"Go on—I understand," I said. "Tell me—was there anything at all unusual about Patrick when he was born?"

"Not a thing," said Miss Cargill emphatically. "He was a sweet, placid, normal sort of baby—*completely* ordinary! Well, I stayed at Killeen until he was about eight months old, and then I went off with Hammond on a tour of the world, which I'd always wanted to do, and that kept me wandering about for about two years. I didn't hurry. I was alone in the world and had plenty of money, and though I worried about Aggie rather from time to time, I couldn't live with them indefinitely. Man and wife must thrash out their troubles together in the long run...

"Well, at last I came back to London and took a flat, and while it was being decorated and got ready I ran over to Ireland again to see Aggie... Patrick was then getting on for three years old, and a chubby, jolly little fellow, as normal as could be, and the greatest comfort to Aggie, I could see. She was far from being either well or happy. The golf-course—after incredible delays and difficulties—was approaching completion, and the English Club had been launched, but *that* venture had not proved a success. A few of Dick's raffish old-time friends had bothered to come over, plus a sprinkling of Americans and *nouveaux riches*, most of whom treated Aggie like a super-housekeeper; but they evidently hadn't found life at Killeen sufficiently amusing to want to come again, and as a result, embittered by this last failure, Dick was drinking harder than ever and looking shockingly old and changed. His old swaggering gaiety had given place to a queer sort of half-defiant aggressiveness, and he was terribly nervy, used to jump and fly into a fearful rage if anything startled him, if a door slammed, a dish was dropped, even sometimes at the ringing of the telephone bell—though they were so cold-shouldered by their neighbours now that it was very rarely that anybody rang them up! I didn't stay very long, as I felt so indignant with Dick for letting himself go to pieces so and making Agnes unhappy that I'm afraid I let him see it, and we had some unpleasant quarrels... so, as Aggie still loved him and scenes between us made her suffer acutely, I cut my visit short and came back to London.

"I didn't go to Killeen again. I had a nice flat and an interesting life of my own in London, I entertained a good deal and went abroad a good deal, and so things went on for about two years. I heard often from my sister, of course, but I gathered from her letters that there was no change there—things were just dragging on, and Patrick the only creature that made life worth living at all. Then suddenly I got a telegram from her telling me that Dick had been killed in a car-accident, and she was coming to England just as soon as she could get away! I hurried to Holyhead to meet them, and I shall never forget the look I saw flash into my sister's eyes as she came down the gangway towards me from the boat—a sort of fear and protectiveness at once—and when the child stepped ashore, holding his mother's hand, and looked at me, I got a shock like a cold chill! He was just five years old then, and it was the same chubby little fair face, the same blue eyes… but that which looked out from them was… *different*! Different—and uncanny to a degree."

"Whatever happened to cause the change?" I said. "Have you ever tried to find out from your sister how it came about, or anything about it?"

Miss Cargill nodded.

"Of course I have!" she said with a trace of scorn. "At first, poor soul, she denied hotly that there *was* any change… naturally, she would. But when we took this house and settled down and she slipped gradually back into the old familiar rôle of my little sister, she began to relax that fiercely-protective attitude—and at last, after some time, she broke down and admitted that she knew that Patrick was changed. But how and what had changed him she simply had no idea! He was, she said, a perfectly normal little boy—a darling—until he was about four years old. It sounds crazy, but she said it happened almost overnight. She'd been away with Dick in Dublin for a few days to do some shopping—and when she came back, to use her own words, 'something else looked up at me out of my baby's eyes! Something that wasn't… human!'"

I frowned.

"That's a bit vague," I commented. "Can't you give me anything more definite?"

"Lots!" said Miss Cargill crisply. "But of course it wasn't for some time that Aggie began to sort out the details, as it were. Patrick had been a merry, chattering sort of little fellow, friendly with everybody, loving to be petted,

enjoying games and sweets and toys, and adoring animals, especially dogs…
he had a puppy of his own, and they used to play together, Aggie told me, all
day long, and were never separated. But after she and Dick returned from
Dublin the puppy wouldn't go near Patrick again! Used to howl and bolt
when he approached it… and from being happy, gay and friendly to all the
world, the child was either sly or malicious, or in other moods as silent and
morose as a little monk. He disliked being with people—used to dodge even
his parents, instead of running to meet them, and instead of playing with the
village children as he used to do, he took to creeping away alone, to sit playing and murmuring to himself in a corner, or lie staring vaguely at the fire,
or up to the sky. While he simply wouldn't *look* any more at the toys he used
to play with, and squirmed away from Aggie's arms when she picked him up
to kiss him… and if you don't think that, in a child of only about four years
old, is a profound change, well, *I* do!"

"I agree with you," I said sincerely. "I take it that this mysterious change
took place before his father's death?"

"Oh yes, before," said Miss Cargill. "Aggie told me it was six months or so
before Dick's death that it happened. It happened shortly after I left them,
actually—just after the completion of the golf-course at Killeen."

An odd little feeling seized me as she spoke the last words—a feeling as
though one of the leading pieces in the mental jigsaw puzzle with which I
had been struggling ever since I had accepted the Flaherty case had fallen
suddenly into place. The whole picture was still in a hopeless state of chaos,
but a vital central piece was found and in position…

"How did Dick Flaherty take the change in his son?" I asked. "Did he
notice it? And what were the symptoms, so to speak?"

"Aggie won't tell me much about that," said Miss Cargill. "But I gather
Dick *did* notice it after a while—and feared it. Though it sounds crazy, Aggie
swears that after the 'change' came, even at that age, when he was only four,
that child could make one feel the power of his eyes! He was only a tiny boy,
but sometimes he'd be playing with his bricks or soldiers on the mat before

the fire, and he used to look up and stare at his father, sprawling half-drunk in a chair, until Dick used to stare at him back and suddenly rouse himself and shudder and yell at Aggie that she'd given him a devil's brat, and rush like mad out of the room! After the change came Aggie told me she kept the child away from Dick as much as she could… and then, a few months later, Dick died."

"How did Flaherty die?" I asked.

"Now," said Miss Cargill, "that's another mystery—at least, according to the villagers at Killeen! He was a first-class driver and he was trying out a new car, in perfect condition on a lovely day, roads as dry as a bone… he was driving down the lane that swings round a corner of his property, and for some reason the car skidded, ran full tilt into a tree and somersaulted clean over on to the golf-course, pitching Dick out like a slung shot! They found him sprawling on one of the bunkers, stone dead, with his neck broken— and of course the general conclusion was that he'd been drinking and lost his head. Poor Aggie sent me a frantic wire, put a caretaker and her daughter in charge of Killeen House, and came back to England and sanity… or so she thought! So there you have the beginning of the story—for what it's worth."

"It's worth more to me than you probably know," I said. "I've got some gleams of light stirring at last—and I've been fumbling pretty well in the dark, I don't mind telling you, until now! But now I know at least the next step we must take—we must go to Killeen!"

Miss Cargill looked startled.

"Killeen?" she said. "Yes, of course I see the sense of that—go back to where it all started, eh? But I think we'll have a lot of difficulty with Patrick—he won't want to go."

"Then for once his mother must be firm," I said. "Will you tell her I said so? Something in Ireland caused the malady, and in Ireland lies the cure—and if I'm to find the cure, I must discover the cause. Surely she will see that?"

Miss Cargill nodded.

"She shall!" she said firmly. "I'll see to that. We'll go to Ireland, just as soon as we can get packed."

Miss Cargill certainly wasted no time. That very night she opened the attack. We were half-way through dinner, and Patrick with us for once—which was probably one of the reasons she seized the opportunity—when she said with an admirable appearance of casualness:

"How long is it since you last went over to Killeen, Aggie?"

Mrs. Flaherty's mouth and eyes opened in surprise—and she paused in her eating to stare at her sister. I saw, too, the child Patrick stop eating and turn his eyes upon his aunt—eyes lowered, cautious, but with a gleam in them that might mean anger—or alarm.

"I—why, I've only been once since Dick died. That's about four years ago when you had your accident. Don't you remember, there was all that bother about getting my consent to driving a new road across a corner of the property? Why?"

"Then," said Miss Cargill, "I think it's about time you went again! We've all been very remiss over things out there, I think—we should have gone there more often. No use leaving the care of a valuable estate to an agent who only goes there twice a year, and an old caretaker and her daughter."

Mrs. Flaherty was white to the ears and staring at her sister, but Miss Cargill went smoothly on.

"And there's another thing! After all, Aggie, Killeen is Patrick's inheritance. He is the last of the Flahertys, so it is only right that he should get to see something of his own country and his own people, let alone the property that will be his."

There was a small sound like a snarl from the boy. He had laid down his knife and fork and was shivering violently. The eyes he turned upon his aunt were wide and alive with venom.

"I…" he whispered, "I won't go! You can't make me, I won't go…"

Mrs. Flaherty broke in with a nervous, almost hysterical laugh.

"Oh, you must be joking, Cathie! You know how Pat hates Ireland."

"It's odd that he should do that," I said, watching the boy as I spoke. "After all, he *is* Irish, isn't he? Flaherty couldn't be anything but an Irish name…"

Patrick snarled again—there is no other way to describe the way in which he drew his breath between his teeth and stared at me.

"My name!" he said, and his voice suddenly sounded quite different, much older and more resonant, so that we all started. "What rot is this about my name? It's Irish—but it's not Flaherty. It's… it's…"

He paused and seemed to gag and stifle, as though trying to finish his speech, then with a sharp jerk he sprang to his feet and darted out of the room. We sat transfixed, staring at each other, then Miss Cargill pulled herself together and addressed the thunderstruck Hammond.

"We'll go on with dinner, I think," she said steadily. "And afterwards, Aggie, we will discuss how soon we can get to Ireland…"

I left the ladies together for a while after dinner, and when ultimately I joined them I noticed that Mrs. Flaherty's eyes were red-rimmed; she excused herself on my entrance and went up to her room, and Miss Cargill and I went out to take our coffee on the verandah, for now June had passed into July and the nights were warm and lovely, so that one spent as much time as one could sitting out of doors revelling in the gorgeous display of coolness in the sunset and enjoying the delicious country air.

Patrick had not appeared since his hurried exit from the dining-room, but still he might be lurking near—one never knew—so we confined our conversation to ordinary topics, books, politics, the theatre and so on. I always found Miss Cargill a stimulating and interesting companion, and was thoroughly enjoying myself when Patrick appeared round the corner of the house, silent as a shadow, sat himself down upon the top step, with his back against one of the wooden posts that supported the awning overhead, and appeared to sink into a sort of reverie, hunched upon the step, hands in pockets, his profile towards us, staring towards where the sunset made a flaming background for a slender little moon.

I glanced at the boy, and then at my companion—she answered my glance with a nod, drew the handsome black lace scarf she wore closer about her and rose to her feet.

"I'm going to take a stroll down to the lake before I go to bed," she said aloud. "Good night, Mr. Pennoyer—and good night, Patrick. By the time I come back you ought to be in bed."

The boy vouchsafed no answer, but sat hunched and still as before, as the lady passed down the steps beside him and moved away, with her slightly halting walk, down the long green slope of the lawn.

A silence fell, broken only by the faint whirring of the bats as they darted in and out of the clustering roses and jasmine that climbed up the thick wooden posts of the verandah and hung from the eaves and balconies above like heavy scented pelmets.

I lay back meditating and listening to the eerie sound of their flight, every now and then glancing at the motionless figure of the mysterious little boy who was my charge. Should I speak to him or not?

I determined to make an effort at any rate.

"Patrick," I called. "Come over and talk to me now that your aunt's left me all alone."

He turned his head and looked at me, and in the ruddy-gold light of the sunset I saw a queer derisive smile cross his face.

"I like being alone," he said. "Don't you like being alone, Mr. Pennoyer?"

"Of course I do, at times," I said. "But at the moment I'd like to talk to you."

He rose reluctantly, came over to me and stood with his hands in his pockets, leaning against the arm of the chair his aunt had occupied as I began to talk to him, exerting all the charm and sweet reasonableness I possessed. I talked to him about our coming visit to Ireland... I knew it was best to take the bull by the horns and treat the whole thing as ordinarily as possible. I said how surprising it was that he had not shown more interest in the land of his birth; pointed out that as he would be a land-owner on quite a considerable scale, this visit to his property, from his own point of view, as well as his mother's, was really long overdue, and I was going on generalizing about what a lovely country I knew it was and how much personally I was looking forward to visiting it, when he surprised me by laughing, a low, amused little laugh.

"You think you're awfully clever, don't you, Mr. Pennoyer?" was his comment.

"I don't know about that," I said with as much nonchalance as I could summon, "but I know that I know a great deal more than you know, young man!"

He laughed again.

"You don't know *what* I know!" he said, and I was silent, for it was true. He went on reflectively.

"And I know you know that I *do*—what you call 'show interest'—in Ireland. You saw my books! You went into my room the other night and looked through them."

I was silent from sheer astonishment as he went on, a faint flavour of contempt in his light boyish voice, "Do you think I couldn't *feel* you'd handled them, the very next time I took them out?"

I had nothing to say—I was too amazed to find that this uncanny eleven-year-old could sense an alien touch upon his personal possessions as instantly as I, with my highly-trained powers, could do. Truly the mystery of this boy waxed deeper and deeper the more I delved into it! I answered as normally as I could: "Yes, I examined some of your things, Patrick—not out of curiosity, but because I want to help you."

He shrugged his shoulders and frowned.

"Help… I don't know what you mean. *I* don't want any help! I am quite happy." He glanced round him, and that sinister smile once again crossed his open, childish face. "You've no idea what fun I have—what fun it is to pull strings and set people against each other and make them do what they don't want to do! It is going to be *much* greater fun when I grow up—when I'm a man. I'm only a little boy now, but you wait!" The evil of his grin grew more intense. "I might lose it—that funny power I've got… if I went to Ireland, especially if I went with you. I'll tell you a secret. I've *always* been frightened of going back to Ireland… of anything to do with Ireland… because of that. Because there's *something* there I don't understand… something that calls me, and that I want to go back to, and yet at the same time I don't! I don't know how or why, but I've got a feeling… a feeling that if I went back to Ireland and met that *something*, I might *lose* myself, though that sounds silly, doesn't it?" He slanted an uncanny glance at me. "You'd be glad if I were to lose myself… wouldn't you, Mr. Pennoyer?"

I looked straight at him.

"I could tell you that better if I knew just who '*you*' were, Patrick," I said deliberately. "I don't know… yet. But you are quite right in suspecting that I suggested this move to Ireland because out there I hope to find out just who you are!" I fixed his shifty gaze imperiously. "And why you are here…"

He moved restlessly, fretfully, a step or two along the verandah. Already his quicksilver attention was away…

"I can't think why you don't leave me alone, all of you," he muttered. "And specially I can't think why *you* came? You aren't like an ordinary tutor! I've done nothing to you… *yet*." He giggled, and the sound, while childish enough, had an unpleasant note in it. "But I *could*, you know… I could! When people really make me angry with them… Aunt Cathie, for instance…"

He checked himself suddenly and there was a long pause, while the bats, lulled into security by the momentary silence, swung out again in their aery dance against the stars. Suddenly the boy turned, held out both arms and uttered a low, queer call beneath his breath—and, lo, as though moved by one common impulse, the bats whirled aloft, and descending like a dark cloud, settled upon his outflung arms as pigeons settle upon the hands of those who feed them! He looked down at me and laughed a little arrogant laugh.

"You think I'm lonely—but these, and lots of others, they are my friends! I can do what I want with them—they obey my words, they do what I tell them. I..."

He stopped abruptly and drew his hands into his breast, the bats still clinging, like a grotesque black patterning, to the sleeves and shoulders of his blue linen shirt, and walked down the steps to the lawn below. There he stood for a few minutes with bent head, seeming to whisper and talk to the clustering creatures—then suddenly, flinging both arms wide, he released them. Like a cloud of black gnats, sharply silhouetted against the fading reds and ambers and coral-pink of the sky, they swept off and away down the lawn in the direction of the distant trees—and Patrick, whistling, turned and walked off round the corner of the house without another glance in my direction.

I sat brooding in silence for a moment, staring before me—then suddenly one of those impulses that, thank heaven, I had by that time learnt to obey without analysing them, seized me. Rising, I ran down the verandah steps and down the lawn after Miss Cargill, through the little plantation of flowering trees that in the lowering dusk made a starry patterning, with their foam of pale blossoms, against the belt of darkness that was the strip of woodland on the far side of the fence, jumped the fence, and plunged into the green-scented dusk beneath the trees. The wood, and the little spring-fed lake that it concealed, was a favourite haunt of the ladies in hot weather, and a well-worn footpath led from the garden, winding between the close-growing tree-trunks to the edge of the water on the far side of the copse. Fortunately I had been there several times with the two sisters so knew my way, though it was very dark in the shadow of the trees. I hurried along, calling urgently as I ran, "Miss Cargill, Miss Cargill!"—but there was no reply, and when I came to the verge of the lake, at first I saw no sign of the lady I sought.

The lake lay glimmering quietly in the moonlight, a small oval-shaped sheet of water, set in a heavy frame of trees. Here and there, scattered water-lilies, floating on their palette-shaped leaves, held up porcelain-white cups to the sunset, and at the further end of the lake, at the foot of the trees, a mass of sturdy bulrushes thrust their tall, brown-velvet spearheads upwards… and it was there, after a few minutes' frantic search, that I found Miss Cargill, just in time! She had fainted and fallen face downwards into the water amongst the bulrushes, and I had some difficulty, indeed, in dragging her out without falling in myself—but within a few minutes she lay gasping and dripping on the bank, white, but safe and smiling, and heartily I thanked the impulse that had once again guided me rightly. Her story, when she recovered sufficiently to tell it to me, turned me cold, though fortunately she did not guess its real inwardness, and needless to say, I did not tell her…

It appeared that she had been walking idly along the steep bank near the bulrushes, watching the lovely effect of the sunset colours reflected on the lily-patterned water, when she had been conscious of a group of bats, flitting, in their aery, inconsequential dance, in and out of the tree-trunks beside her. She had paused to watch them, loving the delicate swiftness and grace of their movement, when suddenly they "attacked" her—that was the expression she used! Flew into her face, into her hair, beating their tiny wings fiercely, blinding her, terrifying her, and all the time uttering their pencil-shrill whistling squeaks, like miniature furies, and the poor woman, startled and terrified beyond words, had stepped back, slipped and fallen in amongst the rushes in the deepest part of the pool…

I had no difficulty in guessing what instructions Patrick Flaherty had given to his—friends!

Indeed it was time—and more than time—that the nettle of this mystery was grasped…

Patrick was so startled at the sight of his aunt in her usual place at break-fast—I admit to enjoying the sight of his pop-eyes and open mouth as he entered the breakfast-room!—that he made no further demur about going to Ireland, and within a week we were off.

We took Hammond and the car over with us, as apparently Killeen village and Killeen House were miles from any station; and ultimately, after a long trek by car through glorious green country over roads anything but glorious, we arrived at the gates of a large estate, and turned into a wide drive that ran, gently rising upwards all the time, through a wide and well-wooded stretch of parkland.

The place had obviously been allowed to run badly to seed, for the gravel of the drive was deeply rutted and moss-grown, and the grass and undergrowth stood knee-high about the roots of magnificent old trees. Shrubs and bushes were all grown wild, and the fences in shocking disrepair, but it was a fine place enough, and when we came at last in sight of a handsome white house standing on the crest of the slope we had been climbing, I gave an exclamation of appreciation that drew a faint smile from Mrs. Flaherty. At the last bend of the drive we ran through a water-splash caused by a briskly-bubbling stream that crossed the gravel and ran off down through the park, and on reaching the front door it was opened to us by a bent old woman with a brown and wrinkled face, wearing a grey stuff dress and a large white apron. Behind her a young woman—a pale-faced, rather furtive-looking creature with black hair, wearing a blue print dress—came out to help Hammond remove the luggage from the car. I heard Mrs. Flaherty address the old woman as "Biddy O'Halloran" and the girl as "Kathleen" as she shook hands with them, and both returned her greeting with a sort of half-bob.

But I noticed—for by now there was nothing connected with Patrick Flaherty that escaped me—that neither of them approached Patrick, though they both dipped the same half-curtsy from a discreet distance, nor did he take any notice of them. A fine Irish wolf-hound came bounding out of the house and fawned affectionately upon the sisters, but he slunk away from Patrick with a faint growl, and I remembered the stories I had been told of the dislike dogs had for him.

He took no heed of dog or servants, nor did he follow his aunt and mother into the house, but turning away, walked a few yards along the wide sweep of the drive that made an arc before the entrance and stood staring at the expanse of lovely country, green and lushly beautiful as only Irish country can be, that lay before him. His brow was creased with an odd frown, half-fretful, half-puzzled—he gave the impression of somebody trying in vain to recall a thing once well known, now forgotten, and leaving Hammond and the maid to cope with the boxes, I joined him where he stood, hands in pockets, his eyes roving the scene before him.

I was immensely curious to see his reactions to his birthplace, but for some moments he said nothing, merely stood silently staring at the rich green lands, patched here and there with groups of trees, that spread before us, descending gradually to a wide sweep of rough grassy country beyond the grounds proper, and further down still to a dark stretch of peat jewelled with the glimmer of water-pools, the bog that filled the valley.

The stream that had crossed the drive meandered away down the hillside below us, a bright gleaming ribbon of water that broke here and there into a series of shallow cascades, to lose itself at last in the distant bog—and here and there, in the belt of rough country that lay between the grounds of Killeen House and the valley below, I noticed certain curious patches of vividly-green turf that looked oddly artificial. I wondered what they were, when suddenly Miss Cargill's story flashed into my mind. Of course! I was looking, I felt sure, at the last surviving remnants of the nine-hole course that poor Dick Flaherty had tried to build. Those were the greens, still standing out sharply against the rough hill-and-meadowland in which they had been set…

I pointed.

"Those must be the remains of the golf-course your father made," I said. Patrick turned and looked at me. His face was blank.

"My father?" he queried. "Why should my father build a golf-course? How idiotic…"

"But of course he did," I said. "Have you forgotten? He laid out a nine-hole course here—there are the greens. They're some way off, but you can see them—or some of them, at least—quite well."

Patrick was silent a moment. I glanced down at him and saw that he was laughing. A nasty, silent little laugh that frankly puzzled me… but directly he saw me looking at him the smile vanished on the instant, and he gave a polite little nod.

"Oh! Yes—I see. I had forgotten."

But the conventional rejoinder was quite unconvincing, and vexed, I left the young man to his own devices and went upstairs to unpack my things. My bedroom was a pleasant, roomy chamber overlooking the park, furnished in an old-fashioned but comfortable style, with a large brass bedstead, one or two unmatched chairs, a coloured Turkish rug laid upon a polished floor, and a blue and white cotton quilt to match the blue and white china set on the old-fashioned marble-topped wash-stand. Later I found that the whole house—that is, the part of it that we were using, as several of the larger rooms were shut up—was furnished in a similar patchwork fashion. Mrs. Flaherty had taken all the really good pieces of furniture with her when she came to live in England, and all that was left was a regular *omnium gatherum* of oddments!

I found it difficult to get unpacked, as I kept wandering to the window to stare at the magnificent view outside—wild and remote, and with a loveliness different from anything I had ever seen before. One might easily imagine strange things and strange forces moving silently about this aloof, almost uncannily beautiful spot! Nothing in it of the comfortable homely "prettiness" of the English countryside. One sensed that here one trod on alien land—a ground untouched, aloof, estranged from human life and laws. The distant purple mountains, the rolling hills with their dour dark masses of forest, the parklands that had never known plough or scythe, the wide slope of virgin land on which the links had been made, the far-off stretch of black peat, with pools of gleaming bog-waters, like a scattered handful of crystals, jade and onyx, that sprawled along the folds of the valley… over all these brooded an air of power not of this world.

The entrance of Hammond with an offer to finish my unpacking for me interrupted my thoughts, and I left him to his work. Going down, I met Miss

Cargill in the hall with a message from Mrs. Flaherty to say that she was terribly tired and was going to bed, so we were left to explore the place together. Miss Cargill showed me round with a curious air of mingled pride and dislike—much as she admired the place, its associations had obviously spoilt it for her—but I found it a truly charming old house. There was a beautiful large drawing-room, though this was among those rooms shut up, and we were using a little morning-room instead; there was a music-room—also closed—and a small study, allotted to Patrick and to me for a schoolroom; and there was a library, which was, like the drawing-room and the music-room, shrouded in dust-sheets—but this I insisted upon opening, on the pretext that amongst the books I might find some useful for Patrick's study.

Actually I was in hopes that amongst the books that had been inherited by Dick Flaherty along with Killeen House, I might find something that might help me in my task of solving the riddle of his strange little son; and after several hours of patient rummaging amongst the dusty shelves, I found a group of books on Irish legends, traditions, customs and the like that looked promising, which I carried off at once to study at my leisure.

The first few days after our arrival passed without incident. Patrick was very quiet—indeed, we saw little of him. He spent his time out of doors, often taking a pocketful of biscuits and an apple for his lunch and staying away the entire day. I noticed that he was curiously restless in the house; prowling from one window to another, unable to settle to anything for long at a time, so I deliberately left the question of lessons on one side and sat back studying him, biding my time and continuing avidly to read up all I could about the folk-lore and history of Ireland—and especially about Killeen, the village, the house, the district. It was a part of Ireland which (Miss Cargill informed me) was peculiarly rich in old beliefs... superstitions as she called them, and I did not contradict her. Though is not the belief of one generation the superstition of another?

Hereabout, she said—unless things had greatly changed since she had stayed there with her sister—the peasants still believed firmly in the evil eye, in spells and runes and enchantments, in witches and wizards, leprechauns and the like! It was even said (she added reflectively) by some of the peasants that Dick Flaherty had done something to offend the fairies of the district, and that this was the reason for his death, and for the strange shadow that had fallen on his child. She suddenly produced this story one night after dinner when her sister and Patrick had both gone to bed, and startled, I sat upright, staring reproachfully at her.

"But why in the world," I said, "didn't you tell me that before?"

"Well, it was no more than a story circulated amongst the servants, and to tell the truth I'd entirely forgotten it till this moment," said Miss Cargill. "Probably because we didn't take it seriously—of course not! If we had we'd never have had a moment's peace of mind—the maids were for ever full of something of the sort. Spooks and grave-lights, and warnings by white birds, and banshees, and I don't know what-all. I don't think it would have occurred to me to mention it, if I *had* remembered… it sounds such nonsense!"

"But you remember I said the most irrelevant and unlikely bits of information might still be useful to me!" I said—a little sourly, I admit. "Can you remember precisely *what* was said? If it seemed nonsense to you, it may not seem so to me, you know."

Miss Cargill looked rueful.

"You'd better ask Aggie," she confessed. "She told me. As far as I remember it was some servants she overheard saying something to the effect that Dick had been 'warned', but he *would* do it, and now he'd have to take the consequences."

"'Do' it? What was he being specially insistent upon doing just then?"

"Oh," said Miss Cargill. "They must have meant that crazy laying-out of the golf-course. Everybody was talking about it, and, of course, it *was* an insane thing to do, to try and make even a miniature course on this property—all slopes and trees and bogland! It cost the earth, and everybody knew nobody would ever play on it but Dick himself and maybe one or two of his boozing friends. Aggie did her best to stop him—after all, it was her money he was spending!—but he'd got pig-headed about it, and there was no stopping him…"

She stopped suddenly and looked at me with startled eyes, and my eyes were round as well. I remembered the "nudge" I had felt when I had heard that the "change" in Patrick had taken place *about the time when the golf-course was completed.*

"My goodness, I believe we're on to something? The golf-course—I believe it all hinges on that," I said.

And the next day I tackled Mrs. Flaherty to see if she could elaborate her sister's story.

She was startled, but much excited and interested. Though she confessed that in the passage of time she had forgotten the exact wording of the comments, she remembered hearing on two or three occasions that "the master'd be wise to let things alone", that he "shouldn't go diggin' up and disturbing things". He had been "warned" and if he didn't heed he must "take the consequences"… and it was odd, but true, that the project of the new golf-course had been amazingly unpopular with everybody around Killeen.

For some reason, from the very beginning there had been opposition from all classes of society. Deliberate and obstinate opposition, guarded from the "County", open and fierce from the villagers—though precisely why, neither Mrs. Flaherty nor her husband had been able to make out. There seemed no solid reason why a private gentleman should not, if he chose, lay out a small nine-hole golf-course on his own property! But reason or no, discouragement, obstruction, disapproval, delay surrounded Dick Flaherty from the moment he first mooted his plan—and naturally, in a man of his type, this merely served to intensify his determination. So in the end, in spite of every difficulty, the course was made, opened and seemed launched, like the English Club that Flaherty opened at his house at the same time, on a tide of success. But after a brief initial flare-up of interest, it failed. Not even the temptation of playing on a private golf-course could attract people, it seemed, to Killeen in sufficient numbers to make it a success.

Six months afterwards the strange curse seized upon little Patrick Flaherty, and before this disaster the failure of Dick Flaherty's cherished project faded into insignificance. Alarmed and bewildered at the tragedy that had stricken his little son, Dick threw all else aside and spent his time and money sending wildly for one doctor after another—only to receive the same puzzled answer from them all.

There was nothing whatever wrong with the child, they said. He was altered in manner, tastes, in every way from what he used to be? Well, well, some children did grow up, as it were, very suddenly! That was nothing to worry about! His disposition changed? With all due respect to a mother's partiality, they would need stronger proof than just Mrs. Flaherty's assertion before accepting that! The odds were that a side of the little boy's nature that had hitherto been dormant was asserting itself, that was all. And as regards the "look in the eyes" upon which Mrs. Flaherty laid such stress, well, perhaps sometimes there *was* a certain fixed look in the eyes, a gleam, a look of age perhaps… but it was rank nonsense to talk about "powers of evil"! Pooh, pooh, that was ridiculous! Young children *did* show sometimes a rather curious flash of age in their expression—there was nothing in that. Physically the boy was in splendid health. Mr. and Mrs. Flaherty were disquieting themselves unnecessarily…

So the doctors, in a dismal procession, pocketed their guineas and went their ways, and shortly afterwards poor blundering, boastful Dick Flaherty crashed to his tragic death, and his widow and child, leaving Killeen House to the caretaker and the cobwebs, returned to England, Miss Cargill and the Manor House.

I listened carefully, made various notes as the story unfolded itself, and my heart was thumping with excitement, for now at last I felt I had got hold of a thread that might lead me to the heart of the mystery! I thanked Mrs. Flaherty and went off to bed, with my head full of plans and a heart considerably fuller of hope than before.

*

The next day, taking a certain piece of paper that I had cherished for some time in my pocket, I started off on an exploration of the derelict golf-course. It was a lovely morning, fresh and cool, with tiny clouds tearing over the high blue skies like tufts of thistledown blown before the wind, and with a sparkle in the air like wine. I felt inclined to whistle, partly through sheer happiness at such a glorious day, and partly out of the curious heady sense of excitement that always possesses me when I begin to scent a possible solution of one of my problems—I suppose a doctor of bodies feels much the same when he thinks he has diagnosed, and hopes to cure, a difficult case!

I went straight down through the wild parkland that sloped downwards from the house towards the valley, and it was fairly easy going as far as the sunken fence that marked the dividing line between the actual grounds of Killeen House and the derelict golf-course below it. Here the country was completely wild and unkempt, and but for occasional unexpected patches of finer turf, greener and more level than the rest, that I had seen from the house, patches that betrayed where once a green or a tee had been placed, one would have sworn the land was virginal, untouched.

For the best part of two hours I tramped this stretch of ground, trying to trace the main outline of the almost-obliterated links—and I rarely had a rougher journey! I stumbled over tree-roots and tussocks of rough grass, got held up by fierce thickets of brambles and thorn, twice lost my footing and slid into hidden rabbit-holes or ditches, stepped on an ants' nest and got well nipped before I could brush the brutes off, fell on my face amongst a patch of nettles, waded—or again fell—into unexpected marshy patches, as well as into the stream (which I was forced to cross two or three times), got caught on rusty lengths of barbed wire, and generally enjoyed myself at the expense of a decent tweed suit and my temper! I had more than a suspicion that I was being deliberately hindered in my progress by some force or forces that did not wish me to find out what I was determined to find out—but I struggled on.

Hole by hole, I managed to trace out Dick Flaherty's pitiful little golf-course, and marvelled at the patience and stubborn determination of the man who insisted on trying to make such a thing against all the opposition—human, and, I was sure, inhuman also—that had been marshalled against him! It was only a small course, but had been cleverly planned to make the most of every natural hazard. Every curve and dip and angle of the difficult ground had been utilized, and though nature had done its best to obliterate poor Dick Flaherty's efforts, one could still see where they had been made. Trees had been cut down where they interfered with a clean drive, great banks or bunkers created just where they were necessary, flat spaces of ground cleared for greens… and even as the last thought crossed my mind I felt again that sudden odd little "click" in my mind that meant something had fallen into place—another vitally necessary bit of the jigsaw puzzle! The pattern, though it was still confused, was slowly becoming clearer. Why did those words ring so persistently in my brain "ground cleared"? But cleared of what? What had been dug up, or pulled down or cleared away to make those greens? Somehow I knew now that this phrase "ground cleared" had a vital connection with the secret of Patrick Flaherty.

I was sweating with excitement by now, and almost running, following the mental "scent" that always leads me in these times as the scent leads a bloodhound on the trail. I let myself go and followed my instinct blindly, going downwards towards the valley, till at last I found myself standing on the bank of the little stream, facing a scene oddly familiar.

Behind me sprawled an immense straggling thicket of prickly bush, mainly thorn and brambles. On the far side of the stream lay a cleared space of ground—evidently one of the old greens, probably the last—situated just under the curve of a high escarpment of ground that reared up sharply, like a curling wave, behind it. And the top of the wave, high above the green, was crowned with two tall trees, an oak and an ash.

The stream was about three feet wide here, and running rapidly downhill in a series of shallow cascades towards the bog that stretched far below, its gleaming pools, green rushes and snowy tufts of wild bog-cotton shining against the black patches of peat; and I reflected, as I stood staring at the green, how cleverly planned it was. It would have taken a pretty good golfer to judge his approach-shot over the stream so that it did not hit the steep face of the wall of earth on the far side of the green and bounce back into the water! But that was not important. What *was* important was that—I recognized the place! It was a little altered, but still undoubtedly the place I had seen once before—in a certain drawing!

I put my hand in my pocket and pulled out the bit of paper I had been carrying. It was a sheet of scribbled drawings torn from the sketch-book I had found in Patrick's room. I had known those drawings would ultimately lead me somewhere—and I had been right! It was the sheet on which were the three drawings that had so arrested my attention—the flying figures with the Gaelic phrase beneath them, "*Nai aluinn an sluagh Sidhe*"*... the face with the foxy, unpleasant eyes, and a small landscape sketch. A sketch of the piece of ground at which I was now looking.

Yes, it was unmistakable! There was the sharply-rising escarpment, curling forward over the top like a breaking wave, the twin trees that crowned it, and in the foreground the fast-running stream falling in shallow cascades. But below the escarpment, where lay the present green... ah, there was the difference! In the drawing there was shown a mass of thorny bushes, almost filling the space between the curling bank and the stream, where now there stretched a flat piece of ground covered with rough grass. Evidently the thorny thicket against which I was standing had originally stretched right across the stream—probably forming a tangled arch of green over the water—but on the further side the bushes had been grubbed up one and all, in order to clear the ground for the final green. An ideal green, challenging the best golfer to rise in his highest efforts—but what if the making of it had challenged Something or Somebody else, who had met the challenge in his

---

* "How beautiful are the Shee."

own way, and won? I re-read that line in Gaelic that was written below the boy's sketch of the scene, and it seemed to read now with a faintly sinister emphasis… *"Dail-sheomra ruit Sidhe."**

I put the slip of paper in my pocket, splashed through the stream—I was so wet already that it made little difference—and walked around the green, surveying it inch by inch. Here and there, growing along the bank of the stream or clinging determinedly along the base of the earthwall on the further side, I found a few stunted remnants of the bushes that had once covered the clearing, and examined them. Yes! They were thorn-bushes, as I had suspected—or rather, they had once been thorn-bushes. And the two trees that soared into the blue above the escarpment were—an Oak and an Ash! The Fairy Trinity—my training and my instinct alike, aided by a few lucky pointers, had led me to the heart of the tragedy. It lay here, on this uncanny patch of ground "cleared" by a blundering fool who did not know how bitterly he was offending Those who owned it—and had owned it from time immemorial. I knew now pretty certainly what had happened, and how poor, ignorant, boastful Dick Flaherty had offended against a Folk whose very existence he would have derided. Now I only wanted a few more details, and I thought I knew where to get those… As quickly as I could I made my way back to the house, lunch, and an urgent interview with Miss Cargill.

I wanted to find out whether it was possible to interview the woman who had nursed Patrick when he was a baby—and I was lucky. Miss Cargill told me that Kathleen, the pale dark young woman who had appeared with her mother, the old caretaker, to greet us on our arrival at Killeen House, had been Patrick's nurse—and sent for her at once to come to the library.

She entered, looking, as usual, pale and rather sullen, but when she saw us both waiting, a look of half fear, half suspicion, came into her eyes, and

* "The Council Room of the Shee."

she hesitated on the threshold, seeing no chance of escape, then came slowly forward.

I felt it was no time to beat about the bush, so I spoke quite frankly. "Kathleen, I want to have a little talk to you about Master Patrick."

She whitened and looked away, evidently frightened. After a moment she spoke guardedly.

"I…" She swallowed sharply. "It's not talkin' about Master Patrick I'd want to be, sor."

Her soft brogue was very appealing, her eyes large and scared as a captured bird's, but there was no time to be soft-hearted.

"I'm afraid I shall *have* to ask you a few questions, though you needn't be frightened," I said. "But you know as well as we do that Master Patrick… well, he isn't… *himself.*"

I chose the words deliberately, and I saw her blench and shiver like a frightened horse. She glanced behind her and, seeing Miss Cargill standing near the door, hesitated—then, abandoning the idea of a hasty flight, took refuge in silence. Her eyes were fixed on the ground as I went quietly on— there would be nothing gained, I knew, by trying to frighten the girl. Our one hope was to "gentle" her as one gentles a frightened horse—to appeal to the soft heart that lies so close to the surface in the Irish race.

"Don't think that anybody is going to be angry with you, or reproach you, or anything like that," I said. "I am here to try and cure Master Patrick—to bring him back to himself, shall we say…"

She threw me a quick, scared glance.

"Ye won't do that, sor," she muttered. "Them that… them that took him knows how to hold fast."

My heart was beginning to thump with excitement. I was on the right track—I knew it, at last! If I could only persuade the girl to tell us all she knew… Miss Cargill spoke, and her voice held an appealing note, surprising from one of usually rather bluntly-direct speech.

"Kathleen, help us—*do* help us, if you can? You know what a darling baby Master Patrick was—once. You know how much you loved him! You know how terrible it was when he changed—when he became like this. Don't you want to help us to find a cure, if there *is* one? Kathleen, *please*, for the sake of the little baby you used to love, tell us all you know."

The girl's face, which had been working oddly as the older woman spoke, suddenly broke into the piteous grimace of tears, and she hid her face in her hands.

"Och, I'll tell, I'll tell!" she sobbed. "And mebbe it'll bring the peace to me sowl at last that it hasn't known for years an' years. I'll tell—and be able to face the praste again widout blushin' at the black shame of the thing I've been hidin' all these years..."

She broke down and wept violently, and it took Miss Cargill several minutes to soothe her into a condition sufficiently tranquil to recount the story that she obviously had to tell us. And a sad story and a mysterious one it was...

It appeared that a few months after the completion of the golf-course Dick Flaherty had to go to Dublin on business connected with the estate, and his wife went with him, to do some necessary shopping for herself and her baby boy. She had been reluctant to leave Patrick, but Dick had pointed out that a very young child would be a great nuisance in an hotel; moreover, that they would both get through their business more quickly if they were not hampered; and finally, that to take him with them would imply lack of trust in Kathleen and her mother—then the cook-housekeeper—which would greatly upset them. So, fortified by her husband's assurances, Mrs. Flaherty departed with her spouse to Dublin...

But the day after they left Mrs. O'Halloran fell ill with an attack of rheumatism, and the entire charge of the child devolved upon Kathleen, who adored little Patrick and fully intended to carry out her charge with faithfulness. But youth and heedlessness, and that ancient mantrap, love, combined to thwart her good intentions...

She was in the habit of taking Patrick out for a short walk about five o'clock in the afternoon, for a final breath of air before his supper and bed. And on leaving the house, was tempted, by seeing a red-capped figure moving about on the bog down in the valley, to go down across the golf-course towards it—though actually she had been forbidden by her mother even to set foot on the course, as apart from its being hard walking for a child, it was considered "dangerous ground" at all times, and doubly dangerous now, since the venturesome Englishman had aroused the enmity of Those whose exclusive property it had been as long as local memory could recollect! But the red cap in the valley below happened to be on the head of tall Danny Rea, cutting peats for market on the bog; he was the handsomest lad in the village and the girls all mad for him, and the chance of meeting him alone was more than Kathleen, ardent, romantic and only nineteen, could bear to lose.

So down the slope of the parklands and across the golf-course she went, carrying little Patrick pick-a-back when the ground became too rough for his little legs to struggle along, and hailed her Danny—and he, only too willing to leave work for an hour's dalliance with a pretty girl, left his peats and his spade, and together they wandered away, leaving the little boy, weary with his long walk, sleeping on the newly-cleared green, wrapped in Kathleen's coat, in the shadow of the curving escarpment.

"I tied me coat-belt round him and it to a root, dear knows," sobbed Kathleen, "so that he shouldn't roll loose in his sleep and into the water, the darlint, nor go wandering away if he woke up! I thought he'd be as safe as if he was tied up in his play-pen and I thought it was only a little while I'd be away, kissing that Danny—bad cess to him, for it was no more to him than a good meal, and to me it was everything, because I'd gone wi' no man till then—in the tumbledown old ancient hut that was down there on the edge of the bog. Glory be to God, I was a silly girl lost in love, and everything went clean out o' my head so that I forgot the time and my duty and everything except that Danny, the spalpeen, and his wicked kisses… and when I came out at last it was dark, and the stars laughing down at me, and I broke away from Danny, and with my heart in my mouth wint running off up the hill to the bushes under the cliff where I'd left my baby! And when I saw him lying, still in the same place, I drew me breath free, and when I stooped over him, and he still seemed sleeping, I thanked the saints and lifted him into my arms, and made up the hill as quick as I could to the house, where I found my mother waiting for me half-mad, the creature, pacing up and down! She took one look at the baby and gave a cry like a soul in torment, for it opened its eyes and looked at her… and then, Mother of Mercies, it looked at me…" She shivered and closed her eyes a moment. "And I looked at the clock and saw it was after twelve o'clock and I knew I'd left the blessed child out there in Their power while I dallied with Danny, God help me, hours and hours without realizing it… and while I was away, They had taken their chance!"

"What do you mean?" demanded Miss Cargill.

Kathleen looked at her and then at me.

"Mother of God!" she whispered. "Is't possible ye don't know, mam, even now?"

I nodded.

"I know, Kathleen. I'll explain to Miss Cargill. I know now, thanks to you, what to do. You have more than atoned for your fault, because you have told me what I needed to make sure my diagnosis is right. So go, and don't worry about it any more. I think and believe—all will be well!"

As the door closed behind her, Miss Cargill looked at me in blank bewilderment.

"Tell me," she demanded. "You mean you really know what happened while she left the child?"

"I do," I said. "I've suspected it, to be honest, for some time—I guessed it shortly after I came here. But I wanted confirmation, and details of how it all happened. Patrick is a changeling, Miss Cargill."

Her face whitened.

"A *changeling*!" she breathed. "But… *do* such things happen? I've read about them when I was a child, as one reads about magic wands and fairy rings and spells and enchanted castles, and all the rest. But to think that it could really happen…"

"If we didn't pooh-pooh what we learn as children in the form of fable and fairy-tale we should be a great deal wiser," I said brusquely. "And I could tell you a lot about all the things you mention that would change your views about their being merely fairy 'tales'! But that can keep. Here in your hands is the solid proof that a changeling is, or can be, a horrible reality! Patrick is not Patrick at all, but a fairy child—and from some none too kind and pleasant branch of the fairy family too, from the way he behaves! Obviously Dick Flaherty incurred the wrath of some of the Folk by making this golf-course on what they regarded as ground peculiarly their own… If I had the chance of digging up the ancient history connected with Killeen House and the hill it stands on, I've no doubt I should find that it had been known as the 'Fairy Hill', or something of the sort, for untold ages past!"

"It *was*," said Miss Cargill, and I hurried on.

"And actually it seems that that particular plot of ground that he cleared, for the last green, was a special meeting-place of the Folk."

"I know," said Miss Cargill unexpectedly, "that several of the greens had names—the last green was called the Council Green. I always wondered why."

"Well, now you know," I said. "In Gaelic '*Dail-sheomra ruit Sidhe*' is 'The Council Room of the Shee'! Well, evidently this roused the wrath of the Shee to boiling-point, and they wreaked revenge on the despoiler of their land via his child when this silly girl gave them the opportunity by leaving him unguarded on the very heart of their quarrel—the Council Green itself! They carried him away, and substituted one of their own weird offspring who resembles him in nothing but physical appearance. And when not even *that* drove Dick Flaherty and his wife away… well, you know what happened to Dick! I've not the least doubt that the Folk caused that skid—somehow. Sounds pretty beastly, but from their point of view they had good reason to hate him." I showed her the thorny twig. "That's thorn—the fairy bush. Without knowing what he was doing, that fool of a brother-in-law of yours first invades their territory, then chooses the most sacred spot on the whole hillside—their Council Room—for his last green, and to make things a thousand times worse, clears it by grubbing up their sacred bush—the Magic Thorn—growing on the brink of running water too, and with an Oak and an Ash standing above on the escarpment! D'you see? The Shee, outraged, their sacred symbols violated, their most precious ground ruined and destroyed, took their revenge—and it remains to be seen whether I have the power or the knowledge enough to force them to release their prisoner and bring him back to us."

"Shall I tell Agnes?" said Miss Cargill.

I shook my head.

"No—please. We *may* fail—in which case she would only suffer the most terrible disappointment, after having her hopes raised. Also, she will want to know—perhaps to take part in—the cure. And you know…" I looked straight at the grey-haired woman before me. "The cure is no easy one, Miss Cargill! It's a grim ordeal, and takes some nerve to carry through, and we couldn't depend on Mrs. Flaherty. It is no job for a mother to share in—it would not be fair to ask her. But I shall need helpers—two if I can get them. I believe I can depend on Hammond—he will do anything to help your sister. Can I depend on *you*—no matter what happens? Remember that if you weaken, or cry out, or funk or disobey my orders, that this one chance of driving out the Changeling, this Child of the Shee, that now wears his body and speaks with his lips, and bringing back the boy Patrick into possession of his own body will be lost—and we can never try again. He will be prisoned eternally with the Folk, and this creature will remain here—with us. Can you do it?"

She looked at me, and her lips set in a firm line.

"I can!" she said. "Only tell me what to do…"

To diagnose a disease is the first step towards finding a cure. And luckily, since I had suspected for some time what the disease really was, I had studied its cure—the only sure cure, according to the ancient books I had borrowed from the great library; a cure at least proved and trusted for many hundreds of years past, when this strange happening was more frequently known. But the cure, as I had warned Miss Cargill, was a grim one, and courage would be needed to carry it out... and there was no time to spare! Hallowe'en was upon us, when the borderline between the two worlds grows so slender that one may step across it more easily than at any other time of the year—and this was the time on which I wanted to seize.

I realized the difficulty of the task that lay before me! Not willingly would Patrick—or rather, this strange being that had dispossessed Patrick of his flesh—join with me in the ritual that was to divorce him from his place amongst the human race and send him back where he belonged! Not that he was—or could be—either happy or at ease with us. But it was plain that he had been "sent" into the human race in order to wreak vengeance on it as far as possible—to create fear and pain and distress as far round him as he could reach. And he would not only fight to retain his footing in the enemy territory he had entered, but his Folk would fight to keep him there—now I understood his reluctance to contact the vibrations of his own land! He knew that once in contact with those vibrations, once he felt their irresistible "pull", his link with the human race *must* become ever so little weakened as his blood called to those who shared that blood—that strange lucent ichor that fills the veins of Those who are neither of Earth nor Heaven, but some-where in between...

I knew that urge, that call of blood to blood would be a factor on our side that I could use—but still, it would be hard. Force might have to be tried—though I devoutly hoped not. Pain and fear are not weapons that those who tread my path like to handle. But there might be nothing else for it...

I explained the situation to Hammond as best I could, hoping that I could manage to make it sound convincing—though in the light of day it certainly sounded, even to me, like some crazy dream! But to my relief and surprise Hammond not only agreed at once to help me, but showed little surprise at my story.

I know now, of course, that he had not told me one-half of the queer or uncanny experiences he had been through with the boy, for fear of being laughed at or disbelieved—but I was thankful for his response, and set about making my preparations, for Hallowe'en was due within the coming week, and coincided with a full moon—which again would be a help. The only thing that remained was to wait—and hope that Patrick would not try on anything particularly devilish during the time of waiting.

I had planned every move of the night's work with the greatest care, but nevertheless we were all three pretty well keyed-up when at last the fateful evening arrived!

I had arranged with Miss Cargill that a sleeping draught should be slipped into the cup of cocoa that Patrick always drank the last thing before going to bed, and to my relief it worked like a charm. Within a few minutes after swallowing it he was nodding, and his mother packed him off to bed with a lecture about over doing things—which would have made me smile had I not been so anxious and strung-up!

Shortly afterwards the good lady also took her departure upstairs with her sister, who sent me a glance of understanding as the door closed behind them. I sat in the little "drawing-room" waiting and listening and trying to read, and half an hour later a cautious tap came at the door, and there entered Hammond, warmly clad in a sweater and corduroy trousers, with his feet thrust into soft rubber "sneakers", carrying a length of fine strawberry netting over one arm. We shook hands and conversed in whispers until a cautious knock on the ceiling told us that Miss Cargill, who slept overhead, was likewise ready, and her sister safely asleep—and leaving the door and window ajar and one light burning, we went softly out of the room and up the stairs to Patrick's bedroom. We passed the door of Miss Cargill's room, and she stepped softly out and joined us, wrapped in a thick coat and scarf, with rubber goloshes muffling the sound of her shoes on the polished floor.

I don't mind admitting that my heart was in my mouth as softly I turned the handle of the door. I had done my best to make the boy's sleep sure, not only by the use of a drug, but by mental "willing"—I had spent the half-hour I had sat waiting in the drawing-room for Hammond and Miss Cargill on building about Patrick a "shell" of sleep that should endure until I myself removed it. But I was younger then at this business than I am now, and less sure of my own powers... also I had not before contacted these strange Folk, and I did not know their powers and how far they might be able to counteract my own. Further, tonight was All Hallow's Eve, which gave them added strength, and the boy himself, of course, being *of* them, was allied with them, and so probably, either consciously or unconsciously, on the alert against me. It might well be that he was already awake and aware of our approach, and if he made an outcry or a struggle, that would awaken Mrs. Flaherty and ruin the whole scheme! I knew that her soft-heartedness would never permit the body of her child, no matter who or what inhabited it, to go through the ordeal that lay ahead... not even to regain his freedom. But all was well.

Patrick was sleeping soundly when I went in, and it was only a matter of a few moments for me then to make the usual passes over him and send him into a profound hypnotic trance, from which I forbade him to wake until I gave him permission. He lay inert, breathing steadily as Miss Cargill and I drew a thick dressing-gown over his pyjamas, put slippers on his feet and wrapped a heavy blanket over all—then I called Hammond in with his strawberry net, which he had fashioned into a sort of small hammock that swung, rucksack fashion, on his back from two strong webbing straps slung across his chest and shoulders. Patrick was a solid, well-grown youngster, and to carry him like a baby in one's arms a couple of miles over rough grounds, streams, bushes, ditches and the rest, would have been more than either Hammond or I could have done... whereas when Miss Cargill and I lifted Patrick into the "cradle", he settled to sleep quite comfortably, encased in the netting, against Hammond's broad back.

I paused on our way downstairs to pick up a certain bundle from my room, and together we went down and out of the front door, which Hammond had carefully left unfastened, into the night and our grim task. It was an eerie-looking scene that spread before us as we went across the drive—an eerie scene, painted in the icy whiteness and dead black of midnight! The moonlight was brilliant, and the trees and their shadows lay like pools of ink on the shimmering whiteness, like hoar-frost, of the dew-wet grass, across which our going left a passage like a dark smeared path. The little pools and the tumbling cascades of the stream glittered uncannily, and the stars overhead in the dark blue sky seemed as large as the tinsel rosettes on a Christmas-tree, with the moon in the middle like a big white face staring down at us; and as we went, I swear Things gathered about us till the whole mountain-side was alive and palpitant with unseen Folk, all alert and stirring, watching us, suspicious, wondering…

We made the best speed we could, but the boy was heavy and the going none too good, and again I had the horrible feeling that endeavours were being made to hinder our advance… yet though Miss Cargill lost her footing twice, once in a rabbit hole, where she almost sprained her ankle, and again when a stone slipped beneath her foot, and I scraped myself cruelly with an unseen strand of barbed wire, Hammond—perhaps because he was bearing Their child—escaped any accident, and at last we crossed the stream and stood below the high-curving bank upon the so-sadly-denuded Council Ground.

Hammond, unslinging his burden, laid it carefully on the ground, and Miss Cargill dropped on her knees and examined the sleeping child carefully. He still slept peacefully and she choked on a little sob as she said in a low voice, "Go on—let's get it over quickly!" and I nodded.

Hammond and I were already busy building a fire—but we were not finding things easy. I had brought down in my bundle charcoal, petrol-soaked rags, bits of paper and wood to make a fire, and for several minutes we strove to build one, but without effect—the things seemed to slide away from beneath our hands, the matches went out, the sticks would not catch fire, and at last I realized that I should have to make a magic Circle all round us, or the fire could not be built. The Folk had taken alarm—and they were bent on thwarting us…

I glanced at Miss Cargill and saw that she looked queer, white and rather tense. She was staring steadily across the stream towards where, on the far side of the water, the great dark thicket of thorn sprawled its length down the mountain-side towards where the bog gleamed lividly in the moonlight. I followed her eyes, and it seemed as though against the darkness of the thicket vague wreath-like shapes were forming… it might have been my excited fancy, or it might not, but in any case the quicker I "fenced" us all in the better, if the Forces of that strange land were already taking shape!

Now there are several methods of forming that magical Circle within which is safety. The best-known, of course, is that drawn within the Pentacle, the Double Triangle that forms a Star, drawn in chalk, with lighted candles at the Points, and little cups of Holy Water standing within the "valleys", or the hollows of the Points. But there are many occasions when it is not feasible to use this Circle—as now. What could one do on wet grass, on a windswept hillside, with chalk and lighted candles? There is the Electric Pentacle, one of the finest and most reliable forms of protection against the forces of the Outer Dark. But again, for obvious reasons, this would have been useless in our present situation, and I had to fall back, not for the first time by many, on that lesser-known protection called the "Holy Rope" or the "Blessed Girdle"—I've heard it called by both names.

Now this is no easy thing to obtain! It must be made by an ordained priest, in the correct way at the correct time—and nowadays there are few priests who know how to make it, and fewer still who *will* make it, even when they know. But I had done a service to a certain priest two years ago, and in reward he had consented to make one for me—and I never travelled without it, especially when engaged on a case. It is a length of new rope, made of twelve strands to represent the Disciples; this is first soaked in Holy Water, then knotted in threefold knots (to represent the Trinity) in seven places, to represent the Holy Number, and then it is left for a night under the High Altar while Mass is said above it. This length of rope, laid in a circle on the ground and held in place either by weights made from lead taken from a church roof, or with split pegs cut from holy wood (meaning wood cut from any tree growing in a churchyard), will keep any force of evil at bay, and it was with a sense of considerable relief that I drew it out of my pocket and pegged it securely down round the four of us and the fire we were trying to make.

Its effect was immediate. Within three minutes the fire we had been unable to light was roaring up fiercely, casting a weird scarlet glow upon the tangled bushes about us, the dew-wet grass and the bubbling stream a few feet away. And we turned to the part of the business we liked least...

The boy was still sleeping, and as though to melt my heart he looked, as he lay there in the leaping firelight, as handsome and as innocent as a child could ever hope to look. His tousled fair hair curled in a crest over his smooth brow, his ruddy young face was flushed with sleep, and the young lips I had so often seen curled in ugly derision or twisted in mockery were pouted now in as innocent a half-smile as ever sculptured cherub bore.

I glanced at Hammond, bending close at my shoulder, and Miss Cargill at my side.

"You're going to go through with it, both of you—for the child's sake?" I asked. "I told you what would have to be done, and if you weaken, you know, I warned you... I don't know what may not happen to all of us."

Both met my glance sturdily.

"I'll stand fast," said Miss Cargill briefly. "But let's get on—quickly!"

"You said it, miss," said Hammond. "Go on, sir, we're behind you. The sooner it's over the better."

Together we dragged the still insensible boy into such a position that he lay with his feet towards the fire, and then, with my heart pounding and a nasty sick feeling at my throat, I loosened the blanket about his legs and removed his slippers. Hammond knelt at his head, holding each arm down, so that he could not move, even if in struggling he wriggled out of the blanket that still swathed him like a giant cocoon, and I beckoned Miss Cargill to kneel opposite me so that she gripped one ankle while I gripped the other. Then I made the passes that released the boy from trance, but—to my great relief— he remained for the moment in a natural sleep. I looked up at last across the stream towards where, I knew, *They* were gathered watching us, and spoke, hoping my voice sounded stronger and more determined than it felt.

"People of the Hills, I know you are there—and I know that this is your child, born of you, of your own green blood and race, thrust by you, out of revenge, into the human family to wreak mischief and distress because of a wrong done to you! Now I come to promise you that that wrong shall be righted—if you in your turn will right the wrong you have done to this human child whose body, inhabited by your Own, lies at my mercy here."

I paused. No answer! And yet, *was* there no answer? The air seemed full of far-off rushing and whispering noises—of constant movement and murmur, yet there was nothing definite enough to call actual *sound*. It was as though one heard from an immense distance off, a mighty multitude rustling and muttering agitatedly, excitedly, together. Yet there was nothing to be seen but the moonlit hillside, the black trees and their shadows, and the sprawling length of undergrowth on the further side of the stream, like a long dark cloud against which still that strange effect of swirling vapour persisted, as though steam was rising from some hidden kettle, faint yet just visible in a stir of barely-perceptible movement against the dusk of the tangled bushes. I waited a moment longer and then drew a long breath and spoke again.

"You do not answer me—so I must act! This child of yours has done grievous harm—and so now I punish him, and you in him, in this physical body he has stolen."

I steeled my heart, snatched a burning brand from the fire and laid it to the soles of Patrick's feet—and as I did so it seemed that all hell broke loose about me! The wild shriek of the boy as the agony aroused him rose high, cutting the air like a steel spearhead of anguished sound, and at the same moment a furious wind sprang up and swept swirling about us, and the flames and smoke of the fire bent and flattened out, sweeping towards us so that Miss Cargill drew back, ducking her head in fright—but she did not let go her hold of the boy and the flames flared high again as the Holy Rope threw back the Forces that were trying to smite us within it. As if in baffled fury the wind roared and buffeted wildly around the Circle, bringing with it, it seemed, a faint crying echo of a million voices.

It was again, as though one heard the clamour of a furious mob a thousand miles away and yet close at hand, the strangest thing—and easily the most horribly uncanny!—I had ever known. And through and over it soared the cries of the boy Patrick in his agony, and I smelt that horrible smell, the stench of singed live flesh…

I cried out too, in my own horror at the thing I had to do, and even as I cried out the wind dropped and the sound with it, leaving utter silence, broken only by the sobbing of the boy as he writhed in the strong grip of the three of us—and as I looked across the stream I knew that I had won the first round of this strange battle. From out of the dim swirling vapours that had curled and wreathed themselves against the thicket, a Shape was slowly emerging—a shape strangely fluid, uncertain, changing as a shadow thrown on running water changes. Indeed, the simile is the best I know; the figure looked like the reflection of something seen on a gliding stream, ever shifting and changing—altering slightly, as ripples from a thrown stone or branch will alter it, yet in its general outlines remaining always the same…

The impression I got was that of a tall, male figure, incredibly lean and clad in some skin-fitting garments of, I thought, darkest green—though precisely what they were like it was impossible in the darkness to discern.

But the face! I had no difficulty in recognizing that face—I had already seen it, drawn in Patrick's sketch-book! *"An Ciar"*—the Dark One… A narrow, fox-like face like a pallid mask lit by a pair of eyes colourless as the grey pools in the bog, with a thin mouth, long and cruel and beautiful, that curved above the sharply-pointed chin, and above the face wreathed wild strands of dark red hair, the colour of dried blood...

The silence was almost uncanny after that hurricane of wind, and I knew that a myriad unseen eyes watched me as I faced that sinister Shape, saw it ripple and shift and quiver against the dark background of the bushes, fade and grow strong again, as always I held my brand firmly over the boy's shuddering feet. Vaguely as I spoke I heard Miss Cargill's voice behind me muttering prayers, and I knew that Hammond's face, like mine, was running with sweat...

"*Taoiseach na muintir na cruta,*" I greet you! You know this child?"

I don't know how I can tell you that I received an answer, because I do not think that, with my *physical* ears, I heard any actual voice. Nor did the others hear any reply—and afterwards Miss Cargill told me how queer and awesome it was to hear me speak into the voice of the night, listen as though to a reply, and speak again. But my inner senses heard the answer clearly enough, given in a clear, thin, distant voice that raised a horrid sense of gooseflesh down my spine, so utterly inhuman was it. It spoke the ancient tongue of Eire—the tongue that was sung and spoken many a thousand years before England and the English were even dreamt about.

"*Seadh aithnighim an leanbh so!*"†

As the voice spoke, in a flash Patrick stopped his moaning and writhed and stiffened into attention. So he heard it, too? No wonder, if my theory was right—and now I was excitedly, triumphantly certain that it was! Blood was calling to blood... and even as the thought came to me the boy Patrick spoke loudly into the stillness.

"*M'athair!*"‡ he said.

There was a pause, as though the world was frozen into utter stillness to listen—and then arose about us a curious sound that was at one and

* "Chief of the Folk of the Hills."
† "Yes, I know this child."
‡ "My father!"

the same time like rushing water, like thunder, like a mighty wind and like the crying of a thousand voices in greeting, in lamentation, in fear, wonder, amaze, acclaim, and the child on the ground beside me shook from head to foot and cried out too, in a woeful voice of pain and longing mixed.

I shut my eyes and held my burning brand tightly, for we were not yet the victors in this strange battle, and I called again, above the appalling, unearthly din about me, to the Figure that I knew still stood there beyond the stream, against the thicket of the Magic Thorn.

"Who is this child?"

A pause, and then high above the clamour rose that thin voice that never belonged to humankind, faint but clear.

"*Leannabh Sidhe! Leannabh Sidhe!*"*

And the child, groaning and rolling in his pain at my feet, echoed the cry, and his voice seemed now thin and eerily inhuman like that of the other who spoke to me across the mists!

"*M'athair—m'athair e shin!*"†

The Child of the Shee—and his father! Father and son… father and son. Now I knew the truth, and my quest ended. I drew myself erect and cried aloud above the wild sea of calling voices that still surrounded us.

"Now you know my power and my purpose, O Chief *Taoiseach Sidhe*!‡ Take back your son and give us our own, and let there be peace between us now, for ever and a day! He who wrought you ill is dead, and the land filched from you shall be returned to you, never to be defiled again. Surely, O King, your vengeance is complete and your son, Prince of the Shee, can return to his own?"

There was a sudden silence. As though a wand had waved, all sound and movement and vibration ceased upon the hillside as though the very night held its breath in suspense, and the Shadow against the thicket flickered and

---

* "The Child of the Shee."
† "My father—that is my father!"
‡ "Lord of the Shee."

wavered like a dark flame in a draught, as though it hesitated. And after a moment the strange uncanny voice came again to my ears. There was a steely note in it.

"*Aoibhinn le haois Sidhe an dioghaltas!*"*

"Then," I said—and I thrust the flaming brand I held deep into the heart of the fire once more as I spoke—"if you choose vengeance—then vengeance shall be *my* choice also, for the harm this child has done! This body of earth that houses your only son shall go crippled all its days from the burning brand here in my hand! The issue is clear between us, so choose! Choose!"

"Choose!" muttered Miss Cargill beside me, and it seemed that echoing all round the vast dark hillside, from every hillock and tree, every tussock of grass, every burrow and ditch and hollow, I heard voices that repeated the word again in appeal, in supplication...

"*Do rogha fein fuit, a Ri! Do rogha fein fuit!*"†

There was another pause, and then faint but clear came the voice of the Figure that stood within the dark thicket on the further side of the stream.

"*Ni beag e! Fill oven a mhic!*"‡

There was a pause. The child at my feet, who had lain curled, moveless, in an agony of attention while this strange conversation lasted, reared himself, bound as he was, into a half-sitting position, and his voice shrilled across the dark—a voice from which the human quality had now entirely vanished, giving place to a high, sweet, almost chanting note of wonder and utter joy.

"*Ta me leat—ta me leat, m'athair!*"§

I don't quite know what actually happened then, because the whole world seemed to spin and rock round me as I flung the brand into the fire and, gathering the child up in my arms, reached out and placed him on the ground outside the circle of the Holy Rope—but I was careful not to place

---

* "Vengeance is dear to the Shee!"
† "Yours is the choice, O Chief! Yours is the choice!"
‡ "It is enough! Return to me, my son—return!"
§ "I come, I come, my father!"

my foot outside the Rope. I did not trust that fox-eyed Shape with the voice of dawn winds and cold stars! Even thus, a sudden vicious gust of wind beat furiously up at me as I leant out of the Circle, Miss Cargill cried out and clutched me, and I fell back just in time as something seemed to rise and soar away from us with a sort of whistling roar... and lo, the child had vanished!

As I lay panting, safe within the Circle, my head was whirling, for the sound of many waters, of thunder, of the beating of wings, and of a thousand tearing, joyous winds was in my ears, and with them, mounting louder and more triumphant every minute, a chorus, high and magical and almost agonizingly sweet, of distant voices—then suddenly it seemed my eyes were opened and I saw that the whole hillside was alive with multitudes of the Shee! Swift arrowy figures sweeping up from the hillside like smoke from a burning prairie, thousands and thousands of them, great and small—and in the midst a lean, green-clad Figure with flying dark-red hair and eyes like pale water-pools bestrode a shadowy horse whose mane trailed amongst the stars and whose hooves were shod with silver! And behind that lean Figure, clinging to his waist, rode a slim boy, green-clad also, whose mop of fair hair, luminous as thistledown, streamed wildly behind him in the speed of his passing, and whose voice rose high and shrill above the others as he shouted for joy...

Some of the Folk were horsed also, and some seemed to half-fly, half-run beside the horses, as running footmen used to do, and others were riding pillion and others still seemed to fly high and swift alone, but all followed the two green-clad shapes on the mighty horse as swarming bees follow their Queen! Some were helmed and seemed to bear sword and shield, some wore trailing robes or cloaks, some seemed clad in shining tatters, and some were naked as dawn, with wild hair flying—a vaporous flood of movement and colour, green and purple and indigo, dark as peatwater or silverwhite as moonlight, olive and brown and grey, blue and palest lilac, every colour of hill and forest, vale and river, of field and sky and sea mingled in a dazzling stream like a living rainbow. Up and away they swept, full speed, and the very air tingled with the swiftness of their passing and the vibration of their high sweet singing.

"Nac aluinn iad an mhuintir
Righeainhail daib astreabh na cruic…,"*

And even as I saw them whirl up and away, the terrible lovely Folk, a cloud swept over the face of the moon, and all was dark—and when the cloud passed a few minutes afterwards that horde of misty flying shapes was gone. There was no sign of anything upon the quiet hillside. The Sidhe had passed, and taken their Own with them… and I had looked upon that sight which is granted to few men to know and live! The Ride of the Shee, the Folk of the Hills, back to their own Place…

I do not quite know how long I stood there, but I knew that suddenly I realized that I was cold, that Miss Cargill was weeping softly at my feet, and that Hammond was pulling my coat.

"Look, sir," he said excitedly. "Look!"

I looked down. There, outside the Circle, where I had placed the child and whence I had seen it vanish, Patrick lay asleep, a faint smile curving his boyish mouth, one cheek pillowed on his hand! His feet were curled comfortably under him, and there were no marks of burning on them, and even as I looked he opened his eyes and blinked, puzzled, at the three of us bending over him. The glare of the fire caught his eyes first and he frowned, puzzled.

"What a jolly good blaze!" he said with appreciation. "But what for—and why are we all here?"

He sat up and held his hands out to the fire, and looked from one to the other of us, hanging almost breathlessly, had he only known it, on his words.

---

* "How beautiful they are,
The Lordly Ones
Who live in the Hills…"

"Hallo, Hammond… have you been poaching with that net, or what? And what on earth am I doing in pyjamas out here, with my shoes off? And auntie…"

He looked at me in a faintly puzzled way and paused a moment—and Miss Cargill, whom I had previously prepared for this somewhat difficult moment, bent over him.

"That's Mr. Pennoyer, Patrick," she said nervously. "You've been rather ill for some time, you know, and he had been looking after you."

The boy frowned faintly and shook his head.

"I don't remember being ill," he remarked, "but I feel as though I've been away a long time somehow! I suppose that's it. Why, *auntie!*" His tone rose with affectionate amazement as he turned to Miss Cargill, and he put up a puzzled hand to touch the tears on her cheeks. "Dear old auntie—why on earth are you crying? Please don't cry…"

*　　*　　*

Pennoyer paused effectively.

"Well, that's the story. Patrick accepted the situation without any apparent wonder or question after those first few moments, and went back to bed and slept as any normal boy would have done. And *was*, indeed, as normal, from that instant, as anyone in the world would be—thank goodness! The Dark One—the King of the Shee—had been as good as his word. He had taken his own and returned us—ours."

"What happened afterwards?" I asked, fascinated.

"Oh," said Pennoyer. "On my advice his mother sold the Manor House, and they all went back to live at Killeen. I knew that the Folk would welcome and help them now instead of hating and hindering, so I urged them to go, and I was perfectly right. Patrick found his feet—and an excellent school—almost at once, and the ladies soon became as popular as poor Dick Flaherty had been unpopular. Everything was all right."

"Weren't there any awkward moments—even at the start?" I asked. "After all, to bridge such a gap..."

"Yes, but you see to Patrick there *wasn't* a gap," said Pennoyer... "though, of course, there were one or two rather difficult moments to start with! He was a trifle puzzled and astonished, I remember, on the following day when he came down to breakfast and met his mother. I had told Mrs. Flaherty the good news that her son was cured (though I omitted the details of the cure!), and though I had begged her to treat him quite ordinarily, when he appeared she burst into tears and fell on his neck, despite the careful warnings I had given her! Patrick endured the little scene politely, but was obviously much bewildered... however, I smoothed things over by reminding him how delicate and emotional his mother was, and he speedily forgot about it. The fact that he remembers nothing of several years of his boyhood he puts down to having been ill, and regarding the years that he spent as a guest of the Shee, in the hollow of their hills, his mind is a complete blank..."

"Would he be kindly treated there?" I asked curiously.

Pennoyer smiled.

"The few who remember their visit, on their return to human life again, seem to spend their days pining for the delights of the Land of Faery!" he said. "So probably it is a good thing that the King of the Shee wiped away all memory from Patrick's mind before he let him come back!"

"Wasn't it rather a risk to let them all go back to Killeen?" I began. "Supposing the Shee..."

Pennoyer shook his head.

"I had made a pact with the King of the Shee," he said, "and if I kept my word I knew he would keep his. Also, I made quite certain, *before* I let the Flahertys return to Killeen, that neither they, nor any of their descendants, would ever be able to break the word I had given—that the land that had been taken from the Folk should be returned to Them. When Mrs. Flaherty asked me what I would take as a fee—she was kind enough to say that nothing would be too much—I asked her if she would make a deed of gift, to Killeen village, of the Fairy Hill, that piece of ground on which poor Dick Flaherty made his ill-fated golf-course. I asked her to arrange matters so that it might be kept in perpetuity as open ground or common-land, for the people of Killeen to wander on, to play and rest and enjoy as their own for ever. She consented at once—and the gift of the 'Fairy Hill' to the people of Killeen created such surprise and pleasure that Agnes Flaherty and her sister were promptly taken to everybody's bosom, where they have remained ever since! The Folk have their ground again, and all is well. That's some years ago now—and I am glad to say that when I last went to visit Killeen House I saw that the two trees, the Oak and the Ash, on the top of the escarpment that overhangs the 'Council Room of the Shee', were green and strong. And best of all, the Fairy Thorn is once more growing thickly over the clearing."

1946

THE TROD

Algernon Blackwood

Algernon Blackwood (1869–1951) was born the son of a fashionable dandy (known as "Beauty Blackwood") turned zealous Christian evangelist, and escaped from his repressive, isolating upbringing by turning to nature. His 1923 memoir *Episodes Before Thirty* describes his early convictions that "everything was alive, a dim sense that some kind of consciousness struggled through every form, even that a sort of inarticulate communication with this 'other life' was possible, could I but discover the way."

After a precarious post-university decade working in North America, where his occupations included dairy farmer, publican, occasional morphine user and court reporter, a friend of his secretly submitted some of Blackwood's "strange, wild, improbable tales akin to ghost-stories" to a publisher. The enthusiastic response allowed him to stop attempting to make a living in the dried milk business and devote himself to writing full-time.

Blackwood's love for nature and his fascination with supernatural forces hidden from (or by) the everyday world can be seen throughout his weird fiction. Sometimes nature takes a more corporeal form, appearing as fairies, nature spirits, or even sentient forests. His stories frequently explore the clash between confidently macho modernity and older, wilder entities, with sports enthusiast heroes like the ice-skating writer of "The Glamour of the Snow" and the grouse-shooting narrator of "The Trod" unsettled by eerie encounters they hadn't bargained for.

Y OUNG Norman was being whirled in one of the newest stream-lined expresses towards the north. He leaned back in his first-class Smoker and lit a cigarette. On the rack in front of him was his gun-case with the pair of guns he never willingly allowed out of his sight, his magazine with over a thousand cartridges beside it, and the rest of his luggage, he knew, was safely in the van. He was looking forward to a really good week's shooting at Greystones, one of the best moors in England.

He realized that he was uncommonly lucky to have been invited at all. Yet a question mark lay in him. Why precisely, he wondered, had he been asked? For one thing, he knew his host, Sir Hiram Digby, very slightly. He had met him once or twice at various shoots in Norfolk, and while he had acquitted himself well when standing near him, he could not honestly think this was the reason for the invitation. There had been too many good shots present, and far better shots, for him to have been specially picked out. There was another reason, he was certain. His thoughts, as he puffed his cigarette reflectively, turned easily enough in another direction—towards Diana Travers, Sir Hiram Digby's niece.

The wish, he remembered, is often father to the thought, yet he clung to it obstinately, and with lingering enjoyment. It was Diana Travers who had suggested his name; it well might be, it probably was, and the more he thought it over, the more positive he felt. It explained the invitation, at any rate.

A curious thrill of excitement and delight ran through him as memory went backwards and played about her. A curious being, he saw her, quite unlike the usual run of girls, but curious, in the way that he himself perhaps was curious, for he was just old enough to have discovered that he *was* curious, standing apart somehow from the young men of his age and station. Well born, rich, sporting and all the rest, he yet did not quite belong to his time in certain ways. He could drink, revel, go wild, enjoy himself with his companions, but up to a point only—when he withdrew unsatisfied. There were "other things" that claimed him with some terrible inner power; and the two could not mix. These other things he could not quite explain even to himself, but to his boon companions—never. Were they things of the spirit? He could not say. Wild, pagan things belonging to an older day. He knew not. They were of unspeakable loveliness and power, drawing him away from ordinary modern life—*that* he knew. He could not define them to himself, much less speak of them to others.

And then he met Diana Travers and knew, though he did not dare put his discovery into actual words, that she felt something similar.

He came across her first at a dance in town, he remembered, remembering also how bored he had been until the casual introduction, and after it, how happy, enchanted, satisfied. It was assuredly not that he had fallen suddenly in love, nor that she was wildly beautiful—a tall, fair girl with a radiant, yet not lovely face, soft voice, graceful movements—for there were thousands, Norman knew, who excelled her in all these qualities. No, it was not the usual love attack, the mating fever, the herd-instinct that she might be *his* girl, but the old conviction, rather, that there lay concealed in her the same nameless, mysterious longings that lay also in himself—the terrible and lovely power that drew him from his human kind towards unknown "other things".

As they stood together on the balcony, where they had escaped from the heat and clamour of the ball-room, he acknowledged to himself, yet without utterance, this overpowering, strange conviction that their fates were in some way linked together. He could not explain it at the time, he could not explain it now—while he thought it over in the railway carriage, and his conscious mind rejected it as imagination. Yet it remained. Their talk, indeed, had been ordinary enough, nor was he conscious of the slightest desire to flirt or make love; it was just that, as the saying is, they "clicked" and that each felt delightfully easy in the other's company, happy and at home. It was almost, he reflected, as though they shared some rather wonderful deep secret that had no need of words, a secret that lay, indeed, beyond the reach of words altogether.

They had met several times since, and on each occasion he had been aware of the same feeling; and once when he ran across her by chance in the park they walked together for over an hour and she had talked more freely. Talked suddenly about herself, moreover, openly and naturally, as though she knew he would understand. In the open air, it struck him, she was more spontaneous than in the artificial surroundings of walls and furniture. It was not so much that she said anything significant, but rather the voice and manner and gestures that she used.

She had been admitting how she disliked London and all its works, loathing especially the Season with its glittering routine of so-called gaiety, adding that she always longed to get back to Marston, Sir Hiram's place in Essex. "There are the marshes," she said, with quiet enthusiasm, "and the sea, and I go with my uncle duck-flighting in the twilight, or in the dawn when the sun comes up like a red ball out of the sea, and the mists over the marshes drift away… and things, you know, may happen…"

He had been watching her movements with admiration as she spoke, thinking the name of huntress was well chosen, and now there was a note of strange passion in her voice that he heard for the first time. Her whole being, moreover, conveyed the sense that he would understand some emotional yearning in her that her actual words omitted.

He stopped and stared at her.

"That's to be alive," she added with a laugh that made her eyes shine. "The wind and the rain blowing in your face and the ducks streaming by. You feel yourself part of nature. Gates open, as it were. It was how we were meant to live, I'm sure."

Such phrases from any other girl must have made him feel shy and embarrassed, from her they were merely natural and true. He had not taken her up, however, beyond confessing that he agreed with her, and the conversation had passed on to other things. Yet the reason he had not become enthusiastic or taken up the little clue she offered, was because his inmost heart knew what she meant.

Her confession, not striking in itself, concealed, while it revealed, a whole region of significant, mysterious "other things" best left alone in words. "You and I think alike," was what she had really said. "You and I share this strange, unearthly longing, only for God's sake, don't let us talk about it…!"

"A queer girl, anyhow," he now smiled to himself, as the train rushed northwards, and then asked himself what exactly he knew about her? Very little, practically nothing, beyond that, both parents being dead, she lived with her elderly bachelor uncle and was doing the London Season. "A thoroughbred anyhow," he told himself, "lovely as a nymph into the bargain…" and his thoughts went dreaming rather foolishly. Then suddenly, as he lit another cigarette, a much more definite thought emerged. It gave him something of a start, for it sprang up abruptly out of his mood of reverie in the way that a true judgment sometimes leaps to recognition in the state between sleeping and waking.

"She *knows*. Knows about these other lovely and mysterious things that have always haunted me. She has—yes, experienced them. She can explain them to me. She wants to share them with me…"

Norman sat up with a jerk, as though something had scared him. He had been dreaming, these ideas were the phantasmagoria of a dream. Yet his heart, he noticed, was beating rather rapidly, as though a deep inner excitement had touched him in his condition of half-dream.

He looked up at his gun-cases and cartridges in the rack, then shaded his eyes and gazed out of the window. The train was doing at least sixty. The character of the country it rushed through was changing. The hedges of the midlands had gone, and stone walls were beginning to take their place. The country was getting wilder, lonelier, less inhabited. He drew unconsciously a deep breath of satisfaction. He must actually have slept for a considerable time, he realized, for his watch told him that in a few minutes he would reach the junction where he had to change. Bracendale, the local station for Greystones, he remembered, was on a little branch line that wandered away among the hills. And some fifteen minutes later he found himself, luggage and all, in the creaky, grunting train that would land him at Bracendale towards five o'clock. The dusk had fallen when, with great effort apparently, the struggling engine deposited him with his precious guns and cartridges on the deserted platform amid swirling mists a damp wind prepared for his reception. To his considerable relief a car was there to carry him the remaining ten miles to the Lodge, and he was soon comfortably installed among its luxurious rugs for the drive across the hills.

He settled back comfortably to enjoy the keen mountain air.

After leaving the station, the car followed a road up a narrow valley for a time; a small beck fell tumbling from the hills on the left, where occasionally dark plantations of fir trooped down to the side of the road; but what struck him chiefly was the air of desolation and loneliness that hung over all the countryside. The landscape seemed to him wilder and less inhabited even than the Scottish Highlands. Not a house, not a croft, was to be seen. A sense of desertion, due partly to the dusk no doubt, hung brooding over everything, as though human influence was not welcomed here, perhaps not possible. Bleak and inhospitable it looked certainly, though for himself this loneliness held a thrill of wild beauty that appealed to him.

A few black-faced sheep strung occasionally across the road, and once they passed a bearded shepherd hurrying downhill with his dog. They vanished into the mist like wraiths. It seemed impossible to Norman that the country could be so desolate and uninhabited when he knew that only a few score miles away lay the large manufacturing towns of Lancashire. The car, meanwhile, was steadily climbing up the valley and presently they came to more open country and passed a few scattered farmhouses with an occasional field of oats beside them.

Norman asked the chauffeur if many people lived hereabouts, and the man was clearly delighted to be spoken to.

"No, sir," he said, "it's a right desolate spot at the best of times, and I'm glad enough," he added, "when it's time for us to go back south again." It had been a wonderful season for the grouse, and there was every promise of a record year.

Norman noticed an odd thing about the farmhouses they passed, for many of them, if not all, had a large cross carved over the lintel of the doors, and even some of the gates leading from the road into the fields had a smaller cross cut into the top bar. The car's flash-light picked them out. It reminded him of the shrines and crosses scattered over the countryside in Catholic countries abroad, but seemed a little incongruous in England. He asked the chauffeur if most of the people hereabout were Catholics, and the man's answer, given with emphasis, touched his curiosity.

"Oh, no, I don't think so," was the reply. "In fact, sir, if you ask me, the people round here are about as heathen as you could find in any Christian country."

Norman drew his attention to the crosses everywhere, asking him how he accounted for them if the inhabitants were heathen, and the man hesitated a moment before replying, as though, glad to talk otherwise, the subject was not wholly to his liking.

"Well, sir," he said at length, watching the road carefully in front of him, "they don't tell *me* much about what they think, counting me for a foreigner like, as I come from the south. But they're a rum lot to my way of thinking. What I'm told," he added after a further pause, "is that they carve these crosses to protect themselves."

"Protect themselves!" exclaimed Norman a little startled. "Protect themselves from—what?"

"Ah, there, sir," said the man after hesitating again, "that's more than I can say. I've heard of a haunted house before now, but never a haunted country-side. Yet that's what they believe, I take it. It's all haunted, sir—everywhere. It's the devil of a job to get any of them to turn out after dark, as I know well, and even in the daytime they won't stir far without a crucifix hung round their neck. Even the men won't."

The car had put on speed while he spoke and Norman had to ask him to ease up a bit; the man, he felt sure, was prey to a touch of superstitious fear as they raced along the darkening road, yet glad enough to talk, provided he was not laughed at. After his last burst of speech he had drawn a deep breath, as though glad to have got it off his chest.

"What you tell me is most interesting," Norman commented invitingly. "I've come across that sort of thing abroad, but never yet in England. There's something in it, you know," he added persuasively, "if we only knew what. I wish I knew the reason, for I'm sure it's a mistake just to laugh it all away." He lit a cigarette, handing one also to his companion, and making him slow down while they lighted them. "You're an observant fellow, I see," he went on, "and I'll be bound you've come across some queer things. I wish I had your opportunity. It interests me very much."

"You're right, sir," the chauffeur agreed, as they drove on again, "and it can't be laughed away, not *all* of it. There's something about the whole place 'ere that ain't right, as you might say. It 'got' me a bit when I first came 'ere some years ago, but now I'm kind of used to it."

"I don't think I should ever get *quite* used to it," said Norman, "till I'd got to the bottom of it. Do tell me anything you've noticed. I'd like to know—and I'll keep it to myself."

Feeling sure the man had interesting things to tell and having now won his confidence, he begged him to drive more slowly; he was afraid they would reach the house before there had been time to tell more, possibly even some personal experiences.

"There's a funny sort of road, or track rather, you may be seeing out shooting," the chauffeur went on eagerly enough, yet half nervously. "It leads across the moor, and no man or woman will set foot on it to save their lives, not even in the daytime, let alone at night."

Norman said eagerly that he would like to see it, asking its whereabouts, but of course the directions only puzzled him.

"You'll be seeing it, sir, one of these days out shooting and if you watch the natives, you'll find I'm telling you right."

"What's wrong with it?" Norman asked. "Haunted—eh?"

"That's it, sir," the man admitted, after a longish pause. "But a queer kind of 'aunting. They do say it's just too lovely to look at—and keep your senses."

It was the other's turn to hesitate, for something in him trembled.

Now, young Norman was aware of two things very clearly: first, that it wasn't quite the thing to pump his host's employee in this way; second, that what the man told him held an extraordinary, almost alarming interest for him. All folk-lore interested him intensely, legends and local superstitions included. Was this, perhaps a "fairy-ridden" stretch of country, he asked himself? Yet he was not in Ireland, where it would have been natural, but in stolid, matter-of-fact England. The chauffeur was obviously an observant, commonplace southerner, and yet he had become impressed, even a little scared, by what he had noticed. That lay beyond question: the man was relieved to talk to someone who would not laugh at him, while at the same time he was obviously a bit frightened.

A third question rose in his mind as well: this talk of haunted country, of bogies, fairies and the rest, fantastic though it was, perhaps, stirred a queer, yet delicious feeling in him—in his heart, doubtless—that his host's niece, Diana, had a link with it somewhere. The origin of a deep intuition is hardly discoverable. He made no attempt to probe it. This was Diana's country, she must know all the chauffeur hinted, and more besides. There must be something in the atmosphere that attracted her. She had been instrumental in making her uncle invite him. She wanted him to come, she wanted him to taste and share things, "other things", that to her were vital.

These thoughts flashed across him with an elaboration of detail impossible to describe. That the wish was, again, father to the thoughts, doubtless operated, yet the conviction persistently remained and the intuitive flash provided, apparently, inspiration, so that he plied the chauffeur with further questions that produced valuable results. He referred even to the Little People, the Fairies, without exciting contempt or laughter—with the result that the man gave him finally a somewhat dangerous confidence. Solemnly warning his passenger that "Sir Hiram mustn't hear of it" or he'd lose his job, the man described a remarkable incident that had happened, so to speak, under his own eyes. Sir Hiram's sister was lost on the moors some years ago and was never found... and the local talk and belief had it that she had been "carried off". Yet not carried off against her will: she had wanted to go.

"Would that be Mrs. Travers?" Norman asked.

"That's who it was, sir, exactly, seeing as 'ow you know the family. And it was the strangest disappearance that ever came *my* way." He gave a slight shudder and, if not quite to his listener's surprise, suddenly crossed himself.

Diana's mother!

A pause followed the extraordinary story, and then, for once, Norman used words first spoken (to Horatio) to a man who had never heard them before and received them with appropriate satisfaction.

"Yes, sir," he went on, "and now he's got her up here for the first time since it happened years ago—in the very country where her mother was taken—and I'm told his idea is that he 'opes it will put her right—"

"Put her right?"

"I should say—cure her, sir. She's supposed to have the same—the same"—he fumbled for a word—"unbalance as wot her mother had." A strange rush of hope and terror swept across Norman's heart and mind, but he made a great effort and denied them both, so that his companion little guessed this raging storm. Changing the subject as best he could, controlling his voice with difficulty so as to make it sound normal, he asked casually: "Do other people—I mean, *have* other people disappeared here?"

"They do say so, sir," was the reply. "I've heard many a tale, though I couldn't say as I proved anything. Natives, according to the talk, 'ave disappeared, nor no trace of them ever found. Children mostly. But the people round here won't speak of it and it's difficult to find out, as they never go to the Police and keep it dark among themselves—"

"Couldn't they have fallen into potholes, or something like that?" Norman interrupted, to which the man replied that there was only one pothole in the whole district and the danger spot most carefully fenced round. "It's the place itself, sir," he added finally with conviction, as though he could tell of a first-hand personal experience if he dared, "it's the whole country that's so strange."

Norman risked the direct question.

"And what you've seen yourself, with your own eyes," he asked, "did it—sort of frighten you? I mean, you observe so carefully that anything you reported would be valuable."

"Well, sir," came the reply after a little hesitation, "I can't say 'frightened' exactly, though—if you ask me—I didn't like it. It made me feel queer all over, and I ain't a religious man—"

"Do tell me," Norman pressed, feeling the house was now not far away and time was short. "I shall keep it to myself—and I shall believe you. I've had odd experiences myself."

The man needed no urging, however: he seemed glad to tell his tale.

"It's not really very much," he said lowering his voice. "It was like this, you see, sir. The garage and my rooms lie down at an old farmhouse about a quarter-mile from the Lodge, and from my bedroom window I can see across the moor quite a way. It takes in that trail I was speaking of before, and along that track exactly I sometimes saw lights moving in a sort of wavering line. A bit faint, they were, and sort of dancing about and going out and coming on again, and at first I took them for marsh lights—I've seen marsh lights down at our marshes at home—marsh gas we call it. That's what I thought at first, but I know better now."

"You never went out to examine them closer?"

"No, sir, I did *not*," came the emphatic reply.

"Or asked any of the natives what they thought?"

The chauffeur gave a curious little laugh; it was a half shy, half embarrassed laugh. Yes, he had once got a native who was willing to say something, but it was only with difficulty that Norman persuaded him to repeat it.

"Well, sir, what he told me"—again that embarrassed little laugh—"the words *he* used were 'It was the Gay People changing their hunting grounds.' That's what *he* said and crossed himself as he said it. They always changed their grounds at what he called the Equinox."

"The Gay People… the Equinox…"

The odd phrases were not new to Norman, but he heard them now as though for the first time, they had meaning. The equinox, the solstice, he knew naturally what the words meant, but the "Gay People" belonged to some inner phantasmagoria of his own he had hitherto thought of only imaginatively. It pertained, that is, to some private "imaginative creed" he believed in when he had been reading Yeats, James Stephens, A.E., or when he was trying to write poetry of his own.

Now, side by side with this burly chauffeur from the sceptical South, he came up against it—bang. And he admitted frankly to himself, it gave him a half-incredible thrill of wonder, delight and passion.

"The Gay People," he repeated, half to himself, half to the driver. "The fellow called them *that?*"

"That's wot he called them," repeated the matter-of-fact chauffeur. "And they were passing," he added, almost defiantly, as though he expected to be called a liar and deserved it, "passing in a stream of dancing lights along the Trod."

"The Trod," murmured Norman under his breath.

"The Trod," repeated the man in a whisper, "that track I spoke of—" and the car swerved, as though the touch on the wheel was unsteady for a second, though it instantly recovered itself as they swung into the drive.

The Lodge flew past, carrying a cross, Norman noticed, like all the other buildings; and a few minutes later the grey stone shooting-box, small and unpretentious, came in sight. Diana herself was on the step to welcome him, to his great delight.

"What a picture," he thought, as he saw her in her tweeds, her retriever beside her, the hall lamp blazing on her golden hair, one hand shading her eyes. Radiant, intoxicating, delicious, unearthly—he could not find the words—and he knew in that sudden instant that he loved her far beyond all that language could express. The dark background of the grey stone building, with the dim, mysterious moors behind, was exactly right. She stood there, framed in the wonder of two worlds—his girl!

Yet her reception chilled him to the bone. Excited, bubbling over as he was, his words of pleasure ready to tumble about each other, his heart primed with fairy tales and wonder, she had nothing to say except that tea was waiting, and that she hoped he had had a good journey. Response to his own inner convulsions there was none: she was polite, genial, cordial even, but beyond that—nothing. They exchanged commonplaces and she mentioned that the grouse were plentiful, that her uncle had got some of the best "guns" in England—which pleased his vanity for a moment—and that she hoped he would enjoy himself.

Her leaden reaction left him speechless. He felt convicted of boyish, idiotic fantasy.

"I asked particularly for you to come," she admitted frankly, as they crossed the hall. "I had an idea somehow you'd like to be here."

He thanked her, but betrayed nothing of his first delight, now chilled and rendered voiceless.

"It's your sort of country," she added, turning towards him with a swish of her skirts. "At least, I think it is."

"If *you* like it," he returned quietly, "I certainly shall like it too."

She stopped a moment and looked hard at him. "But of course I like it," she said with conviction. "And it's much lovelier than those Essex marshes."

Remembering her first description of those Essex marshes, he thought of a hundred answers, but before the right one came to him he found himself in the drawing-room chatting to his hostess, Lady Digby. The rest of the house-party were still out on the moor.

"Diana will show you the garden before the darkness comes," Lady Digby suggested presently. "It's quite a pretty view."

The "pretty view" thrilled Norman with its wild beauty, for the moor beyond stretched right down to the sea at Saltbeck, and in the other direction the hills ran away, fold upon fold, into a dim blue distance. The Lodge and its garden seemed an oasis in a wilderness of primeval loveliness, unkempt and wild as when God first made it. He was aware of its intense, seductive loveliness that appealed to all the strange, unearthly side of him, but at the same time he felt the powerful, enticing human seductiveness of the girl who was showing him round. And the two conflicted violently in his soul. The conflict left him puzzled, distraught, stupid, since first one, then the other, took the upper hand. What saved him from a sudden tumultuous confession of his imagined passion, probably, was the girls' calm, almost cold, indifference. Obviously without response she felt nothing of the tumult that possessed him.

Exchanging commonplaces, they admired the "pretty view" together, then turned back in due course to the house. "I catch their voices," remarked Diana. "Let's go in and hear all about it and how many birds they got." And it was on the door of the french window that she suddenly amazed—and, truth to tell—almost frightened him.

"Dick," she said, using his first name, to his utter bewilderment and delight, and grasping his hand tightly in both of her own, "I may need your help." She spoke with a fiery intensity. Her eyes went blazing suddenly. "It was here, you know, that mother—went. And I think—I'm certain of it—they're *after me, too*. And I don't know which is right—to go or to stay. All this"—she swept her arm to include the house, the chattering room, the garden—"is such rubbish—cheap, nasty, worthless. The other is so satisfying—its eternal loveliness, and yet"—her voice dropped to a whisper—"*soulless*, without hope or future. You may help me." Her eyes turned upon him with a sudden amazing fire. "That's why I asked you here."

She kissed him on the eyes—an impersonal, passionless kiss, and the next minute they were in the room, crowded, with the "guns" from a large shooting brake which had just arrived.

How Norman staggered in among the noisy throng and played his part as a fellow guest, he never understood. He managed it somehow, while in his heart sang the wild music of the Irish Fairy's enticing whisper: "I kiss you and the world begins to fade." A queer feeling came to him that he was going lost to life as he knew it, that Diana with her sweet passionless kiss had sealed his fate, that the known world must fade and die because she knew the way to another, lovelier region where nothing could ever pass or die because it was literally everlasting—the state of evolution belonging to fairyland, the land of the deathless Gay People...

Sir Hiram welcomed him cordially, then introduced him to the others, upon which followed the usual description by the guns of the day's sport. They drank their whiskies and sodas, in due course they went up to dress for dinner, but after dinner there was no carousing, for their host bundled them all off to an early bed. The next day they were going to shoot the best beat on the moor and clear eyes and steady hands were important. The two drives for which Greystones was celebrated were to be taken—Telegraph Hill and Silvermine—both well known wherever shooting men congregated so that anticipation and excitement were understandable. An early bed was a small price to pay and Norman, keen and eager as any of them, was glad enough to get to his room when the others trooped upstairs. To be included as a crack shot among all these famous guns was, naturally, a great event to him. He longed to justify himself.

Yet his heart was heavy and dissatisfied, a strange uneasiness gnawed at him despite all his efforts to think only of the morrow's thrill. For Diana had not come down to dinner, nor had he set eyes on her the whole evening.

His polite enquiry about her was met by his host's cheery laugh: "Oh, she's all right, Norman, thank ee; she keeps to herself a bit when a shoot's on. Shooting, you see, ain't her line exactly, but she may come out with us tomorrow." He brushed her tastes aside. "Try and persuade her, if you can. The air'll do her good."

Once in his room, his thoughts and emotions tried in vain to sort themselves out satisfactorily: there was a strange confusion in his mind, an uneasy sense of excitement that was half delight, half fearful anticipation, yet anticipation of he knew not exactly what. That sudden use of his familiar first name, the extraordinary kiss, establishing an unprepared intimacy, deep if passionless, had left him the entire evening in a state of hungry expectancy with nerves on edge. If only she had made an appearance at dinner, if only he could have had a further word with her! He wondered how he would ever get to sleep with this inner turmoil in his brain, and if he slept badly he would shoot badly.

It was this reflection about shooting badly that convinced him abruptly that his sudden "love" was not of the ordinary accepted kind; had he been humanly "in love", no consideration of that sort could have entered his head for a moment. His queer uneasiness, half mixed with delight as it was, increased. The tie was surely of another sort.

Turning out the electric light, he looked from his window across the moor, wondering if he might see the strange lights the chauffeur had told him about. He saw only the dim carpet of the rolling moorland fading into darkness where a moon hid behind fleecy, drifting clouds. A soft, sweet, fragrant air went past him; there was a murmur of falling water. It was intoxicating; he drew in a deep delicious breath. For a second he imagined a golden-haired Diana, with flying hair and flaming eyes, pursuing her lost mother midway between the silvery clouds and shadowy moor... then turned back into his room and flooded it with light... in which instant he saw something concrete lying on his pillow—a scrap of paper—no, an envelope. He tore it open.

"Always wear this when you go out. I wear one too. They cannot come up with you unless you wish, if you wear it. Mother…"

The word "mother", full of imaginative suggestion, was crossed out; the signature was "Diana". With a faint musical tinkle, a little silver crucifix slipped from the pencilled note and fell to the floor.

As Norman stood beside the bed with the note in his hand, and before he stooped to recover the crucifix, there fell upon him with an amazing certainty the eerie conviction that all this had happened before. As a rule this odd sensation is too fleeting to be retained for analysis; yet he held it now for several seconds without effort. Startled, he saw quite clearly that it was not passing in ordinary time, but somewhere outside ordinary time as he knew it. It had happened "before" because it was happening "always". He had caught it in the act.

For a flashing instant he understood; the crucifix symbolized security among known conditions, and if he held to it he would be protected, mentally and spiritually, against a terrific draw into unknown conditions. It meant no more than that—a support to the mind.

That antagonistic "draw" of terrific power, involved the nameless, secret yearnings of his fundamental nature. Diana, aware of this inner conflict, shared the terror and the joy. Her mother, whence she derived the opportunity, had yielded—and had disappeared from life as humans know it. Diana herself was now tempted and afraid. She asked his help. Both he and she together, in some condition outside ordinary time, had met this conflict many times already. He had experienced all this before—the incident of the crucifix, its appeal for help, the delight, the joy, the fear involved. And even as he realized all this, the strange, eerie sensation vanished and was gone, as though it never had been. It became unseizable, lost beyond recapture. It left him with a sensation of loss, of cold, of isolation, a realization of homelessness, yet of intense attraction towards a world unrealized.

He stooped, picked up the small silver crucifix, re-read the pencilled note letter by letter, kissed the paper that her hand had touched, then sat down on the bed and smiled with a sudden gush of human relief and happiness.

The eerie sensation had gone its way beyond recovery. That Diana had thought about him was all that mattered. This little superstition about wearing the crucifix was sweet and touching, and of course he would wear the thing against his heart. And see that she came out tomorrow with him too! His relief was sincere. Now he could sleep. And tomorrow he might not shoot too badly. But before he climbed into bed, he looked in his diary to find out when the equinox was due, and found to his astonishment that it was on the 23rd of September, and that tonight was the 21st! The discovery gave him something of a turn, but he soon fell asleep with the letter against his cheek and the little silver crucifix hung round his neck.

He woke next morning when he was called to find the sun streaming into his room, promising perfect shooting weather. In broad daylight the normal reactions followed as they usually do; the incidents of the day before now seemed slightly ridiculous—his talk with Diana, the crucifix, the chauffeur's fairy-tales above all. He had stumbled upon a nest of hysterical delusions, born of a mysterious disappearance many years ago. It was natural he thought, as he shaved himself, that his host disliked all reference to the subject and its aftermath. For all that, as he went down to breakfast, he felt secretly comforted that he had hung the little silver crucifix round his neck. No one, at any rate, he reflected, could see it.

He had done full justice to the well stocked sideboard and was just finishing his coffee when Diana came into the empty room, and his mind, now charged with the prosaic prospects of the coming shoot, acknowledged a shock. Fact and imagination clashed. The girl was white and drawn. Before he could rise to greet her, she came straight across to the chair beside him.

"Dick," she began at once, "have you got it on?"

He produced the crucifix after a moment's fumbling.

"Of course I have," he said. "You asked me to wear it." Remembering the hesitation in his bedroom, he felt rather foolish. He felt foolish anyhow, wearing a superstitious crucifix on a day's shooting.

Her next words dispelled the feeling of incongruity.

"I was out early," she said in a tense, low voice, "and I heard mother's voice calling me on the moor. It was unmistakable. Close in my ear, then far away. I was with the dog and the dog heard it too and ran for shelter. His hair was up."

"What did you hear?" Norman asked gently, taking her hand.

"My pet name—'Dis'," she told him, "the name only mother used."

"What words did you hear?" he asked, trembling in spite of himself.

"Quite distinctly—in that distant muffled voice—I heard her call: 'Come to me, Dis, oh, come to me quickly!'"

For a moment Norman made no answer. He felt her hand trembling in his. Then he turned and looked straight into her eyes.

"Did you *want* to go?" he asked.

There was a pause before she replied. "Dick," she said, "when I heard that voice, *nothing else in the world seemed to matter*—!" at which moment her uncle's figure, bursting in through the door, shouted that the cars were ready and waiting, and the conversation came to an abrupt end.

This abrupt interruption at the moment of deepest interest left Norman, as may be imagined, excusably and dreadfully disturbed. A word from his host on this particular shooting party was, of course, a command. He dared not keep these great "guns" waiting. Diana, too, shot out as though a bullet had hit her. But her last words went on ringing in his ears, in his heart as well: "Nothing else in the world seemed to matter." He understood in his deepest being what she meant. There was a "call" away from human things, a call into some unimaginable state of bliss no words described, and she had heard it, heard it in her *mother's* voice—the strongest tie humanity knows. Her mother, having left the world, sent back a message.

Norman, trembling unaccountably, hurried to fetch his gun and join the car, and Diana, obeying the orders of her uncle, was shoved into the Ford with her retriever. She had just time to whisper to him "Keep off the Trod—don't put a foot on it," and the two cars whisked off and separated them.

The "shoot" took place, nevertheless, ordinarily, so far as Norman was concerned, for the hunter's passion was too strong in him to be smothered. If his mind was mystical, his body was primitive. He was by nature a hunter before the Lord. The imaginative, mystical view of life, as with peasants and woodsmen, lay deep below, the first birds put an end to all reflection. He was soon too busy to bother about anything else but firing as fast as he could and changing his guns swiftly and smoothly. Breaking through this practical excitement, none the less, flashed swift, haunting thoughts and fancies—Diana's face and voice and eyes, her mother's supernatural call, his own secret yearnings, and, above all, her warning about the Trod. Both sides of his mixed nature operated furiously. Apparently, he shot well, but how he managed it, heaven only knew.

The drive in due course was over and the pick-up completed. Sir Hiram came over and asked if he would mind taking the outside butt at the next drive.

"You see," he explained courteously, "I always ask the youngest of the party to take the outside, as it's a devil of a walk for the old 'uns. Probably," he added, "you'll get more shooting than anyone, as the birds slip away over yonder butt down a little gully. So you'll find it worth the extra swot!"

Norman and his loader set off on their long tramp, while the rest of the guns made their way down to the road where the cars would carry them as far as the track allowed. After nearly a mile's detour Norman was puzzled by his loader striking across the heather instead of following the obvious path. He himself, naturally, kept to the smooth track. He had not gone ten yards along the track before the loader's startled voice shouted at him:

"For the love of God, sir, come off! You're walking on the Trod!"

"It's a good path," cried Norman. "What's wrong with it?" The man eyed him a moment. "It's the Trod, sir," he said gravely, as though that were enough. "We don't walk on it—not at this time o' year especially." He crossed himself. "Come off it, sir, into the heather."

The two men stood facing one another for a minute.

"If you don't believe me, sir, just watch them sheep," said the man in a voice full of excitement and emotion. "You'll see they won't put foot on it. Nor any other animal either."

Norman watched a band of black-faced sheep move hesitatingly down the moorland slope. He was impatient to get on, half angry. For the moment he had forgotten all about Diana's warning. Fuming and annoyed, he watched. To his amazement, the little band of black-faced sheep, on reaching the obvious path, jumped clear over it. They jumped the Trod. Not one of them would touch it. It was an astonishing sight. Each animal leapt across, as though the Trod might burn or injure them. They went their way across the rough heather and disappeared from sight.

Norman, remembering the warning uncomfortably, paused and lit a cigarette. "That's odd," he said. "It's the easiest way."

"Maybe," replied the loader. "But the easiest way may not be the best—or safest."

"The safest?"

"I've got children of me own," said the loader.

It was a significant statement. It made Norman reflect a moment.

"Safest," he repeated, remembering all he had heard, yet longing eagerly to hear more. "You mean, children especially are in danger? Young folks—eh?—is that it?" A moment later, he added, "I can quite believe it, you know, it's a queer bit of country—to my way of thinking."

The understanding sympathy won the man's confidence, as it was meant to do. "And it's equinox time, isn't it?" Norman ventured further.

The man responded quickly enough, finding a "gun" who wouldn't laugh at him. As with the chauffeur, he was evidently relieved to give some kind of utterance to fears and superstitions he was at heart ashamed of and yet believed in.

"I don't mind for myself, sir," he broke out, obviously glad to talk, "for I'm leaving these parts as soon as the grouse shooting's over, but I've two little 'uns up here just now, and I want to keep 'em. Too many young 'uns get lost on the moor for my liking. I'm sending 'em tomorrow down to my aunt at Crossways—"

"Good for you," put in Norman. "It's the equinox just now, isn't it? And that's the dangerous time, they say."

The loader eyed him cautiously a moment, weighing perhaps his value as a recipient of private fears, beliefs, fancies and the rest, yet deciding finally that Norman was worthy of his confidences.

"That's what my father always said," he agreed.

"Your father? It's always wise to listen to what a father tells," the other suggested. "No doubt he'd seen something—worth seeing."

A silence fell between them. Norman felt he had been, perhaps, too eager to draw the man out; yet the loader was reflecting merely. There was something he yearned to tell.

"Worth seeing," the man repeated, "well—that's as may be. But not of this world, and wonderful, it certainly was. It put ice into his bones, that's all I can swear to. And he wasn't the sort to be fooled easy, let me tell you. It was on his dying bed he told me—and a man doesn't lie with death in his eyes."

That Norman was standing idly on this important shoot was sufficient proof of his tremendous interest, and the man beyond question was aware of it.

"In daylight," Norman asked quietly, assuming the truth of what he hoped to hear.

"It was just at nightfall," the other said, "and he was coming from a sick friend at a farm beyond the Garage. The doctor had frightened him, I take it, so it was a bit late when he started for home across the moor and, without realizing that it was equinox time, he found himself on the Trod before he knew it. And, to his terror, the whole place was lit up, and he saw a column of figures moving down it towards him. They was all bright and lovely, he described 'em, gay and terrible, laughing and singing and crying, and jewels shining in their hair, and—worst of all—he swears he saw young children who had gone lost on the moor years before, and a girl he had loved these twenty years back, no older than when he saw her last, and as gay and happy and laughing as though the passing years was nothing—"

"They called to him?" asked Norman, strangely moved. "They asked him to join them?"

"The girl did," replied the man. "The girl, he said, with no years to her back, drew him something terrible. 'Come with us,' he swears she sang to him, 'come with us and be happy and young forever,' and, if my father hadn't clutched hold of his crucifix in time—my God—he would have gone—"

The loader stopped, embarrassed lest he had told too much.

"If he'd gone, he'd have lost his soul," put in Norman, guided by a horrible intuition of his own.

"That's what they say, sir," agreed the man, obviously relieved.

Simultaneously, they hurried on, Sir Hiram's practical world breaking in upon this strange interlude. A big shoot was in progress. They must not be late at their appointed place.

"And where does the Trod start?" Norman asked presently, and the man described the little cave of the Black Waters whence the beck, dark with the peat, ran thence towards the sea across the bleak moors. The scenery provided an admirable setting for the "fairy-tale" he had just listened to; yet his thoughts, as they ploughed forward through the heather, went back to the lovely, fascinating tale, to the superstitious dream of the "Gay People" changing their hunting grounds along that unholy Trod when the equinox flamed with unearthly blazing, when the human young, unsatisfied with earthly pleasures, might be invited to join another ageless evolution that, if it knew no hope, shared at least an unstained, eternal, happy present. Diana's temptation, her mother's incredible disappearance, his own heart-searing yearnings in the balance to boot, took strange shape as practical possibilities.

The cumulative effect of all he had heard, from chauffeur, loader, and from the girl herself, began, it may be, to operate, since the human mind, especially the imaginative human mind, is ever open to attack along the line of least resistance.

He stumbled on, holding his gun firmly, as though a modern weapon of destruction helped to steady his feet, to say nothing of his mind, now full of seething dreams. They reached the appointed butt. And hardly had they settled themselves in it than the first birds began to come, and all conversation was impossible. This was the celebrated "Silvermine Drive", and Norman had never in his life seen so many grouse as he now saw. His guns got too hot to hold, yet still the grouse poured over…

The Drive finished in due course, and after a hurried lunch came the equally famous Telegraph Hill Drive, where there were even more birds than before, and when this came to an end Norman found that his shoulder was sore from the recoil and that he had developed a slight gun-headache, so that he was glad enough to climb into the car that took him back to the Lodge and tea. The excitement, naturally, had been great, the nervous hope that he had shot well enough to justify his inclusion in the great shoot had also played upon his vitality. He found himself exhausted, and after tea he was relieved to slip up to his bedroom for a quiet hour or two.

Lying comfortably on his sofa with a cigarette, thinking over the fire and fury of the recent hours, his thoughts turned gradually aside to other things. The hunter, it seemed, withdrew; the dreamer, never wholly submerged, re-appeared. His mind reviewed the tales he had heard from the chauffeur and the loader, while the story of Diana's mother, the strange words of the girl herself, took possession of his thoughts. Too weary to be critical, he remembered them. His own natural leaning enforced their possible truth, while fatigue made analysis too difficult to bother about, so that imagination cast its spell of glamour undefied… He burned to know the truth. In the end he made up his mind to creep out the following night and watch the Trod. It would be the night of the equinox. That ought to settle things one way or the other—proof or disproof. Only he must examine it in the daylight first.

It was disturbing at dinner to find that the girl was absent, had in fact, according to Sir Hiram, gone away for a day or so to see an old school-friend in a neighbouring town. She would be back, however, for the final shoot, he added, an explanation which Norman interpreted to mean that her uncle had deliberately sent her out of danger. He felt positive he was right. Sir Hiram might scorn such "rubbishy tales", but he was taking no chances. It was at the equinox that his sister had mysteriously disappeared. The girl was best elsewhere. Nor could all the pleasant compliments about Norman's good shooting on the two Drives conceal his host's genuine uneasiness. Diana was "best elsewhere".

Norman fell asleep with the firm determination that he must explore the Trod next day in good light, making sure of his landmarks and then creep out at night when the household was quiet, and see what happened.

There was no shooting next day. His task was easy. Keepers and dogs went out to pick up any birds that had been left from the previous day. After breakfast he slipped off across the waste of heather and soon found it—a deep smooth groove running through occasional hollows where no water lay, nor any faintest track of man or beast upon its soft, black peaty surface. Obviously, it was a track through the deep heather no one—neither man nor animal—used. He again noted the landmarks carefully, and felt sure he could find it again in the darkness… and, in due course, the day passed along its normal course, the "guns" after dinner discussed the next day's beat, and all turned in early in pleasurable anticipation of the shoot to come.

Norman went up to bed with a beating heart, for his plan to slip out of the sleeping house later and explore the moorland with its "haunted Trod", was not exactly what a host expected of a guest. The absence of Diana, moreover, deliberately planned, added to his deep uneasiness. Her sudden disappearance to visit "an old school-friend" was not convincing. Nor had she even left a line of explanation. It came to him that others besides the chauffeur and the loader took these fantastic fairy-tales seriously. His thoughts flew buzzing like bees outside a beehive…

From his window he looked out upon the night. The moon, in her second quarter, shone brightly at moments, then became hidden behind fleecy clouds. Higher up, evidently, a raging wind was driving, but below over the moorland a deathly stillness reigned. This stillness touched his nerves, and the dogs, howling in their kennels, added to a sense of superstitious uneasiness in his blood. The deep stillness seemed to hide a busy activity behind the silence. Something was stirring in the night, something out on the moor.

He turned back from the window and saw the lighted room, its cosy comfort, its well-lit luxury, its delicious bed waiting for weary limbs. He hesitated. The two sides of his nature clashed… but in the end the strange absence of Diana, her words, her abrupt sensational kiss, her odd silence… the quixotic feeling that he *might* help—these finally decided him.

Changing quickly into his shooting clothes, and making sure that the lights in all the bedroom windows he could see were out, he crept down in stockinged feet to the front door, carrying a pair of tennis shoes in his hand. The front door was unlocked, opening without noise, so that he slipped quietly across the gravel drive on to the grass, and thence, having now put on his shoes, on to the moor beyond.

The house faded behind him, patches of silvery moonlight shone through thin racing clouds, the taste of the night air was intoxicating. How could he ever have hesitated? The wonder and mystery of the wild countryside, haunted or otherwise, caught him by the throat. As he climbed the railings leading from the cultivated garden to the moor, there came a faint odd whispering sound behind him, so that he paused and listened for a moment. Was it wind or footsteps? It was neither—merely the flap of his open coat trailing across the fence. Bah! his nerves were jumpy. He laughed—almost laughed aloud, such was the exhilaration in him—and moved on quickly through the weird half lights. And for some reason his spirits rose, his blood went racing: here was an adventure the other side of his nature delighted in, yet his "other side" now took ominously the upper hand.

How primitive, after all, these "shooting parties" were! For men of brains and character, the best that England could produce, to spend all this time and money, hunting as the cave-men hunted the fox, the deer, the bird— earlier men needed these for food, yet thousands of years later the finest males of the twentieth century—sportsmen all—spent millions on superior weapons, which gave the hunted animal no chance, to bring them down. Not to be a "sportsman" was to be an inferior Englishman…! The "sports-man" was the flower of the race. It struck him, not for the first time, as a grim, a cheap, ideal. Was there no other climax of chivalric achievement more desirable?

This flashed across his mind as a hundred times before, while yet he him-self, admittedly, was a "sportsman" born. Against it, at the same time, rose some strange glamour of eternal, deathless things that took no account of killing, things that caught his soul away in ecstasy. Fairy tales, of course, were fairy tales, yet they enshrined the undying truths of life and human nature within their golden "nonsense", catching at the skirts of radiant wonder, whispering ageless secrets of the soul, giving hints of ineffable glories that lay outside the normal scales of space and time as accepted by the reasoning mind. And this attitude now rose upon him like a wild ungovernable wind of spring, fragrant, delicious, intoxicating. Fairies, the Little People, the "Gay People", happy dwellers in some non-human state…

Diana's mother had disappeared, yearning with secret, surreptitious calls for her daughter to come and join her. The girl herself acknowledged the call and was afraid, while yet her practical, hard-boiled uncle took particular trouble to keep her out of the way. Even for him, typical "sportsman", the time of the equinox was dangerous. These reflections, tumbling about his mind and heart, flooded Norman's being, while his yearning and desire for the girl came over him like a flame.

The moor, meanwhile, easy enough to walk on in the daytime, seemed unexpectedly difficult at night, the heather longer, the ground very uneven. He was always putting his legs into little hollows that he could not see, and he was relieved when at last he could make out the loom of the garage which was one of his landmarks. He knew that he had not much further to go before he reached the Trod.

The turmoil in his mind had been such that he had paid little attention to the occasional slight sounds he heard as though somebody were at his heels, but now, on reaching the Trod, he became uneasily convinced that someone was not far behind him. So certain, indeed, was he of someone else that he let himself down silently into the deep heather and waited.

He listened intently, breathing very softly. The same instant he knew that he was right. Those sounds were not imagination. Footsteps were at his heels. The swish through the heather of a moving body was unmistakable. He caught distinct footsteps then. The footsteps came to a pause quite near to where he crouched. At which moment exactly, the clouds raced past the moon, letting down a clear space of silvery light, so that he saw the "follower" brilliantly defined.

It was Diana.

"I knew it," he said half aloud, "I was sure of it long ago," while his heart, faced with a yearning hope and fear, both half fulfilled, yet gave no leap of relief or pleasure. A shiver ran up and down his spine. Crouching there deep among the heather on the edge of the Trod, he knew more of terror than of happiness. It was all too clear for misunderstanding. She had been drawn irresistibly on the night of the equinox to the danger zone where her mother had so mysteriously "disappeared".

"I'm here," he added with a great effort in the same low whisper. "You asked my help. I'm here to meet you… dear…"

The words, even if he actually uttered them, died on his lips. The girl, he saw, stood still a moment, gazing in a dazed way, as though puzzled by something that obstructed her passage. Like a sleep walker, she stared about her, beautiful as a dream, yet only half conscious of her surroundings. Her eyes shone in the moonlight, her hands were half outstretched, yet not towards himself.

"Diana," he heard himself crying, "can you see me? Do you see who I am? Don't you recognize me? I've come to help—to save—you!"

It was plain she neither heard nor saw him standing there in front of her. She was aware of an obstructing presence, no more than that. Her glazed, shining eyes looked far beyond him—along the Trod. And a terror clutched him that, unless he quickly did the right thing, she would be lost to him for ever.

He sprang to his feet and went towards her, but with the extraordinary sensation that he at once came up against some intervening wall of resistance that made normal movement difficult. It was almost like forcing his way through moving water or a drift of wind, and it was with an effort that he reached her side and stood now close against her.

"Diana!" he cried, "Dis—Dis," using the name her mother used. "Can't you see who I am?" Don't you know me? I've come to save you—" and he stretched his hands towards her.

There was no response; she made no sign.

"I've come to lead you back—to lead you home—for God's sake, answer me, look into my eyes!"

She turned her head in his direction, as though to look into his face, but her eyes went past him towards the moonlit moor beyond. He noticed only, while she stared with those unseeing eyes, that her left hand fumbled weakly at a tiny crucifix that hung on a thin silver chain about her neck. He put out his hand and seized her by the arm, but the instant he touched her he found himself suddenly powerless to move. There came this strange arrest. And at the same instant, the whole Trod became startlingly lit up with a kind of unearthly radiance, and a strange greenish light shone upon the track right across the moor beyond where they stood. A deep terror for himself as well as for her rose over him simultaneously. It came to him, with a shock of ice, that his own soul as well as hers, lay in sudden danger.

His eyes turned irresistibly towards the Trod, so strangely shining in the night. Though his hand still touched the girl, his mind was caught away in phantasmal possibilities. For two passions seized and fought within him: the fierce desire to possess her in the world of men and women, or to go with her headlong, recklessly, and share some ineffable ecstasy of happiness beyond the familiar world where ordinary time and space held sway. Her own nature already held the key and knew the danger… His whole being rocked.

The two incompatible passions gored the very heart in him. In a flash he realized his alternative—the dreary desolation of human progress with its grinding future, the joy and glory of a soulless happiness that reason denied and yet the heart welcomed as an ultimate truth. These two!

Yet of what value and meaning could she ever be to him as wife and mother if she were now drawn away—away to where her mother now eternally passed her golden, time-less life? How could he face this daily exile of her soul, this hourly isolation, this rape of her normal being his earthly nature held so dear and precious? While—should he save her, keeping her safe against the *human* hearth—how should he hold her to him, he himself tainted with the golden poison…?

Norman saw both sides with remorseless clarity in that swift instant while the Trod took on its shining radiance. His reasoning mind, he knew, had sunk away; his heart, wildly beating, was uppermost. With a supreme effort he kept his touch upon Diana's arm. His fingers clutched at the rough tweed of her sleeve. His entire being seemed rapt in some incredible ecstasy. He stood, he stared, he wondered, lost in an ineffable dream of beauty. One link only with the normal he held to like a vice—his touch upon her tough tweed sleeve, and, in his fading memory, the picture of a crucifix her weakening fingers weakly fumbled.

Figures were now moving fast and furious along the Trod; he could see them approaching from the distance. It was an inspiring, an intoxicating vision, and yet quite credible, with no foolish phantasmagoria of any childish sort. He saw everything as plainly as though he watched a parade in Whitehall, or a procession at some southern Battle of Flowers. Yet lovely, happy, radiant—and irresistibly enticing. As the figures came nearer, the light increased, so that it was obvious *they* emanated light of their own against the dark moorland. Nor were the individual figures particularly striking, least of all sensational. They seemed "natural", yet natural only because they were true and justified.

In the lead, as they drew nearer, Norman saw a tall dark man riding a white horse, close behind him a fair shining woman in a green dress, her long, golden hair falling to her waist. On her head he saw a circlet of gold in which was set a red stone that shone and glowed like burning flame. Beside her was another woman, dark and beautiful, with white stones sparkling in her hair as diamonds or crystals sparkle. It was a gorgeous and a radiant sight. Their faces shone with the ecstasy of youth. In some indescribable way they all spread happiness and joy about them, their eyes blazing with a peace and beneficence he had never seen in any human eyes.

These passed, and more and more poured by, some riding, some walking, young and old and children, men with hunting spears and unstrung bows, then youthful figures with harps and lyres, and one and all making friendly gestures of invitation to come and join them, as they flowed past silently. Silently, yes, silently, without a sound of footsteps or of rustling heather, silently along the illuminated Trod, and yet, silent though their passing was, there came to him an impression of singing, laughter, even an air of dancing. Such figures, he realized, could not move without rhythm, rhythm of sound and gesture, for it was as essential to them as breathing. Happy, radiant, gay they were for ever from the grinding effort and struggle of the world's strenuous evolutionary battles—free, if soulless. The "Gay People" as the natives called them. And the sight wrenched at the deepest roots of his own mixed being. To go with them and share their soulless bliss forever... or to stay and face the grim battle of Humanity's terrific—noble, yes—but almost hopeless, evolution?

That he was torn in two seemed an understatement. The pain seared and burned him in his very vitals. Diana, the girl, drew him as with some power of the stars themselves, and his hand still felt the tweed of her cloth beneath his fingers. His mind and heart, his nerves, his straining muscles, seemed fused in a fury of contradictions and acceptances. The glorious procession flowed streaming by, as though the stars had touched the common moorland earth, dripping their lavish gold in quiet glory—when suddenly Diana wrenched herself away and ran headlong towards them.

A golden-haired woman, he saw, had stepped out of the actual Trod, and had come to a halt directly in front of where he stood. Radiant and wonderful, she stood for a moment poised.

"Dis… Dis…" he heard in tones like music. "Come… come to me. Come and join us! The way is always open. There are no regrets…!"

The girl was half way to her mother before he could break the awful spell that held him motionless. But the rough cloth of her sleeve held clutched between his fingers, and with it the broken chain that caught her little crucifix. The silver cross swung and dangled a moment, then dropped among the heather.

It was as he stooped frantically to recover in that Fate played that strange, unusual card she keeps in reserve for moments when the world seems lost; for, as he fell, his own chain and crucifix, to which he had not once given a thought, flicked up and caught him on the lip. Thinking it was a broken edge of torn heather that stung him into pain, he dashed it aside—only to find it was the foolish metal symbol Diana had made him promise to wear, in his own safety. It was the sharp stab of pain, not the superstitious mental reaction, that roused immediate action in him.

In a second he was on his feet again, and a second later he had overtaken the striding girl and had both arms possessively round her figure. An instant afterwards his lips were on her own, her head and shoulders torn backwards against his breast.

"Dis!" he cried wildly, "we must stay here together! You belong to me. I hold you tight—forever… here!"

What else he cried he hardly knows. He felt her weight sink back into his arms. It seems he carried her. He felt her convulsive weeping sobs against his heart. Her arms clung tightly round him.

In the distance he saw the line of moving figures die fading off into the enveloping moorland, dipping down into the curving dimness. Clouds raced back across the moon. There was no sound, the wind lay still, no tumbling beck was audible, the peewits slept.

Putting his own coat about her, he carried her home… and in due course he married her; he married Diana, he married Dis as well, a queer, lovely girl, but a girl without a soul, almost without a mind—a girl as commonplace as the radiant nonentity pictured with shining teeth on the cover of a popular magazine—a standardized creature whose essence had "gone elsewhere".

THE ERL-KING

Angela Carter

Angela Carter (1940–1992) was born Angela Olive Stalker in Eastbourne, and was almost immediately evacuated to Yorkshire to spend her early childhood with her grandmother. There, she recalled, her grandmother would act out the story of Little Red Riding Hood with gleeful relish, "which made me squeak and gibber with excited pleasure." Beginning her first fairy tale-horror novel *Shadow Dance* during her second summer vacation at the University of Bristol, her early delight in the macabre, the fantastical and the Gothic would weave itself throughout all her work.

Fairies themselves are scattered throughout Carter's writing, too, from her sardonic take on Shakespeare's Oberon and Titania in 1985's "Overture and Incidental Music for a Midsummer Night's Dream" to the tinseltown spangles of her 1991 masterpiece *Wise Children*. However, in her 1979 collection of reimagined fairy tales *The Bloody Chamber* she explores a much more Gothic type of fairy in her eerily autumnal "The Erl-King". Drawing on Goethe's 1782 ballad *Erlkönig* ("The Erlking, father, has done me harm"), Rosetti's *Goblin Market*, green man tales and murder ballads, Carter creates a seductive, green-eyed devourer who lures the unwary into his woodland lair.

Dear father, oh father, and do you not hear
What th' Erlking whispers so close to my ear? –
Be quiet, do be quiet, my son,
Through leaves the wind is rustling anon. –

"Do come, my darling, oh come with me!
Good care my daughters will take of thee,
My daughters will dance about thee in a ring,
Will rock thee to sleep and will prettily sing."

Dear father, oh father, and do you not see
The Erlking's daughters so near to me? –
My son, my son, no one's in our way,
The willows are looking unusually gray. –

"I love thee, thy beauty I covet and choose,
Be willing, my darling, or force I shall use!"
Dear father, oh father, he seizes my arm!
The Erlking, father, has done me harm.

From Johann Wolfgang von Goethe,
Erlkönig (1782), trans. Paul Dyrsen (1878)

T HE lucidity, the clarity of the light that afternoon was sufficient to itself; perfect transparency must be impenetrable, these vertical bars of a brass-coloured distillation of light coming down from sulphur-yellow interstices in a sky hunkered with grey clouds that bulge with more rain. It struck the wood with nicotine-stained fingers, the leaves glittered. A cold day of late October, when the withered blackberries dangled like their own dour spooks on the discoloured brambles. There were crisp husks of beechmast and cast acorn cups underfoot in the russet slime of dead bracken where the rains of the equinox had so soaked the earth that the cold oozed up through the soles of the shoes, lancinating cold of the approach of winter that grips hold of your belly and squeezes it tight. Now the stark elders have an anorexic look; there is not much in the autumn wood to make you smile but it is not yet, not quite yet, the saddest time of the year. Only, there is a haunting sense of the imminent cessation of being; the year, in turning, turns in on itself. Introspective weather, a sickroom hush.

The woods enclose. You step between the first trees and then you are no longer in the open air; the wood swallows you up. There is no way through the wood any more, this wood has reverted to its original privacy. Once you are inside it, you must stay there until it lets you out again for there is no clue to guide you through in perfect safety; grass grew over the track years ago and now the rabbits and the foxes make their own runs in the subtle labyrinth and nobody comes. The trees stir with a noise like taffeta skirts of women who have lost themselves in the woods and hunt round hopelessly for the way out. Tumbling crows play tig in the branches of the elms they clotted with their nests, now and then raucously cawing. A little stream with soft margins of marsh runs through the wood but it has grown sullen with the time of the year; the silent, blackish water thickens, now, to ice. All will fall still, all lapse.

A young girl would go into the wood as trustingly as Red Riding Hood to her granny's house but this light admits of no ambiguities and, here, she will be trapped in her own illusion because everything in the wood is exactly as it seems.

The woods enclose and then enclose again, like a system of Chinese boxes opening one into another; the intimate perspectives of the wood changed endlessly around the interloper, the imaginary traveller walking towards an invented distance that perpetually receded before me. It is easy to lose yourself in these woods.

The two notes of the song of a bird rose on the still air, as if my girlish and delicious loneliness had been made into a sound. There was a little tangled mist in the thickets, mimicking the tufts of old man's beard that flossed the lower branches of the trees and bushes; heavy bunches of red berries as ripe and delicious as goblin or enchanted fruit hung on the hawthorns but the old grass withers, retreats. One by one, the ferns have curled up their hundred eyes and curled back into the earth. The trees threaded a cat's cradle of half-stripped branches over me so that I felt I was in a house of nets and though the cold wind that always heralds your presence, had I but known it then, blew gentle around me, I thought that nobody was in the wood but me.

Erl-King will do you grievous harm.

Piercingly, now, there came again the call of the bird, as desolate as if it came from the throat of the last bird left alive. That call, with all the melancholy of the failing year in it, went directly to my heart.

I walked through the wood until all its perspectives converged upon a darkening clearing; as soon as I saw them, I knew at once that all its occupants had been waiting for me from the moment I first stepped into the wood, with the endless patience of wild things, who have all the time in the world.

It was a garden where all the flowers were birds and beasts; ash-soft doves, diminutive wrens, freckled thrushes, robins in their tawny bibs, huge, helmeted crows that shone like patent leather, a blackbird with a yellow bill, voles, shrews, fieldfares, little brown bunnies with their ears laid together along their backs like spoons, crouching at his feet. A lean, tall, reddish hare, up on its great hind legs, nose a-twitch. The rusty fox, its muzzle sharpened to a point, laid its head upon his knee. On the trunk of a scarlet rowan a squirrel clung, to watch him; a cock pheasant delicately stretched his shimmering neck from a brake of thorn to peer at him. There was a goat of uncanny whiteness, gleaming like a goat of snow, who turned her mild eyes towards me and bleated softly, so that he knew I had arrived.

He smiles. He lays down his pipe, his elder bird-call. He lays upon me his irrevocable hand.

His eyes are quite green, as if from too much looking at the wood.

There are some eyes can eat you.

The Erl-King lives by himself all alone in the heart of the wood in a house which has only the one room. His house is made of sticks and stones and has grown a pelt of yellow lichen. Grass and weeds grow in the mossy roof. He chops fallen branches for his fire and draws his water from the stream in a tin pail.

What does he eat? Why, the bounty of the woodland! Stewed nettles; savoury messes of chickweed sprinkled with nutmeg; he cooks the foliage of shepherd's purse as if it were cabbage. He knows which of the frilled, blotched, rotted fungi are fit to eat; he understands their eldritch ways, how they spring up overnight in lightless places and thrive on dead things. Even the homely wood blewits, that you cook like tripe, with milk and onions, and the egg-yolk yellow chanterelle with its fan-vaulting and faint scent of apricots, all spring up overnight like bubbles of earth, unsustained by nature, existing in a void. And I could believe that it has been the same with him; he came alive from the desire of the woods.

He goes out in the morning to gather his unnatural treasures, he handles them as delicately as he does pigeons' eggs, he lays them in one of the baskets he weaves from osiers. He makes salads of the dandelion that he calls rude names, "bum-pipes" or "piss-the-beds", and flavours them with a few leaves of wild strawberry but he will not touch the brambles, he says the Devil spits on them at Michaelmas.

His nanny goat, the colour of whey, gives him her abundant milk and he can make soft cheese that has a unique, rank, amniotic taste. Sometimes he traps a rabbit in a snare of string and makes a soup or stew, seasoned with wild garlic. He knows all about the wood and the creatures in it. He told me about the grass snakes, how the old ones open their mouths wide when they smell danger and the thin little ones disappear down the old ones' throats until the fright is over and out they come again, to run around as usual. He told me how the wise toad who squats among the kingcups by the stream in summer has a very precious jewel in his head. He said the owl was a baker's daughter; then he smiled at me. He showed me how to thread mats from reeds and weave osier twigs into baskets and into the little cages in which he keeps his singing birds.

His kitchen shakes and shivers with birdsong from cage upon cage of singing birds, larks and linnets, which he piles up one on another against the wall, a wall of trapped birds. How cruel it is, to keep wild birds in cages! But he laughs at me when I say that; laughs, and shows his white, pointed teeth with the spittle gleaming on them.

He is an excellent housewife. His rustic home is spick and span. He puts his well-scoured saucepan and skillet neatly on the hearth side by side, like a pair of polished shoes. Over the hearth hang bunches of drying mushrooms, the thin, curling kind they call jew's-ears, which have grown on the elder trees since Judas hanged himself on one; this is the kind of lore he tells me, tempting my half-belief. He hangs up herbs in bunches to dry, too—thyme, marjoram, sage, vervain, southernwood, yarrow. The room is musical and aromatic and there is always a wood fire crackling in the grate, a sweet, acrid smoke, a bright, glancing flame. But you cannot get a tune out of the old fiddle hanging on the wall beside the birds because all its strings are broken.

Now, when I go for walks, sometimes in the mornings when the frost has put its shiny thumbprint on the undergrowth or sometimes, though less frequently, yet more enticingly, in the evenings when the cold darkness settles down, I always go to the Erl-King and he lays me down on his bed of rustling straw where I lie at the mercy of his huge hands.

He is the tender butcher who showed me how the price of flesh is love; skin the rabbit, he says! Off come all my clothes.

When he combs his hair that is the colour of dead leaves, dead leaves fall out of it; they rustle and drift to the ground as though he were a tree and he can stand as still as a tree, when he wants the doves to flutter softly, crooning as they come, down upon his shoulders, those silly, fat, trusting woodies with the pretty wedding rings round their necks. He makes his whistles out of an elder twig and that is what he uses to call the birds out of the air—all the birds come; and the sweetest singers he will keep in cages.

The wind stirs the dark wood; it blows through the bushes. A little of the cold air that blows over graveyards always goes with him, it crisps the hairs on the back of my neck but I am not afraid of him; only, afraid of vertigo, of the vertigo with which he seizes me. Afraid of falling down.

Falling as a bird would fall through the air if the Erl-King tied up the winds in his handkerchief and knotted the ends together so they could not get out. Then the moving currents of the air would no longer sustain them and all the birds would fall at the imperative of gravity, as I fall down for him, and I know it is only because he is kind to me that I do not fall still further. The earth with its fragile fleece of last summer's dying leaves and grasses supports me only out of complicity with him, because his flesh is of the same substance as those leaves that are slowly turning into earth.

He could thrust me into the seed-bed of next year's generation and I would have to wait until he whistled me up from my darkness before I could come back again.

Yet, when he shakes out those two clear notes from his bird call, I come, like any other trusting thing that perches on the crook of his wrist.

I found the Erl-King sitting on an ivy-covered stump winding all the birds in the wood to him on a diatonic spool of sound, one rising note, one falling note; such a sweet piercing call that down there came a soft, chirruping jostle of birds. The clearing was cluttered with dead leaves, some the colour of honey, some the colour of cinders, some the colour of earth. He seemed so much the spirit of the place I saw without surprise how the fox laid its muzzle fearlessly upon his knee. The brown light of the end of the day drained into the moist, heavy earth; all silent, all still and the cool smell of night coming. The first drops of rain fell. In the wood, no shelter but his cottage.

That was the way I walked into the bird-haunted solitude of the Erl-King, who keeps his feathered things in little cages he has woven out of osier twigs and there they sit and sing for him.

Goat's milk to drink, from a chipped tin mug; we shall eat the oatcakes he has baked on the hearthstone. Rattle of the rain on the roof. The latch clanks on the door; we are shut up inside with one another, in the brown room crisp with the scent of burning logs that shiver with tiny flame, and I lie down on the Erl-King's creaking palliasse of straw. His skin is the tint and texture of sour cream, he has stiff, russet nipples ripe as berries. Like a tree that bears bloom and fruit on the same bough together, how pleasing, how lovely.

And now—ach! I feel your sharp teeth in the subaqueous depths of your kisses. The equinoctial gales seize the bare elms and make them whizz and whirl like dervishes; you sink your teeth into my throat and make me scream.

The white moon above the clearing coldly illuminates the still tableaux of our embracements. How sweet I roamed, or, rather, used to roam; once I was the perfect child of the meadows of summer, but then the year turned, the light clarified and I saw the gaunt Erl-King, tall as a tree with birds in its branches, and he drew me towards him on his magic lasso of inhuman music.

If I strung that old fiddle with your hair, we could waltz together to the music as the exhausted daylight founders among the trees; we should have better music than the shrill prothalamions of the larks stacked in their pretty cages as the roof creaks with the freight of birds you've lured to it while we engage in your profane mysteries under the leaves.

He strips me to my last nakedness, that underskin of mauve, pearlized satin, like a skinned rabbit; then dresses me again in an embrace so lucid and encompassing it might be made of water. And shakes over me dead leaves as if into the stream I have become.

Sometimes the birds, at random, all singing, strike a chord.

His skin covers me entirely; we are like two halves of a seed, enclosed in the same integument. I should like to grow enormously small, so that you could swallow me, like those queens in fairy tales who conceive when they swallow a grain of corn or a sesame seed. Then I could lodge inside your body and you would bear me.

The candle flutters and goes out. His touch both consoles and devastates me; I feel my heart pulse, then wither, naked as a stone on the roaring mattress while the lovely, moony night slides through the window to dapple the flanks of this innocent who makes cages to keep the sweet birds in. Eat me, drink me; thirsty, cankered, goblin-ridden, I go back and back to him to have his fingers strip the tattered skin away and clothe me in his dress of water, this garment that drenches me, its slithering odour, its capacity for drowning.

Now the crows drop winter from their wings, invoke the harshest season with their cry.

It is growing colder. Scarcely a leaf left on the trees and the birds come to him in even greater numbers because, in this hard weather, it is lean pickings. The blackbirds and thrushes must hunt the snails from hedge bottoms and crack the shells on stones. But the Erl-King gives them corn and when he whistles to them, a moment later you cannot see him for the birds that have covered him like a soft fall of feathered snow. He spreads out a goblin feast of fruit for me, such appalling succulence; I lie above him and see the light from the fire sucked into the black vortex of his eye, the omission of light at the centre, there, that exerts on me such a tremendous pressure, it draws me inwards.

Eyes green as apples. Green as dead sea fruit.

A wind rises; it makes a singular, wild, low, rushing sound.

What big eyes you have. Eyes of an incomparable luminosity, the numinous phosphorescence of the eyes of lycanthropes. The gelid green of your eyes fixes my reflective face; It is a preservative, like a green liquid amber; it catches me. I am afraid I will be trapped in it for ever like the poor little ants and flies that stuck their feet in resin before the sea covered the Baltic. He winds me into the circle of his eye on a reel of birdsong. There is a black hole in the middle of both your eyes; it is their still centre, looking there makes me giddy, as if I might fall into it.

Your green eye is a reducing chamber. If I look into it long enough, I will become as small as my own reflection, I will diminish to a point and vanish. I will be drawn down into that black whirlpool and be consumed by you. I shall become so small you can keep me in one of your osier cages and mock my loss of liberty. I have seen the cage you are weaving for me; it is a very pretty one and I shall sit, hereafter, in my cage among the other singing birds but I—I shall be dumb, from spite.

When I realized what the Erl-King meant to do to me, I was shaken with a terrible fear and I did not know what to do for I loved him with all my heart and yet I had no wish to join the whistling congregation he kept in his cages although he looked after them very affectionately, gave them fresh water every day and fed them well. His embraces were his enticements and yet, oh yet! they were the branches of which the trap itself was woven. But in his innocence he never knew he might be the death of me, although I knew from the first moment I saw him how Erl-King would do me grievous harm.

Although the bow hangs beside the old fiddle on the wall, all the strings are broken so you cannot play it. I don't know what kind of tunes you might play on it, if it were strung again; lullabies for foolish virgins, perhaps, and now I know the birds don't sing, they only cry because they can't find their way out of the wood, have lost their flesh when they were dipped in the corrosive pools of his regard and now must live in cages.

Sometimes he lays his head on my lap and lets me comb his lovely hair for him; his combings are leaves of every tree in the wood and dryly susurrate around my feet. His hair falls down over my knees. Silence like a dream in front of the spitting fire while he lies at my feet and I comb the dead leaves out of his languorous hair. The robin has built his nest in the thatch again, this year; he perches on an unburnt log, cleans his beak, ruffles his plumage. There is a plaintive sweetness in his song and a certain melancholy, because the year is over—the robin, the friend of man, in spite of the wound in his breast from which Erl-King tore out his heart.

Lay your head on my knee so that I can't see the greenish inward-turning suns of your eyes any more.

My hands shake.

I shall take two huge handfuls of his rustling hair as he lies half dreaming, half waking, and wind them into ropes, very softly, so he will not wake up, and, softly, with hands as gentle as rain, I shall strangle him with them.

Then she will open all the cages and let the birds free; they will change back into young girls, every one, each with the crimson imprint of his lovebite on their throats.

She will carve off his great mane with the knife he uses to skin the rabbits; she will string the old fiddle with five single strings of ash-brown hair.

Then it will play discordant music without a hand touching it. The bow will dance over the new strings of its own accord and they will cry out: "Mother, mother, you have murdered me!"

CONCERNING A BOY AND A GIRL EMERGING FROM THE EARTH

Randolph Stow

Randolph Stow (1935–2010) was an Australian-born writer who published his first novel *The Haunted Land* (1956), a Gothic tale set in a decaying homestead in Western Australia, when he was just 21. In 1960 he made the first of his visits to England, and would come to spend much of his subsequent life there.

In the late 1960s he moved to Suffolk, where his ancestors had lived, and used the folklore of the area to create his haunting 1980 novel *The Girl Green as Elderflower*. It tells the story of Crispin Clare, a young antipodean living with relatives in Suffolk while recovering from malaria, who translates and rewrites medieval Latin tales as part of his recovery. The book weaves together a number of strange "marvels" found in twelfth- and thirteenth-century chronicles—a "fantastic sprite" named Malekin, a merman, and the green children of Woolpit—shifting between the 1960s and the Middle Ages as the boundaries between time periods become increasingly blurred.

The extract here retells the mysterious tale of the green-skinned children who claimed to have come from a land without sunlight, found in Ralph of Coggeshall's *Chronicon Anglicanum* and William of Newburgh's *Historia Rerum Anglicarum*. In Stow's hands, the story becomes an exploration of exile, alienation and a search for home.

"Another wonderful thing," says Ralph of Coggeshall, "happened in Suffolk, at St. Mary's of the Wolf-pits. A boy and his sister were found by the inhabitants of that place near the mouth of a pit which is there, who had the form of all their limbs like to those of other men, but they differed in the colour of their skin from all the people of our habitable world; for the whole surface of their skin was tinged of a green colour. No one could understand their speech. When they were brought as curiosities to the house of a certain knight, Sir Richard de Calne, at Wikes, they wept bitterly. Bread and other victuals were set before them, but they would touch none of them, though they were tormented by great hunger, as the girl afterwards acknowledged. At length, when some beans just cut, with their stalks, were brought into the house, they made signs, with great avidity, that they should be given to them. When they were brought, they opened the stalks instead of the pods, thinking the beans were in the hollow of them; but not finding them there, they began to weep anew. When those who were present saw this, they opened the pods, and showed them the naked beans. They fed on these with delight, and for a long time tasted no other food. The boy, however, was always languid and depressed, and he died within a short time. The girl enjoyed continual good health; and becoming accustomed to various kinds of food, lost completely that green colour, and gradually recovered the sanguine habit of her entire body. She was afterwards regenerated by the laver of holy baptism, and lived for many years in the service of that knight (as I have frequently heard from him and his family), and was rather loose and wanton in her conduct. Being frequently asked about the people of her country, she asserted that the inhabitants, and all they had in that country, were of a green colour; and that they saw no sun, but enjoyed a degree of light like what is after sunset."

Ralph of Coggeshall, *Chronicon Anglicanum* (*c.* 1200–1299),
translation in Thomas Keightley, *The Fairy Mythology* (1850)

(De quodam puero et puella de terra emergentibus)

A NOTHER wonder not unlike the appearance of the Wild Man occurred in Suffolk at St. Mary Woolpit. On the manor at this place belonging to Richard Calne, a soldier, a great throng of reapers was proceeding along the harvest field. The day was bright and hot, which, as afterwards appeared, was not without bearing on what followed; poppies and may weed stared in the yellow grain as yet unapproached by the reapers and gleaners; and over the summer-darkened hedgerows tangled with woodbine and traveller's joy, invisible larks sang.

Some way from the field, in a sandy place grown with gorse, there were certain hollows or pits, which ignorant people called the Wolf Pits, to explain to themselves the name of the village. Towards these pits, during a pause in the work, a young reaper strayed on some business of his own, and so became (with round eyes and gaping mouth) the first to observe the prodigy over which the Abbot of Coggeshall and many more have marvelled.

Crouched near the edge of one of the pits this John observed two children, whom at first he took to be the children of neighbours playing at some game; for the sun was in his eyes and they were a little shadowed by a clump of brambles. But at the sound of his feet in the gorse the children rose and looked towards him, their eyes narrowed against the light, and seeming to see him only dimly, if at all. They were a girl and boy of perhaps seven and six years old, comely in form and in every way like any children of our world. But their hair and their eyes and all their skins were of the green of leeks.

The young reaper for some minutes only stared at their fear, with fear of his own in which there was pity too. Then he turned about and ran back to the harvest field, shouting to the lord of the harvest: "Roger! Roger, see what's here!"

In a narrow vale stood the manor house of Wikes, looking out over its fish-ponds to a little wood which closed the view. Built of stone, whitewashed within and without, with a steep thatched roof adapted to the line of its curved ends, the house rose with a modest ceremony out of a ceremonious garden on the same small scale. A plot of fine grass lay before the hall door, bordered by other plots of herbs and roses. At the south end a wall enclosed an orchard of pears, apples, quinces, cherries, plums and a single vine, and there the strawberries also lurked brightly. In that weather the garden and the house itself, with its open door and narrow glassless windows, moaned with the many doves from its cote throughout the day.

At the time when the children came, the knight sat in the airy hall with only his wife for company. The lady, who after many disappointments was expecting her second child, was at her spinning, though a harp was within her reach should her husband wish for cheer. For the knight was melancholy, his blue eyes shadowed, his brown beard uncombed. A wound in battle had caused him a long illness, and though a man in the prime of his age he would never fight or tourney or hunt as he had done before. By his chair there rested a stick, curiously carved, where his hand gripped, with the leafed face of the Green Man.

When the reapers descended upon the house the knight was at first too rapt in thought to attend to their noise, brooding perhaps on his wound, or perhaps, as he now often did, on his only son, a boy being educated in the household of the bishop. So the lady too, for his peace, feigned to give all her attention to her spinning, though her ear was intent on the voice of Peter Butler disputing with Roger the lord of the harvest, and on the exclamations which came from Kit of Kersey, her faithful servant and friend.

At length, rising, she went some way towards the door, and called twice, not loudly: "Kit! Oh, Kit!"

The young woman heard, and had indeed been hovering outside the door for such a call, and she came quickly, but shyly (for it was understood that at that hour the hall was the knight's alone) to her mistress. Her rosy face was a complexity of every feeling between wonder and tenderness.

"Oh Madam," she cried. "Oh Madam."

"Why, Kit," said the lady, "how strange you look. And what is this crowd of folk in the garden? I hope it does not mean some poor soul is hurt in the harvest field."

"Thass no wonder if I look strange," said Kit, "for my eyes have sin the strangest thing under the sun. Madam, they all want to come in to the master, and Peter he won't let none of them, but Madam, let Roger and John come and bring the children with them."

"What children, Kit?" asked the lady.

"The ones John find, Madam, near the harvest field. Two children lost or strayed, but so uncommon, Madam, that it won't do no good for me to try to tell you. But have them fetched, and oh Madam, only see."

"Tell Peter, then," said the lady, "that those two men and the children may enter." And returning to her husband she said: "The reapers have found some poor children, who are lost, it seems."

The knight looked on idly as his sturdy butler, in a yellow tunic, marched in before the reapers. Those two, dark silent Roger and hay-haired young John, walked close together, which the knight set down to the diffidence of such men inside his house. But when the butler stopped before him, said: "Sir, the strangers," and stepped aside; when the knight saw what the reapers held in a manner trapped between them; then he felt like a man shocked from a long day-dream, and grasping his stick leaped up, crying: "Holy Virgin!"

Being now out of the sun the children gazed at the knight, the most imposing man in the room, wide-eyed, and the beauty of their eyes amazed him like some stone never seen before. They were not of one unmixed green, but flecked or lined with different greens, and in each child's eyes there was a different promise; for in the boy's there was, as it were, a misting of blue, while in the girl's was a haze of pale bird-breast brown.

Nor were their skins all of a single colour, but as there is variation with us (whose arms, for example, are darker above than below), so the skins of the green children verged in some places on the fairness of ladies. Noticing this, the knight thought first of the green of leeks, where that green meets white. But his second thought was of green elderbuds, at the point where they are transfigured into bloom.

The children's hair was like silk, and green as barley, but like barley presaging gold. As for their clothes, the Yorkshireman William Petit has written that they were covered with raiment of unknown material; but the Abbot of Coggeshall, who heard these things from the knight himself, says nothing of such raiment, and for good reason. For what touched the knight and his lady more than the girl's elfin face, more than the boy's little warrior's mouth and chin, was their likeness to pictures of our first father and mother before their fall. As if unaware, both covered their nakedness under small hands with nails like hazel leaves. And like our first parents, but later, both began to weep inconsolably.

That evening, when the long trestle table was set out in the hall, the green children sat not with the other children, but with the knight and his lady and with a certain priest, a true friend to the knight and himself a man of soldierly bearing, though grave. This priest looked continually at the children with wonder in which there was something of pity and of trepidation.

From all the food which was offered them, from beer and from wine, the children turned their heads away, and wept. And no delicacy prepared for them by kindly Kit, whose own child was of their age and was then in the hall, could tempt their appetite or bring a pause to their weeping.

At last the priest, who had meditated long, said to the children: "*Ydor ydorum?*" And then, touching a handsome ewer of bronze in the form of a knight on horseback, from whose horse's mouth the water poured, he added: "*Hydriai?*" But the children merely looked at the ewer and wept. And when he asked, touching the salt: "*Halgein ydorum?*" they gazed at him greenly, but evidently understood nothing, and wept again.

"What are those words, father?" inquired the knight's lady.

"I thought, Madam," said the priest, a little discomfited, "that in the story of the priest Elidorus there might be an answer to the marvel of these children. This Elidorus, as a boy of twelve, ran away from his studies, and hid himself in the hollow bank of a river near Neath, in Wales. And when he was in great hunger, two men of small stature came upon him and said: 'If you will go with us, we shall take you to a land full of sports and delights.' The boy went willingly, at first down a path under the earth which was lightless, and came at length to a most beautiful country of rivers and meadows, woods and plains, but somewhat gloomy, for the sun never shone there, nor the moon or stars. Brought to the King, he was received with wonder and with great kindness, and the King gave him into the care of his own son, also a boy.

"These men were of handsome form, with long fair hair to their shoulders like women, but very small, and their horses were the size of greyhounds. Though there was no cult of religion among them, they were strict in honour; and returning from our hemisphere, they often spoke in reprobation of our ambitions, infidelities and inconstancies, which things were unknown among them.

"The boy Elidorus soon learned their language, and was permitted to visit our world as he liked, and so came to be rejoined with his mother, to whom he told all these things. But the woman, being greedy, asked him to bring her back a present of gold from that kingdom. So, on an unlucky day, while playing at ball with the King's son, he seized the ball, which was of gold, and made off with it to his mother's house.

"But as he entered, his foot stuck fast on the threshold, and he fell. And two of those subterranean beings, following him, seized the ball, and with the greatest contempt and derision spat upon him, and he saw them no more. Nor could he ever again find the passage into their world, which was behind a waterfall, though he searched for a full year.

"Almost inconsolable, the boy took again to his studies, and at last became a priest. But even in old age he could not speak of that land and its people without tears, and their language he never quite forgot. He remembered, and told the bishop when he was well stricken in years, that *ydor ydorum* meant with them: 'Bring water'; and *halgein ydorum*, 'Bring salt'; and *hydriai* water-pots or ewers such as this. All these matters are told by Gerald the Welshman, and are a most powerful lesson against greed, which is the destruction of all felicity."

"And yet, father," said the soldier, "these are no pygmy men, but children, and they have recognized nothing of those words remembered by the priest Elidorus."

"My test has failed," admitted the priest. "And therefore I am forced back to my first position, which is that they have fallen from the moon."

The knight and the lady said nothing to that, but the lady at length suggested: "Let us take them into the garden, and show them the moon."

To the moon and the stars the stubborn-faced boy paid little attention. But the girl, who seemed the older, gazed up at all the immensity above with a look of terror.

The priest spoke kindly to her, and as men will sometimes do with foreigners, made use of the one foreign tongue he knew, which was Latin. So he said, pointing: "*Luna.*" And finding that her eyes seemed to return to the red planet, he told her: "*Stella Martialis.*"

Then for the first time the child spoke. She repeated the priest's words, but strangely, so that it seemed to him that she said: "*Terra Martinianit.*" And then both children, weak with fear and hunger, began to weep again.

*

Some days later Kit of Kersey was passing through the hall, where the children lay on the rushes as ever in tears, carrying with her beans which her little daughter had torn roughly in the garden.

The boy, raising his head, saw the green things, and with a shout rushed at the woman, snatched the beans, and carried them to the girl. With cries they began, joyfully, starvingly, to tear at their booty, seeking the beans, however, not in the pods but in the stalks. And not finding them, they began to weep again.

But kindly Kit, forgiving the hungry child his robber's manners, came to them and showed them where the beans were to be found. And then, chattering in their unknown tongue, they eagerly devoured them, and by signs asked for more. And for a long time they nourished themselves with beans entirely.

Concerning this the priest had many doubts, for beans are condemned by Pythagoras, and are thought by some to contain departed souls. And as Bartholomew the Englishman has written: "By oft use thereof the wits are dulled and they cause many dreams." But the children, growing by degrees stronger and ceasing to bewail their outcast condition, became accustomed to eat whatever was set before them, and by signs made the priest understand that until then they had refused other food only because of its strangeness, and from fear that it would poison them. But once their trust in Kit was firm, they would accept any dish from her hand; and from her their trust was extended to all the people of the manor, and they became happy, hearty children. But the boy was often shaken by fits of passion, and the soldier, who was growing to love him, said: "Out of this bean will sprout a terrible knight."

The lady's time drew near, and her son, a boy of nine years, came to visit the manor from the bishop's household where he was being schooled. And being so young, and vain of his little learning, as well as charmed by the pointed face and strange eyes of the green girl, he made a doggerel rhyme about her in Latin, calling her Viridia. And he sang it to his mother's harp.

Viridia mirabilis
Tum pulchra quam amabilis

Colloquium nemo intelligit,
Quod puto esse habilis.

By which he meant, or wished to mean:

Viridia the marvellous,
As amiable as fair;
Her speech no man can understand,
Which shows her wit, I swear.

In due course the lady was delivered of a daughter, whom the knight welcomed with a good grace, though he had prayed for a boy, for his son Mark, he felt sure, was destined for the clergy or the court, and he longed for a little soldier. At the baptism of the child, whose name was Lucy, the green children watched intently, and the girl, pointing at the baby and at Mark, and then at herself and the green boy, made it understood that they too were brother and sister.

After that baptism the priest took to spending much time with the children, and began to teach the boy his letters, from a feeling that he might in this way come to have some knowledge of their language. The boy was no diligent scholar, having an adoration for horses and hawks, but the girl, very strangely for a female, took to learning with the ardour of a clerk, and soon not only wrote fairly, copying both English and Latin, but acquired a knowledge of our tongue, which she spoke with sometimes comical grammar, but in a clear precise accent like a lady.

So through her the priest instructed the boy in the tenets of our faith, and in time both were regenerated by the holy waters of baptism. The priest had wished to name them Barbara and Peregrine: each name, as he said, meaning "stranger". But because of the boy Mark's rhyme, the girl had long been called either Amabel or Mirabel, and at the lady's insistence both names were given to her at the font. As for the boy, the knight said that he was made to be a warrior, and must carry the name of the most glorious and holy of warriors, and he was therefore baptized Michael.

But not long afterwards the boy began to dwindle and pine, and when he grew too weak to walk was laid in a truckle bed in the hall, where at meal times his green eyes watched the company wistfully. He could eat little, though kind Kit brought him, in his own silver-rimmed mazer, many delicacies easy to stomach. The priest and the lady were frequently with him, and his sister always, and just as often the lame knight's chair was beside the bed. The two never spoke, but the soldier would look with a yearning helplessness into the child's eyes, in which there was more blue than formerly.

There came an evening when the soldier took his usual place, carrying with him a handful of beans which he himself had gathered in the moonlit garden. The child accepted them with a wan smile, and after swallowing one or two, said in English the word: "Grace."

Then a change came over his face, and reaching out he took the stick which leaned against the knight's leg, and gazed long at the face which was carved on it. And to himself he murmured one word in his own tongue.

"Amabel," said the soldier, "what does he say?"

The boy murmured again, and the girl said, her face thin with dread: "He says: 'Green.' He says: 'Home.' He says: 'Green home.'"

The boy's green-blue eyes, fixed on the carved face, slowly closed. With his free hand he touched the knight's crippled knee, and then he died.

The soldier and the girl, leaving him to the priest and the woman, went out into the garden. And under the stars and the moon, looking up, the knight said: "There, perhaps, he goes, into that awful vastness, where the warrior-archangel will receive him with loving-kindness and guide him to his green home."

As a star fell, the girl, who had been disturbingly still, burst into a passion of tears. The soldier, with tears on his own lean cheeks, clutched her to him, and stroking her hair, which in the moonlight was blonde, said: "Oh Amabel, oh little Mirabel. There are more green homes than one."

*

Seven years passed. The girl, growing perfect in our tongue, also most surprisingly showed herself at fourteen very skilled in music, and a scholar the
equal of any abbess in the land. The priest somewhat ruefully admitted her
his superior. Yet she was no abbess in the making, but chambermaid to the
lady and nursemaid to her little daughter, and as a foundling and a stranger
there was no girl or man on the manor who did not think her of lower station.

Among the youths of the manor was one Robin, a dark lad of pleasing
and humorous countenance, foster-brother to the knight's son Mark. For
months he had watched the girl with an admiration in which there was
something curious and sly. And one day in late May he said to her: "Mirabel,
you used to be partial to beans. Shouldn't you like to come with me and
smell the beanfield in flower?"

When they came to the beanfield, the sweetness of it was an intoxication
to the girl, and she stood among the flowers with her elfin face rapt, as if
ecstatic with wine. Her skin, by that time, was between green and white, as at
that moment the elderflower was. Her fair hair, though streaked with green,
had turned lightest blonde, and her eyes were a confusion of green and hazel.

The boy Robin, with a secretive grin, loosened the drawstring of his linen
breeches, and said: "Hey, Mirabel, ever seen one of these?"

The girl's beautiful eyes showed shock, and some disgust. But the boy,
quite gently yet with his customary indifference, simply clasped her and laid
her down among the beanflowers.

Long afterwards, Robin told everything to a crony. "She have all the
clothes off me," he said. "It was like she want to swallow me whole. She
keep calling out in her foreign lingo. And she say: 'Oh, you're warm,' she say,
'you're mine.' She say: 'Robin, love me, love me.' She say: 'Oh, I was alone.'
When I couldn't do no more, she just hold me like a baby, and she say:
'You're mine,' she say 'you're mine.'

For weeks after that the green girl and the dark boy were lovers. But
because of her strange intensity, or because, more likely, of a coolness in his
own nature, he began to avoid her, and took up with Margery, she who was the

laughing-stock of the dairy because, for beauty's sake, she had been seen to wash herself in milk. For a long time thereafter the green girl seemed in her inscrutable way to mourn. But some yearning had been awakened in her by the lad's body, and when cheerfulness returned she became (as the knight afterwards told the Lord Abbot) *nimium lasciva et petulans*, that is, very lascivious and wanton.

One day the girl came upon Roger, the man who had been lord of the harvest when she and her brother were discovered, alone in a wood, sitting on a log to take his noonday bread and beer. She seated herself beside him, and accepted some beer. At last the man broke his silence to ask a question which had been in his mind for nearly eight years. "Tell me straight, gal, where was you and young Mikey from?"

Without answering, the girl took the knife from his waist, and choosing a piece of rotten wood began very skilfully to carve. When she had finished, she showed the man her work.

"Oh-ah," said Roger. "A woman, and up the stick."

The rude figure was indeed of a grinning woman, large-breasted and hugely pregnant.

"That," the girl said, "is our goddess. We were children of the flint-mines. Day after day, year after year, century after century, we crawled along the galleries of our mines, loosening flints with our picks made from the antlers of red deer. I do not understand our life. I do not understand how we came here. But suddenly we found ourselves in that pit, in the blinding sun and stunning heat, and could discover no hole leading back to the gallery. And so we lay there weeping, until seized away."

"I do believe," said Roger, "that you might be talking about Grime's Graves."

"I have never heard that name," the girl said. "I remember only our mines and galleries, and our goddess, before whose figure carved in chalk a little lamp burned."

"And what about your god?" asked Roger, and sniggered. "She didn't get that way on her own, if I recall the facts of life."

The girl took up the knife again, and turning aside, her long greenish-fair hair dangling, began to carve once more. When she had finished, she held out to Roger a phallus, the glans and testicles painstakingly distinct.

"That," she said, "is our god."

"Something tell me," said Roger, "I sin him before. Yes, and not so very far from here."

For answer the girl pulled the drawstring of his breeches.

Afterwards she said, or pleaded: "Roger, you love me?"

"Love?" said the taciturn man. "Why, gal, that int one of my words. But," he said, giving her a slap on the rump, "I'll say this for you, you int a bad little old poke."

The girl liked to haunt the woods and the heaths, and in another wood one day the soldier, walking for exercise of his leg, found her lying among last year's leaves. Over her head an elderbush, its flowers in their last fragile fullness, smelled overpoweringly heavy.

"Mirabel," he said, with the help of his stick and with a little difficulty sitting beside her, "Mirabel, you are no longer a green girl. You are the fairest and whitest of girls, as white as elderflower."

The girl said nothing, but taking the knight's stick she gazed intently at the carved face, as the dying boy had done, a memory which softened the melancholy soldier.

"This," she said, "is our god."

"A strange god," said the knight. "One would say a cruel one."

"He is," said the girl, "the bringer into being, and the destroyer. He is neither cruel nor merciful, but dances for joy at the variousness of everything that is."

"Then, Mirabel," said the knight, "having said so much, you may tell me now from where you and Michael came."

The girl thought, and taking his hand, once so sunburned and strong, now so thin, she said: "I shall tell you.

"We are people," she said, "of the land of the Antipodes, where, years ago, a man from your world made a visit. He was a swineherd of Derbyshire, and had lost a sow of great value, about to farrow down. In dismay at the thought of the steward's anger, he followed it to a certain cave near the Peak, which is called in the British tongue *With Guint*, and in English the Devil's Arse, because of a violent wind which blows from it continually. Overcoming his fear, the swineherd traced the swine into the cave, and as at that time it was free of wind, he followed long and long through the darkness. At last he came upon a lighted place, and from there emerged into a fair land of spacious fields, where he found reapers harvesting the ripe corn, and among the hanging ears of corn recognized his sow, which had brought forth her litter.

"Marvelling and congratulating himself on this event, the swineherd spoke for a time with the chief man of our land, letting him know what had occurred. And then, taking a joyful leave, he returned with his charges into the darkness of the cave.

"Emerging from its mouth, fresh from the harvest fields of the Antipodes, he was amazed to find that in Derbyshire winter frosts persisted everywhere. And some have said that the winter sun is not the real sun, but as it were a deputy. But of this I understand nothing, though of the swineherd's visit I have often heard, but only know that Michael and I, straying into a cave and wandering far through the darkness, found ourselves at length not in Derbyshire but in Suffolk, in great affright and with mourning for our land which will never see us again."

"Poor child," said the knight, and stroked her elder-soft hair. "But mourn no more, my pretty."

The girl bent her head to kiss his other hand, and then looked at him with eyes in which there was only one meaning.

Long afterwards, kneeling beside his lean body, she kissed his scarred and twisted leg (for for her pleasure he had made himself naked as a worm), and cried, "Oh my fair love, oh my warm, wounded love."

And that was not the last time that the knight and the girl had such commerce. But a sort of shame was on him, because of his wife and because the girl, so young, had grown up in his household. So ever afterwards there was in company a constraint between them, and on some evenings in the hall the girl would look at him with leaf-shaped eyes in which there was a little hurt, but more compassion.

In the hall one winter night, seated with the priest before the fire, the girl took up the lady's harp and sang a hymn, beginning:

> *Martine te deprecor,*
> *Pro me rogaris Patrem,*
> *Christum ac Spiritum Sanctum*
> *Habentem Mariam matrem.*

Which is in English:

> *Saint Martin, I beseech thee,*
> *For me entreat the Father,*
> *Christ Jesu and the Holy Ghost*
> *Who Mary had for mother.*

When she had ended, the priest said: "A beautiful hymn. Where have you learned it?"

"It came out of Ireland," said the girl, "I believe. But it might be a song of my own land, for Saint Martin is the chief saint among us."

"Indeed?" said the priest. "Then there are churches in your land?"

"Many, many churches," said the girl, "all dedicated to Saint Martin. But our churches do not shine like yours. In our land there is little light, but as it were a perpetual gloaming, and not far from us is a certain luminous country, divided from us by a great stream."

"Indeed?" repeated the priest. "Then I take you for one of the Antoikoi or the Antichthones, who live south of the equatorial ocean. And I think that the land you have seen is the edge of Africa, lighted from above like the rim of a plate, by the sun which never descends to your hemisphere."

"Of that I understand nothing," said the girl, "nor of how my brother and I came here. I only know that we were minding our father's flock, and strayed into a cave. And after wandering far, we heard a certain delectable sound of bells, as when in Bury they all chime together, and at the sound we were entranced, caught up in the spirit, and knew no more until we found ourselves near the harvest field."

"And the people of your land," said the priest, "they are all green, these Christians?"

"Yes," said the girl, "green in every part and member. As I was once, and am still, between my thighs."

The girl looked at the priest with eyes in which there was only one question. The priest's own eyes were shadowed. Though his body was large, his mouth was that of a good little boy.

"Would you love me?" asked the girl.

"No, Mirabel," said the priest, tearing his wistful eyes away from the hazel mists of hers, and staring at his own clasped hands. "It would be sin, it would be folly, it would be pain. But," he said, and gazed at her again with a boyish candour, "I have loved you, and do, as no other child of God. So try me no more, but believe in my love, and I shall bring you from Bury, done by a clever monk there, the hymn to Saint Martin with a picture of the saint dividing his cloak with the beggar. And the naked man will be green, and will look like Michael."

The soldier's son, now a clerk of nineteen years, came to visit his parents and his sister. And by strategy he waylaid Mirabel beside a haystack.

"Tell me," he said, "of Saint Martin, your land's patron saint."

The girl looked at the coltish youth with a shrewd understanding. "On top of the stack," she said, "that is where I will tell you."

When they lay side by side, she said: "Saint Martin is of the Devil."

"Holy Virgin!" exclaimed the clerk. "This is heresy."

"We, who are ancient Britons," said the girl, "call him Merddin. He was begotten of Satan upon a nun, and is the high priest of his father, whom in our orgies we name Manogan. And in Manogan's name we dye our skins green, for that is his favoured colour, and in that colour he appears at our conventicles, or rites, to take his pleasure of woman or man.

"For long after Christianity came to the British countries, Merddin lay asleep beneath the earth in a forest of Brittany called Brocelien, which in our tongue means 'the land of concealment'. But in time he rose again, and gave his name as Martin, and was made bishop of Tours. He was the son, he said, of Florus the Hun, and therefore first cousin to the Seven Sleepers, whom Martin ordained, and sent into the cave where they lie breathing still. Their turning in their sleep, as happened in the time of Edward the Confessor and was miraculously made known to him, is a portent of dreadful calamities in the world, but happens perhaps once in two centuries.

"The bishop Saint Martin was a potent sorcerer, as Christians may read. When the Emperor Valentinian refused to receive him, he passed with the aid of a demon through bolts and bars, and stood suddenly before the throne. And when the great monarch would not rise to greet him, flames covered that seat and scorched him *ea parte corporis qua sedebat*, that is, on the part of the body where he sat down.

"Christians also know of my people because of Priscillian, who travelled Gaul with processions of women, before whom he appeared naked to perform his rites, his magical orgies and obscene discourses. In such a fashion we honour Manogan, or Satan, and his son Merddin, or Saint Martin, who is not dead but sleeps in a prison of air beneath a hawthorn."

The long-legged youth moved yet closer to the girl, and panting said: "Mirabel, let us honour Saint Martin."

"Kiss me," said the girl.

The youth kissed her, long and long, lying upon her body. But suddenly he groaned, and rolled away.

"It is no matter," said the girl, gazing with her strange eyes into the sky. "The god knows that all things rise again."

But the youth was shamed. "I don't want to," he muttered, "now. It is sin, it is the risk of eternal perdition." And leaping down from the stack, he made his way home to the manor house, and never saw the green girl again.

A pedlar came to the manor, a young man with brown curling hair, and was well received by all the women, for the sake of his gewgaws but also for himself, for his tongue was sharp but his smile was warm, and he seemed to admire all of them. But most often his sea-grey eyes were on the green girl.

He slept that night among the straw in the stables, and when all the household was abed the girl came to him. He drew her down to where he lay naked, and long and joyously they honoured Saint Martin.

When they were still, the girl murmured, stroking his shaggy chest: "Oh love me, love me. I am alone. Oh, be mine."

"I am yours," said Matthew, for that was his name, "and love you truly, and we shall never part."

She buried her face in his breast, and sobbed, as when she was new to our world.

"You are strange," said her lover. "You are like no one else here. Tell me from where you came."

The girl meditated, listening to the stirring of the horses. "I shall tell you," she said, "when I know all there is to know of you."

"Of me?" said the young man, and she glimpsed his white wild-man's grin. "If you keep secrets, as I am sure you do, I shall tell you. I am a Jew of Lynn."

At the bleakness in his voice, she comforted him with her whole body.

"How much of the blame," said Matthew, "for the fate of our people, for the horrors of York, may lie on a single man. I do not mean King Richard, though his favour was soon a curse to us. I mean one Jew of Lynn, who chose for himself the Christian faith, so enraging the rich and numerous Jewish merchants of the town that in their arrogance they took up arms against him, and calling him deserter and renegade, pursued him to a Christian church. It was for our sake that he fled the house, for he was my father.

"The huge noise, as they besieged the church and broke down the doors, and dragged my father away to punishment, attracted many Christians, who already hated us for our wealth and pride and the King's favours. And many came running with arms, among them a crowd of young strangers from the ships, who traded in Lynn. And all of them fell upon our people, who could not withstand them. Many were hewn down in flight, and with them my father, though whether a Jew or a Christian killed him I shall never know.

"From there the Christians went to our houses, looting and killing, and at last burning everywhere. So my mother and brothers and sisters died, either by fire or the sword. That night, since I was at Norwich, there was not a living Jew in Lynn.

"The next day a Jewish physician arrived, a man much respected by Christians for his art and manners. But in his grief he expressed himself immoderately, seeming to prophesy revenge, and so the Christians made him the last victim of the Jewish fever. And the young foreigners, laden with our wealth, made off again in their ships, and on them the people of Lynn blame everything."

"And yet," said the green girl softly, "you live there still."

"I should have gone," said Matthew. "I should have gone to York. If only that had been my fate. I would have died with them proudly, by my own hand. Masada," he murmured to himself, in a voice like a groan. "Masada."

"And what have you to return to," the girl asked, "there in Lynn?"

"A hut by the sea," said the young man. "A squalid hut, for me orphaned by riches. I am pedlar or sailor or what work comes to hand. I am not known to be a Jew. We were so many, I was not noticed among so many. Now we are one."

He stopped, his breath coming fast, then rolled on his side to face her. "And you, my Mirabel?"

"We were people," said the girl, in her quietest voice, "of a far foreign land, which I think you would call Tartary. As children, my brother and I were stolen away. We were brought by sailors to Ipswich to be sold as slaves."

The young man stroked her hair, all his speech in his eyes.

"There we escaped," said the girl, "and lived in the woods, on the heaths. We were very young. How long it lasted is all unclear. We lived like deer or squirrels, on whatever fruit or green things we dared try. The greatest joy I remember was discovering a field of beans.

"As we weakened, our skins began to change. We became green children. When we fell into the pit near the harvest field, we were weak to the point of death. And my brother's end I attribute to that weakness, that long green hunger."

"Mirabel," said the young man, "are you telling me the truth?"

"Does it matter?" asked the girl, with a shy laugh. "I have so many truths to tell."

The young man stood up in his nakedness and searched for his clothes. "We shall go tonight," he said. "To these people who have been kind to you you will write, for I know you can write. But tonight you and I must vanish, vanish for ever, into a hut by the sea at Lynn."

The girl rose beside him, and twined around him her elder-white body. "Oh my love," she said. "Oh my own one. Oh my home."

Many years later the priest received from a traveller a grimy letter. "I am sick and alone," it said, "and would wish to speak with you. For the love you vowed, undertake the journey. I am the widow of Matthew Pedlar of Lynn."

In a hut by the grey winter sea, with a leaking roof and a window rimmed with snow, on a musty bed tossed by fever, the grey-haired priest discovered the green girl. But green no longer, and a girl no longer, for her silken hair was white, and in her wandering eyes there was only a freckling of their old hue.

The priest, kneeling beside her, said the prayer of intercession to Saint Martin, and then the Pater Noster. But she seemed not to understand, nor to know him, so he took her hand and made her his farewell.

"In love is grief," he said, "in grief is love. As your grief for him is love, so is my grief for you. Pity my grief. Let my grief teach you to love mankind.

"Truly there is in the world nothing so strange, so fathomless as love. Our home is not here, it is in Heaven; our time is not now, it is eternity; we are here as shipwrecked mariners on an island, moving among strangers, darkly. Why should we love these shadows, which will be gone at the first light? It is because in exile we grieve for one another, it is because we remember the same home, it is because we remember the same father, that there is love in our island.

"In the garden of God are regions of darkness, waste heaths and wan waters, gulfs of mystery, where the bewildered soul may wander aghast. Do not think to rest in your village, in your church, in your land always secure. For God is wider than middle earth, vaster than time, and as His love is infinite, so also is His strangeness. For His love we love Him, and for His strangeness we ought to fear Him, lest to chastise us He bring us into those dark and humbling places.

"I, even I, have known a prodigy and a marvel, and I have wept for two children, and feared in their plight to see an image of my own. Nevertheless I did not despair, for them or for myself, knowing that even in their wandering they rested still in reach of God's hand. For no man is lost, no man goes astray in God's garden; which is here, which is now, which is tomorrow, which is always, time and time again."

Mirabel's eyes, which had been closed, slowly fluttered open. Into them there seemed to come the paradox of a green flush as she died.

"This I believe and must," said Jacques Maunoir. "I believe, and must."

2014

IN YON GREEN HILL TO DWELL

Jane Alexander

Jane Alexander is an Edinburgh-based writer, lecturer and researcher whose work explores hauntings, the magic mirror of the media, and the contemporary uncanny. Her first novel, Glasgow-set morality tale *The Last Treasure Hunt*, was selected as a Waterstones Debut of the Year in 2015, while 2020's *A User's Guide to Make-Believe* explores the darker side of virtual reality. Her most recent book is an M.R. James meets *Black Mirror* collection of eerie tales with accompanying essay, *The Flicker Against the Light and Writing the Contemporary Uncanny* (2021).

Her shivery twenty-first-century folktale "In Yon Green Hill to Dwell", winner of the 2014 Fiction Desk competition and originally published in its *New Ghost Stories II* anthology, revisits the Border ballad of Tam Lin to explore what might happen next in the tale. In the ballad, pregnant heroine Janet saves her lover Tam from being taken by the Fairy Queen by holding onto him "at the mirk and midnight hour" while he shapeshifts into a snake, a lion and a red-hot rod of iron. But seven years later, has he changed again— or has she?

"O tell me, tell me, Tam Lin," she says,
"For's sake that died on tree,
If eer ye was in holy chapel,
Or christendom did see?"

"Roxbrugh he was my grandfather,
Took me with him to bide
And ance it fell upon a day
That wae did me betide.

"And ance it fell upon a day
A cauld day and a snell,
When we were frae the hunting come,
That frae my horse I fell,

The Queen o' Fairies she caught me,
In yon green hill to dwell.
"And pleasant is the fairy land,
But, an eerie tale to tell,

Ay at the end of seven years,
We pay a tiend to hell,
I am sae fair and fu o flesh,
I'm feard it be mysel.

"But the night is Halloween, lady,
The morn is Hallowday,
Then win me, win me, an ye will,
For weel I wat ye may.

"Just at the mirk and midnight hour
The fairy folk will ride,
And they that wad their true-love win,
At Miles Cross they maun bide."

Lines from the Border ballad Tam Lin communicated
by Robert Burns, 1792, from Francis James Child,
The English and Scottish Popular Ballads (1882–1892)

O I forbid you, maidens a',
That wear gowd on your hair,
To come or gae by Carterhaugh,
For young Tam Lin is there.

"FORBIDDEN," I say. "That had something to do with it." The word sounds like an invitation. That lift in its middle, flicking up: like raised eyebrows, or the hook of a glance. I say it again, for the hard-and-soft sound of it, for the way it contains its opposite.

"When you're that age—what was I? Sixteen—"

"Seventeen," says Tam. It's the first he's said, all session. As if it matters.

"My dad should've known," I say. "I mean. I was off the rails anyway." I can feel my mouth tugging into a smile: I was wild, once.

"Tam?" says the counsellor. "What about you? Was it significant for you, that Janet's father disapproved?"

"Ach," he says, and though I'm not looking at him, I know he's shaking his head. I can *hear* it. "No. Maybe. I don't know."

What a way he has with words: my silver-tongued poet.

He was the prize, back then. He'd turn up every now and then, in the woods by the well where we used to hang out: tight black jeans and a military coat, silver hipflask wedged in his pocket. He was older than the rest of us. When he said he was a poet, we laughed, but despite ourselves we were impressed. I'd never thought of a poet as someone alive, let alone blue-eyed and beautiful.

While the rest of the lassies fluttered about him, hitching up skirts and tugging down necklines, I acted like he wasn't there. Like he wasn't in my dreams at night, golden, glowing; like I didn't wake feverish at dawn, clutching a sweat-damp pillow. I was hooked on the high of his eyes on me, his watchful half-smiles, the way he saw straight through me. It was a game, addictive, and we kept on playing till the day I skived school to turn up alone. Till the day it was just us two.

It happens occasionally, in this bland pastel room: a moment when it's us two alone. When the counsellor's listening to the words, but deaf to their significance.

"Change," he says now, "can be positive in a relationship. But it can be hard, as well." He nods his head, agreeing with himself.

"Well," I say, "we've certainly had our share of change." I glance at Tam, who's avoiding my gaze, looking off into the corner; see the muscles shift under his skin. Not a smile, but at least the suggestion of one. The counsellor keeps on nodding. I notice him noticing, catching at our hidden current of meaning. How his face slips—the open face he wears as a mask—and how he hides the slip with an all-purpose smile. It makes me want to stir things up.

"It was *her* that did it," I say. "It was her that changed him."

"When you say *her*, you're talking about the woman Tam was seeing—"

"I'd hardly call her a woman!"

The counsellor's face slips even further. He thinks I'm reduced by burning jealousy to insults and insinuations. But there's an upward twitch at the corner of Tam's lips, and for a moment—just a moment—it's me and him together. The things that bind you: shared traumas, shared secrets. I thought we'd be bound right till the end. Tighter than promises, tighter than rings.

"She wasn't a woman," I say. "She was impossible."

In the woods by the well, just us two. When he tipped his head to swig from that silver flask, the curve of his white throat begged to be touched. He told me I was special, precious, I was The One. I raised his flask to my lips, a burning kiss: spiced, bright, nothing I had a name for. I'd worked my way through the boys my age, so plain and tame and tongue-tied. I was ready for something wilder. Minutes later, his hand up my skirt, my hands unsnaking his belt. No-one for miles around: still, I felt watched.

After, curled into each other, bedded in ivy; that's when he told me. Said he belonged to someone else. Save me, he said. His face was naked, his blue eyes haunted. *Save me.* I thought he meant he was married—my wife doesn't understand me—but when I laughed, he started to shake. Drugs, I thought then, a proper habit, and scanned his arms for trackmarks. But he was smooth skinned, life strong in his veins.

No wonder she took a fancy to him; claimed him for her own.

What made me believe him, in the end? His impossible story? Why didn't I think he was mad, or tripping? His silver tongue, it must have been. I lay in his arms, and promised him. I lay in his arms: inside of me, everything changing. A magic spell. A spell of division, of doubling and doubling.

The counsellor reckons we've got issues with trust. Well. Tam might have told me first, before he knocked me up.

All the last hour I've done the talking while Tam's sat there like a pudding: single words dragged out of him, given up like gold coins. Now, in the car, I keep my mouth shut. I don't start the engine, or turn on the radio. Dusk presses against the windscreen. A line of trees, newly stripped, shivers its branches in the wind. A small witch clings to her hat as she skips down the street; behind her a skeleton, not much taller, shields the guttering flame of his turnip lantern. I sit—wait—swallow the starts of a dozen sentences, till finally Tam caves in, and cracks the stubborn silence.

"We'll need to be heading back," he says.

A skirl of leaves blows past the window. Six words: it's a start. "Used to be," I say, "I couldn't shut you up."

"Two hours, I said to Ann-Marie. She'll be wanting to get away."

"Not that I wanted to shut you up. But now…"

"Janet, come on—"

"No!" I bang the heel of my hand against the steering wheel. "No: you come on. What are we doing? What's the point of this? Are we giving up, is that it? Because I don't give up, I hang on, that's what I do—of all people, you know that. But what am I hanging on to?"

For a minute, I'm sure I've talked him back into silence. Then: "All that," he says. "In there. What you were saying, how she was impossible." I nod, not wanting to open my mouth in case it gives him an excuse to shut his. "And so she was," he says. "But what you want… that's more impossible still." He looks at me. "Well, unless you've got a time machine? To turn us back, that's what you want. Back seven years."

I'm ready to argue, but he raises a hand like a wall between us.

"Listen," he says. He sounds tired. Defeated. "I'm yours. Yours and Caitlin's. I stay home, keep it nice, look after my daughter. That's all I need, and there's not many men would do that. But that's not enough for you. It's not how you want me. You want me on loan."

He looks at me like he's asked me a question, but the arguments have died on my lips.

"You want me bewitched by her, still."

> And pleasant is the fairy land,
> But, an eerie tale to tell,
> Ay at the end of seven years
> We pay a tiend to hell;
> I am sae fair and fu o flesh,
> I'm feard it be mysel.

There's a flash of it when he thanks the babysitter, after I've paid her. The lassie from over the road: almost the age I was when we met. He turns it on just a wee bit, the old warmth, the spark, holding her eyes a second too long—and I should be smashing plates, shouldn't I, yelling that he never looks at me that way. But I don't. I shove the fish fingers under the grill and slop the baked beans into the pan and tell Caitlin ten minutes until tea.

"Look," says Caitlin, "we made hats!"

I'm wrestling with the gas which is all sorts of temperamental and thinking how we can't afford a new hob and wondering whether Tam can fix it, and she's dancing about waiting for me to admire, singing about witches and black cats. Eventually I get the gas to stay lit, and turn to look at my daughter. She's sporting a black paper hat, wonky brimmed and crusted with glitter stars, accessorized with a pair of pink gauze wings.

"I'm a witch," she tells me, hand on hips.

"A witch, are you? Or a fairy?"

"I'm a princess-witch."

I can't tell her to take it off. I can't tell her there's no such thing. I look to Tam for help.

"You look magic," he says, manfully, and she does a spin, waves a wand made out of drinking straws.

The two of them head out after tea: he's promised to take her guising. I open a bottle of cheap wine, close my eyes as I drink. I imagine the glass is a hip flask, heavy silver, its threaded neck teasing the tip of my tongue; the alcohol heady with unnamed spices. In reality, it's sharp and watery. I swallow it down like medicine, pour some more.

Just once, he spoke to me. It was not long afterwards: we were at the start of our happy ending, and I still believed that, since it hadn't killed us, the trauma we'd shared made us indestructible. But if ever I spoke about what had happened, he changed the subject. Turned on the TV. Left the room.

That night, I was up feeding Caitlin, in the chair by the bedroom window; Tam muttering, twisting in his sleep, covers kicked onto the floor.

"What was it like?" I said, softly. "Tam. I wish you'd speak to me. I wish you'd tell me."

He opened his eyes, stared straight at me. I clutched at Caitlin, holding her closer.

"I was there," he said. His voice was flat. "I wasn't absent. I was the snake. I was the deer. I was the red-hot iron, and the ember. She pulled me apart, re-made me. She destroyed me, again, again, again. Bones jagging into hooves. Tearing the skin. Poison still singing in the needles of my teeth. A rope of cold flesh—a tongue split in two—a scream of white heat—"

His face was pale, shined with sweat, his eyes unseeing. He looked like a dead man conjured back into life.

"But then," I said, "I saved you." I stretched a hand towards him: to comfort? To plead? "Remember, Tam? I saved you?"

In the morning, he'd forgotten he'd ever spoken.

The bottle's half gone by the time they get back. Caitlin's high on sweets and attention—she's been performing her party piece for the neighbours, her Halloween song about the witch's cat. She gives one last rendition: each time I think it's finished, there's another verse to come. When I'm certain she's done, I give her a round of applause and offer a bedtime story.

"No," she says. "I want Daddy to read it." Nine times out of ten it's Daddy she wants.

"Okay, sleep tight, love you," I say, and I sit back on the sagging couch and cradle my glass.

Sometimes, I think that's what spoiled us—my saving him. He begged me to do it: *hold me fast, don't let me pass*. But being saved is so passive. I won't read those stories to Caitlin about princesses waiting to be rescued, though god knows what Tam lets her do when I'm out earning our living. God knows what stories he's telling her now.

More often than not he'll fall asleep up there, stretched alongside her, feet hanging off the edge of the bed. When that happens, I don't wake him. But tonight, we're meant to be talking. Homework, the counsellor called it, as though we're studying for an exam, as though our performance will be assessed and graded: pass or fail. Tonight's exam topic is expectations; our objective, to find some middle ground. So I wait a while, long enough to finish the wine, then I haul myself up off the sofa and climb the stairs.

In Caitlin's room the nightlight is on, spinning stars around the ceiling. She's face down, breathing loud and deep, dead to the world. Beside her, Tam lies tense, chest barely lifting. I know he is faking.

I say his name, and his eyelids flicker.

"Homework," I say. "Expectations."

A heavier breath: a sigh.

I speak softly, so as not to wake Caitlin. "Are you thinking of her?"

He doesn't respond.

"Seven years with her. How could you not?" I'm making it easy for him to confess. I wish he'd tell me yes, tell me he thinks of her, often, always... "Not even at night?" I say. "Not even in your dreams?" In dreams: that's where I hear her. Cursing me like she did that night, ice and grit—and softer, more insidious: *got what you wanted, did you? Enjoying your fine husband? Your ill-gotten gains?*

He keeps his eyes shut, but he answers at last. "If she's ever inside me," he says, "it's in my nightmares."

I should walk away now, close the door, let him sleep. "But you must... when you think of yourself back then... don't you ever want—"

"Let me tell you what I want," he says. His voice is low and clear. "I want to stay here, safe inside, in our house. I want to look after our daughter. I want to be here for her, always, so she never has to be afraid. This, here. This is what I want."

*

A poet. What did it ever mean? A box of pamphlets I paid to have printed, taking up space, turning yellow. He couldn't give them away. The rhymes he makes for Caitlin, when there's plenty already in books.

I shouldn't drive—I've drunk too much—but I drain a glass of water, then another; grab my keys anyway. If I'm to make it to Milecross by midnight, there's no choice.

I duck through the rain and into the car. Rub my eyes to focus my vision. I set off carefully, watching out for late night guisers and Halloween revellers. For each beat of the windscreen wipers, I count three, four of my heart. The roads are empty, till my headlights illuminate a dark figure crossing ahead of me: a black cat raised up on two legs. She stops, stares at me. Then she laughs, turns tail and vanishes into the dark.

> *Just at the mirk and midnight hour*
> *The fairy folk will ride,*
> *And they that wad their true-love win,*
> *At Miles Cross they maun bide.*

I park across from the Co-op. As I hurry the short distance to the crossroads the church bells ring: once, twice, three times. Fifteen minutes to wait.

Here's where it happened, seven years ago: here, where a crumpled can of Special Brew catches the streetlights, and fag-ends lie scattered across the cobbles. Here's where I held him, held him fast, as he turned and turned in my arms. A red-hot iron burning clean through the skin of my hands. At least I knew I was alive; could feel it in that screaming pain, could smell it in my own roasting flesh.

And after—he couldn't stand. That's when I was most terrified. The shock of his skin, suddenly, and his whole weight on me as he fell to the frozen ground, fitting—kicking and shuddering. I laid my coat over him, put his head on my lap. Rubbed his shoulders, his arms, his body, trying to warm him. All the heat had gone from him, in the red-hot iron, in the burning coal.

Everything that had been fire had turned to ice. And she, the Faerie Queen, was nowhere.

I wrap my arms around myself, pull my hood lower. You want me bewitched, he'd said. Bewitched by her still. And I wonder was it always true, from the first time I saw him; that the glow of him, the gold that drew me, was only the glitter of some other woman's treasure?

It starts with the first chime of midnight: a faint rumble that could be thunder—except that the rain has faded to a smirr; except that it keeps on rolling, building, turning into the drum of unshod hooves on cobblestones. I stare, straining into the street-lit dark. I can't see the riders, though they must be close now. I take a step forward, placing myself in their path. In the dark, a deeper shadow, spreading, growing; the hairs on my arms stand up. I can feel the wind of them, the air shifting—the hoofbeats loud now, deafening—and I close my eyes and raise my arms and pray she'll see me: *stop, stop*—

A sudden stillness. Small sounds all around me. The creak of leather. The shuffle of hooves. Close enough to touch. I open my eyes. Look up.

The horse towers over me, flesh and blood, white and groomed and glossy, all muscle and sinew under its shining coat. Breath plumes from its flaring nostrils—but there's no heat. If I reached to touch, my leather-sheathed fingers would freeze and crack. And if I touched my fingertips to a riding boot, a stockinged knee, or a hiked-up skirt; what then? Above me she sits as on a throne, her face in shadow.

"Bold Janet," she says, and I can hear amusement in her voice, which is icicles on the nape of my neck, is the voice I've dreamed for seven years. She laughs. "Bold, or boneheaded."

I feel it then: the army of riders massed at her back. Not that she needs an army. I've seen what she can do on a whim.

"Or both," I say. "Why not?"

"Careful, Janet. Is that your question?"

"My question?"

She breathes an Arctic sigh. "You've something to ask. Of course you have. Married him, didn't you; had his daughter. But here you are alone. Well, ask carefully. I'll answer just the once."

Perhaps there's a break in the clouds; perhaps up there the moon is full, because for a moment I see her clearly. Her lips are curved, her eyes slanted: cruel, beautiful. She knows. She knows what I've come to ask.

Change him back. Take him back. Change him, one more time.

But I hear his voice. I remember his words. What you want is impossible. I see them together, him and Caitlin. This, here. This is what I want. Curled around each other, sleeping safe. *To never be afraid.*

At the edge of my hearing, a siren rises and falls, its urgency faded by distance; like a reminder of something, like the loosest stitch still tacking me to this town, this life, this world. Then a horse shifts its hooves—sharp, soft, soft: a single bar of a waltz—and its harness shakes, sings, strikes a golden note that hangs in front of me. Close enough, bright enough, almost, to touch.

The smirr has coated me, given me an ice-damp skin. When I press my lips together I taste it: when I open them, I'm ready to ask.

"Take me?" I say. "Take me."

APPENDIX

The Cottingley Fairy Photographs

Images and captions are sourced from *The Coming of the Fairies*, Arthur Conan Doyle, London: Hodder & Stoughton, 1922.

A: FRANCES AND THE FAIRIES

Photograph taken by Elsie. Bright sunny day in July 1917. The "Midg" Camera. Distance, 4ft. Time, 1/50th sec. The original negative is asserted by expert photographers to bear not the slightest trace of combination work, retouching, or anything whatever to mark it as other than a perfectly straight single-exposure photograph, taken in the open air under natural conditions. The negative is sufficiently, indeed somewhat over-exposed.

B: ELSIE AND THE GNOME

Photograph taken by Frances. Fairly bright day in September 1917. The "Midg" camera. Distance, 8ft. Time, 1/50th sec. The original negative has been tested, enlarged, and analysed in the same exhaustive manner as A. This plate was badly-under-exposed. Elsie was playing with the gnome and beckoning to it to come on to her knee. The gnome leapt up just as Frances, who had the camera, snapped the shutter. He is described as wearing black tights, a reddish-brown jersey, and a pointed bright-red cap. The wings are more moth-like than the fairies and of a soft, downy, neutral tint. The music of the pipes held in his left hand can just be heard as a tiny tinkle sometimes if all is still. No weight is perceptible, though when on the bare hand a fairy feels like a "little breath".

C: FRANCES AND THE LEAPING FAIRY *(above, left)*

Photograph taken by Elsie in August 1920. "Cameo" camera. Distance, 3ft. Time, 1/50th sec. This negative and the two following have been as strictly examined as the earlier ones, and similarly disclose no trace of being other than perfectly genuine photographs. Also they proved to have been taken from the packet given them, each plate having been privately marked unknown to the girls. The fairy is leaping up from the leaves below and hovering for a moment—it had done so three or four times. Rising a little higher than before, Frances thought it would touch her face and involuntarily tossed her head back. The fairy is apparently in a close-fitting costume of faint lavender colour.

D: FAIRY OFFERING POSY OF HARE-BELLS TO ELSIE *(above, right)*

The fairy is standing almost still, poised on the bush leaves. The wings are shot with yellow, and upper part of dress is very pale pink.

E: FAIRIES AND THEIR SUN-BATH

This is especially remarkable, as not only would it be exceedingly difficult to produce such a negative by faked work—impossible in the opinion of some experts—but it contains a feature that was quite unknown to the girls. The sheath or cocoon appearing in the midst of the grasses had never been seen by them before, and they had no idea what it was. Fairy lovers and observers, of the New Forest and elsewhere, describe it as a magnetic bath, woven very quickly by the fairies, and used after dull weather to magnetize the interior, and thus provide a "bath" that restores vitality and vigour.